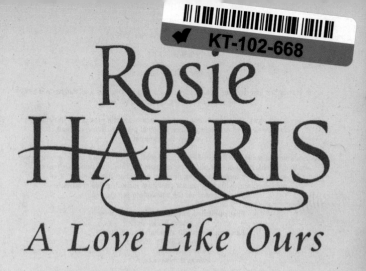

Rosie HARRIS

A Love Like Ours

arrow books

Published by Arrow Books 2008

4 6 8 10 9 7 5

Copyright © Rosie Harris 2008

Rosie Harris has asserted her right under the Copyright, Designs and Patents Act 1988
to be identified as the author of this work

First published in Great Britain in 2008 by
Arrow Books
Random House, 20 Vauxhall Bridge Road,
London SW1V 2SA

www.randomhouse.co.uk

Addresses for companies within The Random House Group Limited can be found at:
www.randomhouse.co.uk/offices.htm

The Random House Group Limited Reg. No. 954009

A CIP catalogue record for this book
is available from the British Library

ISBN 9780099503033

The Random House Group Limited supports The Forest Stewardship
Council® (FSC®), the leading international forest-certification organisation.
Our books carrying the FSC label are printed on FSC®-certified paper.
FSC is the only forest-certification scheme supported by the leading
environmental organisations, including Greenpeace. Our
paper procurement policy can be found at
www.randomhouse.co.uk/environment

Typeset in Palatino by Palimpsest Book Production Limited,
Grangemouth, Stirlingshire
Printed and bound in Great Britain by Clays Ltd, St Ives PLC

For Robert Mackenzie Harris
My Favourite Grandson

Acknowledgements

Once again a warm thank you for all the support I have had from my editor Georgina Hawtrey-Woore and her colleagues at Random House and to my agent Caroline Sheldon.

Chapter One

March 1915

Caitlin Davies stopped stirring the savoury-smelling pot of cawl on the top of the kitchen range and turned round to face her daughter in astonishment. A trimly dressed woman in her late thirties with a plain round face, dark eyes and straight dark hair swept back into a thick knot in the nape of her neck, she had a serene outlook on life and it took a great deal to upset her.

'What was that you said, Ruth?' she gasped, her dark eyes widening with shock as she stared in utter disbelief at her thirteen-year-old daughter.

The look of incredulity on her mother's face alarmed Ruth. For weeks she'd been trying to break the news, but she'd always held back at the last moment because she was so afraid of what her mam's reaction was going to be. By the look of things now she'd had every right to be worried.

Caitlin Davies shook her head from side to side, almost as if she couldn't believe her ears. 'Duw anwyl! Did you really say what I think you did?'

1

Ruth bit down on her lower lip, blinking back her tears. She knew she was shaking all over and it wasn't from the cold, even though it was one of the bitterest March days she'd ever known. She'd been glad to get into the warm kitchen when she'd come home from school, even though she knew that what she had to tell her mother was going to be difficult.

Now, pushing her shoulder-length dark hair back behind her ears, she squared her slim shoulders and faced her mother with an air of bravado.

'I'm pretty sure you heard what I said, Mam, now didn't you?' she challenged.

'Oh, I heard all right, but I can't believe my ears!'

'Well, it's quite true,' Ruth affirmed, avoiding her mother's eyes. 'I'm pregnant. In fact, I've been trying to tell you for ages,' she added petulantly.

'Ages! I see, and exactly how many weeks would we be talking about, then?' her mother demanded as she turned back to her cooking, stirring the pot of cawl so vigorously that some of the hot liquid splashed on to her hand making her wince.

'Does it matter?'

'Matter! Of course it does. And, even more importantly, when is this baby you're talking about due?' Caitlin asked, as she grabbed a tea towel to wipe the hot liquid from the back of her hand and from the front of the flowered cotton pinafore that she'd put on to protect her plain dark red dress from just such accidents.

'I'm not too sure,' Ruth admitted uneasily.

'There's rubbish! You must have some idea!' her mother exclaimed as she turned round, her dark eyes unusually hard and angry.

'I think it will be later in the year, probably about the end of August.'

Caitlin's eyes narrowed as she quickly did some mental calculations then she shook her head in despair. 'A special Christmas present, was it?' she commented sarcastically.

Ruth bit her lip and said nothing.

'You don't leave school until Easter,' her mother went on. 'You're supposed to be starting work in May as soon as we get back from our family holiday. What is going to happen now?'

'I don't know, Mam. That's why I've been trying to tell you about the baby.'

'You won't be able to go to work, that's for sure,' Caitlin went on almost as if Ruth hadn't spoken.

'Why ever not? Of course I can go to work; the baby isn't due for months and months.'

'That's as maybe, but by the beginning of June every man and his monkey will probably be able to guess what's happening. Apart from the disgrace you are bringing to our heads, no one is going to employ you when they find out you are expecting, now are they, girl?' Caitlin pointed out angrily.

'I don't see why not.'

3

'Stop acting so twp. Who on earth will want to spend their time training you to do a job when they know you'll be leaving in a few weeks?'

'I'm not stupid so—'

'Duw anwyl, you are damned twp or you wouldn't be in this condition,' her mother exclaimed furiously. 'So who's the boyo responsible for this mess, then?'

'There's no boy, Mam,' Ruth mumbled, hot colour rushing to her heart-shaped face. Her throat tightened with fear as she saw the anger in her mother's eyes. This was even harder than she'd thought it was going to be; if only her mother wasn't so high-minded and worried about what other people thought. She was only too aware how silly she'd been to believe that Glyn would stand by her, or to let herself be taken in by his words of love. She'd dreaded having to tell her mother and now, seeing her reaction, she was suddenly scared stiff that her mother might turn her out because if that happened she had no idea what she would do

'Oh damnio di! A miracle, is it? That's one tall story that I'm not going to believe, so speak out and tell me his name. Come on now, girl, that's the least you can do. With a bit of luck we can have you married off before the baba's born; otherwise the poor dab is going to be a little bastard.'

'There won't be any wedding, Mam, so don't start going on about it.'

4

'Oh and why's that, then? Has he scarpered already, suddenly become all patriotic and joined the army and gone off to the war and left you in the lurch?' she asked bitterly.

'He's already married.'

The colour drained from Caitlin's face. 'He's married and you knew! So what were you doing messing around with someone like that?'

'He said he loved me and that what we were doing proved that I felt the same way about him.'

'Duw anwyl!' Caitlin looked dumbfounded. 'Ruth, what's wrong with you, cariad? You've got a loving family, a good home and we've given you everything you could possibly want. We've brought you up properly, regular chapel, nice clothes, good meals, and then you let a married man spin you some daft yarn like that. Surely you must have realised that he was taking advantage of you, you silly girl. Now come on, tell me who it is.'

'Glyn Jenkins.'

The admission made Ruth draw in a deep breath of relief. It was as if it was no longer a burden she had to bear alone. She knew her mother was shocked, and she realised that there would be ructions – especially when her father was told – but the sense of relief that swept through her was tremendous.

It was a guilty secret no longer. Her mother was upset, but deep down she knew she'd help her and tell her what she must do. She wondered if she would let her leave school right away so that she wouldn't have to see Glyn Jenkins every day.

She'd been so sure that when she told him her news about the baby he would be absolutely overjoyed and would want to marry her. His refusal to even discuss their future, and his adamant assertion that he not only didn't love her, but had also never considered leaving his wife and family, had been the biggest shock of all.

He'd told her so many times that his wife didn't understand him and that he wasn't happy at home, and even that he'd give anything for the chance of the two of them being together, so she'd thought he would be delighted at the thought of being with her and making a home for her and their baby. She still found it hard to believe how wrong she'd been and that he'd never had any intention of marrying her after all.

'Glyn Jenkins! Duw anwyl, this gets worse by the minute.' Her mother's voice, now almost a shriek, sliced through Ruth's thoughts like a sharp knife through paper. 'He's not just a married man, he's got a young family. Three little ones and the youngest is a mere mite not yet three. What the hell has been going on? And him the school caretaker and all. I've a good mind to report this to the authorities. He shouldn't be allowed anywhere near young girls, not when they are as twp as you are,' she added scathingly.

6

'Please, Mam, don't go doing anything like that. I've learned my lesson. I'm not even speaking to him now.'

'Chucked you, has he, and told you to keep your mouth shut?' her mother commented caustically.

'Please, Mam, promise you won't go causing trouble for him,' Ruth implored.

'I'll think about it. You keep quiet as well until I've decide what to do. Who else knows that the pair of you have been carrying on and that you're pregnant?'

'No one. I haven't breathed a word to anyone about the baby except to Glyn and now you.'

'Well, let's keep it that way for the moment. He won't be telling anyone, you can be sure of that, and if you say anything then in all probability he'll only deny it. Meeting you in the boiler room and round the back of the bike sheds, was he?'

'Something like that,' Ruth admitted, hanging her head.

'Right. Well, go and lay the table for our meal. Your dad will be home any minute and you know how he likes his food to be ready the minute he gets in, especially on a cold day like this. Go on, then, and stop moping. Just remember to keep your mouth shut about all this until I have had time to consider what we must do for the best.'

'Yes, Mam,' Ruth agreed contritely.

'We must think carefully; think of the scandal

if this gets out. Pity you didn't tell me earlier, then we could have got rid of it,' she added reflectively.

'Mam!' The horror in Ruth's voice brought a tightening to Caitlin's lips. 'That would be murder.'

'It will be murder once your dad gets to hear about what's happened, let me tell you. I don't know how he'll react. He'll probably blame me for being too lenient with you and not keeping a firmer rein on what you get up to. Mind you, seeing as you rarely go anywhere without us, how I could do that when I thought you were safe and sound in school, I don't know,' her mother retorted sharply. 'By rights the authorities ought to be told and he should be drummed out of the school,' she went on angrily. 'Wicked thing to do, leading an innocent young girl on, taking advantage of her, and then refusing to accept any responsibility.'

'I'm sorry, Mam.' Ruth scrubbed away the tears which were now streaming down her face. As she made to put her arms round her mother, hoping for a reassuring cuddle, there was the sound of the front door key that hung on a string being pulled through the letter box, signalling that Tomas Davies was home from work.

'Quick!' Caitlin pushed her daughter away. 'Dry your eyes, girl, and try and behave normally. Not a word to your dad, mind. Get on with laying that table. Hurry.'

By the time her father had taken off his overcoat, muffler and cap and hung them up on a peg in the hallway and come through into the kitchen, rubbing his hands together and grumbling about how cold he was, Ruth had hastily laid out the knives, forks and spoons for their meal and put the crusty loaf on the bread board, placing it in the centre of the table along with a dish of butter. She had also set out three cups and saucers in a group, together with a small jug of milk and the teapot stand, ready for when their meal ended.

Her mother dished out the cawl and Ruth carried their plates of savoury-smelling stew from the kitchen to the table, putting the largest helping in front of her dad who was already sitting at the table waiting for his meal.

'That smells good!' he commented as he picked up his knife and fork. 'You managed to get some lamb, then. Hard to believe there's a shortage when there are so many sheep on the hills just outside Cardiff. This war has a lot to answer for and no mistake, and it has only just started. Things will get worse, you mark my words,' he added gloomily.

'Lamb or mutton, I'm not sure which it is,' Caitlin laughed. 'I've marinated it well and then cooked it nice and slowly so it should be lovely and tender.'

They ate in silence. Ruth didn't feel hungry and started pushing the meat and vegetables around on her plate but a warning look from

9

her mother stopped her. With an effort she began eating; her mind was still full of the revelations she had made to her mother and she wondered what the outcome was going to be. The earlier feeling of relief was dissipating as she began worrying about what her mother intended to do about it now that she knew. Sooner or later they would have to tell her father and she wasn't at all sure that he'd accept the situation as well as her mother had done. He was a kind and caring man but as the wage earner he felt responsible for his family's welfare and he'd be shocked and hurt when he heard the news.

Every Friday night he handed over house-keeping money to her mother and gave Ruth a sixpence for pocket money. 'Save half and spend the rest,' he always told her. And she did. Three pennies went straight into her money box, the remaining threepence she spent on sweets and a comic.

Sixpence wouldn't be much use to her when she had a baby, she thought wryly. There was so much to worry about, not only the actual act of having it, which was something of a mystery to her, but also how to provide it with food and clothes once it was born. She dared not even start to think about all that because she had no idea what it was going to cost.

She studied her father. He was almost as broad as he was tall. A rotund man, thickset with a barrel chest. His short dark hair was beginning to recede and his shiny forehead was becoming more and more pronounced so that it looked like a giant egg when he stood underneath the gas light. Yet it wasn't because he was old; he was not yet forty. It was something that ran in his family. Grandpa Jenkins had been completely bald and her dad claimed that he'd started to lose his hair when he was still in his twenties, which was even before she was born.

He was a manager at Mostyn Mouldings and in charge of over thirty men so he was used to ordering people around. He had a hard, curt voice and a decisive manner. He stood no nonsense from anybody and never argued. It was as if what he said was law. Once or twice she had tried to contradict something he'd said, but he'd completely ignored her. After that she noticed he did the same when her mother expressed an opinion that was different from his.

Her mam was plump and placid and although she appeared to do exactly what he told her to do Ruth knew that really she ran things exactly the way she wanted to. She never argued with him and it seemed that, as long as their home was run efficiently, his meals were on time and his clothes always washed, ironed and ready to wear whenever he wanted them, he rarely queried what she did.

He never questioned how she managed to find the money for new clothes or even things for their home, which was probably just as well since her mam liked to look smart and well dressed and was always buying things.

It was as if he had no idea about the price of food or anything else. As long as he was well fed and they had a fire burning brightly in the grate when he arrived home, he was content to let her spend the housekeeping money as she thought best and to run things her way. Their house was probably the best furnished in Harriett Street. They had a lovely Axminster rug in front of the fire in the living room, not a rag rug made out of scraps of cloth from old clothes like some of their neighbours had. They changed their curtains twice a year; thick heavy ones in the winter to keep out the draughts and pretty cotton ones in the summer. Her mam never turned sides to middle when their sheets or towels became worn but bought new ones and cut up the old ones and used them as cleaning rags or polishing cloths.

She wasn't expected to wear any of her mother's cut-down dresses or skirts. Her mam bought her a new dress for summer every Easter and a hat and shoes to go with it. She had a thick winter coat and when it was too small for her she had a new one; often her mam gave her old one away to a younger child in the street.

They were never in debt, nor did they ever have a tally man banging on their door because that was one thing that her dad wouldn't tolerate. They celebrated at Christmas with a big fat chicken for their dinner and there'd always been a stocking at the end of her bed as well as a special present like a big doll, or something else that she'd been longing for. There'd always been an Easter egg for her ever since she could remember.

Compared to some people in Harriett Street their life was as smooth as a mill pond. Leastwise, it had been until now, Ruth thought guiltily. She didn't see how her mam was going to break the news to her dad without causing ructions, but she knew better than to question her decision.

His job was both physically and mentally tiring and all Tomas Davies wanted to do when he got home at night was have his meal, put on his slippers and sit and read the evening paper until it was time for a cup of hot cocoa before bed.

That was except on a Saturday night; that was his night out. He went on his own to the local pub where he mingled with friends he had known all his life, played a game of darts, drank two or three pints of beer, and then came home again by ten o'clock.

His routine rarely varied. On Sundays, he accompanied Ruth and her mother to chapel in the morning and after their midday meal he often slept in the afternoon for an hour or so. In the summer, though, he took her and her mother out for a stroll or to Cathays Park to listen to the band.

During the week her mam made sure that her housework was done before midday and then she'd get dressed up and go out with her friend Phoebe Parsons who lived in the next road. Sometimes they went to the pictures or else into the centre of Cardiff and walked around the posh shops admiring all the things they would like to buy.

Usually her mam brought home some little luxury from one of the stalls in the Hayes. Her father didn't approve of shop cake; he liked the ones her mother baked, like apple tarts, Welsh cakes and Bara Brith. He liked to take one or the other in his lunch box each day, so what Caitlin bought was always put away in the larder. Ruth and her mam would share them as a special treat when she came in from school, or sometimes on a Saturday evening while her dad was out at the pub.

It had been fun to share the secret of these special treats with her mam when she'd been younger, but as she grew older they lost their appeal. Living such a well-ordered life was so dull. The other girls in her class at school were allowed out to the pictures or even to local dances but her mam would never let her go because she always said that her dad wouldn't approve.

It meant she had no excitement at all in her life like the other girls had, which was probably why she'd fallen for Glyn Jenkins's glib tongue so easily, she thought ruefully. He was extremely attractive; very tall and handsome with thick black curly hair, flashing blue eyes, a thin dark moustache and an infectious smile. He was always making witty comments or telling a snappy joke. Whenever he had to tell anyone off he always spoke to them in such a way that they never felt guilty or uncomfortable but were eager to do as he asked.

At one time when the other girls talked about their flirtations with one of their classmates, or one of the boys who'd left school a year or so before and were now out working, she'd felt jealous. But from the moment Glyn Jenkins had singled her out and started paying her attention she'd felt so special. Her classmates' boyfriends were only raw youths; hers was an experienced man.

He'd told her that he thought she was pretty; no one had ever said that before. The first time he'd kissed her had been magical. She relived the memory of it every night for weeks afterwards.

After that, every day had brought some new exciting memory to treasure. At first they had mostly talked, telling each other all about their home life. He'd gently stroke her face or hold her hand and tell her how much she meant to him and that no one had ever shown him so much affection before.

These snatched moments together, the thrill

of knowing that she was the one he loved, and the scheming to be with him, without anyone else at school finding out what was going on, made every school day exciting.

Life suddenly become a wonderful adventure. She never knew when she was going to see him or what he was going to say or do next. He would convey messages to her with a special smile, a knowing wink, or raise his eyebrows questioningly so that words were hardly ever necessary when there was anyone else around.

He aroused feelings deep inside her and turbulent emotions she'd never known before. It was thrilling and frightening. Whenever they were alone he was so loving and gentle that she never for one moment considered that what they were doing was wrong.

She still couldn't believe how he'd changed the moment she'd told him that she was expecting his baby. The twinkle went out of his eyes, there were no more secret meetings in the boiler room or light touches on her arm when they passed each other in the corridors.

He was so cold and formal towards her that she felt deeply hurt. Whenever she tried to catch him on his own to talk to him about it and ask what they were going to do and when he was going to leave his wife, he made some excuse or the other.

When he finally told her to stop pestering him and that he'd no intention of breaking up his own home life she had felt as if the bottom had dropped out of her world. All the promises he'd made and the dreams they'd woven together as she lay in his arms after they'd made love turned to ashes.

That was when she knew that she would have to tell her mother the sordid unhappy news that now she was expecting his baby he wanted nothing more to do with her.

She'd tried so hard to do it, lying awake for hours at night, going over and over in her mind how she would lead up to telling her. Then when it came to it tonight she had blurted it out knowing that it was the only way she could do it.

Chapter Two

Ruth waited anxiously for her mother to tell her father that she was pregnant. She knew there was bound to be a tremendous row and the thought of it hung over her head like a threatening cloud.

She wished they'd had time to talk more before her dad had come home. Now she was in turmoil wondering what her mam was going to do; the waiting was a greater punishment than any telling off would have been.

Two days, three days, then four, and she decided she could stand it no longer. She'd tell him herself. She mightn't do it as tactfully as her mother would, but that didn't matter. At least it would be out in the open and she wouldn't be on tenterhooks all the time wondering when the storm was going to break.

She resolved she'd do it on Saturday morning when they all sat down to breakfast together, and she spent the next couple of days going over and over in her mind exactly what she would say.

The opportunity to carry out her plan never materialised. On Friday, when she arrived home from school, she found her mother white faced and apprehensive. A letter from the war authorities addressed to Tomas Davies had arrived by the midday post and she was full of gloom about what the contents might be.

Caitlin waited until they had finished eating their evening meal before she produced the letter. 'This came for you this morning, Tomas,' she commented as she took it out of her pinafore pocket and passed it across the table to him.

Her husband frowned as he took it from her. Thoughtfully he turned it over, studying the markings on the envelope and shaking his head as if mystified. Then, wiping his knife clean on the side of his plate he inserted the blade under the flap and sliced it open.

Ruth and Caitlin held their breath as he drew out the sheet of paper and studied it in silence.

'Damnio di!' he muttered. 'Things must be in a pretty bad state when they need to conscript a man of my age.'

'Conscript? You mean you've been called up, Tomas?' Caitlin asked in a shocked voice, her eyes widening in dismay as her worst fears were confirmed.

'Here, read it for yourself,' he said, shaking his head in disbelief as he passed the letter across to his wife.

Caitlin's mouth tightened as she read the curt notification. 'Duw! I can't believe it's come to this, boyo!' she said, shaking her head sadly. 'What are they going to say about this at work when you tell them?'

Tomas pushed back his chair and stood up. 'What can they say or do? If you get your call-up papers then that's it.'

'There must be some exemptions – your age, the sort of work you do, that sort of thing,' Caitlin protested.

'Maybe there are, but by the look of things none of them apply to me or they wouldn't have sent me that dratted letter. They're not going to waste time writing to those they know can wriggle out of going, now are they?'

'No, I suppose not,' Caitlin agreed slowly. 'This is such a shock though. It's going to make such a difference to our lives. You may be away months—'

'Or even years,' Tomas interrupted.

'Oh, don't go saying things like that. They are probably calling up all the men they possibly can so as to make a huge attack on the enemy and settle this silly war quickly and put an end to such conflicts once and for all.'

Tomas shook his head. 'I doubt if they will manage to do either, cariad. I think we are all in for a tough time. With the men away you women will have to manage as best you can and there will be shortages of everything from food to clothes, so you won't find life easy-going, I can tell you.'

'It won't be all that easy for you either, Dad,' Ruth added.

'No, cariad, you're right there. We're all going to find our lives changing and there is

nothing at all we can do about it. It's out of
our hands and we have to rely on those at the
top, the ones in authority, to do their damn-
dest to get us through this lot – and I'm not
all that sure that they know what they're doing.
Time will tell, though, time will tell,' he added
morosely.

'Cheer up, Dad.' Ruth smiled. 'It will be quite
an adventure for you going off and meeting
lots of other men and leaving Mam and me at
home on our own.'

'Adventure!' He gave a bitter laugh. 'It's an
adventure I can well do without. I'm happy
enough where I am. I have a good job, regular
pay at the end of each week, so what more
does any man want? Security is a wonderful
thing. We've just about finished scrimping and
saving to get a home together and we've finally
got things as we want them. You'll be starting
work in a few weeks' time and then we'll even
be able to afford a few more of life's little
luxuries.'

'Well, I may not . . .' Ruth started to speak,
intent on telling him about what was going
to happen, since her mother didn't seem to
be prepared to do so, and explain that she
might not be starting work for a while. She
caught Caitlin's warning look and her slight
shake of the head and realised that her mother
didn't want her to speak out at this moment.

She felt slightly irritated. Surely if they were
going to break the news to her dad then they

must do it quickly, because from the contents of the letter it appeared he would be leaving within the next few days and he ought to be told before then. If they put it off until the very last moment it would be a terrible shock for him and she didn't want him to go away with the impression that she had avoided telling him until the very last moment in order to escape a good telling off.

If she told him now it might even help to take his mind off being called up, Ruth thought wryly. He certainly didn't seem to like the idea of going into the army, which rather surprised her because he was a man who always liked to be seen doing and saying the right thing. She knew he didn't approve of physical violence, but surely when it came to defending your country against the enemy then that was slightly different and he had always seemed to be very patriotic.

As she helped her mother to clear away the dishes and carry them through into the scullery to be washed, she managed to waylay her out of earshot of her father and ask why she wasn't telling him about the baby.

Again Caitlin shushed her to keep quiet and, frowning, shook her head, even more vigorously this time. 'Leave it!' she hissed. 'I'll deal with it all in good time.'

Ruth knew it was pointless arguing with her mother when she was in one of her determined moods, so she said no more but she couldn't help wishing she'd hurry up and get on with it. The sooner her dad knew and the lecture was over, the better she would feel. It had dragged on now for almost a week and she found the suspense was like some form of torture. She even wondered if it was her mother's idea of punishing her.

There was no opportunity for her to speak to her mother again that evening because both her parents seemed to be too intent on discussing how things were to be handled in her father's absence.

Long after she went to bed Ruth tossed and turned because she was so worried about the situation. She was full of regrets about what had happened. What on earth had she been thinking about to let herself be taken in by the smooth tongue and handsome looks of Glyn Jenkins? She knew all the girls in her class at school fancied him and they were always talking and joking about it, but she was the one he'd picked out for special attention.

In the beginning it had merely been roguish smiles and amusing quips whenever he had a chance to speak to her. Then it had become more daring; the hand on the small of her back, a gentle squeeze or an arm around her shoulders as he pretended to move her out of his way. Gradually, one familiarity had led to another: the snatched kiss; the raised eyebrows signalling that he would meet her later. Then came the dallying after school so that they could meet secretly when she was supposed to be with her friends or staying late at school for some reason.

At first it had been merely a crazy flirtation on her part; and probably on his as well. Then, after the school end-of-term party at Christmas things had really got serious. It had been the only time that he had actually made love to her and it had scared her stiff. She realised they had gone too far.

He'd joked about it, but she had been in a terrible state for days afterwards, frightened in case her parents or someone at school discovered what had happened. She'd found it so scary that she didn't even tell her best friend Veronwy Williams, in case she blurted it out to someone. Anyway, there wasn't much to be gained from doing so because she knew Veronwy would be forbidden to have anything more to do with her once it was known she was having a baby.

Her mam was so right; Glyn Jenkins was a married man with young children and there was no excuse at all for him to be playing around. She should have known better than to trust him. The minute he saw how upset she was he'd cut and run. The next day he hadn't even spoken to her. He'd passed her in the corridor and simply carried on walking, whistling away as though he hadn't even seen her.

A couple of days later and he was chatting

up Freda Francis, another girl in her class; winking at her, raising his eyebrows and nodding suggestively towards the janitor's office where he kept all his mops and buckets.

She'd been on the point of warning Freda but then thought better of it. She could hardly justify doing so without disclosing what had happened to her and, once she told one person, then she was pretty sure that the entire class would get to hear of it, possibly the whole school, and she couldn't bear for everyone to find out what an idiot she'd been.

A couple of months later exactly how stupid she'd been came home to her even more forcibly. At first she tried to ignore the signs, telling herself it was because she'd had a cold, or because she was so worried that she was run down. When nothing happened the following month she knew it was pointless to go on kidding herself.

Even so, it took her ages before she could pluck up the courage to tell her mam. She would have avoided doing so if she could, but she kept being sick in the morning and refusing her breakfast and her mother was concerned.

She'd thought her mam would tell her dad about it straight away; keeping her waiting was adding to her mental torment. She realised what a dreadful blow it must have been for her mother because friends and neighbours would think it a terrible disgrace. More than likely, as her mother had already said, they would put some of the blame on her. Her dad certainly would, which was no doubt why her mam was so hesitant about telling him, especially now. Even so, she wondered what was going on in her mam's mind and why she was holding back from telling him.

Perhaps she thought he had enough already on his plate and so she wasn't going to tell him right to his face. If they waited until after he'd actually left home then one of them could tell him in a letter. It seemed rather a cowardly way out, though, and she was sure that it would upset him far more than if he was told now.

She simply had to talk to her mam about it. She was still thinking it over when she fell asleep, and next morning she was so late getting up that there was no time to discuss anything. Her dad had already gone out, probably to work, anxious to break the news to his boss and colleagues that he had received his call-up papers and to see if any of them had done so as well.

Her mother was not in a very talkative mood over breakfast. There were dark shadows under her eyes and she looked as though she'd hardly had any sleep.

'Your dad being called up for the army is going to affect us all,' she said worriedly. 'I have no idea what sort of pay a soldier receives, but I'm pretty certain it won't be as much as he earns as a manager at Mostyn's.'

'I'll be leaving school and—'

'Yes, I'd been counting on you going out to

work and being able to hand over some house-keeping money and perhaps even being able to buy your own clothes in the future,' her mother interrupted. 'Now it seems you are going to be more dependent on us than ever. We'll not only have to keep you, but this baby as well.'

'I'm sorry, Mam.'

'It will probably mean that I'll have to go out to work like one or two of the other women around here whose husbands are out of work or not earning very much money.'

'Dad would hate for that to happen,' Ruth told her. 'He's always said that he doesn't approve of wives working and that their place is in the home, caring for their family, cooking and cleaning, not out in the workplace.'

'He won't be here to do anything about it, though, or even to know if I go out to work or not, now will he? I'd rather find myself a job than be short of money.'

The thought intrigued Ruth; she wondered what sort of job her mother would want to do. As far as she knew, she hadn't worked since the day she got married. Before that she had been an assistant in a ladies fashion department in David Morgan's, which was one of the top department stores in Cardiff.

In the past she'd always loved hearing the stories her mam sometimes told her about those days. All the apprentices and shop assistants had to live in, so they had slept in dormitories and had had to obey all sorts of rules.

Of course she wouldn't have to do that now, because she was a grown woman and had a home to run. But, although she still loved clothes and took a great interest in all the new, modern styles, it was such a long time since her mam had actually worked behind a shop counter that they might not think she was suitable any more.

She might have to take on some other kind of work, such as dressmaking, which she was quite good at, or perhaps making curtains and things like that since she was very good with her needle.

Ruth was quite sure her mam would never go out cleaning or looking after sick people. She didn't think she'd even like minding other people's children while they went out to work because she was far too house-proud. She wouldn't want little sticky fingers touching everything, or toys and muddle all over the place.

In fact, the more she thought about it the more she wondered how her mother would react to working for other people. She was so used to doing things her way and no one criticising her at all that she'd probably take it very hard if she had to conform to other people's demands.

Chapter Three

It was a crisp, bright Monday morning in late March when Tomas Davies pulled on his heavy grey coat over his dark blue suit, kissed Caitlin goodbye, and set off for work from his comfortable little terraced house in Harriett Street.

He felt unusually alert as he set off at a brisk pace for the tram stop in Newport Road and made the journey to Mostyn Mouldings at East Moors. Tucked into the inside pocket of his jacket was the letter that had been waiting for him when he'd arrived home the previous Friday night; a letter that he was well aware was going to change his entire life and that of his family.

He'd spent many years as a young man getting his hands dirty and ingrained grimy-grey from the metal components they handled on the factory floor, but he'd stuck at it, doggedly working his way up the promotional ladder. He'd succeeded; he'd become one of the youngest charge hands in the company.

He'd been determined to do even better for himself and he'd felt it had been very worthwhile when he'd been promoted to under-manager for the entire components section some three years earlier.

It meant that not only was he able to discard his overalls and wear a suit to work, but he also had his own office. True, it only consisted of a flat-top metal desk, a couple of chairs and a four-drawer filing cabinet in a partitioned-off corner of the factory floor, but it was a mark of his authority.

Now it seemed he was about to lose all he had achieved. A single sheet of paper from someone he'd never heard of was going to ruin his entire life. He would no longer be a man of some importance and authority, but would be demoted to being a mere number.

As a raw army rookie he'd have to jump to attention whenever a corporal or sergeant issued an order. He'd have to wear a khaki uniform and, once more, he'd be at the bottom of the pile. It was a bitter pill to swallow.

It seemed so unfair after all the effort he'd put into making good in his chosen career. If he'd played around like some of the boyos who'd signed on at Mostyn Mouldings when they left school, and remained one of the over-alled workers of the factory floor, then he would probably have been exempt from army service.

They would have regarded what he was doing as helping towards the war effort, but because he was a white-collar worker, his services could be dispensed with; he was not considered to be an essential cog in the war machine. It was all so unfair, yet he knew there was nothing he could do about it.

The contents of the letter in his pocket were imprinted on his brain; he'd thought of nothing else since he'd read it. He'd wondered if it was a mistake since surely he ought to be exempt. Without him organising everything on the factory floor things would quickly go to pot. He had strict rules and he made sure that the men adhered to them. He was very methodical so there were never any mix-ups with the orders. He was so organised that he was never behind with an order; in fact, if anything, he was always ahead of schedule. Things wouldn't remain like that for long if he wasn't there, he thought grimly.

Surely, since the items they manufactured were needed indirectly by the army, his work should be regarded as essential and he should be exempt. He certainly intended to take his case to the top; he'd arrange to see one of the directors so that he could ask if they could intervene on his behalf.

The letter had only given him a week before he had to report and already two days had gone by. There was barely enough time left to get his affairs in order. As well as handing over all his files and details of the outstanding orders to someone else and instructing them in what had to be done and exactly how it should be carried out, there were things at home to be organised.

Caitlin was a good wife; she'd never been in debt and she organised things in their home almost as efficiently as he ran his own job. Of course, she'd always had enough money to do so, unlike some poor dabs in their street whose husbands went on a blinder every weekend as soon as they were paid, and he was always there in the background to discuss matters with her and to advise her.

He would make her an allowance out of his army pay, but he had no idea exactly what that would be or how much he'd be able to send her each week. It certainly wouldn't be anywhere near as much as he handed over now.

Leaving later in the week meant that he was going to miss Ruth's fourteenth birthday by a few days. She was due to start work in May and he had already advised her on the kind of job she ought to apply for, but of course it all depended on what sort of a school report she received when she finally left at Easter.

Her marks had always been good and he was pretty certain that she'd get a first-class reference from the head teacher, so there was really no problem there. Nevertheless, he would have preferred to be on hand to guide her in her choice and iron out any problems she might come across in the first few weeks.

Going out to work was very different to spending time in school. It was a longer day for a start, and there wouldn't be breaks or changes of lessons to provide variety. Most jobs became humdrum in a very short time. He'd noticed that the young apprentices were always eager and willing for the first few months, but after that their interest waned as they found that they were repeating the same processes day in, day out.

He'd also miss out on the family holiday they'd intended to have at Easter, before Ruth started work. He had planned to take them up the Valleys to visit Caitlin's mother, Maggie Hughes. She'd left Cardiff after her husband had died a few years earlier to go and live with her younger sister, Edyth, who was also a widow. Edyth's husband had been a miner and had died from silicosis a few years earlier.

Edyth herself had died just before Christmas and he knew that Caitlin was worried about her mother living on her own. Maggie Hughes was no longer in the best of health and it would set Caitlin's mind at rest to go and visit her and make sure that she was able to manage.

Perhaps if he did have to go into the army then it might be an idea to move the old lady back to Cardiff, Tomas mused. Caitlin could keep an eye on her and it might help to take her mind off the fact that he wasn't at home.

Still, he hoped none of this would be necessary. If they could manage to plead his case and he didn't have to go into the army, then life could carry on just as it had always done.

Tomas Davies's hopes were dashed the moment he was shown into the managing director's office.

Mervyn Mostyn came straight to the point. 'I understand, Davies, that you want to see me because you've received your call-up papers,' he said without any preamble.

'That's right. I think there must be some mistake. I'm sure you will agree that I am needed here and that the work I am doing is very valuable war work.'

'I'm afraid not,' Mervyn Mostyn said curtly. 'You're classified as a white-collar worker and therefore not essential to production. Nothing we can do, I'm afraid. We'll try and keep your job open for you when you are discharged, but I can't promise anything. None of us know exactly how things will change or how long this war will last. You can certainly apply to come back when it's all over, but I'm unable to guarantee anything at all.'

Tomas stared at him in disbelief. Mervyn Mostyn was still in his twenties, almost young enough to be his son. He'd taken over the managing directorship when his father Martyn had a heart attack while in his mid-sixties, and although Mervyn was figuratively in charge, Martyn was still Chairman and the power in the business; all major decisions were still made by him, so Tomas resented being spoken to in such a manner by his son. The wondered if he should demand to speak to Martyn Mostyn to see if he could intervene with the authorities on his behalf, but he decided it would probably be a complete waste of time.

The interview took less than ten minutes and Tomas found himself outside the managing director's office once more, reluctantly accepting that there was not going to be a reprieve of any kind whatsoever.

He felt both hurt and angry. He'd devoted his life to Mostyn Mouldings, and always placed his work commitments before anything else, even his own family. He'd struggled in to work when he was feeling far from well rather than let them down, and this was his reward. It all seemed to be so terribly unfair; it was enough to make a man lose all respect for those in charge.

He would have to break the news to Caitlin and he hoped that she would understand that there was absolutely nothing more he could do. At the moment, since his promotion, they were quite well off compared to most of their neighbours, and when Ruth started work in May things would be even easier. At least, that was what he'd thought, but now it was all a pipe dream. As a private in the army he'd be on such a miserable wage that he didn't see how Caitlin would be able to manage, he thought gloomily

They'd talked about it endlessly over the weekend and she'd even pointed out that it might mean she would have to go out to work. He didn't like that idea one bit. He'd always maintained that a woman's place was at home. What sort of work could she do, anyway? She'd not had a job since the day they were married sixteen years ago, except to cook and clean and look after him and Ruth.

She'd said something about doing war work,

but that meant going into one of the munitions factories and he didn't like the sound of that. He'd seen some of the women who worked in the factories down near the docks and at Curran's munitions on the Taff Embankment. They were a rough crowd and he couldn't see his Caitlin settling into something of that sort.

There was also the question of Ruth finding work. Caitlin had told her so much about the job she'd had as a young girl that Ruth hankered to do something similar. He didn't know how much things had changed but Caitlin had been expected to live in when she was a young apprentice and he didn't think that was a good idea now, when he would be away from home, because it would leave Caitlin on her own.

Tomas felt so frustrated that he didn't know what to do for the best. The trouble was, he had only three days to get himself and Caitlin and Ruth organised and then he had to report to barracks. He knew enough about the army to know that there was no way he could put it off; he only had to be a few hours late to be in trouble.

There were so many last-minute things to compete that he was going to be rushed off his feet. He certainly wouldn't bother coming into work for the next couple of days, not after Mervyn Mostyn's curt dismissal. In fact, he resolved to make the announcement to the chaps on the floor right away and then he'd go to the accounts office and demand a day's pay and his cards and leave right away.

Saying goodbye was a bigger wrench than he'd expected. The men on the shop floor seemed to be as angry as he was that the company weren't doing anything to see if they could get him exempt from call up or, at least, get the date deferred.

To his surprise most of them seemed sorry to see him go. 'Better the devil you know,' the foreman quipped as he shook hands and said goodbye. There was backslapping and hand-shaking all round after that, and Tomas felt a lump in his throat as he walked out of his office for the last time.

He didn't go straight home. Instead, he made his way to the Pier Head, bought himself a cup of tea and a bacon sandwich at one of the cafés there, and sat watching the boats sailing in and out of the harbour as he ate it.

Given the choice he would have preferred to have been called up for the navy rather than the army. He'd always wanted to go to sea. Even the huge coal barges that moved in and out of the busy port each day had fascinated him when he was a lad, although he wouldn't have wanted a job on one of them because it was such heavy work and they were so dirty. You were black from coal dust from morning until night and, like the miners who worked underground in the pits up in the Valleys, you found that it became so ingrained in your skin that you could never really get clean.

No, he would have liked to work on one of

the passenger liners, though in what capacity he wasn't sure; possibly working as an engineer, or maybe even as a steward waiting on the passengers.

It must be an exciting life, setting out from Cardiff for a port on the other side of the world, he mused. You'd be visiting countless strange cities, meeting unusual people, and listening to languages you'd never heard before.

You only had to walk down Bute Road, and go into any of the maze of streets in Tiger Bay, to realise what a tremendous variety of people there were in the world. Streets around Loudon Square and James Street were packed with men and women of all races. There were Africans, Asians, Chinese, and even white people from places like Poland, Holland and America. Some had come in search of a better life than they'd had in their own country. Others had jumped ship because they didn't like the conditions they had to endure on board and when they found that they could scrape a decent living in Cardiff they'd stayed, married, and now had families.

He realised he'd probably meet a host of different people in the army; men not only from Cardiff and South Wales, but probably from places like Yorkshire or even Cornwall. Some would be good, hard-working men like himself while others would be loafers or out of work through no fault of their own. They'd all be thrown together, expected to live in barracks, drill every day and learn how to use guns and take care of themselves ready for when they were sent over to the Front in France where the actual war was going on.

As he boarded a tram at the Pier Head he wondered when he would see it all again. Would it be months or years before things returned to normal? he wondered as he settled back on the wooden seat and handed over his pennies to the conductor.

The tram swayed and clanged its way up Bute Road, past the Hayes and along St Mary's Street towards the castle, before turning into Queen Street on its way to Newport Road, and he was conscious of how busy the streets were with people shopping, or going about their daily business.

He was proud of the city with its outstanding gleaming white new City Hall and its fine parks. He'd lived there all his life; he'd been born in Roath and had gone to school less than half a mile from Harriett Street where he was living now. As he studied all the familiar shops and buildings as the tram passed by them, he wondered when he would be back.

Everything would probably have changed by then. Ruth would have left school and would be working. She'd always been a good scholar and he was proud of the way she'd worked so hard. They'd never had a moment's worry over her and he was sure she'd get a worthwhile job even though it was wartime; that, at least, was something to look forward to.

Chapter Four

The remaining few days in March were taken up by the many last-minute things that had to be done prior to Tomas leaving home. Finally, though, all that remained was for him to say goodbye to friends and neighbours.

Ruth took the day off school so that she could be at home the morning he left. She was unable to hold back her tears when it came to the final parting. Up until then she had thought of it as an exciting adventure for her dad, but now that his case was packed, and he was standing in the hallway with his hat and overcoat on, the realisation of what it was going to mean hit her forcibly.

She knew her mam was holding back her own tears, and she could see she was very upset; it would be the first time her parents had been parted since they'd been married and it was going to be so lonely for her without him.

They would miss him, but he had to establish a whole new life for himself with people he didn't know. He wasn't the sort of man who enjoyed the company of strangers so he was probably going to find it extremely difficult.

Tomas had to report to Maindy Barracks

which was in Cardiff and not very far away. Caitlin had wanted to go as far as the gates with him, but he was adamant that they said goodbye within the privacy of their own home.

'I'd look a complete fool if you were there, standing at the gates blubbering and crying your eyes out,' he said sternly. 'Have some pride, cariad!'

Caitlin didn't argue, but then she rarely did. She knew he liked to think that his word was law.

After they'd said their farewells and the front door had closed behind him, Ruth immediately asked her mother why she'd said nothing about the baby.

'No point, cariad, there isn't anything he can do about it now, is there, and he's got enough on his plate at the moment,' her mother said crisply. She blew her nose and wiped the tears from her eyes. 'Right, let's get the breakfast dishes washed up and then the pair of us can pop along to the Hayes and do a spot of shopping to cheer ourselves up,' she pronounced briskly.

'Mam! Dad's only just this minute walked out of the door and we don't know when we will see him again and you're talking about gallivanting off on a shopping spree.'

'Why not?' Her mother frowned. 'What good is it going to do if we sit here and mope? I would have gone as far as the Barracks with him, but he didn't want that so what else can

41

we do but get on with our lives? If a trip out to the shops cheers us up, then surely it's the best thing to do.'

'It doesn't seem right somehow,' Ruth protested.

'If you don't want to come with me, then instead of taking the day off you can cut along to school. I'm sure they'll understand why you're late if you tell them that your dad joined the army today. Anyway, decide for yourself. You break up tomorrow for the holidays so you won't be missing very much if you do come to the Hayes with me.'

As Ruth collected up a pile of dishes and followed her mother into the scullery she felt at a loss to understand her mother's reasoning about the baby. Still, there was no point in arguing. She'd have to be patient and wait and see what her mam wanted to do about it.

It would be Easter next week and she had been looking forward to leaving school. It should have been the start of a whole new life, going to work, earning money and gradually becoming independent, but now she wasn't at all sure what was going to happen.

She didn't even know if she wanted to keep the baby. She'd never had a baby brother or sister so she had no idea how difficult it was to bring them up.

Even though her mother had pooh-poohed the idea of her going to work she still didn't see why she couldn't get a job of some sort, even if it was only for a few months. It would give her the chance to earn some money and to start buying things for the baby.

As they wandered around the various stalls at the Hayes, Ruth was surprised to see her mother lingering at one where they sold baby clothes and fingering one of the delicately knitted layettes. She didn't buy it, but it prompted Ruth to ask her mother when they arrived home if they were still going on holiday after Easter to visit Granny Hughes as they'd planned.

'No, we won't be going yet,' her mother told her. 'We'll leave it for a month or so.'

'I thought you were worried about her because she wrote and said she wasn't too well,' Ruth murmured.

'Well, I want to see her, but I don't think there is all that much rush,' her mother prevaricated. 'I thought we'd leave it until after we'd heard from your dad and found out where he's going to be stationed after he's finished his training.'

'Surely he'll be sent over to France,' Ruth said, pushing her hair back behind her ears and looking at her mother in surprise. 'That's why Dad has been called up, isn't it, so that he can go over there and fight the enemy?'

'Yes, of course it is, but it doesn't necessarily mean that he will go out to France straight away.'

'You mean that you think he might get some leave after he's finished his training and then we could all go to Caerphilly to see Granny?'

'I don't know about that. I just want to wait and find out exactly what is going to happen.'

'Why, Mam? I don't understand why the two of us can't go. Granny will be ever so disappointed if we don't.'

'No, I don't suppose you do understand; that's because you don't know what I have in mind,' her mother replied in a tight voice.

'Perhaps you'd better tell me, then, because if it concerns me I need to know.'

There was a long silence as her mother considered this idea. 'Go and put the kettle on and make us a cup of tea and while we drink it I'll try and explain.'

Although she felt utterly mystified, Ruth did as she was told. When they were both sitting down with a cup of tea in front of them she looked at her mother expectantly. 'Well then, Mam. What is it that you have to say to me?'

'I want you to listen to me very carefully,' her mother said, reaching out and squeezing her hand.

Ruth looked at her in alarm because she sounded so on edge. The memory of her mother handling the baby clothes on the stall at the Hayes came flashing into her mind and she immediately felt anxious. It was something to do with the baby, she was sure about that.

Caitlin sat back and sipped her tea, added more milk to it, and then some more sugar, and stirred it vigorously before she spoke again. The longer she had to wait the more tense Ruth felt.

'I've been thinking about what we must do about this baby,' her mother said at last. 'It all depends on what happens to your dad, of course.'

'Why? What do you mean?'

Caitlin took another sip of her tea. 'It depends on whether he is sent overseas to the front or whether he stays here in this country.'

Ruth frowned and waited in silence for her to continue.

'If he goes overseas, then we'll go up to Caerphilly and see Granny Hughes sometime in June and stay there for two or three months, until after the baby is born.'

'Why? Whatever for?' Ruth frowned. 'She won't want the worry of all that, not if she isn't too well.'

'Don't be twp, cariad, we'll be there to look after her.'

'Yes, but wouldn't it be better to have the baby here, at home? Our house is bigger than Granny's.'

'No, we're going up there and we'll come back here again as soon as you are recovered enough to do so,' her mother said firmly.

Ruth thought about it for a moment while her mother poured herself another cup of tea. An uneasy thought had invaded her mind. It was the only reason she could think of as to why they should go to Caerphilly. Her mother was planning for the baby to be born while they were there, so that she could arrange to have it adopted before they came back home. People would think they'd been in Caerphilly looking after Granny Hughes and no one would know the truth about what had happened.

It was a clever idea, she could see that, but she was confused as well as astounded that her mother would go to such extremes to conceal the fact that she'd had a baby.

As she finished her own cup of tea anger bubbled up inside her. She knew she couldn't simply hand her baby over to strangers. Glyn Jenkins mightn't want her or the baby, but she didn't intend to abandon it and she was astonished that her mother would even think that she'd do so.

'No,' she said determinedly as she replaced her cup in the saucer. 'I know what you're planning. You intend to have the baby adopted, but I won't let you.'

'Shush, shush, don't upset yourself, and don't talk so twp,' her mother said quickly. 'I have no idea of asking you to give the baby up.' She gave a complacent smile. 'I have a much better idea than that.'

'You have?'

Her mother nodded and pursed her lips thoughtfully. 'Well, we stay up in Caerphilly like I said, until after you've had the baby, and then we come back here to Cardiff with the baby, but we tell everybody that it is mine,' she pronounced triumphantly.

46

Ruth stared at her mother in disbelief. 'Yours! How can we say that?'

'Why not? If you haven't told anyone about it except me, then who is to know?'

'Glyn Jenkins will know.'

'Huh, I can't see that cowardly boyo saying anything,' her mother told her scornfully. 'He'll keep his mouth shut because he knows that if he doesn't he'll land himself in deep trouble. No, Glyn Jenkins will keep quiet to save his own skin, so you needn't worry your head about him saying anything.'

'Surely some people will be bound to guess the truth, Mam,' Ruth protested.

'Why should they? I'm not that old, cariad.'

'I know that, Mam, but people are going to think it strange. And what about Dad, what is he going to say?'

'If your dad is over in France we can hood-wink him easily. As soon as he goes overseas I'll write and tell him I'm expecting and, with any luck, he won't be home again before the baby is born. When he does come home then he will have a new little son or daughter to gladden his eye. What could be nicer?'

'It's risky, Mam. Supposing he isn't sent to France, or supposing that even if he is, he comes back on leave between now and when the baby is born?'

'Fat chance of that, cariad,' her mother said dismissively. 'Once he's out there he'll be there until the war ends, you mark my words.'

47

'It may end quite soon, like in a month or so,' Ruth said thoughtfully.

'Well . . .' Her mother stood up and started clearing away their cups. 'If that happens and he does come home, then we'll have to tell him the truth. When I write I'll be very careful how I word the letter, don't you worry. If he should come back before it is born, then I'll let him think that he misunderstood what I wrote and told him.'

'How can you do that? He may have saved the letter so he'll be able to check out what you said.'

'Oh stop worrying about it, cariad. I know what I'm doing. Leave it to me. Why do you think I was so insistent that you said nothing to him before he went away? The moment he received his call-up papers the idea came to me like a bolt out of the blue, but I needed time to think it through. It's the ideal solution to all our problems.'

Ruth mulled over her mother's suggestion long after she went to bed that night. It was a clever idea, she had to admit that, but it didn't seem right to hoodwink her dad like that. She would rather that they had told him, perhaps even included him in their subterfuge, rather than do it her mother's way. It was better than having an abortion or having the baby adopted, she readily admitted that, but it was all going to be so terribly confusing.

Everyone would think that the baby was her

brother or sister and once they started misleading people then they'd have to go on doing so for ever more. It would mean that the baby would grow up thinking that she was its sister.

It was such a risky undertaking that she wasn't sure if she could go through with it. For the rest of her life she would be living a lie and, for that matter, so would her mother, but what choice did they have? She was astonished and grateful that her mother was prepared to do such a thing for her.

When her father came home from the war he would have the responsibility of raising a young child. What would he think about that? He had been a good father to her, but he was inclined to be strict and he might be much worse with the new child not only because he was quite a lot older, but also because he might have changed in so many other ways after being in the army.

She remembered clearly how, when she'd been very small, he had objected if she made too much noise when she was playing in the house or in the small backyard. He had never liked her bringing her friends home, because he said that they made a mess in the house or else that they caused too much commotion. He was bound to be the same with the new baby and she'd probably find it hard not to say anything.

It was a lot for her mam to undertake as well.

She was easier going than her dad, but even so she didn't like her home being untidy and for a long time there would be toys around the place. There would be sticky little fingers everywhere, too. Could her mam cope with all that? she wondered.

She knew her mam was doing all this to help her and because she thought it was the best way out of a difficult situation, but nevertheless it was very risky. What if someone from Caerphilly met someone from Harriett Street who knew them and blurted out the truth? How would her mother deal with that?

Another thing that worried her was that it would be fourteen years before the child was old enough to leave school and by then her mam would be quite old and so would her dad. They'd both be in their fifties and wanting a quiet life. She'd be nearly thirty herself and that was approaching middle-age.

The really big problem, of course, was that there would be a fourteen-year difference in age between her and her so-called new brother or sister and that was an awfully big gap; surely people would talk or even suspect that it wasn't her mam's child?

It was a bold plan and she knew she ought to be very grateful, but there were so many drawbacks that she felt frightened in case it all went wrong and if it did, then the consequences might be overwhelming for all of them.

Her mam must have thought about all this

so there was probably no point in raising any of these issues with her as it would only make her cross. Probably the best thing to do would be to go along with her mother's plan and hope that everything turned out all right.

If only she was older and had a job and was earning money then perhaps she could be the one to make the decisions. As it was, she knew she must be grateful to her mother – after all, she could have refused to help and thrown her out.

Chapter Five

It was ten days before they heard from Tomas. Even then it was only a few lines to give them his army number and a box number where they could write to him, and to say that he was at a training depot, but was unable to tell them where it was.

He said he was quite well but finding all the drilling very tiring and he missed his comfortable chair and bed. He hoped they were both well and managing without him.

'Not got much choice, have we?' Caitlin observed as she took the brief letter back from Ruth, folded it up, and put it on the mantelpiece behind the clock.

'He doesn't say anything about getting any leave or whether or not he'll be going overseas,' Ruth commented.

'I don't suppose he knows,' her mother told her. 'As a private you only hear rumours until the day they line you up on the barrack square and tell you that you'll be leaving within the next hour.'

'Oh, Mam, you do make things up. You don't know that for sure, now do you?'

'It's what happened to Phoebe Parson's young

brother. He was one of the first to be recruited. He went straight to a training camp and after three weeks he was sent over to France.'

'Is that the one who was killed?'

'Yes, poor dab. A sniper got him. He'd only been over there a week. It happened on the eve of his twenty-first birthday, broke his mother's heart, so Phoebe said.'

'That's terrible.' Ruth shuddered. 'I hope Dad doesn't get sent to the Front.'

'He probably will and there's nothing we can do about it. We probably won't even know he's gone until days afterwards.'

'Surely he'll write and tell us?'

'Of course he will, I made him promise to do that, but it doesn't mean we will get the letter right away. He has to hand his letters over so that they can be censored to make sure he doesn't tell us anything that would be of use to the enemy.'

'You mean like where he is while he is training, or when they are going to the Front?'

'That's right, and the army people hang on to the letters for a few days so that the men are all over there before their families know anything about it.'

'You and Phoebe seem to tell each other everything; have you said anything to her about the baby?'

'Of course I haven't, don't be so twp.'

'I wish you'd stop telling me that I'm daft all the time,' Ruth protested sulkily.

'Sorry, cariad, but sometimes I think you are very silly. I told you in the first place that we wouldn't breathe a word to anyone. As long as no one else except Glyn Jenkins knows, and as I said before he won't say anything, then things will go the way we want them to.'

'Surely though, Mam, she'll think it strange if you go off to Caerphilly and then come back a few months later with a young baby.'

'Not if I handle things carefully. As soon as I know what's happening with your dad, then I can start preparing Phoebe and one or two of the neighbours.'

'You mean you are going to drop hints that you are expecting a baby?'

'That's right, but not yet; not until a couple of days before we leave for Caerphilly. I shall tell them in confidence, of course, which means it will get round the place like wildfire,' she said with a wry smile.

'Is that what you want to happen?'

'Of course!'

'Surely they'll take one look at you and know it's not true,' Ruth said with a puzzled frown.

'Not a bit of it. From now on I shall wear loose blouses and then when they hear the news they'll think I was being modest and trying to disguise the fact.'

'You can't do that for ever, though, Mam. Someone's bound to guess that it's me, not you, that's getting bigger and having the baby. My skirts are tight around the waist already.'

'It will only be for a few weeks and from now on you'll have to wear loose dresses or something, or else stay indoors out of people's way. As soon as it is possible to do so we'll be going off to Caerphilly to look after Granny Hughes.'

'Won't Phoebe think it strange we're going up there when you made such a fuss about doing that a few weeks back and said it would be better if she came down here?'

'She'll understand when I tell her that it's for the best. People of Granny Hughes's age prefer to stay in their own place where everything is familiar, so all we are doing is humouring the old lady.'

'That sounds OK, but if Phoebe also believes that you are expecting a baby then surely she'll be puzzled as to why you want to go there when you would be far more comfortable in your own home.'

'Oh, Ruth, stop picking holes in my plan. I've already explained that I will be telling her that it's to keep Granny Hughes happy,' Caitlin told her irritably.

'So what are you going to tell Granny Hughes?'

Caitlin smoothed down the front of her dress thoughtfully. 'We'll have to tell her the truth, I suppose.'

It was mid-May before they heard that Tomas had been sent to the Front. Although they were both saddened by the news they were also in some way relieved. Ruth was finding it increasingly difficult to disguise the fact that she was putting on weight and that her shape was already changing.

She'd been so looking forward to discarding her school uniform of black skirt and white blouse for ever, but apart from having to breathe in when she wanted to fasten her skirt they seemed to disguise her burgeoning figure better than anything.

It was all right for her mother, she thought despondently, she simply kept her loose cotton overall on over her dress or blouse and skirt, and in the afternoons she wore a pretty, fancy little apron so that people had a job telling what shape she was.

The moment Caitlin was sure that Tomas wouldn't be coming home on leave she started talking openly about the baby she was expecting. She stayed fairly vague about the date when it was due. To make it look as if her stomach was getting bigger she began pulling in her apron so tight at the waist that it made it look as though she had quite a bulge underneath it.

'You shouldn't have to go all the way to Caerphilly to look after your mother, not in your condition,' her friend Phoebe sympathised one afternoon when she dropped in for a cup of tea and a chat. 'At your age you're bound to find that you want to put your feet up every afternoon, not have to wait hand and foot on an old lady.'

'True, but don't forget Ruth will be up there

with me and she'll be able to help us both, won't you, cariad?' Caitlin smiled as Ruth refilled Phoebe's cup and passed her the plate of Bara Brith that they'd made that morning.

'Poor little Ruth. She was so looking forward to leaving school and going out to work. They do at that age,' Phoebe went on garrulously. 'A couple of years' time, mind you, and she'll be thinking differently. Work seems to be so exciting before you leave school; it's only later on that it becomes a drudge.'

'And then we get married and find we have more responsibility and more hard work to do than ever and wish that we were back at work,' Caitlin said, smiling.

'Well, you're certainly going to have a busy time of it,' Phoebe agreed. 'How on earth will you manage it all? A new baby, Tomas away and your mother getting ever frailer.'

'You've already asked me that and I've already told you that Ruth will be on hand to help me.'

'I meant after you come home again. Surely you're not going to keep poor little Ruth at home to help with the baby. She needs to get a job and stand on her own feet . . .'

'Oh, don't let's try looking that far ahead,' Caitlin cut in quickly. 'I'll take things as they come and work it all out when I have to. Tomas might be home again by then, who knows.'

'I wouldn't think that was very likely. This old war is not going at all well. More and more men are being called up for service and there's so many of them being killed or injured that it makes you afraid to read the newspaper. I see they've even started putting big printed notices up all over the place, even on the pillar boxes, saying "A Call to Arms; Your King and Country Need You".'

'That's Kitchener for you!' Caitlin agreed. 'Pointing his finger and making all the men feel they've got to rush off and do their bit in case anyone considers them to be a conscientious objector. I understand that the way they are treating the "conchies" in some places is absolutely disgraceful.'

'Well, up until now they've said they'll wait for volunteers, but now they've started conscripting, none of the men are safe.'

'What about your lot then, Phoebe? I don't suppose your Idris will be called up because he's nearly fifty and working in a munitions factory. He will probably be exempt, but what about your Cedric? He's coming up for nineteen, and working in a butcher's shop is hardly likely to be regarded as war work, is it?'

'Cedric keeps saying that he wants to volunteer, but I told him he'd find things in the army different to things at home and to wait; it'll be time enough to go when they send for him.'

'You'd miss getting all the best cuts of meat, too, if he left there,' Caitlin joked.

'He treats me just the same as he does every other customer,' Phoebe said quickly. She stood up. 'I'd better be off home to get the meal started for when he and Idris get home from work. I have them to think about, not just myself like you. Now that Tomas isn't coming home hungry you don't need to cook every night if you don't feel like it.'

'That's true.' Caitlin smiled. 'I may as well take it easy before we go to look after my mam.'

'Let me know when you're going and you can leave your key with me if you want to, so that I can keep an eye on things here while you're away and send on any letters.'

'When are we going to Granny's?' Ruth asked the minute Phoebe had left. 'Can we do it soon? I'm scared stiff someone is going to find out the truth. I'm really starting to put on weight so someone is bound to guess.'

'Nonsense! They'll put it down to puppy fat. They're all too busy gossiping about me having another baby at my age,' Caitlin told her dismissively.

Nevertheless, Caitlin did heed what Ruth had said and began making definite plans to go to Caerphilly. It was now almost June and the weather was getting warmer by the day so Ruth couldn't go on wearing a thick dark skirt and long-sleeved blouse much longer.

She couldn't make up her mind whether or not to give her house key to Phoebe. She wouldn't have done so in the normal scheme of things because Tomas didn't like the idea of someone else being in their house and being free to go through their things in their absence.

On the other hand, since they were going to be away for at least four months it was a long time to leave the place shut up. If she left a key with Phoebe then she could write and ask her to open the windows now and then to give the place an airing. Also, Phoebe could forward on any letters from Tomas. It wasn't worth writing and telling him that they were going to Caerphilly because by the time he received her letter they'd probably be home again.

She hoped that there would be no other problems to do with the house which might need her attention. If there were, then she'd have to make some excuse about not being able to come down to Cardiff, even for the day, but she was sure she could do that in a convincing manner if she really had to.

When everything was eventually ready for their departure, she breathed a sigh of relief. Although Caerphilly was less than ten miles away, she felt that once they were there she and Ruth could relax and finally assume their proper roles.

Caitlin had explained to Ruth that it would be best if they didn't tell Granny Hughes that she was pregnant just yet.

'Let's get settled in and see what state she's in before we say anything. We don't want to upset her the moment we land on her doorstep, now do we?'

'Mam, she has only to look at me to guess there is something wrong,' Ruth said hesitantly.

'Nonsense! Her eyesight isn't all that good these days, cariad, and if she does think you're putting on a bit of weight, well, what of it? We haven't been to see her for months so she'll just think you've developed into a big girl since the last time she saw you.'

'You make it all sound so simple, Mam, but it scares me stiff. You know what she's like; when she does find out that I'm having a baby she'll be aghast.'

'Yes, she probably will. I know I was,' Caitlin agreed. 'I've managed to come to terms with it and so will she if we give her time. She probably doesn't remember how old you are anyway. Don't go letting on that you've only just left school, mind.'

'The way things are going I'll be afraid to even say hello to her in case I say something wrong,' Ruth sighed.

'Stop being so twp, girl,' Caitlin said crossly. 'You got yourself into this mess so now it's up to you to do all you can to make sure you don't upset my plans if you are going to get through it.'

'I really will try,' Ruth promised as they carried their cases from Caerphilly station to Herbert Place, the row of small cottages where Granny Hughes lived.

'Remember now, careful what you say,' Caitlin warned as she knocked on the door and

61

they heard the shuffling of feet from inside as her mother came to answer it.

Both of them were shocked by the appearance of the old lady when, after much fumbling, she finally managed to open the door. The front of her dress was covered in food stains and she looked so pale and frail that Ruth thought she was going to collapse at any minute.

'Who is it, who's there?' she asked, staring out at them as if unable to get them into focus.

'It's me, Mam. It's Caitlin, and I've got Ruth with me. I wrote a letter to you last week to tell you that we were coming up to see you, so can we come in?'

'Just visiting, are you?'

'Well no, not exactly, we've come for a couple of weeks,' Caitlin told her as they carried their cases into the hallway.

'Did you say you were going to stay?' the old lady asked in a querulous voice.

'That's right, Mam. In your last letter you said you weren't feeling so good so I thought it would be a good idea if we came up here and looked after you for a bit.'

'I don't know about you staying,' Maggie Hughes said worriedly. 'I don't think I am up to having visitors; not at the moment. It takes me all my time to look after myself.'

'I know that, Mam,' Caitlin told her patiently, 'that's why we've come up. We'll look after you for a few weeks and get you back on your feet again.'

'I'm not well enough to be bothered with visitors,' her mother said petulantly, shaking her head so violently that her hairpins became dislodged and her thin grey hair that she'd caught up in an untidy bun fell down at one side.

'We're not visitors, Mam, we're your family. You won't have to wait on us; we're here to take care of you,' Caitlin said with a smile.

'I'm not well, you see,' Maggie Hughes said. 'I've got pains, see, in my chest,' she went on. 'Sometimes they're stabbing like red-hot needles and then at other times my chest feels as tight as a drum and I can hardly get my breath.'

'Have you been to see the doctor?'

'Who?' Maggie Hughes cupped her hand to her ear and tilted her head to one side.

'The doctor, Mam. Have you been to see the doctor about the pains in your chest?' Caitlin repeated more loudly.

'I think I did some time ago, but I can't remember. He gave me some pills, but I'm not sure where I've put them. Not that they've done me any good, mind.'

'Well, they won't if you're not taking them regularly. Come on, come and sit down and Ruth will go and put the kettle on and make us all a nice cup of tea.'

'Oh, you're going to stay for a bit, are you?' Mrs Hughes said in a surprised voice.

Ruth and her mother exchanged looks and

Caitlin shook her head in despair. 'Go and put the kettle on, Ruth, while I try and sort this out. Your granny seems to be far worse than I thought she was.'

Chapter Six

Over the next few days both Caitlin and Ruth were dismayed by the state of Granny Hughes's home. It was obvious that not only had her eyesight been declining in the few months since they'd last visited her, but also that she seemed to have lost all interest in keeping the place clean and tidy.

'It's so sad because my mother was always so house proud,' Caitlin sighed as she and Ruth began the task of clearing and cleaning and restoring order to the house.

Most of the time Maggie Hughes seemed to move around in a daze and ignore what Caitlin and Ruth were doing. Then she would have sudden flashes of normality and start upbraiding Caitlin for messing about with her things and changing everything.

'You know I don't like other people interfering,' she would scold. 'I don't like you going into my drawers and cupboards, so keep out of them, do you understand?'

Realising that it was pointless arguing with her mother, Caitlin always nodded in agreement and then made them all a cup of tea and sat down and chatted to her mother until the old lady had calmed down.

She and Ruth had quickly decided that there was no need to tell Granny Hughes anything at all about the baby.

'She'll probably have forgotten all about it five minutes later anyway,' Caitlin pointed out.

'It would depend on which of her moods she was in,' Ruth said smiling. 'If she did understand then she'd probably severely lecture me and tell me what a disgrace I was to the family name.'

'Oh yes, she'd do that all right. My mother was always very straight-laced and she'd be horrified to think that you were bringing a fatherless baby into the world. If she knew he was a married man with a young family she'd be beside herself with worry so it is just as well she doesn't understand.'

In the weeks that followed, Maggie Hughes grew even frailer. By the middle of July she was staying in bed most of the time, only coming downstairs for an hour or so in the afternoons on the days when she felt well enough to do so.

'I must say, it's a good thing you two are here with her,' Rhiannon Evans, Maggie's next door neighbour, told them. 'I'm too old to be doing much for her, though I was doing a bit of shopping for her when she wasn't feeling well enough to get out. I'll be sixty-five in a few weeks' time and I'm beginning to feel my years;

breathless most of the time, see,' she puffed. 'My daughter says it's because I'm too fat, but as I keep telling her it's not that I eat a lot. In fact, I don't eat any more than I've ever done. I sit around too much, I suppose, but then it's my legs. Ache, they do, from morning till night. And they swell up; they're like great balloons sometimes.'

'Well, thank you for what you have done for her in the past, Mrs Evans, and if there is anything we can do to help you while we are here then you have only to let us know.'

'Thanks, cariad.' Rhiannon smiled at Caitlin. 'Your girl, Ruth, is a big girl now; I remember when she was just a tiny tot clinging to your skirts. They grow up so quickly these days and most of them are twice the size of us,' she added meaningfully as she stared at Ruth over the top of her steel-rimmed glasses.

Caitlin merely smiled, but she didn't offer any explanation, or make any comment. Once she and Ruth were on their own, however, she broached the subject of what they were going to tell Rhiannon Evans and her mother's other friends and neighbours.

'It's obvious that some of them have noticed that you are pregnant, so we've got to think of a convincing story that will put a stop to any gossip,' she pointed out.

'You mean tell the truth?'

'Don't be so naïve, girl,' Caitlin said crossly. 'If they know the truth, that you are not married to the father, or ever likely to be, then you'll be drummed out of the place. They're strongly religious around here, remember. If the truth gets out, neither of us will be able to hold our heads up around here ever again.'

'So what are we going to tell them?' Ruth asked, her eyes filling with tears as the enormity of the situation hit home. 'I'm so sorry, Mam, to be causing you so much trouble,' she added in a tremulous voice.

'Tears aren't going to solve anything, cariad,' Caitlin told her. 'Think yourself lucky that I'm prepared to stand by you. Now, sit down and listen to what I think we should say.'

Ruth listened in ever increasing dismay as her mother outlined the deception. 'We're going to say that you were going to be married and that your boy was called up for the army before you could go through with it. You'll be getting wed the moment he comes home on leave and hopefully that will be before the baby is born.'

'But that's all lies, Mam,' Ruth protested.

'I know that and so do you, but there's no need for anyone around here to know it,' her mother said sharply.

'Mrs Evans next door and lots of Granny Hughes's friends will know that I've only just left school so they'll know I'm barely fourteen and too young to get married,' Ruth wailed.

'The state my mother's been in for a while will make it easy enough to convince them that you're sixteen and that she has got it wrong,'

Caitlin said calmly. 'All you've got to do is go along with what I say and don't argue and don't go adding to the story.'

'So what's this boy's name, the one that I'm supposed to be marrying?'

'Call him anything you like as long as it isn't Glyn Jenkins,' her mother told her tartly. 'Now come on, go over the details with me so that we are both singing from the same hymn sheet. Put a smile on your face; you're supposed to be feeling happy and wanting this baby, not being gloomy and depressed.'

'Would I be happy, though, Mam, if he'd been called up and sent overseas and we mightn't be able to get married before the baby is born?'

'Not all the time, maybe, but they'll think you are putting a brave face on things. Remember, most of them will have sons or some relation or the other called up and they'll be full of sympathy for you. It's only for a couple of months, cariad. Surely you can manage to play your part rather than plunge us all into disgrace. Think of your Granny; it would kill her if she learned the truth.'

'Yes, all right,' Ruth agreed reluctantly. 'I don't think we should say anything, though, unless people ask.'

'Fair do's! At least we know now what we are going to tell everyone, and as long as we both say the same thing then we've nothing to worry about.'

She held wide her arms. 'Come here and let

me give you a cuddle. I know how worried you are about all this, but believe me, what I'm telling you to do is for the best, cariad.'

Ruth felt fresh tears brimming in her eyes as her mother took her in her arms, smoothing her hair and kissing the top of her head. Not for the first time she wished she could turn the clock back, become once again the innocent little school girl, full of dreams for the future, that she'd been before she'd got involved with Glyn Jenkins.

As she stared at her reflection in the mirror she hated what she saw; even her face looked bloated. She was no longer slim and pretty; she was fatter than her mother.

Feeling the baby move inside her was so alarming. Even though she wasn't sure if she really wanted it, she was scared all the time that she was going to do something that might harm it. Her mother was standing by her and being very practical but she wouldn't talk about what would actually happen when it was time for the baby to be born.

It was all so frightening and, apart from her mother, there was no one she could talk to about it.

She wondered if she would ever return to normal. If she was this big now, what was she going to look like over the next two months? The loose dresses her mother had made for her before they left Cardiff were already becoming strained across her enlarged stomach.

If only she could persuade her mother to let her stay indoors from now on so that she wouldn't have to face the curious, pitying stares from strangers in the street. She felt sure that they realised she was only fourteen. What else they thought she wasn't sure; it didn't bear thinking about.

Although she hated to see Granny Hughes looking so frail and finding it so difficult to understand what was going on, it was a relief that she didn't have to be told anything about the baby. How they were going to explain things to her once it was born was still a problem that would have to be faced.

As the birth drew ever nearer Ruth had a fresh quandary to face. She had no idea what was going to happen when she went into labour, or even how she'd know when her labour had started.

'You'll know when its started,' her mother told her. 'You'll get terrible backache and then grinding pains. Believe me, you won't be in any doubt about what's happening.'

'So what do I have to do, then?' Ruth asked.

'Get to bed and wait for it to be born,' her mother said dismissively. 'Don't worry; I'll be on hand to help you.'

'Do I have to have a doctor or someone there?' Ruth asked apprehensively.

'In the ordinary way you'd have a midwife, but we daren't risk that for fear of what she might say. No, I'll have to handle everything myself. Now stop worrying about it, I know what to do, I've done it before and everything worked out well.'

Towards the end of August, on one of the hottest days of the year, Maggie Hughes collapsed. Caitlin and Ruth did their best to revive her. They tried sitting her up, giving her sips of water, and dabbing her face and hands with a cool wet flannel, but all to no avail. She was gasping for breath and moaning as if in pain.

Caitlin managed to support her while Ruth slipped a pillow under her head then they covered her over with a blanket.

'Stay here with her; I'd better go and fetch the doctor,' Caitlin said worriedly.

'Don't be long, Mam, I don't know what to do.'

'Sit by her, hold her hand and bathe her face with a wet flannel now and again,' her mother advised. 'I won't be long; he's only around the corner.'

The doctor came back with Caitlin. After he'd examined Mrs Hughes he shook his head. 'She's in a bad way, she should be in hospital, but I don't think she's strong enough to stand the journey. It might be better to make her comfortable where she is for the moment and I'll prescribe something to ease her breathing. The next few hours will be critical,' he warned.

Although they did everything they could for her and the doctor called back again twice,

Maggie Hughes remained in a coma. Three days later she died without ever regaining consciousness.

Ruth was very upset, but Caitlin accepted it as being inevitable and tried to console Ruth by pointing out that they'd done everything in their power to help her.

The funeral took place a week later. It was a very quiet affair. Ruth and Caitlin and one or two neighbours paid their last respects by attending the service and then went to the cemetery, but none of them came back to the house for any refreshments.

'What are we going to do now, Mam?' Ruth asked worriedly. 'We won't be able to stay on in Granny's house, will we?'

'Oh I think it will be all right for a couple of weeks,' her mother assured her. 'They'll want us out, but they have to give us time to clean the place out and dispose of all her belongings. We can probably hang on until after you've had the baby; it should be due any time now. Look at you, cariad; you're the size of a mountain.'

'I know that, Mam,' Ruth said uncomfortably, 'but I still don't know when it is going to be born.'

'Of course you don't. All in good time, though. Let nature take its course. I'd say it will be any day now.'

Caitlin was right; shortly afterwards, Ruth went into labour. It was a fairly quick birth and although she found the pain more excruciating

73

than anything she had ever experienced in her life, the first glimpse of her baby daughter soon erased the experience from her mind.

'She's absolutely beautiful, Mam,' she exclaimed in awe as she cradled the tiny bundle in her arms.

'She is now, but wait until she grows up a bit and starts causing you worry and heartache,' Caitlin said cynically.

'Oh, Mam, I am sorry about all this happening, I really am.'

'I know, I know, cariad. Do you still want to keep the baby or shall we try and arrange to have her adopted?'

The colour drained from Ruth's face as she stared at her mother in disbelief. 'You can't even think that I'd want to do that, Mam,' she exclaimed.

'Think about it carefully,' Caitlin warned. 'It's going to be fourteen years before she is old enough to go out to work; fourteen years of responsibility and a lifetime of worrying about her even after that. You're only a child yourself; you should be out testing your own wings. You should be planning to start your first job, going on holiday with your friends, and having a good time. How can you do all that if you have a young baby to look after?'

'I know all that, Mam. I've thought of nothing else for weeks, but I don't want to have her adopted.'

'She might stand a better chance in life if you

74

did. She might go to someone who could afford to give her far more things than you'll ever be able to do.'

'Can they give her a mother's love, though?' Ruth asked softly.

'No,' Caitlin sighed, 'you're probably right there. Your own flesh and blood are always there ready to stand by you when you need them, that's for sure.'

'Like you've stood by me, Mam; and I am truly grateful,' Ruth told her, reaching out to squeeze her hand.

'Yes, well, if you're determined to keep her then we'd better go through with the rest of our plan, hadn't we? We said that when we went back to Cardiff we'd tell people that she was mine.'

Ruth pressed her lips together thoughtfully. 'Do you still want to do that?' she asked doubtfully.

'It will save you from scandal; stop all the gossip and make life easier for her when she's growing up.'

'I know, but it means I'll have to treat her as my little sister.'

'In name only, cariad. I've brought up one child and I don't want to go through sleepless nights and all the other things having a young baby entails. No, when we get back to Cardiff you're the one who is going to have to look after this baby. You'll prepare her feeds and if she wakes in the night you'll be the one who gets up to see to her, not me. Don't you ever forget that. To the outside world she might be your little sister, but as far as I'm concerned she's your baby and your responsibility.'

'That means that I won't be able to go out to work so I won't be earning any money to pay for my keep or for all the things the baby is going to need,' Ruth said balefully.

'That's true enough; but that's the way it's going to be. Perhaps later on, when she's a toddler, or ready for school, we can re-think all this and change how we do things. For the moment, though, you'll be the one looking after her.'

'People are bound to talk if I don't get a job.'

'We'll make sure they don't. Most people will realise that having a baby at my age can be quite an undertaking and if I have to keep you at home to help me for a while then that's quite understandable.'

'So when are we going back to Cardiff?'

'Not for another week or so. You need to rest to get over this and the time we spend up here will help you to come to terms with the situation. The one thing I don't want you to do is make any mistakes. One slip up, like calling it "your baby", and the cat will be out of the bag.'

'I do understand that, Mam. It's just that it's going to seem so strange.'

'From this moment on, Ruth, as far as everyone else is concerned, you have to think of her as your little sister, not your baby. Now, is that understood?'

'Yes, Mam. We've already agreed about that.'

'You must never tell her the truth, either. As far as she is aware she is your sister.'

'Yes; yes, I do understand.'

'So what do you want to call her?'

Ruth looked at her mother uneasily, colour rushing to her face.

'Something else you haven't given any thought to, isn't it?'

'As a matter of fact I have. I want to call her Glynis.'

'Glynis! Duw anwyl! You mean you are naming her after that scoundrel Glyn Jenkins! What on earth has got into you, girl? You want to put him out of your mind once and for all so come on, think of some other name.'

'No, Mam. I'm going to call her Glynis, so it will remind me of my folly every time I use her name or think about her,' Ruth said quietly.

Chapter Seven

Both Ruth and Caitlin were pleased to be back in Cardiff. They planned their homecoming for early evening in the hope that it was the time when most people would be indoors having their meal so that they would arrive unnoticed.

Settling in and making arrangements for Glynis and feeding her took them most of the evening. They didn't have anywhere for her to sleep so as a temporary measure they left her in the crib they'd brought her in from Caerphilly.

'Tomorrow we will have to do some serious shopping,' Caitlin said worriedly. 'We need a proper cradle or else a cot so we must measure up and see how much space there is in your room for it.'

'In my room?'

'Yes, Ruth, in your room. I told you from the start that I have no intention of getting up in the middle of the night to see to her.'

'I know that's what you said, Mam, but you've been doing so ever since she was born.'

'Only because I didn't think you were quite strong enough to look after her. From now on, cariad, she is your responsibility and don't you forget it.'

'I won't, Mam, but people are bound to think it strange if they see you sitting back and me doing everything for her?'

'No they won't, why should they? You're her devoted big sister and you are staying home to help your mam because I'm not feeling strong enough to cope with everything myself.'

As soon as Glynis had been fed and settled to sleep they decided to have an early night in preparation for meeting their neighbours and answering the thousand and one questions they expected to be bombarded with the next day.

'Remember now, cariad, the past is over and best forgotten about; tomorrow will be the first day of the rest of our lives for all of us. When your dad comes home he's going to find it almost as strange as we do to have a baby in the place, but by then we should be into a routine and so used to thinking of Glynis as your little sister that we won't make any slip-ups.'

Long after she was in her narrow single bed, Ruth lay awake thinking over all that had taken place that summer. How could she have been so foolish as to give in to him as she'd done? She'd enjoyed the flirting and found it exciting so why couldn't she have been content with that? Deep in her heart she knew she'd been afraid to refuse his ultimate demand when he said it was the only way she could prove that she really loved him. Yet, she'd lost him just the same, she thought unhappily. Since then it was almost as though they'd never meant anything to each other.

She loved Glynis with all her heart; nothing would make her give the baby up, but she also realised what an onerous burden she was going to be. There would be no more carefree times with her girlfriends. Going off to Caerphilly with her mam and staying there for such a long time she'd probably lost most of them anyway. Those who'd been leaving school at Easter would have been out working for over six months and probably made new friends. Anyway, she'd only be able to see them in the evenings or at weekends and she didn't think they'd want to go out with her if she always took the baby along. Yet she'd have to because her mam had made it quite clear that she was going to have to be the one who looked after Glynis.

Perhaps it would be best if she stopped seeing them, because it would only take a careless word for them to find out that the baby was hers and that she'd been foolish enough to fall for Glyn Jenkins. She couldn't risk that happening because it would bring disgrace on her family and then even though her mother had been so supportive she might become upset, change her mind, and throw her out after all.

It was such a tremendous responsibility that she wasn't sure if she was going to be capable of doing so, even with her mother there to support her. Yet she had no alternative.

The only way out was to have Glynis adopted and now that they'd brought her back to Cardiff and her mother had claimed that Glynis was her baby, there was no chance of that happening.

Tomorrow would be the real test, when their friends and neighbours realised that they were back home. They'd all want to see the baby and enquire about its birth, what it had weighed, what it was called and whether or not it was good at night. All attention would be fixed on her mother, on what sort of time she'd had and how she was feeling now.

There was no doubt that she'd also have to answer countless questions and possible teasing about what it was like to have a baby sister after all these years. People would probably praise her for being such a dutiful daughter and helping her mother so much; they might even marvel at her confidence as she handled the new baby and perhaps even express surprise at how expertly she coped.

Whatever happened she had to play her part and pretend that she did all these things because she loved her little sister so much.

She knew her mother would play her part well, but could she manage to do the same? It was the question uppermost in her mind as she fell asleep and it was still there when, a few hours later, baby Glynis woke, crying for a feed.

It took her several minutes to realise that even though she was half asleep herself she was the one who had to struggle out of her warm, comfortable bed and attend to her.

As she settled the baby back down in her makeshift crib after feeding her and changing her wet nappy she willed her to go back to sleep so that she could do the same because she felt so tired.

Glynis didn't settle. The crib was too small for her to be comfortable and Ruth reminded her mother the next morning that she'd said they would go and buy a proper cradle or cot.

'We'll have to go to the market, or possibly the Hayes and see what we can find. We might even have to try the pawnbroker's and see if he has anything in there to sell.'

'Mam! Do we have to do that? Can't we buy her something new?'

'No, cariad, we most certainly can't. The allowance I'm receiving from the army is only about half what your dad was earning at Mostyn Mouldings. From now on we're going to have to watch our pennies. It's lucky for you that I have some money saved up and put away for emergencies. That's what we'll be spending and when that's gone, it's gone. There's no more.'

'You said we'd get a pram as well,' Ruth reminded her.

'So we will, as soon as I've worked out how much we can spend on it. Today, let's settle for something for the baby to sleep in. You'll have to carry her for now. I'll find a big shawl and then you can wind it over your shoulder and round your body Welsh fashion so that she won't feel so heavy.'

'I'll just carry her in my arms, she's not that heavy.'

'She may not be when you're walking around indoors with her, but when you go out in the street, or on a tram and are walking round the shops in town, you'll soon be complaining. She'll make your arm ache, I can tell you, so do what I say and use a shawl.'

Reluctantly, Ruth agreed. With the huge black flannel shawl wrapped round her with the baby tucked inside she felt middle-aged and cumbersome. But it did leave one arm free and she had to admit it was a safe and comfortable way to carry Glynis.

In fact, she quite enjoyed their first trip out although she was feeling exhausted by the time they came home again. They'd managed to find a second-hand drop-side cot that would be suitable for Glynis until she was three or four years old and ready to sleep in a proper bed. The stall holder said he'd deliver it later that day on his way home after he finished for the night.

They'd also made an offer on a lovely dark blue pram which looked as good as new. The pawnbroker had promised her that she could collect it in two weeks' time if the woman who'd pawned it hadn't redeemed it by then. Ruth hoped she would get it because it would be so much warmer and comfortable for Glynis during the winter, even if it was going to take up rather a lot of space indoors.

She was well aware that the disruption in their home was annoying her mother a great deal: the pail with nappies soaking in it under the sink in the scullery, the nappies and baby clothes drying indoors when it was too wet to put them out on the line, and then having to be aired on the clothes horse, either in front of the dying embers of the fire when they went to bed at night or in front of the fire during the daytime if they went out.

'This place looks like a Chinese laundry these days with all this washing about,' Caitlin grumbled. It's a good thing your father isn't here; it would drive him mad.'

Her mother didn't like the way the baby's routine interfered with her timetable either, but, as Ruth pointed out, there was nothing they could do about that.

To the outside world, Caitlin was the perfect doting mother. Whenever they were stopped by neighbours in the street who wanted to take a peek at the new baby she was full of enthusiasm about how wonderful it was to have another daughter and what a wonderful baby Glynis was.

If they commented that they often saw Ruth taking her out in the pram she was full of praise for her older daughter and eager to tell people how besotted Ruth was with her new sister.

'I only wish it had happened years ago,' she

would sigh. 'It would have been so nice for them to have grown up side by side.'

Usually people shook their heads and told her how fortunate she was that Ruth was old enough to help look after the baby.

'If they were of a similar age then they might have been squabbling all the time, you know what sisters are like. Or else borrowing each other's clothes and falling out over that. This way you have the best of all worlds. You have the time to enjoy having her and a daughter old enough to help take care of her.'

Indoors, it was a very different story; Caitlin hardly ever went near the baby. She complained grumpily about the noise whenever Glynis was crying or needed attention, especially on the rare occasion when she cried in the night and Ruth didn't waken in time to quieten her before she disturbed Caitlin.

The only time she was prepared to keep an eye on the baby was when she wanted Ruth to do something for her; like the shopping when it was a wet day. Then, and only then, would she agree to look after Glynis, but she preferred it if Ruth fitted in whatever chore it was with a time when Glynis was sleeping.

Ruth took Glynis out most afternoons. If any of the neighbours stopped to chat she always said her mother was having a rest and most of them fully understood that at her age Caitlin was probably feeling the strain of having a young baby. They complimented and praised

Ruth for being such a good daughter and said how lucky her mother was to be able to keep her at home.

Each time she did go out, Ruth was worried in case she bumped into Glyn Jenkins. There was only one occasion when this happened, and he simply walked straight by after glancing briefly in her direction. He gave neither a smile nor a nod to indicate that he had seen her, or that she was carrying his baby daughter in her arms.

The incident upset Ruth because it reminded her all too poignantly of how foolish she'd been and what a mess she'd made of her life. Then anger and resentment took over, giving her the strength to pull back her shoulders, hold her head high and, even though her heart was breaking, walk on as though nothing had happened.

After that, she was reluctant to go out in case she saw him again. A couple of weeks later her mother told her that one of the neighbours had said that Glyn Jenkins had been called up for the army.

'His wife and family will have to move out of the house they live in because it is intended for the school caretaker and they'll have to hire a new one. It seems they are going to live with relations in another part of Cardiff,' she told Ruth.

Ruth felt such a sense of freedom that she cried with relief. There would be no need to hide away any more; she would probably never see Glyn Jenkins ever again.

Even so, the next few months were fraught with problems. Caitlin still had to tell Tomas about the baby. The letters that passed between them were infrequent and took so long that, in the end, she took a risk and pretended that she'd already told him that she was pregnant and asked him why he'd said nothing about it.

It was weeks before she heard from him and then he seemed to be stunned by the news and his letters were full of questions about when the baby was due and asking her how was she managing.

She wrote back saying that she had been away looking after her mother until Maggie Hughes had died, but that she was now home again and the baby was already born and was now three months old and doing well. She also made a point of saying how much Ruth was helping her with the baby and so she hadn't yet started work.

It all sounded so plausible in a letter, but as she held baby Glynis in her arms and studied her little face Ruth wondered if her father would still believe it when he returned home.

Glynis was a lovely baby, but she didn't take after any of them. Now that she had started to put on weight and fill out it was obvious that she was going to be quite pretty. She had a round chubby face, very dark curly hair and huge dark eyes.

Already she was taking a lively interest in all that was going on around her. Even so, she was also fairly placid and much of the time she would lie contentedly in her pram or cot, waving her podgy little arms and legs in the air and making little cooing noises until it was time for her next feed.

Ruth found that she loved her more intensely with each passing day. She couldn't imagine life without her and couldn't do enough to make her happy.

Although it was Glynis's first Christmas, Caitlin didn't see much point in making an occasion of it since, at three months, she was too young to understand what was going on. Nevertheless, Ruth twined some pretty tinsel around the window in their bedroom and was delighted that Glynis seemed to take an interest in that as the candlelight made it flicker.

Immediately after Christmas the weather turned exceptionally cold and Ruth was forced to leave Glynis with her mother while she went to the shop for groceries and to the butcher. Supplies of even basic foodstuffs were beginning to be spasmodic and often it meant going to more than one shop to find what they required.

The brief letters they received from Tomas confirmed the lurid newspaper reports that things were even worse over in France. They both read the details of the battles going on with sinking hearts, but then tried to put them out of their minds since there was nothing they could do about them.

Caitlin wrote to him regularly and always said how well Glynis was progressing, but Tomas barely mentioned her in his letters; it was as if he had not yet accepted that he had another child.

'Wait until he comes home on leave and sees her, and then he won't be able to resist her,' Caitlin assured Ruth. 'He'll be devoted to her in next to no time.'

Ruth hoped her mother was right, but she felt uneasy in case her father saw through their subterfuge, and she was afraid of what might happen if he did.

She wasn't sure why she felt like this since everyone in Harriett Street had accepted their story; even close friends, like Phoebe Parsons, had as well.

'It's your guilty conscience,' her mother told her when Ruth confided in her about her fears. 'I'm not going to let the cat out of the bag, and Glyn Jenkins has gone away, so there is no one at all who can ruin things now except you, Ruth.'

The expenses incurred in bringing Glynis up
were a constant source of friction between Ruth
and Caitlin. When she was a small baby, she'd
needed special foods, though after she was
weaned they minced or mashed up whatever
they were eating themselves and fed her with
that.

Chapter Eight

The expenses incurred in bringing Glynis up
were a constant source of friction between Ruth
and Caitlin. When she was a small baby, she'd
needed special foods, though after she was
weaned they minced or mashed up whatever
they were eating themselves and fed her with
that.

When she was teething, Ruth liked to give
her a Farley's rusk, but Caitlin thought these
were unnecessary. In her opinion a dry crust
cut from the edge of the loaf was just as good.
She would save up any stale bread and put it
in the oven after she'd finished baking to harden
it off.

Ruth protested that Farley's rusks were never
a waste because if Glynis didn't eat them all,
they could be softened with milk and fed to
her with a spoon. Caitlin argued that pobs made
from ordinary bread, broken up into pieces and
soaked in warm milk, were just as good and
that the child would never know the difference.

Once Glynis started walking there was the
need for proper shoes instead of knitted
bootees, and Caitlin grumbled about how much
these cost.

'What you've got to remember is that the army allowance I'm getting is nowhere near as much as your dad was earning,' she repeated over and over again.

Caitlin had also begun cutting back on what she spent on their own food and she refused to buy new clothes for either herself or Ruth.

'Mam, I've outgrown all the things I was wearing when I was at school,' Ruth protested when her mother told her to go on wearing her old school skirt and blouse.

'Then wear something of mine. We haven't the money for you to have anything new.'

'You're at least four inches shorter than me,' Ruth wailed. 'I can't go round in any of your things.'

'You've no choice; it's either that or what you already have,' her mother told her. 'You want to remember, you haven't earned a penny piece all your life and now that my savings are gone there's nothing in the kitty. You'll either have to let the hems of my stuff down or cut up something else and put in a band of a different colour.'

Ruth wasn't happy about the situation and wondered if there was any way she could earn some money. She would have to come to some arrangement with her mother to look after Glynis for a few hours each day, but right from the start she'd said that she wouldn't do this. Perhaps now, since they were so hard up, she'd change her mind.

At first Caitlin refused to even consider the idea. 'You should have asked me a long time ago, when she was still a small baby and sleeping most of the time. Now that she's toddling around she's into everything. I wouldn't be able to take my eyes off her for a single second or she'd be in some sort of trouble.'

'Oh, Mam, she's not that bad. Anyway, if I got a morning job then you could take her out in the pram for an hour and do the shopping at the same time. She always has a nap around mid-morning, so you could plan things so that you were back home by then and have some time to yourself while she was asleep.'

'What happens if you can't find a morning job?'

'If I can only get something in the afternoon then the same thing applies. I'd make sure she didn't have a sleep in the morning so that she would need a nap in the afternoon and that would give you a chance to put your feet up for an hour.'

'So where are you going to find a job like that, to suit the hours you want to work?'

'I've no idea,' Ruth told her, 'but if you are agreeable to an arrangement of this sort, I'll start looking.'

'Well, I can't say I'm very keen on the idea, but there's no doubt about it, we could certainly do with the money,' her mother said reluctantly. 'I suppose we could give it a try and see how it works out. If I find she's too much of a handful for me, then you'll have to pack it in. You'll have to find something around here, though, so that if she has an accident, or there is an emergency, I can get hold of you quickly.'

Within a matter of days Ruth had managed to find herself some part-time work in a little general shop on the corner of Coburn Street and Fitzroy Street. It was hardly any distance away from where they lived, which pleased Caitlin. She wasn't very happy, though, about the fact that Ruth had to be there for eight o'clock in the morning and that she wouldn't finish work until one o'clock.

'That means I'm going to have to wash and dress Glynis and give her some breakfast every day,' she grumbled, 'and I like to get all my jobs around the house done first thing in the morning so that the place looks tidy.'

'After she's had her breakfast, if you leave her to play on her own or let her follow you around while you wash up and tidy around the place, she'll be happy enough and by then she'll be ready to settle down for her morning nap,' Ruth pointed out.

'Yes, I suppose you're right,' Caitlin admitted grudgingly, 'but it's not going to be easy on a Monday morning when it's washday. I can hardly risk lighting the copper and getting things moving with her underfoot, now can I?'

'Then we'll do the washing on a Sunday, when I'm here to help you,' Ruth promised.

'On a Sunday! We can't do something like that! Think what the neighbours would say. They'd be shocked to the core and we'd be the talk of Harriett Street.'

'Oh, Mam, it's wartime and people make allowances for things they wouldn't dream of doing, normally. If it worries you all that much, then you'll have to leave it until Monday afternoon when I get home from work.'

'Don't be so twp, cariad; we'd still be at it come midnight if we put off starting until then!'

'Do you want me to go ahead and take this job or not?' Ruth said in exasperation.

'Of course I do; I'm just pointing out how difficult it's going to be for me.'

'Well, would you rather be the one to take the job and leave me to stay home and look after Glynis?'

'For heaven's sake, Ruth, don't be so ridiculous. You expect me to go and work behind the counter in a corner shop at my age? Whatever next! What do you think your dad would say if he ever found out I was doing something like that? No, you'll have to go ahead and take it; we're desperate for more money and I'll just have to put up with the upheaval and do my best here.'

Ruth soon found that Caitlin doing her best meant that the routine she'd established since Glynis was a tiny baby was completely forgotten.

Often when she came home at one o'clock it

was to find the baby still in her nightdress and wearing a nappy that was either soiled or soaking wet. If she said anything about it, her mother was quick to remind her that Glynis wasn't her child and that she'd made it clear right from the very beginning that she had no intention of being the one to bring her up.

Ruth was in two minds as to whether or not she should give up her job and stay at home, even though she knew they'd find it hard to manage. Christmas was only a few weeks away, however, and since they'd no spare money to buy anything special for the occasion she felt that it was more important than ever that she was earning.

This year, at fifteen months old, Glynis would take notice of what was going on around her and she wanted to make it as special for her as she possibly could.

She'd already planned that, with the money she'd be earning, she would buy her some new warm clothes and some sturdy little shoes now that she had started to walk. She also wanted to give her a teddy bear, or a soft doll; one that she could cuddle when she went to bed. If she had a few pennies left over then she'd even fill her little sock with odds and ends that would delight her and keep her amused on Christmas morning.

She suspected her mam would disapprove and tell her that a child of that age was too young to understand what Christmas was all about, but Ruth herself would get a great deal of enjoyment from seeing the smile on her little baby's face.

As well as providing some extra food she also wanted to buy a special present for her mam; something to cheer her up and let her know how much she appreciated the way she was trying to help her. She didn't like all the lies and subterfuge one little bit, but if her mam thought that it was necessary, then she had to accept it. Perhaps a new blouse for her mam to wear on Christmas Day would help to lift the black mood she seemed to be in most of the time.

When she'd been growing up they'd always celebrated on Christmas Day with a big plump roast chicken served with roast potatoes, Brussels sprouts, carrots, roasted parsnips and all the other bits and pieces that made it a special feast. That was always followed by Christmas pudding and, later on in the day, there'd be mince pies. At teatime there was always an iced fruit cake, although often they'd eaten so much by then that they could barely find room for it.

They wouldn't be able to manage anything like as good a spread as that, but she was hoping they could have a roast chicken even if they had to forgo some of the trimmings.

Working in a shop, she was able to buy a great many things which were in short supply; not only food, but other items as well. She'd thought that her mam would be pleased about this because it meant she didn't have to go searching around the market or half a dozen different shops to see if they had whatever item it was she wanted; nor did she have to queue up to get them.

Far from being pleased, Caitlin was always carping on that Ruth managing to get so many items which were in short supply ruined her enjoyment.

'I like to go round the shops looking for things. I look forward to all the chat and banter when there's a crowd of people queuing up in the street. You hear all sorts of amusing things while you are waiting,' Caitlin told her. 'It's different for you out working in the shop and meeting up with different people every day of the week; I'm stuck here at home all the time, with a grizzling baby.'

Ruth tried to be patient and ignore her complaining. She knew her mother was on edge because she was alarmed by all the disturbing news about what was happening over in France.

They received letters so infrequently that it was worrying and when they did get a letter it was usually so brief that in fact they were none the wiser about how Tomas was fairing after they'd read it.

They obtained most of their news from the newspaper headlines and some of these were very scary. 1916 had started off badly, with the evacuation from Gallipoli early in January, and that had been followed by harrowing accounts of what had happened at the Battle of Verdun.

Later in the year the Battle of the Somme had been fought, which had stretched over four months and they'd received the startling news that tanks were being used as part of the trench warfare. America joined in the conflict in April 1917 and by the end of June they heard that the American army had arrived in France.

Like everyone else, Caitlin and Ruth had thought that this would bring a swift end to the war, but the fighting had still gone on and more and more men were being conscripted and sent out there.

A few weeks ago, at the beginning of November, there'd been the heartening news that the British had managed to capture the Passchendale Ridge and, once again, hopes had soared. Now, at the beginning of December, there were rumours of a revolution in Russia and once more people became optimistic as there was talk of an armistice between Russia and Germany.

'Perhaps your dad will be home before Christmas after all,' Caitlin said hopefully.

'I hope so, but I doubt it,' Ruth sighed. 'The Kaiser won't surrender to the British that easily and we certainly won't give in to him.'

'Then if our lot want to go on fighting they should let the men who have been out there all this time come back home for a rest and send out a fresh bunch of boyos,' Caitlin declared. 'Your dad was one of the first sent out and from the way things are going it looks as though he's going to be out there the longest.'

'I suppose we should feel grateful that he is still over there fighting,' Ruth commented.

'What's that supposed to mean, for heaven's sake?'

'At least he's alive and able to go on fighting. Look at how many men are being reported killed or so badly injured that they have to be sent home. It's not only the soldiers, either. Think of how many boats have been sunk, with most of the sailors on board drowned, or the men who fly the aeroplanes; some of them only manage to go over to Germany once before they are shot down.'

'All right, all right, you don't have to go on and on about it,' Caitlin told her. 'I lie awake at night worrying as it is without you adding to my misery. If I start thinking about all of them, as well as about what is happening to your dad, then I'll be having even worse nightmares than the ones I'm having now. All I'm interested in is your dad coming back safe and sound.'

'Well, so am I,' Ruth told her. She put her arms around her mother and hugged her. 'I'd like nothing better than for him to be back home with us before Christmas, but I know quite well that it's highly unlikely.'

In that Ruth was wrong. Three days later they received a War Office telegram.

Ruth had come in from work only minutes before and she hadn't even had time to take off her outdoor clothes. She was trying to pacify Glynis who was crying noisily, when there came a knock on the door.

'It's probably someone from next door to complain about the noise she's making,' Caitlin said sourly. 'She's been yelling her head off all morning.'

'She can't help it, poor little thing, she's teething,' Ruth defended her daughter quickly. 'Look at her little cheeks, they're bight red; she's probably in awful pain.'

Ignoring her, Caitlin went to answer the door. When she saw the young boy in his dark blue uniform standing there holding out a buff envelope she let out a scream.

Ruth rushed to see what was wrong and when her mother seemed to be incapable of taking the telegram from the boy she held out her own hand for it.

'Shall I open it, Mam?' she asked.

Her mother nodded. 'Go on; tell me what it says, I'm too frightened to read it,' she moaned.

Ruth scanned the flimsy scrap of paper then turned to her mother with a puzzled smile. 'Dad's coming home!'

'On leave, or for good?'

'I'm not sure . . . well, I don't know. It says here he's being sent to the army hospital at Llandough.'

'That's between here and Penarth. If he's

being sent there then it must mean that he's been badly hurt.' Caitlin was shaking like a leaf as she clutched at Ruth's arm. 'Come on, tell me what's happened to him; how bad is he?'

Ruth shook her head. 'I don't know, Mam. It doesn't give any details. All it says is that he will be arriving at the hospital tomorrow. We'll have to wait until he gets there and then make some enquiries and see what they can tell us.'

Chapter Nine

It was almost a week after receiving the telegram before they were allowed to see him. It was a week filled with tears and frustration as they tried in vain to find out how badly he'd been injured, and to obtain permission to visit him.

'You'll be informed in due course,' was the stock answer to all their enquiries.

Caitlin alternatively cried and berated the heartlessness of the authorities. Ruth tried to pacify her, do her job at the corner shop, care for Glynis, and keep things from getting out of hand at home since Caitlin seemed to have lost all interest in doing any housework, cooking or shopping.

Ruth tried to be patient and understanding, but there were times when she longed to take hold of her mother and give her a good shake, especially when she saw the way she was neglecting Glynis.

Caitlin spent hours each day on the doorstep, looking this way and that, up and down Harriett Street as if expecting Tomas to suddenly come striding along the road. One of Ruth's greatest fears was now that Glynis was so active her mother would leave the front door open and Glynis would run out into the road and be knocked down by a horse and cart or even a van.

When finally they were allowed to visit Tomas his appearance shocked Caitlin so much that Ruth was afraid she was going to collapse on the spot. He looked old and gaunt; he was sitting bolt upright in bed, his eyes bright yet vacant. As they approached his bed he was muttering in a low agonised voice as he stared unseeingly into space.

At first Caitlin refused to believe that he was Tomas. When the nurse escorting them to his bedside insisted that he was, Caitlin let out a shrill scream and covered her face with her hands. She swayed so much that Ruth and the nurse had to each take an arm and guide her to a chair. She sat there, head almost on her knees, shuddering as though she was about to have a fit.

The nurse brought her a drink of water and insisted that she stay seated until she was calmer. Then once more she led them both across the ward to Tomas's bedside.

For a moment he didn't seem to know them; then, when he recognised Caitlin, his face crumpled and as her arms went round his emaciated shoulders their tears mingled.

Ruth felt so overcome that she had to turn away. She picked Glynis up in her arms and buried her face in the child's thick dark curls to hide her own tears.

As Glynis wriggled to be put down, Ruth turned back to her father, smiling weakly and asking him how he was.

He simply frowned and shook his head as if he didn't understand her question; his eyes were fixed on Glynis, as if he was puzzled by her being there and he was trying to work out who she was.

Ruth held her lower lip between her teeth, afraid she might blurt out the truth, and felt an enormous sense of relief when Caitlin pulled herself together and started to explain to him.

'I wrote to you, Tomas, not long after you were called up and told you that I was expecting another baby. Surely you haven't forgotten! This is Glynis, she's just turned two.' Glynis, come here and say hello to your dada.'

Feebly, Tomas held out a hand towards the child. 'Glynis,' he murmured and repeated the name several times as if he was trying to memorise it.

For a moment Glynis played shy then she grabbed hold of his hand so hard that it made Tomas wince.

'Gently, gently,' Ruth admonished. 'Dada isn't feeling very well, that's why he's in bed.'

Even as she spoke she felt a humbug and once again had the overwhelming desire to tell him the truth. It seemed so unfair when he was so desperately ill to burden him with the responsibility of a child who was not his own.

Instinctively, her mother seemed to suspect

her intention and gave her a warning look and picked Glynis up and sat the little girl on her knee as if to prove that it was her child.

At that moment the nurse came bustling up and told them that it was time for them to leave.

'We've only been here a few minutes, we haven't had time to talk about anything,' Caitlin protested. 'I haven't seen my husband for almost three years; there's so much we have to say to each other. He has never seen his little girl before today; she was born after he was sent to the Front.'

'Exactly, and all this excitement is too much for him. He's still very weak, so I'm afraid I must insist that you leave,' the nurse said very briskly.

'You haven't even told me what's wrong with my husband yet,' Caitlin prevaricated.

'He's suffering from shell-shock.'

'Shell-shock? Do you mean he's been hit by a shell?' Caitlin asked in alarm.

'No, no; there's been nothing like that. You've misunderstood me. He hasn't any physical injuries at all.'

'Then why is he being kept here in this hospital?'

The nurse gave a light shrug. 'I'm afraid you will have to talk to one of the doctors to find out those details,' she said dismissively. 'It's probably because he's been in an area where there's been a lot of enemy shell-fire and that seems to damage the brain.'

'You mean that you think my husband's gone

mad?' Caitlin exclaimed, her voice filled with horror.

'Of course not! It simply means that at present he's unable to concentrate and suffers from very severe headaches. Men in his condition are not usually sent back to Blighty for treatment, so he should regard himself as very lucky.'

'Lucky! I would hardly call it that,' Caitlin said in a scathing voice as she stared hostilely at the nurse.

'Believe me, it is,' the nurse told her gravely. 'The treatment they usually dish out is to attach the sufferer to a post, or something similar, for several hours a day for about three months and make sure that they are within range of enemy shell-fire.'

'I thought you said that it was the shell-fire that did the damage?' Ruth interrupted.

'Yes, that's right, but a lot of men say they have shell-shock when in actual fact they are simply malingerers or cowards and use it as an excuse to get sent home, so it's a way of testing them.'

'I'm quite sure my husband would never do a thing like that,' Caitlin said huffily.

'Probably not.' The nurse smiled. 'The doctors over there must have thought that he was a genuine case and that's why they sent him home. He was fortunate in that the doctor he saw believed that with rest and quiet the condition could be cured.'

'So what happens to the men who don't get sent home?' Ruth questioned.

The nurse shook her head sadly. 'They're usually sent back to the front line and many of them commit suicide.'

'Can't they protest?'

'If they refuse to accept their officer's command, then they are usually court-martialled and given severe punishments; or even shot on the spot.'

'That's terrible,' Ruth gasped.

'When can we take my husband home?' Caitlin pleaded. 'I'd make sure he got plenty of rest. I could look after him perfectly well and I'm sure he'd get better more quickly in familiar surroundings than he will do here.'

'That's a matter for the doctors to decide,' the nurse said firmly. 'Now, you really must leave; you have already overstayed your allotted time.'

'When can we see him again?' Caitlin persisted.

'You can visit him on Sunday afternoon. You will find all the visiting times listed on a board in the entrance hall.'

'Sunday! That's three days away. Why can't we come again tomorrow?'

'Visiting is only permitted twice a week. On Wednesdays and Sundays. It is limited to half an hour and only two people are allowed at the patient's bedside at any one time,' she said, looking at Glynis pointedly.

'Two people? You surely don't count a little tot like this as a person, do you?' Caitlin asked huffily, resting her hand on the top of Glynis's head.

'By rights a child of that age shouldn't be in here at all. I've made an exception in this instance, but in future I suggest you leave her at home with someone when you visit or you can take it in turns, because if Sister saw her in here she'd turn you both out right away.'

'Thank you, we'll remember that,' Ruth said quickly as she took her mother by the arm and began moving towards the door before Caitlin could argue any more with the nurse.

Seeing Tomas, and being told what was wrong with him, seemed to depress Caitlin more than ever. She was convinced that because Tomas was suffering from shell-shock it meant that he was mad and nothing Ruth said seemed to convince her otherwise.

Their twice-weekly visits to the hospital seemed to drain Caitlin of every ounce of energy and Ruth was afraid that if it went on for too long, Caitlin would become ill herself. As it was, she usually spent most of the morning following a visit in bed, and this worried Ruth because she knew that while she was out at work Glynis was probably being left to her own devices.

When she found it was impossible to make her mother understand that she must get up first thing in the morning and look after the child, Ruth began rousing Glynis before she went out and making sure that she ate some breakfast. Then, although she would take toys up to the bedroom for Glynis to play with, she'd try and persuade her daughter to go back to bed and have another little sleep.

'I'll leave you a glass of milk and some biscuits for later on,' she'd promise, 'and then you must play quietly until I come back home to get your dinner.'

She knew it was asking a lot from such a young child, but at the moment there was no alternative. They needed her wages even more; they had fares from Cathays to Llandough to find twice a week and they always tried to take some little treat in for her dad when they visited him.

Tomas was in Llandough for just over two months, then, on a bright spring day, shortly before Ruth's seventeenth birthday, the news came that he was being discharged not only from hospital but as unfit for military service.

'Does that mean he'll be coming home?' Caitlin folded up the letter and put it back in the envelope.

'Yes, of course it does, Mam; that's what you want, isn't it?' Ruth smiled as she spread a thick blanket on the table and covered it with an old piece of clean sheet in readiness to do the ironing.

'Well, yes,' Caitlin agreed. 'I suppose it will be better than having to traipse backwards and forwards all the way to Llandough twice a week like we're doing now.'

'So why are you looking so worried, Mam?'

'I'm worried in case it means that my army

allowance will be stopped once he's discharged from hospital. If it is, then how on earth are we going to manage?'

'He'll get a disability pension, won't he?' Ruth frowned. She lifted the iron from the trivet in front of the fire and held it close to her cheek to test if it was the right heat before she started work on the washing piled up on the table.

'I don't know. The first time we went to visit him at Llandough the nurse said he hadn't been injured.'

'She said he hadn't been physically injured, but his mind has been injured. She called it a mental disturbance, if you remember, and said that was why he must have rest and quiet.'

'So does that mean they've cured him? Is his mind all right again now?' Caitlin asked worriedly.

'I don't know.' Ruth paused, setting the flat iron down on its heel; she shrugged helplessly. 'You saw what he was like when we went there last week. He seemed to recognise us and was interested in little Glynis, but he was still staring into space a lot of the time, almost as if he was somewhere else.'

'Back in the trenches, if the look in his eyes was anything to go by.' Caitlin sighed. 'There must have been some terrible things going on over there; ones we know nothing about.'

'When he comes home you've got to try and make him forget about all that, Mam,' Ruth told her gently as she resumed the ironing.

'He seems very taken by little Glynis, so perhaps having her around will help to take his mind off what's happened in the past.'

'I think all the noise she makes will upset him,' Caitlin argued. 'She chatters away all day, non-stop, or else she's singing the same little rhyme over and over again. She makes *my* head ache, so I don't know what it will do to him.'

'Perhaps he will join in and sing with her and that will help him to forget the more unpleasant things that he seems to dwell on,' Ruth said optimistically.

'Yes, perhaps he will,' Caitlin agreed. 'Far more important, of course, is whether or not he'll be well enough to work.'

'I shouldn't think so! He's nothing but skin and bone at the moment and he certainly won't be able to cope with his old job at Mostyn Mouldings, even if they take him back.'

'If he isn't well enough to go back to work, then how much pension do you think they'll give him?' Caitlin asked worriedly. 'If he doesn't get one and our army allowance is stopped, then what are we going to live on? It's going to mean another mouth to feed and we're scrimping and scraping and watching every penny as it is. We're barely managing to keep our heads above water.'

'I know that only too well, Mam, but I don't know what we can do about it, not unless I try and find some full-time work. I suppose I'd get paid more if I went to work at one of the munitions factories, but that would mean you'd have to look after Glynis all day instead of only in the mornings.'

'Take care of her as well as nurse your dad! Talk sense, cariad, how on earth could I do all that? I've only got one pair of hands and I'm not getting any younger.'

'For goodness' sake, Mam, don't start making your age an excuse. Anyone would think you were ninety, to hear you talk; you're only just forty.'

Caitlin's eyes hardened. 'It's all very well for you to talk like that, Ruth, but you'll look at things differently when you're my age. You seem to forget that I have been weighed down with problems over these last couple of years. Even though I've tried very hard to put a brave face on things they've taken their toll on how I feel, believe me,' she exclaimed indignantly.

'Yes, Mam, I do know, and I also realise that I've been the cause of much of your worry,' Ruth agreed penitently as she placed an arm around her mother's shoulders and hugged her.

'Well, we'll say no more about it,' Caitlin said stoically, pulling away. 'We'll have to wait and see how things turn out, I suppose. I just hope that your dad gets a disability pension big enough for us to live on.'

Chapter Ten

Tomas's arrival home caused a tremendous upheaval. Caitlin and Ruth had been on their own for so long that they had forgotten what it was like to have a man around the place.

Tomas was frail, almost skeletal, and the clothes that he had looked so smart in before he went into the army now hung on his bony frame making him look like a scarecrow. Even his shoes seemed to be too big, and he shuffled around the house like a very old man.

He refused to go outside, even though both Caitlin and Ruth did their best to encourage him to do so.

'You need a breath of fresh air to give you an appetite and bring the colour back into your cheeks,' Caitlin told him.

Ruth tried to cajole him into walking as far as the corner shop to meet her when she finished at one o'clock, but he wouldn't listen to her either.

'I don't want to be stopped by people asking me how I am. What does it matter to any of them how I feel? I know I'm a complete wreck and I don't want to talk about it.'

Although he was so adamant about this both

113

Caitlin and Ruth agreed that it was all a question of time and that it was much better to ignore what he said.

'Give him a chance to regain his confidence first and then perhaps we can persuade him to come to the park with us one Sunday afternoon, like he used to, in the old days.'

Even indoors, Tomas was very jumpy and nervous and, as Caitlin had foreseen, Glynis's constant chatter seemed to disturb him. He constantly worried about her being underfoot when he moved around because he was afraid that he was going to fall over her.

'She moves so fast I never know where she's going to be next,' he grumbled. 'One minute she's sitting down on a chair, or playing quietly on the floor, then, the moment I start to walk across the room, she's there in front of me.'

'Try not to worry about her, she'll get out of your way,' Ruth assured him.

'Probably she will, but I am so unsteady on my feet that if she bumps into me I am the one likely to fall over.'

Glynis was equally perturbed by having Tomas around. She'd been happy enough to call him Dada, and to chatter away to him when he'd been in hospital, but she seemed rather frightened at finding him in her home.

Caitlin found herself run off her feet, trying to make sure that Tomas had everything he needed and contending with Glynis as well. Most of the time she was either clutching on to Caitlin's skirt, hiding away behind a chair, or in a corner sucking her thumb and staring wide-eyed at Tomas.

Caitlin tried desperately to reconcile the two of them, hoping that if Tomas would talk to Glynis or play with her, then it would leave her free to get on with things.

'Perhaps if you sat her on your knee and told her a story, she'd get used to you being here and I'd be able to get on with doing things around the house,' she suggested.

'Not much chance of that happening,' he told her sharply. 'She hates the sight of me and I can understand why. I must look like an ogre to the poor little thing.'

'Don't talk such rubbish,' Caitlin scolded. 'Children of that age judge people by how kind and friendly they are towards them not by what they look like.'

'I've forgotten how to be either of those things,' Tomas said bitterly. 'That's what being in the trenches does to you. You can only think about looking out for yourself.'

'Well, you don't have to do that now. We're doing all we can to make you comfortable.'

'I know that!' He blew his nose to conceal his emotions. 'I'm just a burden to you all. I'd have been better off staying in hospital, or not coming back from the Front at all.'

'You're talking nonsense!' Caitlin told him, putting her arms around him and hugging him close. 'It might be taking Glynis a little while to get used to you, but remember she's your little daughter. Try and get to know her a bit better. The pair of you could be good company for each other if you made the effort.'

'It's you she wants or else our Ruth. Those two seem to dote on each other. The moment Ruth arrives home, Glynis makes a beeline for her and won't leave her side for a moment.'

'Yes, our Ruth spoils her. It's a pity she didn't have a little sister years ago.'

'Then they would have grown up together and things would have been so much easier for you,' Tomas sighed.

'Still, we should be thankful we've got her now,' Caitlin commented quickly.

'And that Ruth is so willing to do so much for her. I've noticed that when it comes to her bedtime, if Ruth walks out of the room before little Glynis is asleep, she's in floods of tears. Ruth has to stay in there, putting away clothes, tidying up, or even doing some mending until Glynis finally falls asleep. I'm pretty sure it's because she's scared of me and it's no good you trying to tell me anything different.'

'Yes, but it is only a temporary setback. As soon she's more used to you being home she'll go off to bed quite happily. Ever since she was quite small she has been content to lie there in her cot singing to herself until she finally falls asleep.'

When later Caitlin repeated all this to Ruth she begged her to say something to Tomas to see if she could reassure him. 'Nothing I say to him seems to make any different and I do so hate seeing him upset like this. I'm always afraid it's going to bring on one of his erratic moods like the doctors warned me would happen if he was worried or upset, and then I never know how to deal with him.'

'Of course I will,' Ruth promised. 'Do try and stop worrying, Mam.' She gave her a big hug and a kiss. 'Give it time and things will work out fine, you'll see.'

Although Ruth was pleased that her mother was once again house proud and running their home as efficiently as she'd done before Tomas had been called up, she was also aware that her mother was desperately worried when he became angry or erratic and didn't appear to be able to make allowances for it.

'These bouts of despair, mental confusion and irritability are like an illness, Mam,' she kept telling her. 'They're caused by the stress he's been under because of what he has had to endure.'

'At the hospital they put it down to the shells exploding so close to him,' Caitlin reminded her.

'That was only part of it; think of the conditions he was living in when he was in the trenches. All that mud and wet; hardly any food; bombs making great craters all around him; no wonder he was in a state of shock.'

'You are only surmising all that,' her mother

argued. 'You don't know it for certain because he won't talk about it.'

When Caitlin tried discussing it with some of the neighbours when she met them out shopping most of them were full of sympathy for Tomas, but they seemed surprised by her attitude.

'At least you've got your man back home with you while the rest of us have husbands and sons still over there fighting,' several of them pointed out.

'You're not on tenterhooks all the time dreading that there'll be news that he's been killed or badly injured,' another neighbour told her dismissively.

The general opinion seemed to be that Caitlin was one of the lucky ones.

'Get on with your life, Caitlin Davies, and stop worrying so much about everything,' several of them told her.

'I might be able to do that if I wasn't so worried about money,' she pointed out. 'My poor Tomas is a very sick man; he's not fit to work and he needs good food to build him up, but we can't afford it. The disability pension they've given him is less than half what his army pay was and that was a mere pittance.'

'Well, you've got him home, you're fit and well yourself, so there's nothing to stop you going out to work and earning a crust, is there?' one woman asked scathingly as she stowed her groceries away in her canvas shopping bag.

'If I go out to work, then who's going to look after little Glynis?' Caitlin sighed. 'She's still only a baby and needs watching all the time.'

'Get yourself a day job, then, and let your Ruth work nights so that there's always one of you in the house to see to Tomas and look after the baby. They're crying out for women to work shifts at the munitions factory.'

Caitlin felt shocked by the suggestion. When she mentioned it to Ruth, though, she was surprised to find that her daughter thought it might be a good solution.

'It could be the answer,' Ruth said thoughtfully. 'Hard on little Glynis, mind, since it will upset her routine and she won't know where she is half the time.'

'What about me, how do you think I'd feel about having to go and work in a factory at my age?'

'I know, Mam, but there is a war on and it would be better than being hard up all the time. We certainly can't manage on the money I'm getting part-time and, as you say, the pension Dad has been given is so small that it's hardly any help at all.'

Caitlin still didn't like the idea, but in the end she suggested that perhaps Ruth should find out about factory work and what sort of hours would be involved if they did do shifts.

'We could give it a try,' she suggested as they washed up after their midday meal the following Sunday. 'What about you doing evening or night shifts first, to see how you get on. There's always the possibility that you might find it too much for you.'

'Well, if I was working at night I'd need to sleep during the day,' Ruth pointed out thoughtfully, as she dried a pile of plates and put them away in the kitchen cupboard.

'Not much chance of doing that, not with the noise young Glynis makes around the place,' Caitlin commented as she emptied out the bowl of dirty water and began wiping out the sink. 'And then there's your dad to think about. He doesn't do anything to help himself,' she added, giving the dishcloth a vicious twist as she wrung it out and then draped it over the tap.

'You never know, perhaps if he realised that it was necessary for both of us to go out to work he'd make more of an effort. He's not injured in any way so he's quite capable of making a cup of tea for himself; or getting a meal on if it comes to that.' Ruth smiled as she filled the kettle.

'That would be a shock, mind,' her mother said scathingly, as she took three cups and saucers from the cupboard and put them on the table with a clatter. 'He's never lifted a finger in the house since the day we were first married. He's always considered cooking and cleaning to be women's work. He always said that as he earned the money it was up to me to see that it was spent wisely and that everything in the home was run to his satisfaction.'

'That might have been the case in the past, when you were first married, Mam, but times have changed and we've all got to do things we've never done before.'

'Well, see what you can find out about shift work at the munitions factory and whether or not they'll take you on,' Caitlin suggested as she poured boiling water into the teapot.

A week later Ruth had found herself a job at Curran's Munitions factory on the Taff Embankment. The hours were from ten o'clock at night until six o'clock the next morning.

'Funny hours,' Caitlin complained. You'll wake us all up, if you come home at that time in the morning.'

'By the time I get home it will be almost seven o'clock and you're usually up by half past seven, so I don't see that it's going to disturb you at all,' Ruth told her.

'No, perhaps not. Then I suppose you'll want to go to bed right away and you'll expect me to keep Glynis quiet all morning while you get some sleep.'

'I'm not sure. By the time I've given you a hand to dress Glynis, have some breakfast and then clean and tidy around the house, it will be getting on for mid-morning. That's when Glynis normally has a nap so I could take her upstairs with me for a sleep. That would leave you free to go shopping or whatever else you wanted to do.'

'Got it all planned out, haven't you,' her

mother sighed as she started sorting out the clean washing. 'I suppose after a couple of weeks you'll expect me to go and work at the factory during the daytime.'

'I thought that was the idea, Mam? We would both work shifts and double the money coming in each week,' Ruth said as she took hold of one end of a sheet to help fold it.

'I see! So what sort of hours have you got lined up for me to do, may I ask?'

'Well, if you are going to work in the munitions factory, the same as me, there's a two o'clock till ten o'clock shift, or there's one from six in the morning till two in the afternoon.'

'Six o'clock in the morning! That would mean leaving here just after five o'clock and that's the middle of the night. If you think I'm going to make my way down to the Taff Embankment at that time in the morning, you must be mad. The trams don't start running until six. Anyway, it's on the edge of Tiger Bay. I'd probably get my throat cut on the first morning. Apart from that, I'd never be able to get out of bed as early as that. When would I get any sleep?'

'In that case, you'd better think about the two o'clock till ten o'clock shift.' Ruth smiled.

'That's out of the question as well because I wouldn't get home until half past ten at the earliest and you'd have to leave at half past nine to be in time for your shift.'

'By the time I left home, Dad would either be going to bed, or even in bed, and Glynis would not only be in bed but sound asleep,' Ruth pointed out.

'And what happens if Glynis wakes up and starts howling for a drink or something?'

'Dad would either have to take one up to her or else ignore her till you got home. It would only be for a few minutes.'

'I don't know.' Caitlin made a pile of the folded sheets. 'I'm not sure I like the sound of it. He's a bag of nerves as it is, and having her crying or calling out for attention could make him a lot worse.'

'We won't know unless we try it out, now will we? Why don't you talk to Dad about it and see what he says. I'm sure he'll agree with me that there's no real problem.'

'Except that I will have to tear round all morning trying to get all the cleaning and shopping done,' Caitlin pointed out.

'No you won't, I've already said that I'll give you a hand when I get home before I go to bed. I'm sure we can work a routine out between us so that I do my fair share of those things. You never know, when Dad realises what is going on he may start to help. He might even be prepared to do some of the shopping for us.'

'Don't be so twp, Ruth. You know damn well that your dad hasn't set a foot outside the front door since the day he came home from the hospital. He says that he can't bear the thought of people asking him how he is or seeing the pitying look in their eyes when they see what he looks like these days.'

'That was weeks ago. He doesn't look anywhere near as gaunt as he did when he first came home.'

'He still has these terrible mood swings, though. One minute he's as nice as pie and then the next he bites your head off. Supposing he acted like that when one of the neighbours spoke to him and said something he didn't like?'

'I'm sure most people would understand. He's not the only man in the world to have suffered shell-shock, you know, Mam. People talk about these things and most of them not only know how the soldiers are affected by it, but are also ready to make allowances; which is what we should do as well.'

'Are you saying that I'm not treating him right?' Caitlin demanded huffily.

'No, of course I'm not. I know it has been very difficult for you to cope with him and with little Glynis at the same time. I know she looks like a little angel when she's asleep.' Ruth smiled as she looked fondly at Glynis who was curled up with one little hand under her cheek. 'But she can be very demanding when she's awake.'

'I'll think about it and let you know what I decide after I've had a chance to talk it over with your dad,' Caitlin told her cautiously. 'Going out to work is a big step for me to have

to take at my age; you must try and understand that.'

'I do, Mam; really I do,' Ruth told her, putting
her arms around her mother's shoulders. 'I
think you've been wonderful and it often makes
me feel guilty that you have so little time to be
with other people.'

'Yes,' Caitlin sighed, 'I do sometimes get a
bit fed up and it makes me irritable, I know.
Still, going out to work and meeting other
people might make all the difference.'

'I really think so, Mam. This could be the
start of a whole new life for all of us. Let's give
it a try, Mam; that's all I'm asking.'

Chapter Eleven

Much to Ruth's surprise, Caitlin not only settled in to working at the munitions factory, but she also seemed to enjoy it far more than Ruth did herself.

She'd expected her mother to hate having to wear the drab long-sleeved uniform that reached down to their ankles and the cap that hid all their hair, but it didn't seem to bother her at all.

They seemed to have so much more in common that they became more like friends rather than mother and daughter and enjoyed sharing their work experiences.

When she arrived home at the end of her shift, early in the morning, Ruth found that her mother was usually already up, had lit the fire and had a pot of tea brewed and waiting for her. Caitlin seemed to like to sit down with her and, while they drank their tea, chat about what had gone on at the factory the previous night.

As soon as they heard either Tomas or Glynis stirring, Caitlin would take Tomas up a cup of tea and when she came back downstairs she'd start getting the breakfast ready while Ruth went up and dressed Glynis ready for the day.

After breakfast they shared the various chores

that had to be done and, more often than not, Caitlin popped Glynis into her pram and took her out to the shops. Ruth would finish off any jobs that still needed doing and then go upstairs to get ready to go to sleep. By the time Caitlin returned she was usually already in bed and her mother would put Glynis in alongside her and in next to no time the two of them would be sound asleep.

Glynis quickly learned that when she woke up it was all right for her to go downstairs to her mam and dada, but that she must do it quietly so as not to waken her big sister.

At first Tomas seemed to be mesmerised by the change in routine and all that was going on around him. Gradually, though, he adjusted and even began to try and help. Often he'd lay the table ready for a meal, or put coal on the fire when it started to die down. He even began to take more notice of the baby.

Glynis thrived on his attention and quickly learned how to persuade him to play with her or to tell her a story. Even if he was tired or not feeling too well, she only had to give him one of her beaming smiles, or roguish looks, to make him notice her and do as she asked.

He still refused to set foot over the doorstep; he wouldn't even answer the door if someone knocked. Caitlin and Ruth both tried to reason with him over this but he was adamant.

'It might be the enemy,' he said worriedly. 'They get everywhere; they're probably looking for me right this minute. That's why I don't want to see anybody. I'm safe while I'm indoors. I've got everything I want, so leave me be.'

'Why would they come looking for you, Dad?' Ruth murmured gently. 'You've got nothing to do with the war now.'

'I was over there, I was fighting them, and they have spies and snipers everywhere you turn. They're out for revenge, so you want to watch out. Don't trust anyone, understand?'

He was so positive about this and became so distressed when he talked about it that Ruth assured him that she'd be on her guard at all times.

'You don't want to believe all you read in the newspapers either; a lot of the things they say about the war aren't true. They're saying it's going to end soon, but it will never be over.'

'He'll come round, Mam,' Ruth assured her mother. 'Look at how well he's adjusted to us both going out to work.'

Although Caitlin agreed with her on this point she still felt concerned about Tomas.

'Give it time. We have more money now, so you can buy meat, milk, butter and those things you need to build him up,' Ruth reminded her. 'Once he regains his strength and puts on some weight it will make him feel so much better and then there'll be no stopping him. He'll want to be out every day and perhaps he'll even take Glynis out for a walk in her pram.'

'Your dad wouldn't dream of doing that!'

Caitlin laughed derisively. 'He'd never be seen pushing the pram when you were a baby, except to put a hand to it if we were going up a really steep hill, and even then I had to ask him to do it.'

'Well, I don't suppose it matters very much at the moment. It's almost the winter and no one wants to go out for walks when it's cold and wet. By next spring things will be a lot different. Dad may have forgotten about the enemy because he's bound to be feeling fitter, and who knows, the war may be over. If we can get a pushchair for Glynis, perhaps he won't mind being seen with one of those.'

A few weeks later, at the beginning of November, their dreams came true: the war was over, and peace had been declared.

At first no one could believe it, then people went wild; there was celebrating in the streets and everyone who had men at the Front waited eagerly for them to come home. Christmas 1918 was going to be the best one ever. Families would be reunited; 1919 would see the start of a bright new world. This was the war to end all wars. In future, negotiations would take place peacefully; the future was full of hope.

Even Tomas seemed to take a turn for the better. With the war over there was no enemy, no one to fear. He still had days when he was depressed and morbid, but these became less frequent and not nearly as intense. Ruth hoped that after Christmas, once the cold winter weather was over, he'd be willing to go out and perhaps even take Glynis with him.

Apart from his reluctance to do this one thing, she felt that life was really quite good for them all at the moment. With her mother working as well they were going to be able to afford extras for Christmas, even though so many things were still in short supply and expensive.

Feelings in Harriett Street towards the Davies family were still very mixed. Most people realised that Tomas had been too unfit to continue as a soldier and they admired the way that Ruth and Caitlin had both gone out to work and made the best of things.

But as Tomas's health and appearance improved, there were some, who were still mourning the loss of loved ones, or still waiting to hear when their husband, son or brother was going to come home and be demobbed, who resented the fact that Tomas was already home.

'Take no notice, Mam, they're only jealous. We're doing fine so let's enjoy what we have. The war is over so even though their men folk are still in the army they're no longer in any danger from the enemy.'

'Things shouldn't take this long to get back to normal, though,' Caitlin sighed.

'Everything will be in place by Easter, you'll see,' Ruth told her confidently. 'Now that Dad is starting to go out it's certainly going to be good for us. If we save up hard, we might even be able to go on holiday this summer. Think how lovely it would be for all of us to go to the seaside for a whole week. Imagine how excited Glynis will be when we take her paddling.'

'Will our jobs last, though?' Caitlin pondered. 'They won't need any more munitions now that the war is over.'

'No, but Curran's will probably go back to making all the tinware they did before the war started. There will be plenty of demand for bowls and buckets because people haven't been able to buy things for their kitchens for ages as all the metal was being used to make armaments.'

Although Ruth was quite right in what she surmised, she'd been too optimistic. Once the men were demobbed they wanted their old jobs back and expected the women to return to the domestic life they'd known before.

Caitlin was the first to be sacked. She was in tears; her wage packet had been so important to her. Without it she knew she'd be back to scrimping and scraping to make ends meet.

'Never mind, Mam, you've done your bit. You always said you were too old to do war work,' Ruth joked, hoping to bring a smile to her face.

'I've proved I'm every bit as fit as you,' Caitlin claimed hotly. 'With only your wage and your dad's disability pension we'll find it a hard job to manage.'

'Perhaps you can get a part-time job somewhere,' Ruth suggested. 'What about one of the corner shops around here? It might be less strenuous than shift work in a factory.'

'It would certainly be a much smaller pay packet,' Caitlin retorted.

A month or so later, Ruth was also given her cards. She was shocked; she tried to protest, to reason with the foreman, but it was all to no avail.

'There are men with families to support and they worked here long before you came,' he told her. 'Get back home to your knitting and think yourself lucky you can take it easy.'

'I have a family to support,' Ruth told him sharply. 'My dad's been shell-shocked and can't work, and you sacked my mam only a short time ago.'

'Your dad will have his pension, so you're not destitute,' he told her callously. 'Now, do you want this pay packet or not?'

Caitlin was in tears when Ruth told her what had happened. 'Don't say anything to your dad, cariad, it will only worry him,' she warned.

'He's going to find out sooner or later when he sees me around the place all the time.'

'Let's delay it for a couple of weeks. See if you can get another job first of all. If you can, then we'll simply tell him that you've changed your hours.'

For the next two weeks, Ruth pretended she'd changed her shift and went out of the house just after one o'clock as if she was going to the factory to work. She spent every afternoon scouring the shops to see if there were any vacancies. She walked from one side of Cardiff to the other, afraid to spend money on tram fares and existing on a bottle of cold tea and jam sandwiches which she took with her.

The strain on both Ruth and her mother was intense. They started snapping at each other and constantly arguing over every penny that was spent.

The money they'd saved up for a holiday was their mainstay, but as it began to disappear Caitlin became frantic with worry.

'I owe the rent man for three weeks,' she confessed, 'but I had to use the money to put a decent meal on the table. Your dad has got his appetite back and he'd notice if I didn't. As it is, we've had cawl and stale bread for three days running – that's if you can call it cawl; it's more like vegetable water than nourishing stew.'

Ever since they'd told Tomas that they'd both lost their jobs he kept insisting that he should be the one out looking for work, not Caitlin or Ruth.

'If you get a job we'd probably be worse off,' Caitlin pointed out, 'because they'll stop your pension.'

'You're always grumbling about what a meagre amount it is, so would that really matter?'

'It might. At least we know we're going to get it every week. If you get a job, and then later you don't suit, or the man whose job it was before the war insists on having it back when he's demobbed, we'll be in trouble.'

'That's a load of old rubbish!'

'No it's not; it's the reason that both Ruth and I got the sack from Curran's. The same thing will happen with the job our Ruth's got now at the baker's. When the chap who was working there before the war is demobbed, they'll have to give him his old job back.'

'If he isn't home by now, then he probably isn't coming back.'

'I know I shouldn't say this,' Caitlin sighed, 'but the truth is I hope he doesn't come back.'

Three weeks later her hopes were dashed. Ruth came home from work looking so downcast that Caitlin didn't even have to ask her what had happened.

Two days later the rent collector turned up to tell her that unless she paid the back arrears in full they'd have to vacate the house in Harriett Street.

'Duw anwyl! Don't talk such rubbish,' she protested. 'Where do you think we'll go? There's not only me and my husband, but our two daughters, and one of them is little more than a toddler.'

'Where you go is no concern of mine,' he told her. 'All I'm here for is to collect the rent, and to inform you that the bailiffs will be here in three days' time if you don't pay.'

'Bailiffs? What do they think they can do? If I haven't got the money, then I can't pay you.'

'If you haven't got the money, then they'll take goods to meet what's outstanding and, by the size of your arrears, I imagine that will be everything you have in this house.'

'Damnio di! That's criminal!'

'No, not paying your rent is what's criminal,' he told her. 'As well as losing all your belongings you might even find yourself in jail if you don't pay up.'

Caitlin was in floods of tears when Ruth came home. 'That old rent man said that the bailiffs could take everything,' she sobbed. 'My lovely home; it's taken me over twenty years to get it together and now I'm going to lose every stick of it.'

'Unless we move first, before they get here.'

'Move! Don't be so twp, Ruth.' Caitlin sobbed. 'Where would we move, we've no family left, so where would we go?'

'I don't know; somewhere cheaper, I suppose. How much money is there left in the savings pot? Is there enough to put down a couple of weeks' rent somewhere else?'

'Somewhere else? What do you mean? All the houses around here are about the same rent.'

'I know that, Mam. It would mean moving away from here, probably even away from Cathays.'

'The houses in Roath are even dearer, so exactly where were you thinking we should go? It's no good moving out of Cardiff to somewhere like Caerphilly or Tonypandy, because there's hardly any work there; not unless you're a miner.'

'No, you're right, Mam, it's far better for us to stay in Cardiff.'

'So where can we move, then?' Caitlin persisted with a puzzled frown.

'You're not going to like this, Mam, but the only place we can afford move to is down towards the docks.'

Both women looked up guiltily as Tomas came into the room. It was obvious he had heard part of their conversation. Caitlin was all for trying to pass it off, but Ruth shook her head to silence her. 'Dad has to know, Mam. Let's hear what he thinks about my idea, shall we?'

Tomas listened in silence as Ruth told him that they were unable to feed themselves, let alone pay the rent, and if they didn't want everything they owned to be seized by the bailiffs in a couple of days' time, then they had to act fast.

When she'd finished he nodded in agreement with her. 'You'd best get your coat on, then, cariad, and go and see what you can find for us. Me and your Mam will start sorting out the bits and pieces that are worth taking.'

'Shall I take Glynis with me or can you keep an eye on her?'

'Leave her here with us; you'll get around quicker on your own.'

It took Ruth two days to find somewhere they could afford to rent and then it was only two rooms. How they were going to manage cramped up in them she didn't know, but at least they appeared to be reasonably clean. There was a double bed for her mam and dad, but she and Glynis would have to sleep in the living room for the time being. The landlady had told her there was a small boxroom she could have when the chap who was using it now moved out.

'So where is this paradise you've managed to find for us?' Caitlin asked bitterly.

'It's in Adelaide Place.'

'I've never heard of it. Where is it, over in Canton or out at Splott?'

'Neither; it's down in Tiger Bay,' Tomas told her.

'Tiger Bay!' The horrified look on Caitlin's face said it all. 'Over my dead body! You can't make me move there,' Caitlin said defiantly.

'What other choice do we have?' Tomas asked.

'Tiger Bay's full of foreigners, drug users, thieves and robbers,' she exclaimed aghast.

'I'm sure there are plenty of honest, hard-working people living down there as well,' Ruth defended. 'People unable to afford the high rents they charge for places around here.'

'The alternative is probably the poor house,' Tomas told her.

Caitlin refused to believe him. 'They can't treat ex-soldiers like this,' she protested.

'They can and they do,' he told her bitterly. 'Let's start packing before you find out just how merciless they can be.'

Chapter Twelve

They spent all evening and late into the night packing up their belongings. First thing next morning Tomas said he was going out to see if he could find someone with a horse and cart who was willing to take their belongings along to the rooms in Adelaide Place which Ruth had rented.

'We shouldn't have let him go on his own,' Caitlin said worriedly, pushing her hair back from her face. 'He might get lost or have one of his nervous attacks.'

'He'll manage; he's trying to help, Mam, so don't start undermining his confidence. You go and finish dressing and do your hair and then make a pot of tea. I'll get Glynis up and dressed so that we're ready to leave the minute he gets back.'

When it came to the afternoon and Tomas still had not returned, Caitlin became more and more distressed. She was convinced that he'd come to some harm or had wandered off and couldn't remember where he was.

'I can't sit here any longer, I'm going out to see if I can find him,' she declared, putting on her outdoor coat and hat.

'Whatever good will that do, Mam? You've no idea at all where he might have gone, so where would you start looking? He might come back at any minute and want to leave right away and then we wouldn't know where to find you,' Ruth pointed out.

'He's been gone so long, though, he must be starving hungry. He only had a cup of tea and a crust with a bit of jam on it for his breakfast,' Caitlin reminded her in a concerned voice.

When Tomas finally returned it was mid-afternoon and he not only looked exhausted, but he smelled of beer.

Caitlin was furious. 'Have you been and spent that last couple of shillings I had on beer while we've been sitting here hungry?' she fumed. 'You ought to be ashamed of yourself.'

'Damnio di, woman, talk some sense,' he flared. 'How else did you think I was going to find someone to take our bits and pieces down to Tiger Bay? I had to check out the pubs to find a chap who'd do it and then bribe him with a drink before he'd even consider talking about the idea.'

'And you had to have one yourself into the bargain, did you?' Caitlin retorted.

'Of course I did. Anyway, we'll argue about it later. His name's Elwyn and he'll be here any minute, so get all our bits and pieces together and start moving everything out into the hallway.'

He sounded so sure of himself, so much more

139

in charge of what was going on, and like the Tomas she'd known before the war, that Caitlin felt utterly bemused.

'What can we take?'

'Well, it's furnished, Mam. There's a double bed and a table and chairs—'

'You'll need your pots and pans, some cups and plates and stuff like that,' Tomas interrupted. 'We'll take our clothes as well and any ornaments and knick-knacks that we might be able to sell off later on for a bob or two to help us out if none of us can find work right away. Fill the pram with oddments like that after you've wrapped them up in some clothes and use the big tin bath for all the china.'

He continued to issue instructions as they rushed around trying to do what he asked.

'Tie up the bedding and blankets in one of the big sheets and if you can't find anything better to put all our clothes in, then use another big sheet for those as well.'

'Everything will get so creased,' Caitlin protested, but no one took any notice of her.

'Ruth, when you've got everything together, start piling it all up on the pavement outside the front door so that it is ready to load up.'

'Oh no we don't, Tomas Davies, You're not putting any of my things out there for all the neighbours to gawp at,' Caitlin said heatedly. 'Folks will know right away that we were scarpering and I haven't said a word to any of them about our sorry plight.'

'Mam's right, Dad,' Ruth intervened. 'The less people that know about what's happening the better. If they don't see us moving all our stuff out then they can't tell the bailiffs anything about us when they turn up.'

'It's the middle of the day so people are bound to see us going,' he argued.

'Maybe, but we don't want to make it any easier for them than we have to and we don't have to tell them where we're going.'

Before they could discuss it any further Elwyn appeared at the door.

The next hour was a concentrated effort on the part of all of them. Even little Glynis dashed to and fro, carrying some of the lighter bundles and handing them up to Elwyn who was standing in the back of the cart stowing them away.

'I'll ride on the cart with our stuff. You take a tram and meet me there,' Tomas told them as Caitlin locked the front door for the last time and stood on the pavement dabbing away her tears.

'You're sure you know where Adelaide Place is, Dad?' Ruth asked anxiously.

'I do, so don't you worry about it; we'll have most of this stuff unpacked by the time you get there,' Elwyn assured her.

He was as good as his word. By the time they reached Adelaide Place it was early evening and the two men were carrying in the very last of the load.

Caitlin had alternatively cried and grumbled from the moment the tram trundled down Bute Road on its way to the terminal at the Pier Head.

The nearer they got to the docks the more Caitlin ranted saying she was fearful for her life, and that she couldn't stand the surroundings, the smells, the people or anything else she could grumble about.

Ruth moved into the next seat with Glynis and tried to distract the child by pointing out different things. If her mother objected so much to the general surroundings she was worried about how she was going to react when she saw the two rooms that were to be their new home because they were so drab and poky.

As she'd feared, Caitlin hated the place even before she'd climbed the stone steps to the front door with its peeling paintwork.

She heard her mother's gasp of dismay as she took her up the narrow stairs to the two rooms above.

Ruth thought the rooms seemed to have shrunk since she'd first seen them and that they looked very much shabbier than when she had handed over a week's rent in advance for them, but she decided that it was too late to worry about that now.

'I'll make us all a cup of tea,' she offered. 'You'll stay and have one, won't you, Elwyn?' she invited.

'No, not tea; never drink the stuff,' he guffawed. 'Me and your dad are going to cut along to the pub so that I can buy him a quick half.'

Before either Ruth or Caitlin could say a word the two men had left.

'Make that tea, Ruth; I think I'm about to collapse,' Caitlin moaned. 'Your dad was never a drinking man and here he is going into a pub twice in one day!'

'There's no fire alight to boil the kettle on, so I'll have to go down to the kitchen that we'll be sharing with the rest of the house and use the gas. I expect that means feeding some money into the meter. Have you got a shilling?'

'A shilling to make a cup of tea! Don't talk so daft.'

'Well, I only know that's what the landlady said you have to put into the meter.'

'Only when you want to cook a meal, not to simply boil a kettle. You put that much in and someone else will come along behind you and use it all up before you can boil the kettle again.'

'So what do you want me to do?' Ruth asked exasperatedly. 'Can you wait for your tea while I light the fire and boil up some water or not?'

'Go down there and see if there's enough gas left to make us a cup of tea without you having to put any money in. You can always say you didn't know how to work it. Go on, cariad, I'm parched. Take Glynis with you then if someone is thinking of telling you off you can always say the drink is for her and they probably won't mind so much.'

The ruse worked and ten minutes later they were sitting drinking their tea and wondering where they were going to put all the stuff they'd brought with them and which was piled up in great heaps in both of the rooms.

'This place is terrible, not at all what I'm used to,' Caitlin muttered as she inspected the double bed and the rickety chest of drawers in the bedroom. 'There's nowhere to hang anything!'

'There's a wooden rail across the alcove there, so that will hold a lot of things, and there're all sorts of nails and hooks dotted around the wall where you can hang things as well,' Ruth said.

'First of all, let's take these grubby sheets off the bed and put our own on,' Caitlin pronounced, 'and where on earth are you and Glynis going to sleep?'

'We'll have to make up some sort of bed in the living room. I told you that the landlady said we might be able to rent another small room later on when the chap who's in it moves on.'

'Moves on? What is he, a tramp?'

'No, Mam, he's a merchant seaman who's been waiting for a boat and she said he'd taken the room for a couple of months while he was ashore.'

'Fair do's, but is she expecting extra money for this other room?'

'I imagine so. That's how she makes her living, letting out rooms, so she's not likely to let us have it for nothing.'

'She should be paying us to live in this pigsty, not the other way round,' Caitlin said sourly.

'Look, Mam, it's all we can afford and you don't want to let her hear you saying things like that or she might get nasty and turf us out. We've got to make the best of things and hope that before too long we can move to somewhere better.'

Caitlin was not so easily appeased. She resented having to leave behind the furniture she had saved hard to buy over the years even more than losing the friends and neighbours she had known for so long.

'It can't be helped, Mam,' Ruth consoled her. 'As for friends, well you and Phoebe have hardly spoken to each other since Dad was invalided out, now have you?'

'She'd have come round, given time. Now she's going to think the worst of me and of all of us, disappearing suddenly like this without a word.'

'Why don't you write to her and explain what's happened,' Ruth suggested. 'Sometimes it's easier to say things in a letter than face to face.'

'I may do, later on. I'll see how I feel,' Caitlin agreed. 'Tomorrow things may look different. Probably even worse,' she added grimly as she stood up, put her empty cup on the table, and began to sort out the nearest pile of their belongings. 'Come on; let's get all this stuff put away somewhere so that we can make space for you and Glynis to sleep.'

Helped, or rather hindered, by Glynis they managed to arrange their belongings so that they could find everything. By that time Tomas was back again with a parcel of fish and chips for their supper. Whether he'd been mellowed by the beer or not they weren't sure, but he was certainly both affable and helpful. He refused to let Ruth and Glynis sleep on the floor.

'No, I'm not having that,' he told them. 'You two sleep in the double bed with your Mam and I'll make myself up a bed on the floor, I'm more used to roughing it than you are.'

'You can't do that, Dad; you still need your sleep.'

'Why? I'm not working. If I feel tired then I can always take a nap on the bed during the day. You and your mam are the workers these days,' he added bitterly.

'Only if we find a job,' Ruth said smiling.

'Oh you will, have no fear of that, but you won't be any good at it if you don't have a proper night's sleep. Anyway, it's much better for Glynis; she needs to get to bed long before the rest of us, and how is she going to do that if she has to sleep in the main room with all of us moving about and talking?'

In the next few days, there were a good many other problems that they had to sort out. Four of them living in two small rooms made it very crowded and Glynis seemed to be underfoot all the time.

They'd promised her that after her fourth birthday she'd be allowed to go out and play in the street with other children and she couldn't understand why they had changed their minds.

'There must be other little girls living around here,' she protested. 'If you let me go out, then I would be able to meet them and they could be my friends.'

'No!' Caitlin's voice was much harsher than she'd intended it to be. She'd been horrified the first time she'd looked out of the window to see a couple of dark-skinned children sitting on the steps on the opposite side of the road and several others playing on the pavement.

'Please, Mam. I hate being shut in all the time because there's no room to play.' Glynis pouted. 'You're always saying that I'm in the way or else that I'm making a mess.'

'Find one of your picture books and sit at the table and look at that,' Caitlin told her. 'If you are a good girl then once we've sorted a few things out one of us will take you out for a walk.'

'Yes, we will, cariad,' Ruth said quickly when she saw Glynis was about to argue. 'We'll both come with you because we want to find out where the shops are.'

'And the school?' Glynis asked eagerly. 'I'll be able to go to school soon, won't I?'

There were so many other drawbacks that Ruth was afraid her mother would never settle, even though her dad tried to make light of them and tell them that it was the lap of luxury compared to what he'd had to endure in the trenches.

'Well, you're not out there now and I'm certainly not used to living like this,' Caitlin told him tartly. 'There's nowhere for us to get a wash, we don't even have a sink up here. Whenever we need water for anything we've got to go down and collect some in a jug or bucket and bring it back up here to use it. There's nowhere for us to cook anything unless we go downstairs and use that filthy, dirty kitchen. Heaven alone knows how many other people living in this place are using it as well. Every time I go down there it seems there's someone different either cooking or washing their dirty dishes. Half of them don't even rinse the sink out properly afterwards. How we're going to wash our clothes and our bedding I've no idea at all.'

'We'll find a way, Mam, don't worry,' Ruth told her. 'Anyway, when we bring water up here to have a wash we can always rinse out Glynis's little things at the same time as our own smaller items.'

'Oh yes, and where are we going to dry them?'

'I'll fix you up a line in front of the window and then you can hang them on that and open the window and dry them that way,' Tomas promised.

'Great idea and then we can put them round the fire when we go to bed at night to air them off,' Ruth said quickly before her mother could condemn the idea.

'One thing you are not going to be able to solve is the lavatory,' Caitlin told them triumphantly. 'That's out in the backyard and the only way to get to it is through the kitchen, so that means everyone knows where you're going. What's more, it's disgusting! It's stinking dirty and the door doesn't shut properly.'

'Yes, you're right, but you're going to have to put up with that,' Tomas agreed. 'Most of the time, though, you could use a bucket up here and I'll take it down and empty it.'

Tomas was now so decisive that it surprised them all. He didn't hesitate to go out and do the shopping. In fact, he took it over as one of his main chores when he realised how much it frightened Caitlin to walk through the neighbourhood because of the many coloured people she encountered.

'You and Ruth go up to the Hayes once a week and see if you can pick up any extras. For the rest of the time I'll get what we need from the shops around here,' he told them.

'Oh yes, and what will you use for money?' Caitlin asked. 'We're going to have precious little left after we've paid next week's rent. We'll be lucky if we can afford a pint of milk and a stale loaf.'

'We've all the ornaments we brought from

Harriett Street,' he told her. 'If neither of you find any work before our money runs out then I'll take a couple of things along to the pawn-broker's and see how much I can get for them.'

'Fair do's,' Caitlin agreed, 'but I doubt if it will be enough to tide us over; you know how stingy those people usually are.'

'You leave it to me. When it comes to haggling, I'm your man,' Tomas assured her, and he squared his shoulders defiantly as if he were going in to battle.

Chapter Thirteen

Caitlin was the first to find work as a cook at the Seamen's Mission in Bute Road. Her hours were from eleven in the morning until six at night.

'That's wonderful, Mam, but it's an awfully long day; do you think you're going to be able to do it?' Ruth asked worriedly. 'You don't want to take on too much, you know.'

'It's not as bad as it sounds,' Caitlin told her. 'There's a woman to do all the rough work and prepare all the vegetables every day. I'll only be doing the cooking, making pastry and then supervising the dishing up of the food. They provide hot midday meals from twelve until half past one and then there's a break while we have something to eat ourselves and then start serving hot meals again between five o'clock and six.'

'Won't you have to clear away the dishes afterwards and wash up?' Ruth frowned.

'No, there's someone else to do all that. The only other thing I have to do besides cook the food is decide what I'm going to serve up the next day. I make out a list of what's needed and the man in charge of the place makes sure that it will all be there waiting for me when I get in the next morning.'

'So when are you going to have time to plan the menus?'

'I can work all that out in the afternoon, after I've had my meal and before it is time to start cooking again for the evening.'

'In that case, then it sounds like a great job,' Ruth enthused. 'You've always loved cooking.'

'Yes, but for a long time I've not had the money to buy the sort of ingredients for good nourishing meals. Now I'll be able to make proper stews with great lumps of meat in them; steamed puddings and all the other sorts of things that men enjoy. It's a pity your dad wasn't a sailor instead of being in the army and then perhaps he could have come along and eaten his fill.'

'Never mind; you'll be able to have a good nourishing meal yourself each day,' Ruth reminded her.

'I know that, but I don't need building up like he does.'

'He's not doing so badly.' Ruth smiled. 'He practically fills out his clothes now and he has quite a spring in his walk. What's more, he's having less bouts of depression and he really seems to be trying to help around the place as much as he can.'

A week later, Ruth found a job serving behind the counter in a little general shop in James Street.

'At least I've done something similar before, but I'm afraid the money isn't very good,' she told her mother.

'Better than nothing, cariad. With your dad's pension we should be able to pay our way, though whether or not we can manage to save any money towards moving out of Tiger Bay is another matter.'

'I hope we can do so before Glynis has to start school,' Ruth told her mother.

'I don't like the thought of her going to the one around the corner,' Caitlin agreed, 'because from what I've seen of the children, not only are they every colour and creed under the sun, but also half of them are barefoot and some are in rags.'

'Even so, I suppose we should start letting her go outside to play so that she can make friends with some of the children, otherwise she won't know anyone if she does have to go to that school.'

'I'm hoping that we'll be gone from here long before her birthday,' Caitlin argued. 'I can't stand the place and if I didn't have a job then I think I'd go mad cooped up here in these two awful rooms all the time.'

'I thought that Dad would complain, but he seems to be managing to cope quite well,' Ruth mused. 'I'm amazed at how well he's doing. He's almost back to normal and he doesn't seem to mind that he has to look after Glynis.'

'He's certainly a lot better than he was, but he's not the man I used to know,' Caitlin sighed.

Later, when Ruth was putting Glynis to bed, she tried to find out what she did all the time she and Caitlin were at work and how she and her father spent the day.

'Does Dada read stories to you?' she asked as she took off Glynis's dress, folded it, and laid it on top of the rickety chest of drawers, 'or does he play games with you?'

'We usually go for a walk while you and Mam are at work,' Glynis told her as she climbed up into bed and plumped up her pillow.

'So where do you go? Is it to one of the parks or along the embankment?'

'We go down to the Pier Head and watch all the big boats coming in and we walk along the esplanade wall and we go over the Clarence Road Bridge and look down into the water and see what's going on there. Then we have a rest.'

'Rest? Where do you have that? Do you come back home?' Ruth probed as she tucked Glynis into bed.

'Sometimes,' Glynis said evasively. Quickly she began to talk about something else. When Ruth tried to get her to say more she screwed her eyes tight shut and said that she was tired and wanted to go to sleep.

Ruth thought about what Glynis had said and then dismissed it as childish prattle. She was pleased to hear that her dad was taking Glynis out and about because it was a good idea to get her more used to her surroundings. She was pretty sure that they'd still be living in Adelaide Place when it was time for Glynis to start school, despite Caitlin's hope that they wouldn't be.

She would have liked to know more about where Glynis and her dad went, but it probably wasn't all that important, she decided. It wasn't until several weeks later, when she discovered where their 'rest' took place, that she became alarmed.

It was a Sunday afternoon in March, a couple of weeks before Easter, and as it was fairly mild and sunny Ruth decided that that she'd take Glynis for a walk so that her mam and dad could have an hour or so on their own.

'Come on, put on your best dress and some clean white socks and then you can take me on one of your favourite walks and show me where you and Dada go,' she suggested.

'Couldn't we go somewhere I haven't been before? Could we go to a park and see some flowers?' Glynis begged.

'We can do both, if you like. We're not in a hurry. Why don't we walk down to the Pier Head and look at the boats and then we can catch a tram to Cathays Park. There might even be a band playing.'

As they walked towards the Pier Head, Ruth shuddered as she saw the state of some of the squalid streets and the children who were playing in them. Some were swinging from ropes knotted and thrown over one of the lampposts; a few were kicking at tins; others were sitting in the gutter, poking at the rubbish with sticks. Unless they could move right out of the area and go back to Cathays or somewhere like that, it was going to be a dreadful place for Glynis to grow up in.

Could they manage to save up enough money for them to do so, like her mam hoped? she wondered. It certainly seemed pretty unlikely. Now that both she and her mam had managed to find work, her dad was only handing over half of his pension and pocketing the rest.

'Duw anwyl! I need it for tram fares, and such like,' he blustered when Caitlin protested. 'Half the time the money you leave out for the shopping isn't enough and a man looks a fool if he hasn't got a few coins in his pocket.'

He'd also started going for a drink on a Saturday night. He never stayed very long and he claimed he did it because it was best to keep in with the people living round about. 'What's more, I keep my ear to the ground in case there's any talk of the bailiffs, because we don't want them discovering where we are.'

'Damnio di!' Caitlin exclaimed cynically. 'You must think I'm a bigger fool than I look if you think I believe that nonsense! I know quite well that you've started drinking and I don't like it when you come home reeking of beer with your clothes stinking of pub smells.'

'I have a half-pint of bitter and I sit there and make it last for an hour,' he retaliated. 'A man needs the company of other men; listening to you women nattering on about nothing all the time drives a man senseless.'

He also smoked, and though he had always done so in moderation Caitlin was sure he smoked far more now than he'd done before he'd gone into the army.

'Dirty fag ends and ash everywhere,' she grumbled whenever she caught him lighting up. As a result, rather than argue with her or get her back up, he usually smoked when they were out at work or when he went to the pub.

Ruth thought that her mother was being rather unreasonable. He emptied their slops without being asked; he tidied up around the place when they were at work, and he kept Glynis amused. In fact, she couldn't see that they had very much to grumble about. He'd made such tremendous progress back to health since he'd been demobbed that she thought they should be pleased that he was no longer a walking skeleton who was afraid of his own shadow and leave him alone.

The only thing that puzzled her was this business of 'taking a rest' when he was out with Glynis. He looked so fit and well these days that she couldn't believe that a walk to the Pier Head and back home again could possibly tire him out.

Glynis didn't seem to want to talk about it and she'd probably never have known the truth if they hadn't gone for a walk that

Sunday. As they approached the Pier Head and were passing by the Harp Public House on the corner of Stuart Street and Bute Street, there was a swarthy-looking man standing in the doorway. When he reached out and ruffled Glynis's curls, Ruth's immediate reaction was to pull the little girl closer to her side, worried in case Glynis was frightened by him. To her astonishment Glynis reached up her hand and took his.

'Hello Juan,' she said smiling.

'So you are not with your dada today then, little Glynis.' He smiled. 'Are you going to tell me who this pretty young lady is that you are taking for a walk?'

'This is my big sister, Ruth.' Glynis grinned. 'We're on our way to get a tram from the Pier Head to go Cathays Park and see the flowers and listen to the band.'

'Hello, Ruth!' The man gave her a little bow of his head and a huge broad smile, displaying big white teeth that gleamed brightly against his swarthy skin.

Ruth acknowledged his greeting with a very tight little smile, and then, grabbing Glynis by the hand, hurried along, almost dragging the little girl off her feet in her haste to get away.

'Who on earth is that?' she hissed. 'You've been told before that you mustn't talk to strangers.'

'Juan isn't a stranger, he's a friend,' Glynis protested. 'He always talks to me and he usually gives me a sweetie or a drink of pop while Dada is having his rest there.'

For a moment Ruth couldn't understand what Glynis meant, and then it slowly dawned on her that her dad's 'rest' must mean that he went into the pub for a drink. 'So what do you do when Dada is having a rest?' she asked as calmly as she could.

Glynis giggled. 'All sorts of things. Sometimes I play with other children who are waiting while their dads have a rest; sometimes I just sit on the step. When he takes a rest here then Juan comes out and gives me a sweet; at some of the other places, I just play around with the others until he is ready.'

Ruth felt utterly flummoxed. She didn't want to say any more in case she frightened Glynis, but she was only too aware of the dangers the child could be in.

She pondered on every aspect of it for the rest of the time they were out. She was hardly aware of the pleasure Glynis was deriving from their visit to Cathays Park.

By the time she reached home again she'd decided that the best thing to do was to have a quiet word with her father and to put it to him that it was risky to leave Glynis on her own in the streets around Tiger Bay. He might mend his ways and then perhaps her mother need never know anything about it.

She intended to wait until after Glynis was in bed and then see if she could get her dad on his own but Glynis forestalled her. As they sat down to Sunday tea she began telling them all how she and Ruth had spent the afternoon.

'We saw Juan, Dada. He wanted to know who Ruth was. He said she was very pretty.' She giggled.

'Juan? Who is Juan?' Caitlin asked.

'One of my friends,' Glynis said loftily.

'A little boy and he thought Ruth was pretty!' Caitlin smiled indulgently.

'He's not a little boy; he's a big grown man. He's twice the size of Dada. Isn't he, Ruth?'

Ruth was aware that her mother was looking at her curiously and her father was looking slightly uncomfortable.

'You eat your tea and stop chattering so much,' Ruth admonished, giving Glynis a warning look.

Glynis was not silenced so easily and before Ruth could stop her she was telling Caitlin about Juan and her dada taking 'rests' when they went for a walk.

Pushing back his chair, and leaving the rest of his meal untouched, Tomas stood up, picked up his cap and walked out of the room. The next minute they heard him going down the stairs.

'Where's Dada gone?' Glynis asked bewildered.

'I expect he has remembered something he had to do,' Ruth told her. 'He'll be back later.'

She shot a warning glance at her mother, shaking her head slightly to indicate it was better not to say any more.

Even though Caitlin remained silent Ruth could see the anger in her mother's eyes and she knew there would be a lot more discussion about the matter later on. She only hoped that she'd have a chance to pacify her and that she'd have calmed down before her dad came home.

Chapter Fourteen

There was so much animosity between them all when Caitlin heard about Tomas leaving Glynis outside pubs when he took her out for a walk that Ruth decided to take matters into her own hands.

She was so concerned about the child's welfare that she went along to the school off Adelaide Street to see if they'd let Glynis start attending there after Easter, even though she wouldn't be five until the following September.

'What good is that going to do?' Caitlin railed. 'She'll be mixing with all sorts if she goes there; probably even worse types than she's meeting up with now. Why don't you wait and see if we can scrape enough money together to move.'

'Because I know we can't, Mam. It's taking us all our time to make ends meet as it is.'

'Then why don't you try and find yourself a better job? I'm earning almost twice as much as you,' Caitlin told her sourly.

'I know you are, Mam, and look what it's doing to you. You're so thin that you're a shadow of your former self. It's you, not Dad, who needs building up now.'

'Well, it's not for the want of good food, I can assure you,' Caitlin told her huffily. 'I always make certain that I have the very best of whatever I'm cooking each day.'

'I should hope so, seeing that you eat barely anything at home,' Ruth commented.

'I don't need to, cariad. I have such a big meal at midday and then something else again before I come home at night that I couldn't possibly eat another mouthful.'

'Then all I can say is that working such long hours is too much for you.'

Caitlin didn't argue; she knew it was true. Some mornings she could hardly drag herself out of bed she felt so weary. Once she was in work and became engrossed in whatever she was doing the feeling passed off. By the time she came home at night, though, she barely had the energy to put one foot in front of the other.

She knew she was irritable and snappy with Tomas and Ruth and that she couldn't wait for Glynis to be put to bed so that they could have some peace and quiet.

Caitlin put her symptoms down to the conditions they were living under. Four of them being cramped into two poky little rooms wasn't healthy.

Added to that, the living room was always full of damp clothes because they had to drape everything they'd washed on a clothes horse in front of the fire every night before they went to bed in order to get them dry.

Despite all the efforts she and Ruth made to keep the place clean there were cockroaches and fleas, though where they came from she'd no idea.

'They've probably been here for years,' Tomas said philosophically. 'They only come out after dark. I'll get some Keating's Powder and sprinkle that around the place, but there're so many of them I don't suppose it will do much good.'

'We must find somewhere else, Ruth,' Caitlin grumbled. 'Your dad hasn't been to bed since we arrived here. That room the landlady promised us has never come to anything.'

'Well, she did mention that the sailor chap is leaving in about a week's time,' Ruth told them.

'Have you reminded her that we want his room?'

'No, I wasn't sure we could afford it. We'll have to find another one and sixpence a week if we take it.'

They looked at each other dubiously. 'It would be better than having to sleep on the floor every night,' Tomas affirmed.

'Perhaps if you helped towards paying for it by cutting back on your beer and fags, then we'd be able to manage it,' Caitlin snapped.

Ruth and Glynis moved into the little bedroom three days before Glynis started school. The bed was only a fraction bigger than a single size, but even so it left very little space in the room for anything else. The only storage was a chest of drawers squeezed in sideways at the bottom of the bed and it was very difficult to open the drawers.

Glynis thought it was wonderful being in a room with her big sister and Ruth had to admit that they slept better with only the two of them sharing the bed.

'Since Glynis has to start at that school around the corner, you can make sure that she's up and dressed and see that she has some breakfast in the mornings,' Caitlin told Ruth. 'What's more you can take her along to school on your way to work each day, then me and your dad can sleep on a bit because I don't have to be at work as early as you do.'

Ruth agreed that this sounded like a good idea and promised they'd be as quiet a possible so as not to disturb her. She hoped that it would mean that if her mother managed to get more rest then she'd soon look less drawn and tired. She still felt that her mam was doing too much, but they needed the money she was earning.

With Glynis starting school they'd had to spend some of their precious savings on decent clothes for her. They bought a grey skirt and a white blouse, as well as new shoes, from one of the stalls in the market. This time they'd bought sandals because the summer was coming and they were so much cheaper.

For the first few days Glynis seemed reluctant to go in through the school gates. She clung on to Ruth's hand as if she was scared of mixing with the other children and it took quite a lot of persuasion from Ruth to get her inside. Once she overcame this initial shyness, though, she took to school like a duck to water.

She seemed to love learning and trying to please her teacher. From the minute she came home, until she was in bed and asleep, she drove them all mad as she recited the alphabet and her two times table in a sing-song voice.

'I hope you know what it all means.' Ruth smiled. 'You have it all off so pat that I don't think you do.'

Glynis did, though, and in next to no time she was able to read simple words and even her teacher commented on how well she'd fitted in and how bright she was.

There was only one aspect of school life that neither Ruth nor Caitlin were too happy about and that was the children Glynis had become friendly with and played with out in the street after school.

'You shouldn't let her hang around with them, Tomas,' Caitlin scolded. 'They're little varmints, always up to some kind of mischief.'

'Duw anwyl! Don't talk such rubbish, woman. They're five-year-olds, the same as her. They swing from the lamp-posts, play hopscotch and marbles on the pavement, or chase each other around to run off their energy, so what's wrong with that?'

'They also knock on people's doors and run away again, and tie cans to the dogs' tails. I've seen them doing it with my own eyes, so don't say that I'm talking nonsense.'

'All kids do things like that when they're playing together. I did when I was growing up and I lived in a mining village. They're the sort of pranks children everywhere get up to.'

'Put like that, then I suppose it is better for her to be playing with the other children from around here than it is to be sitting on the doorstep of some old pub and mixing with all the drunks, down-and-outs and heaven knows who else, as they stagger out half-cut,' Caitlin retorted acidly.

Although both Ruth and Caitlin were delighted by the progress Glynis was making with her reading and writing, they were also very concerned about her general behaviour. She was far too quick to answer back, she'd started telling lies, and Ruth suspected that she was also taking things which didn't belong to her. The crowd she mixed with most of the time were utter ragamuffins.

'There's no other word to describe them,' Caitlin protested when Ruth tried to tell her that it wasn't the children's fault that some of them were barefoot and others almost in rags. 'I'm well aware of the fact that it's not really their fault, and I feel sorry for them; that's not what I object to. It's the way they speak to people. They're sly and cheeky and Glynis is picking up all their bad habits. It's high time you had a word with her or spanked her bottom.'

'It's a passing phase,' Ruth defended. 'She thinks it's clever to be like them. Give her a couple of months and she'll start being her old self again.'

'I've always thought you were a bit twp, but this proves that you're not just daft but also unable to see what's happening to the child,' Caitlin retorted.

'She's not going to take much notice of what I say, now is she, when I'm only her sister. Perhaps it's time we told her the truth, but you don't want that so we'd better hope she will grow out of it,' Ruth said stubbornly.

'But will she? Look what happened last week when we let her go on the summer outing with the rest of them.'

'What do you mean? She had a great time.'

'She enjoyed it, there's no doubt about that,' Caitlin said scathingly, 'but remember what she got up to?'

'She took part in the three-legged race, won the egg-and-spoon race, and fell over and hurt her knee in the sack race. All good fun, as far as I can see.'

'Yes, she enjoyed it, I'm not disputing that, but from what I heard she also pinched a lump of toffee off one of the side stalls and sneaked on to one of the donkeys for a ride without paying.'

'She couldn't very well pay because we didn't give her any money,' Ruth pointed out.

'Then she should have done without the toffee and not gone on the donkey.'

'It must have been a big temptation when all the other children were enjoying those things,' Ruth reasoned.

'If you haven't got the money, then you have to do without,' Caitlin said stiffly. 'The sooner she learns that the better because there are going to be an awful lot of things that she's going to have to do without as she grows up.'

'I still think it was our fault for not giving her a penny or two to spend.'

'She never asked for them or even told us she was expected to take them,' Caitlin said indignantly.

'I know that; she probably didn't ask because she knew she wouldn't get any.'

Their shortage of money seemed to cause a lot of friction and Ruth felt more and more guilty that she was earning so little and that as a consequence her mam was working such long hours. Caitlin was becoming more irritable and tired with every passing day. In addition, she had developed a cough. At first it had been a mere irritating tickle, but now it was getting worse. Sometimes she coughed for five or ten minutes non-stop.

'Dad, I think you ought to make Mam see a doctor,' Ruth told him quietly one day.

'Nonsense. A bit of an old cough is nothing to worry about. We all get one from time to time.'

'You might because you're always smoking,' she told him.

He ground out the cigarette he was holding and carefully put the stub back into the packet.

'Perhaps it's the smoke in here that's bothering her,' he admitted, a little shamefaced. 'She's always complaining about it so from now on I won't smoke when I'm indoors.'

'I hope that's not going to mean that you have to go to the pub more often,' Ruth chided.

'Give over, cariad, you're getting as big a nagger as your mam.' He scowled, but there was no animosity in his voice and Ruth knew that he'd taken it in good part.

Caitlin still continued to have coughing spasms. If the fire was smoking, or a high wind caused the smoke to blow back down the chimney into the room, it set her off. At night she found she had to remember to keep a glass of water or a peppermint sweet by her bedside to try and ease the irritation in her throat. If she didn't then her wracking cough disturbed Tomas and woke him up

Glynis soon spotted what was going on and found out where Caitlin kept her supply of peppermint humbugs.

Several times Ruth caught her going to the chest of drawers in Caitlin's bedroom, taking one out, sucking it for several minutes, and then putting it back into the bag again.

When she scolded her for doing it Glynis gave her a cheeky answer. 'I'm not pinching them, only making sure that they're all right,' she said, grinning.

Ruth was well aware that as Caitlin's cough became worse she became less and less able to do things at home and that she found Glynis's noisy chatter extremely aggravating.

Every Sunday afternoon, so that her mother could go and have a lie down on her bed and sleep in peace, Ruth took Glynis out to either Roath Park or Victoria Park.

Going on a tram was something Glynis loved. If they arrived at the Pier Head in plenty of time before the tram started off they'd go upstairs. On the upper deck the wooden seats with their metal backs were laid out in pairs. Sometimes Caitlin wanted to sit so that they could see where they were going; at other times she'd insist they pushed the backs the other way so that she was looking at the road they'd come along.

If they were downstairs, then as the great iron monster clanged and swayed its way up Bute Road towards the Hayes they'd struggle to keep their places on the shiny wooden bench seats that ran the full length of the tram. As the tram began to fill up and more, and more people crowded in alongside them, they were packed in so tight that could hardly move, let alone slide along the wooden seats.

What Glynis liked to do most of all was sit on one of the bench seats that were at either end of the tram upstairs and open the little sliding window and stick her head out. Ruth was always scared stiff that she would fall out when the tram gathered speed or lurched around a corner and usually insisted that they picked one of the other seats.

When the school broke up at the beginning of August for four weeks' summer holidays Ruth was faced with a real dilemma. Although Glynis was not yet five, she was as worldly wise as a child twice her age. The thought of her playing out in the street and running wild for the next four weeks was a real problem.

Tomas promised to keep an eye on her and listened solemnly to Ruth as she begged him not to leave her on any pub doorsteps while he went in for a drink.

'So what am I to do with her? You don't want me to leave her out playing on her own, or with that bunch of little hooligans she goes around with, and you don't want me to leave her outside the pub for ten minutes while I nip inside to have a quick drink, so exactly what am I supposed to do with her?'

'Couldn't you take her along to one of the parks or something?'

'There's nothing for her to do in the parks around here. She mustn't touch the flowers, and in some of them there're notices to say we mustn't go on the grass. When it is a scorching hot August day she doesn't want to walk round and round the gravel paths because she says that makes her feet hurt. It makes mine ache as well, and trudging around all the time only wears our shoes out.'

'You used to like taking her down to the Pier Head to look at the boats.'

'We do that anyway. The minute we go anywhere near water, though, she plagues the life out of me to let her take her shoes and socks off and go for a paddle.'

'Well, she can't do that at the Pier Head.'

'No, but she can do it down by the Clarence Embankment. Half the kids she goes to school with are down there; the girls tuck their frocks up into their knickers, and she wants to join them. She's so wilful that half the time I can't stop her.'

'You mustn't let her do that!' Ruth exclaimed horrified. 'All along the bank is thick with mud; she could easily slip on that and end up being drowned.'

'Not her, she's far too nimble for anything like that to happen to her. You worry about her far too much, Ruth. In fact, you're worse than her mam. Heaven knows what you will be like when you have children of your own.'

Chapter Fifteen

No one was more relieved than Ruth when the summer holidays were finally over and it was time for school again.

Glynis seemed to have shot up in the four weeks since she'd last put on her school clothes. Ruth was shocked to see that they were so small on her that she couldn't possibly wear them when the new school year started. Everything would have to be replaced.

Ruth had agreed with her mother right from the very start that she'd be the one to provide clothes and shoes and anything else Glynis might need and now it meant dipping into her meagre savings to do so.

Glynis was quite excited at the idea of them going on a shopping trip until she learned what they were going to buy and then she became very rebellious.

'I don't want another old grey skirt or a silly white blouse,' she argued. 'Why can't I wear my ordinary dress like all the others do? They all laugh at me when they see what I have to wear.'

Ruth was taken aback. 'I thought you wanted to look smart for school,' she said in surprise.

'I'd sooner look like everyone else. I don't like them laughing at me and calling me "Miss"; even the boys tease me about what I'm wearing,' Glynis told her.

Ruth hesitated. She liked to see Glynis going off to school in her smart grey skirt and white blouse every morning, but she had to admit that it did make her stand out from the rest of the class.

'Can't you ask Mam if I can go back to school in the dresses I've been wearing all through the summer holidays?' Glynis begged. 'I do have two, so if I make the one I'm wearing dirty and you have to wash it, you won't have to try to get it dry and ironed overnight. Please, Ruth. I hate looking different to everybody else.'

'Leave it for now, then, and I'll have a talk with Mam and see what she thinks about it.'

Although she didn't really like the idea she was well aware that the weather was still unusually warm for September and the two summer dresses Glynis was talking about most certainly wouldn't fit her next year, not at the rate she was growing.

If she wore one of her jumpers over them when the weather became colder then they'd last right up to Christmas and she'd buy Glynis a new skirt and two brightly coloured jumpers as her Christmas present. They'd take her right through until next Easter when it would be time for summer dresses again.

The more she thought about it the better Ruth

liked the idea. It meant that she wouldn't have to make inroads into her savings and she was very anxious not to do that in case the money was needed for something else.

She was worried that her mother might have to take time off work because of her cough. It seemed to be getting worse and she wondered what would happen in a few months' time when the weather turned cold and damp.

Ruth's premonition was well founded. Early in October Caitlin had a severe bout of bronchitis. The chemist prescribed some dark brown linctus, but it didn't seem to do very much good. When Ruth told him this when she went back for a second bottle, he advised that she ought to take her mother to see a doctor.

'I know that visiting the doctor costs money,' he said sternly when he saw her hesitate, 'but your mother has an extremely bad cough and if she doesn't take care she might very well end up with pneumonia.'

Caitlin ignored the advice completely and even refused to stay home in bed.

'I can't afford to lose my job,' she insisted next morning as she struggled into her outdoor coat and wrapped a thick black shawl round her shoulders.

She was shivering and shaking even as she spoke and was so unsteady on her feet that it looked as if she was about to keel over. Both Ruth and Tomas pleaded with her to see sense and to stay at home in the warm, even if it was only for the one day.

A couple of hours later she was taken to hospital after collapsing at work. As she had fallen, she had pulled over a pan of hot stew that she'd been stirring and the contents had gone all down one leg and badly scalded it. She was in terrible pain and the manager at the Seamen's Mission sent someone round to Adelaide Place to tell Tomas that she'd been rushed to the infirmary.

He, in turn, went to the corner shop where Ruth was working to tell her the news. It was the busiest time of the day, when all the women were popping in to buy bits for their midday meal, or to prepare a meal for when their families came home, and her boss insisted she couldn't be spared.

'Are you sure you can manage to make your way from here to Newport Road on your own?' Ruth asked him worriedly in between serving customers.

'Damnio di, I travelled on the tram when we lived in Cathays from there to the docks every day of my life before I went in the army; of course I can manage it.'

'Don't worry about getting back for Glynis when she comes out of school. I'll see if I can take a few minutes off and perhaps bring her back here with me.'

'I wouldn't worry about that. She's been coming home on her own ever since the new term started. She plays with some of the others on the way home and I've told her that as long as she's in before it gets too dark it's OK,' he told her.

Ruth was about to tell him that he shouldn't have allowed this, but bit back the words. There seemed to be no point in saying anything about it now. Obviously it had been going on for weeks and at the moment there were more serious matters to worry about.

It was late evening before Tomas arrived home from the hospital.

He looked almost as grey and drawn as her mother had been before she'd left for work that morning. Ruth's heart thudded the moment she saw him because she suspected that there was bad news.

She'd already put Glynis to bed and made a pot of tea so she poured him out a cup and waited until he was sitting down and drinking it before she asked how her mother was.

Tomas shook his head from side to side and seemed to have difficulty in answering.

'She's in a bad way,' he said at last in an uneasy voice, running a hand through his hair.

'Has her cough turned to pneumonia like the chemist said it could, or is it her scalded leg that's giving cause for concern?'

'Her leg's all bandaged up, but things are far worse than that,' he said hoarsely.

'Worse? What do you mean?'

He drained his cup, swallowing the last of

the tea with a noisy gulp. 'They're saying she's got TB.'

'TB?' Ruth looked bemused. 'You mean tuberculosis! Oh, Dad, poor Mam, but how on earth has that happened? Are you sure that's what they said?'

'Oh, I'm sure, cariad. Quite sure.' Tomas put his head in his hands and his shoulders heaved. When he looked up his cheeks were wet with tears.

'Oh, Dad!' Ruth crossed the room and put her arms around him. 'Don't take on so, try not to be so upset. It's terrible news, but it's not your fault.'

'Of course it's my fault,' he said angrily as he pushed her away. 'Having a baby at her age is what's brought it on. And then there was all the extra work and worry of having to look after me when I was sent home from France and now having to go out to work and live in this hovel. It's all my fault! None of it would ever have happened if she hadn't had Glynis. Somehow or other we'd have been able to manage to stay in Harriet Street, with you working and my pension, if there'd only been the three of us. She'd never have gone down with TB if we'd still been living there.'

As he dropped his head into his hands again Ruth felt such an overpowering sense of guilt that she was tempted to tell him the truth about Glynis; tell him that Glynis wasn't his child, that her mother's poor health had nothing at

179

all to do with Glynis being born because Glynis was *her* child.

The thought of what her mother's reaction would be if she did this made her hesitate. Would it be an even bigger blow to her father to discover how they'd both lied and kept such an important matter from him all these years? His health was still not good, and although his mood swings had decreased there were still times when he was sunk in black despair.

Finding out something like this on top of learning that her mother had TB might undo all his recovery and she wasn't sure whether or not she ought to risk it.

The moment passed. Tomas sat bolt upright again, squared his shoulders, and began telling her in more detail about her mother's condition.

'Would you like me to go along and see her right now?' Ruth asked him gently.

'I'm not sure if they'd let you in, cariad, not at this time of night,' he said hesitantly.

'Well, there's no harm in trying, that's if you'll be all right left here with Glynis.'

He nodded. 'Go on, then. It might ease her mind to see you. She seemed so worried about what was going to happen and how we'd manage here without her as well as about losing her job. Perhaps if you went to see her and had a little chat with her then you can reassure her that everything will be all right and that she's not to worry, otherwise she'll never get better.'

As she put on her outdoor things Ruth checked that Glynis was still fast asleep.

'Promise you won't go out and leave her on her own, Dad,' she begged as she was about to leave. 'If she woke up and found herself alone she'd be scared stiff.'

All the way from the Pier Head to Newport Road Ruth worried about what was going to happen. Her mam was earning far more than she was; in fact, her money was their mainstay. Without it there'd certainly be no new clothes for Glynis; she'd be lucky if they could afford something from a second-hand stall when she outgrew what she was wearing.

They'd be on the breadline, there was no doubt at all about that, and how they were going to manage to live all through the winter when they needed more coal as well as good, hot, nourishing meals she really didn't know.

When she arrived at the infirmary there were two ambulances outside and people on stretchers were being lifted out. Ruth was told by the police that there'd been a serious accident and she was asked to stand to one side while the stretchers were being carried in by porters.

When the commotion died down and she decided that it would be all right for her to go in, they still didn't really want to let her do so when they found out that she had nothing to do with the accident because it was far too late for visiting. It took argument, persuasion and tears before anyone would even make enquiries to see if it was possible for her to see her mother.

Much to Ruth's surprise and relief she was finally told that she could see Caitlin. The minute she was taken along to her mother's bedside she could see why they had been so lenient; there was no doubt about it, Caitlin was desperately ill.

Her mother's face was completely drained of colour; even her lips were white, although there was a faint blue tinge around the edge of them.

There were also dark shadows under her eyes. She made hardly a dent under the starched white bedclothes she was so thin.

One of her hands was lying outside the bedclothes and it looked almost lifeless; the veins on the back of it stood out like trails of blue ink. There was a tube in her arm and that was attached by a long trailing wire to a machine at her bedside.

Her breathing was shallow and so terribly laboured that she made a strange wheezing sound with every breath she took. When Ruth bent over and kissed her on the forehead Caitlin gave no sign that she felt anything or that she was even aware of her presence.

For almost an hour Ruth waited patiently at her mother's bedside, willing her to open her eyes, but she seemed to be in too deep a state of sleep for that to happen. A nurse in a blue uniform with a crisply starched white apron and frilled cap came and took Caitlin's pulse, then frowned and asked Ruth to leave.

'It's quite pointless you sitting here at her bedside for half the night,' she said brusquely. 'Your mother is heavily sedated and so it's very unlikely that she'll regain consciousness before midday tomorrow at the earliest. The best thing you can do is to go home and get a good night's rest yourself.'

With a heavy heart, Ruth reluctantly obeyed the nurse. She wanted to stay, but she realised it was doing no good and that she was only in the way.

As she left her mother's bedside the nurse said in a more kindly tone, 'You can come back tomorrow whenever you wish. Mrs Davies is on the danger list so you will be allowed in at any reasonable time.'

'Was she lying here like this when my dad was here a couple of hours ago?' Ruth asked.

The nurse gave an impatient shrug. 'I've no idea, I wasn't on duty then, but I expect she was.'

Ruth tried to hide her concern as well as her tears from Tomas when she arrived back at Adelaide Place.

'Will you go and see her tomorrow morning and then come to the shop and let me know how she is?' she asked as she banked up the fire before going to bed.

He nodded, but didn't answer. He looked

almost as grey and drawn as he'd done when he'd first returned home from France and there was a vacant look in his dark eyes, almost as if he had retreated to some unknown place because he couldn't accept what was happening.

As she went out of the room she saw him reach into his jacket pocket for his cigarettes, take one out of the packet, light up, and take a long hard draw on it.

It was the first time she'd seen him smoking indoors for many weeks. She said nothing, realising that he needed the comfort and strength that having a cigarette gave him.

Once again she wondered if she ought to tell him the truth about Glynis and wished, not for the first time, that they hadn't kept the truth from him in the first place.

The thought was uppermost in Ruth's mind when she went to visit her mother the next day and found Caitlin awake.

Even though her breathing was so laboured that she could barely speak, her mother was anxious to tell her something.

Caitlin clutched at her hand, pulling her closer. 'Ruth, I want you to make me a promise,' she gasped. 'When I die, you're not to tell your father that you are Glynis's mother . . . promise me now.'

'You're not going to die, Mam,' Ruth exclaimed quickly, her eyes filling with tears. 'You're on the mend. Look, you're talking again; the last time I came to see you, all you did was sleep.'

'Promise me, Ruth,' Caitlin begged, struggling to try and sit up in the bed. 'It would kill him if he knew how we'd lied to him all these years. You mustn't tell him. It would upset Glynis as well. Look after her, Ruth, and . . .' Her strength failed and she slumped back against the pillows, her eyes closed as she gasped for breath.

Chapter Sixteen

Caitlin died three days later without ever regaining consciousness.

Tomas was utterly bewildered. 'Damnio di, she's only in her forties,' he muttered over and over again. 'Having Glynis has been such a strain on her,' he added remorsefully.

Ruth shook her head and said nothing. She was sure it would make him feel better if he knew the truth and she wished she'd never promised her mother that she wouldn't tell him.

If only her mother hadn't lost consciousness again then perhaps she could have talked her round but it was too late now.

She tried to push her own grief to one side as she consoled Glynis who cried copiously because she found it so difficult to understand that she would never be seeing her mam again.

'I thought Mam had gone to hospital to be made better,' she said in a bewildered voice.

'We all hoped that, my lovely,' Ruth told her, cuddling her and wiping away her tears, 'but I'm afraid they couldn't make her better.'

'So what's happened to her, has she run away somewhere else?'

'Of course she hasn't, cariad. Whatever makes you think something like that?'

'I thought perhaps she'd gone because I was always being so naughty.'

'No, my lovely! Mam was so tired that she fell asleep and now she's gone to heaven.'

'Why? Didn't she like it here in her own bed? Perhaps it was because I wasn't sleeping with her any more.'

'No, it was nothing to do with that,' Ruth assured her. 'She'd been working too hard, that was why she was so very tired.'

'So has she gone up with the angels?'

'Yes, that's right, cariad. They'll look after her and make her happy.'

'Will she be an angel?' Glynis persisted.

'I'm not too sure,' Ruth prevaricated. 'Why do you want to know that?'

'My teacher says we all have a guardian angel and that she comes and sits at the bottom of our bed and watches over us to keep us safe when we're asleep so I was hoping that perhaps Mam would be my guardian angel.'

'I'm sure she'll be watching over you and loving you just as much as she always did,' Ruth assured her giving her a big hug and drying her tears.

Tomas wasn't anywhere near as easy to consol as Glynis. He really took Caitlin's death to heart and grieved openly. He seemed to lose interest in everything and went downhill so rapidly that Ruth was concerned about him.

She was also desperately worried about money. Caitlin's funeral used up all their meagre savings, and though they'd pawned every possible item they could, they still didn't have enough to meet their bills and she feared they would end up in debt.

Whenever she tried to talk to Tomas about it he got up and walked away, or else became so distressed that she wished she'd never mentioned it at all.

One of the economies she knew they ought to make was to give up the small bedroom, but she didn't know how to explain this tactfully to her father.

Finally the matter was taken out of her hands. The seaman who'd previously occupied it was due home again and so the landlady more or less demanded that she should have it back so that she could rent it out to him.

'So where are you and me going to sleep now?' Glynis asked as they piled their bedding into a corner of the living room and tried to find room for their clothes.

Ruth knew that the obvious answer was that they should use the big double bed that her mam and dad had shared and that he should have a makeshift bed in the living room again, but she didn't know how to tell him this without upsetting him. In the end Glynis was the one who brought about a solution.

'I want to sleep in a proper bed again. I don't like sleeping on the floor,' she announced when the three of them were sitting down to their meal the following Sunday.

Tomas put down his knife and fork and stared over at her in bewilderment. 'What do you mean about having to sleep on the floor, Glynis?'

'That's where I have to sleep now and so does Ruth,' she told him as she speared a piece of potato and popped it into her mouth. 'We have to wait until you go to bed before we can make up our bed,' she added.

He still looked utterly bemused, almost as if he had forgotten all about them giving up the smaller bedroom because they couldn't afford it. 'Well, I've got a bed,' he announced as he picked up his knife and fork and started eating again.

'Yes, a great big one all to yourself,' Glynis told him. 'Can I come and sleep in it with you?'

'No, of course you can't,' Ruth told her quickly. 'Take no notice of her, Dad.'

Once again he put his knife and fork down and looked at them blankly.

'Get on with your dinner, Dad, or it will be cold and you know you hate cold gravy.'

'She's right, though, isn't she?' he said in surprise. 'I've got a great big double bed all to myself so surely it would be better if you two slept in it?'

'And where will you sleep?'

'In the chair or on the floor in here. I can sleep anywhere; on a clothes line, if necessary.

You two must have my bed. I mean it, I should have noticed what was happening long before this.'

There was no further discussion or argument. Glynis took him at his word and when it was time for her to go to bed that night she marched straight into his room and climbed up into the double bed and settled herself down with a huge smile on her face.

Before she went to bed herself, Ruth made up somewhere for Tomas to sleep in the living room and made sure that he was comfortable. Even though he assured her he was she still felt dubious about turning him out of his proper bed.

In the weeks that followed it became clear even to Tomas that they'd have to find somewhere else to live because they simply couldn't remain in Adelaide Place. They already owed two weeks' rent and the landlady refused to wait any longer for it.

'I know perfectly well you're never going to pay me because I have a pretty good idea how much you earn at the corner shop where you're working,' she told Ruth.

'Surely you can give us a little longer. I'm trying to find another job, one that will pay better,' Ruth told her.

'Perhaps you are, but I can't wait until you manage to do that,' the woman sniffed aggressively. 'It may take you months and I'll be on the breadline myself by then.'

'Will you give us another week?' Ruth pleaded.

'My dad isn't well and, as you know, my mam died only a couple of weeks ago . . .'

'We've all got problems of one sort or the other,' the woman cut in dismissively.

'I really am trying,' Ruth affirmed earnestly.

'You've got until next Friday and then I want all the back rent as well as the money for this week, or else it's out you go.'

Ruth could see from her attitude that it was pointless arguing so she simply nodded to signify she understood.

Tomas was perplexed when she told him. 'Duw anwyl! What does she want from us? You've explained things and told her you're trying to earn more money, isn't that enough?'

'It seems not. She obviously doesn't trust us to be able to pay.'

'Then in that case we'll have to disappear one dark night and leave her whistling for what we owe her.'

'Dad! That would be very unfair.'

'No more than the way she's treating us. All the time we've been here we've paid our rent on the dot.'

'Well, if it makes you feel any better, we'll consider doing that,' Ruth said smiling. 'The trouble is, though, we haven't anywhere else to go, now have we?'

'I'll find us somewhere else,' he asserted. 'You say we've got to be out of here by next Friday, well, I'll find a new place before then; you wait and see.'

Although Tomas was as good as his word the room he eventually found for them was even worse than the two poky rooms they had in Adelaide Place.

'I know it isn't as good as where we are,' he told Ruth when he took her to see the one room he'd rented in a basement in Bute Road, 'but at least we'll have a roof over our heads. It's only temporary, to give us breathing space, and so that we can get away from Adelaide Place before Friday. If we can manage to do that we won't have to pay off the arrears, or this week's rent, if it comes to that.'

'I don't see how we can possibly move all our things out without the landlady seeing us do it,' Ruth protested.

'You leave it to me. We haven't got that much to shift, not like when we moved in.'

'That's true!' she sighed. 'When we moved from Cathays we had the big pram for Glynis, all our pictures, ornaments and heaps of other knick-knacks, as well as pots and pans and suit-cases full of clothes. Now, practically all we have is what we stand up in.'

'It makes good sense to travel light. All you need is what you can take on your back. That's what they teach you in the army,' he told her confidently.

Ruth tried to smile to show that she accepted what her father said but, neverthe-less, she felt deeply unhappy as she surveyed their meagre belongings. Life now was so

192

different from what she'd known when she was growing up.

You can't turn the clock back, she told herself firmly. Get on with things and don't let little Glynis become unhappy or despondent by hearing you grumbling or by letting her know that you had a better childhood than she's getting.

There was still the problem of moving everything they owned without the landlady spotting them. Tomas took charge and planned it all like an army manoeuvre.

He started immediately after their meal on Wednesday evening by telling Ruth and Glynis that he was going for a walk. Glynis wanted to go with him.

'No, cariad, that's not a good idea,' he said picking up a big brown paper parcel he'd left ready behind his chair. 'You need your sleep because you have to get up for school in the morning,' he reminded her as he headed for the door.

'What have you got there, Dada?' she asked, scrambling down from her chair and going over to him and squeezing the parcel, trying to feel what was in it.

'Nothing that has anything to do with you,' he said, quickly pulling it away and holding it up high so that she couldn't reach it. 'Now you go and help Ruth to get the dishes washed and put away and then get yourself off to bed.'

Glynis pouted and looked sulky, but Tomas

remained firm. 'Its no good pulling that face at me and pretending you're going to cry because it won't make any difference, I'm not taking you,' he told her.

As the door closed behind him Glynis tried to find out from Ruth where he'd gone, but Ruth claimed she didn't know. She talked about other things and even promised to read to Glynis once she was undressed and in bed.

Glynis was asleep by the time Tomas came back. Ruth had wasted no time, but had packed up the rest of their clothes into a bundle in case he wanted to make yet another trip that night back to the new room in Bute Road.

'Are you quite sure no one saw you going out with that first parcel?' she asked anxiously as he drank a cup of tea and made ready to set off once more.

'You mean the landlady? I don't think so. As far as I was aware there wasn't anyone around. Anyway, what if she did see me going out? A man has a right to go to the pub for a drink in the evening, hasn't he? She's seen me doing it often enough.'

'What will you say if she sees you going out again and asks?'

'I'll tell her that I've left my packet of fags on the counter and that I'm going back to collect them.'

'So why are you carrying that great big parcel, then?'

Tomas shook his head. 'I'm glad you're not

the landlady, you're too sharp by half! Now you get off to bed and I'll come in as quiet as a mouse. I won't do any more trips tonight, but I want to be up as early as possible in the morning to start again.'

'Why don't I take some stuff along on my way to the shop in the morning? It will look less suspicious than for you to be constantly setting off with mysterious-looking parcels.'

'Yes, that's probably a good idea. There won't be all that much left to move anyway, apart from the few bits of crockery that we'll need in the morning and our bedding.'

'You're sure that everything is going to be secure in that place overnight?' Ruth asked anxiously.

'Of course it will be. There's a lock on the door and the key's in my pocket.'

Before she went to bed, Ruth collected together the rest of the things that would have to be moved, and stacked them in a pile. She'd be glad when it was over, she thought uneasily.

She lay there in the dark going over in her mind what they were planning to do and she hoped that her dad was right and that the landlady wouldn't be able to trace them. If she did then there was no knowing what she might do about it. Ruth was afraid that even if they paid her the rent they owed she might take some sort of revenge because they'd tried to cheat her.

'Why are you taking the sheets and blanket

off the bed?' Glynis asked in a puzzled voice as Ruth began to strip their bed next morning.

'They need washing,' Ruth told her. 'I'm going to take them to be done on my way to work.'

'They're not dirty, though,' Glynis persisted, wrinkling up her nose and sniffing them. 'The sheets might be, but the blanket isn't. You've always said that it only needs washing once a year when you do the spring cleaning.'

'Well, it's going to have a wash now,' Ruth told her. 'Eat up your breakfast, because I want to leave a bit early so that I have time to take it along.'

'Can I come with you? It's ever so early so it won't make me late for school.'

'No, you go to school, Glynis. You'll have longer to play with your friends if you're there early.'

'I thought you didn't like me playing with my friends before school because you said I get myself in a mess and look like a ragamuffin,' she answered cheekily.

'I would hope that by now you're old enough to have enough common sense to know that you're expected to stay clean and tidy when you've got to go to school,' Ruth told her sharply. 'By the way,' she added quickly, 'Dada will be coming to meet you this afternoon so don't go running off with any of your friends when you come out. If Dada isn't already at the school gate then wait there until he arrives. Do you understand?'

'Why's he coming to meet me? Is he taking me somewhere special?' Glynis asked excitedly, hopping from one foot to the other, her dark eyes shining.

'You'll have to wait and see, won't you?' Ruth told her as she ran a comb through Glynis's thick dark curls and straightened the neck of her dress.

'You must know,' Glynis persisted. 'Please, Ruth, is he taking me somewhere?'

'Yes, he will be taking you somewhere, so make sure that you wait for him.' She smiled as she kissed Glynis goodbye.

'Will I like it there?'

Ruth looked down at the little girl's eager expectant face and bit her lip. Would Glynis like it there? She didn't think she would; not when she found out that she'd be losing all her friends because she'd be going to a different school.

'I hope so,' she told her optimistically. 'Now run along or you won't have time to play before school starts.'

Chapter Seventeen

The moment Norah Rhys, the landlady of the pub in Bute Road, showed them into the single room in the cellar Ruth knew she didn't like it even though it was quite a lot larger than their living room had been in Adelaide Place.

It was furnished with a rickety table, four straight-backed wooden chairs and one armchair that had the springs hanging out of the bottom of it. There was an old rusty iron range on which they had to cook and boil their water, with a cast-iron fender in front of it and a threadbare rag rug in front of that. The poker, tongs and shovel for coal were balanced up against one side of the range and there was an old bucket to hold the coal on the other.

The only lighting in the room, apart from a candle that was stuck in the neck of an old wine bottle, was a gas mantle which had to be fed by putting pennies in the meter behind the door. The small window had rusty iron bars across it outside and was caked down the sides with green mould.

The room stank of stale beer and men were constantly passing by outside the door as they came down from the bar to use the lavatory in the yard outside.

Often some of them were slightly drunk and were singing or cursing as they made their way outside. They usually swayed up against the battered dark brown door of their room as they went by. Some even tried to open it, thinking that it was the back door that led out into the yard. Ruth and Glynis lived in fear that one night they might forget to lock it and someone would stumble inside.

Their move to Bute Road had also meant that Glynis had to change schools. She was now seven and had to attend the Elementary School in Bute Road where she was in a mixed class of boys and girls. Ruth quickly found out she was associating with the most disruptive children in her class and was frequently being sent to the Head's room to be disciplined.

Whenever she tried to remonstrate with Glynis about this all she got was a cheeky grin or a flippant answer.

'It's very serious, Glynis,' she admonished. 'Do you get told off in class by the teacher?'

'Sometimes. We all do. We're made to sit with our hands on our heads or behind our backs if we are very noisy.'

'Is that all?'

'If one of the boys is very naughty then he has to go over to the other side of the classroom and sit with the girls,' she giggled.

'And what happens if one of the girls misbehaves? Does she have to go and sit with the boys?'

'Sometimes.'

'Have you ever had to do that?'

Glynis didn't answer. She jumped up and went to look for something in a corner of the room.

'Glynis, come back here and sit down. I've asked you a question and I want an answer; a truthful one. Have you ever had to go and sit with the boys?'

'Yes, a couple of times.' She shrugged her shoulders. 'I don't care. You have more fun when you are sitting over with them.'

'So when do you get sent to the Head's room? What do you have to do to be considered that naughty?'

Again Glynis shrugged. 'If you say something cheeky, put your tongue out, pinch someone or pull their hair; things like that,' she mumbled.

'So do you do those sorts of things?' Ruth frowned.

'Only when someone does them to me first,' Glynis muttered, rubbing one shoe over the top of the other and not looking at Ruth while she was speaking.

Ruth felt it was difficult not to smile since she felt that none of those things were terribly serious, but she was careful to hide this from Glynis. They were the usual sorts of misdemeanours most children got up to at some time or other. She could even remember doing some of them herself when she'd been Glynis's age.

What was of real concern, however, was the cheeky remarks Glynis made when she met any of the men coming down from the pub when she was on her way out. Most of them took it in good part and simply laughed, others cuffed her lightly around the ears. Ruth was afraid that one day one of them might hit her really hard.

When the upset did come it wasn't someone hitting Glynis, but Glynis hitting another girl. So hard, in fact, that she ended with a gash on her head that needed hospital treatment.

'She hit me first,' was the only explanation Glynis would offer. What she didn't tell Ruth was that the girl in question was Avryl Robins, the granddaughter of the woman who owned the shop where Ruth worked. Two days later, when the full facts were revealed, Ruth found herself facing an irate employer who gave her the sack.

'Surely we don't need to take their squabble seriously,' Ruth protested. 'I'm very sorry that Glynis hurt Avryl, but at that age they're always falling out over something. By tomorrow they'll probably be best friends again.'

'It's pointless arguing with me, Ruth. My mind is made up,' Mrs Robins told her as she slapped her wage packet down on the counter. 'There's your money. Take it or leave it, that's up to you, but you're no longer wanted here.'

Ruth would have loved to have left it lying on the counter, but she knew she couldn't afford to do that so she picked it up with as much dignity as she could muster and left the shop, making sure that she closed the door very quietly behind her. Once out in the street she felt tears spilling down her cheeks and she hastily brushed them away with the back of her hand.

Finding another job wasn't easy. Although it was 1922 and the war had been over for four years, employers could take their pick; there were plenty of men who'd come out of the army still looking for work. Ruth knew it was pointless going after a job which one of them could fill. In the main employers preferred to take on men because they considered them to be more reliable. A woman usually had family responsibilities and, though they avoided doing so whenever possible, they were the ones who had to stay at home if there was an illness or some other problem to sort.

Not for the first time she wished that she'd not had to leave school so early. She'd make sure that even if Glynis insisted on leaving school at fourteen she was trained to do something other than work in a shop or factory so that she had a skill which would be useful to her all her life.

Ruth searched for almost two weeks, answering every likely advert and asking everybody she came into contact with if they knew where there was a job going, before Tomas told her that he'd heard that a tailor in Bute Road was looking for someone.

'I don't think there's much point my going after that because I don't know anything at all about tailoring,' Ruth said dubiously.

'It wouldn't hurt to give it a try. Even if he only takes you on for a couple of weeks it would bring in a few bob. I'd give it a go myself if I thought I could get away with it, but someone would be sure to squeal on me and I'd lose my pension.'

Todd, the tailor, was Chinese; a wizened little man with sallow skin and small eyes. He studied Ruth in silence for several minutes then said, 'All right. Start tomorrow. Eight o'clock. A week's trial.'

There were a dozen questions that Ruth wanted to ask, but he'd already hopped down from the big flat table in his workroom where he'd been sitting cross legged, and disappeared.

She waited for about five minutes, hoping he might come back, then, when he didn't, she made her way back out into the street. Apart from the fact that she had to be there for eight o'clock she'd no idea at all what the job entailed, what the hours were or how much he was going to pay her.

Nevertheless she turned up promptly at eight o'clock the next morning and was surprised to find that as well as Mr Todd there were ten other people working there.

For the first week all she seemed required to do was to tidy the workroom, brushing the floor to keep it clear of cottons, pins and scraps of material as they trimmed the seams of garments, or to run messages and make tea for them all.

At the end of the week, he handed her a pay envelope and said curtly. 'Right, you will be ripping next week.'

She stared at him blankly, but he offered no explanation so she took the envelope and said nothing. When she got outside and opened it she was amazed to find that there was a ten-shilling note in it; much more than she'd earned at the corner shop.

'Ripping', she discovered, meant the removal of tacking stitches after sections of the garment had been sewn together. Mr Todd did all the cutting out himself. Sometimes he used paper patterns, and at other times he worked on the fabric without anything at all to guide him. Ruth watched in awe as his huge shears cut through several thicknesses of expensive-looking material, transforming a flat piece of cloth into a positive shape that she recognised as the sleeve or back or front of a coat or jacket.

One of the young men did the tacking; working so fast that she couldn't believe how he could achieve such even stitches. After that one of the women working the treadle sewing machines took over. As the machine whirred away she fed the material under the foot, following the tack lines so that one piece was permanently joined to another, or so that a sleeve which had originally been a flat piece of material was suddenly a shaped tube.

Once this was done Ruth found that it was her job to remove the tacking stitches. At first she was very slow, afraid of snipping the cloth or damaging it in some way.

After watching her in silence, Mr Todd took the garment she was working on from her and showed her how to snip both ends of the white cotton thread and then hook the scissors under a largish stitch in the middle and pull so that the cotton came out from both ends simultaneously in a second.

The only time it didn't do so was when the machinist had been careless and gone over the tacking stitch. Whenever this happened the white cotton tack had to be eased out with great care so as not to disturb the small machine stitches.

From 'ripping' she graduated to 'unpicking' which she found much more tedious.

'It is something that has to be done when the machinist makes a mistake and sews two pieces together when they shouldn't have been,' Mr Todd explained.

Ruth found that this was much more difficult because the machine stitches were so small and the colour of the cotton used was invariably the same colour as the fabric.

Often, after a day spent unpicking, she went home with a raging headache or aching eyes. Even so, she enjoyed the constant variety of the work she was given to do and she hoped that one day she might even become a machinist. Apart from the fact that it was more interesting work it carried a wage packet that was almost double what she was earning doing all the less important jobs in the workroom. It would also mean that she'd no longer be at the beck and call of anyone who wanted her to run a message or give them a hand.

Some of the more experienced machinists worked 'piece rate' which meant that the more they did the bigger their pay packet. It was usually these pieceworkers who caused most of the 'unpicking'. They tried to work faster than their fingers and brains could manage. If they did make a mistake, whether they ran over the tacks or made some other error, they were penalised and money was stopped out of their wages.

There was also quite a lot of hand-finishing that had to be done. Sewing on fasteners, hooks or buttons; neatening the inside of collars; tacking stiffening into collars and reveres, neatening turn-ups on the bottoms of trousers, putting in pockets, and even stitching gold braid on to officers' uniforms.

Some of it was tedious; all of it required neatness and precision. Ruth enjoyed it because it took her mind off the problems at home. Glynis was still headstrong and rebellious. There were frequent complaints about her behaviour and, although Ruth did all she could to make her see the error of her ways and behave better, she had little success.

Tomas no longer seemed to be able to exert any influence whatsoever over her. He was not well himself and he'd neither the interest nor the strength to stand up to her even when he knew she'd been naughty.

Apart from breathing problems which became worse when the weather was damp or cold, he was beginning to be very absent minded. He'd completely forget the errands Ruth asked him to do and there were days when he'd simply lie on the bed until she came home from work at night. Often he'd eaten nothing all day.

She asked Glynis to make him a drink and check if he'd eaten when she came in from school, but Glynis rarely came home before Ruth did. After school she ran wild with a crowd who spent their time annoying the neighbours, pinching from the shops and stalls, or going down to play on the Embankment in all the flotsam and jetsam that floated past.

All Ruth's scolding or pleading had no effect at all. Often Glynis was kept in late by her teacher, and sometimes she was even given the cane, but it never made any difference. Indeed, it seemed to make her more rebellious and cheeky than ever.

This faded into second place, though, as Tomas became increasingly frail and the mood swings which made him both irritable and bad tempered returned.

Although they were only paying rent for one room, their other living expenses for food, heating and lighting seemed to be as high as ever. And, even though the money she was now earning was far better than her wages had been at the corner shop, they still found it was difficult to make ends meet. Ruth was afraid Tomas wasn't getting enough to eat, or indeed the right sort of food.

One of the biggest expenses was clothes and shoes for Glynis. She seemed to either outgrow things or wear them out so fast that replacing one thing or another was almost a weekly occurrence.

In desperation, she finally plucked up the courage to ask Mr Todd if there was any extra work she could do so that she could earn a little more money.

'You come here with no experience of tailoring; I teach you much and I pay you well for someone who is inexperienced in the work you are doing. Are you saying that you are not satisfied?' He frowned, his small eyes narrowing.

'No, no, I'm not complaining at all,' she assured him. 'I like my job very much and I think you've been extremely fair. I just wondered if there was some extra work I could do – perhaps something I could do at home in the evening. My father is a sick man and I need to buy plenty of good food for him.'

'I see!' He studied her, his small eyes speculative and thoughtful. 'Work that is outside what you do here?'

'I wouldn't mind what it was,' she said eagerly. 'I thought perhaps I could take some of the hand sewing home to do in the evenings. A bit like piecework,' she said hopefully.

Mr Todd shook his head. 'I'm sure you'd do it well and take the greatest care of it, but I couldn't allow garments to be taken outside my workrooms. I insist on having complete control over what is going on. However,' he said quickly when he saw how disappointed she was, 'it is possible that I might have other kind of work for you. You did say it could be anything?'

'Yes, I did say that,' she said hesitantly, wondering what he was going to suggest. She'd hoped it would be something she could do in her own time at home, but she suspected it was going to mean working late or even coming back again in the evening, and she wasn't too happy about that.

'I haven't time to discuss the matter with you now so the best thing is for you to come back about eight o'clock tonight, and we'll talk about it then. I can promise you it will mean more money and it's not work that you will find difficult.'

Ruth hesitated. It would mean her father would be on his own for most of the evening and she felt he needed her company for part of the day to stop him becoming too morose. Also, it meant leaving Glynis to her own devices and she was pretty sure she couldn't rely on her staying at home even if she promised to do so.

Yet if Glynis went out after dark with the crowd she usually mixed with then there was no knowing what trouble she might be in, Ruth thought worriedly.

Ruth knew Mr Todd was waiting for her answer and as she desperately needed the extra money she felt she had to agree to do as he asked.

At least she could come back and see what it was he had in mind, she told herself. If it was cleaning the workroom after all the others had gone home then she'd ask if she could bring Glynis along with her so that she knew where she was, she decided.

Chapter Eighteen

As soon as she had cleared away the remains of their evening meal and washed up their dishes, Ruth had a wash, changed into a clean blouse, and combed her hair ready to go back to the workroom as she'd agreed to do.

'Where are you going at this time of night? You've only just come home,' Tomas grumbled.

Ruth hesitated. She didn't want to raise his hopes by telling him about the extra money she was hoping to earn in case she didn't get the job after all.

'I left something behind, I'm just nipping back to get it,' she told him.

'Can I come with you, Ruth?' Glynis asked eagerly. 'I'll wait outside if you don't want me to come in with you, but I would like to see where you work.'

'No, I think you ought to stay here with Dad,' Ruth told her. 'I won't be very long.'

'Then it won't matter if I come with you, will it?' Glynis persisted.

'Oh, take her with you, I'll be glad of a bit of peace and quiet,' Tomas said irritably.

'No, I said she was to stay here and I meant it,' Ruth asserted quietly. Without giving either of them the chance to argue any further she headed for the door.

As she hurried down Bute Road she could hear Glynis calling after her and she was tempted to turn round and make sure she went back inside. But if she did, she'd be late, so she hurried on as if she hadn't heard her.

Mr Todd was waiting in the workroom. Telling her to follow him, he went through a side door into a room she'd never been in before. The light was so dim that for a moment Ruth didn't realise that there were also three other men in there. They were all Chinamen and wearing close-fitting embroidered jackets which had tiny high-necked collars. They were sitting around a table with drinks in front of them, smoking long clay pipes which seemed to bubble as they drew on them.

'Come and stand here, by my chair,' Mr Todd ordered as he moved to the vacant chair at the head of the table.

Ruth felt very nervous. No one spoke to her, but they all stared at her, eyeing her up and down as though she was some rare exhibit. Then they started talking amongst themselves in a language she couldn't understand but which she assumed was Chinese. She looked questioningly at Mr Todd, wondering what she was supposed to say or do.

He ignored her completely, but he seemed to be listening intently to what his companions were saying. When they stopped speaking he clapped his hands as though in agreement with what they'd said, before he turned to her, smiling and nodding his head as if very pleased about the decision they'd reached.

'What is it I'm expected to do, Mr Todd?' Ruth asked in a bewildered voice.

His face was inscrutable as he spread his hands wide and shrugged his thin shoulders. 'Serve drinks, fill their pipes, perhaps, but most of all you must keep a check on the counters.'

'Counters? What are counters? I didn't know that you had a shop,' she exclaimed in surprise. 'I had a job in a small corner shop before coming to work for you.'

Mr Todd shrugged dismissively. 'Not that sort of counter. Come, I will show you.'

He walked across the room and pulled back a heavy red velvet curtain revealing a door. Using a key that was hanging on a length of silken twine around his neck he unlocked the door and ushered her through into the room beyond.

Ruth gasped in surprise. Two massive chandeliers hung over two large tables which dominated the room. Even though she knew nothing about such things she could see from the way the tables were marked out that they were used for some sort of gambling.

The room seemed to be full of Chinese men, most of them gathered at the bar which ran right across one end of the room. There was only one woman in the room. She was very tiny with shiny black hair drawn back into a coil which was pinned high up on top of her head and secured there with a number of decorative combs. Her face was a greenish white and her eyes outlined so heavily with mascara that she had a clownish appearance. She was very slender and she was wearing an exotic red silk dress that was slit almost up to her mid thigh on one side. It was beautifully embroidered on the back with gold thread depicting an enormous fiery Eastern dragon.

'This is Mia,' Mr Todd told Ruth as he led her towards the woman. 'She will tell you what you have to do.'

The woman gave her a cold little smile as she bowed very slightly towards them both, then she turned away and shuffled back to one of the gaming tables.

'Go along, Ruth, Mia will show you how to look after the counters. I will come back later,' he ordered as he walked away.

In something of a daze Ruth did as she was told. Mia said very little; it was almost as if she only knew a few words of English. Nevertheless, she managed to make it clear that Ruth was to stack all the counters into different piles according to their colour. Mia explained that they only handed them over to the men who were playing on the table when they told her what colour they wanted and produced the right money to buy them.

As far as Ruth could see there was very little

skill needed to do this and she felt quite confident when Mia left her in charge of the counters at one of the tables while she herself went over to the other one where men were waiting to play.

For the first hour all went well. Men approached holding out a handful of money or bank notes and Ruth exchanged them for the correct number of counters. Then, just as she was beginning to think she'd mastered it with no difficulty at all, one man took his counters, frowned, and then held them out in his closed hand towards her.

'You've cheated me,' he exclaimed angrily, in such a loud voice that everyone stopped what they were doing to listen to what was going on. 'I gave you enough money to buy twenty red counters; you only gave me eighteen.'

'Let me see?'

Ruth touched his hand to indicate that he should open it so that she could check the counters for herself. This seemed to anger him still further. In a matter of seconds several of his friends had joined him, all of them babbling away in their own language. Ruth couldn't understand what they were saying but all of them were pointing accusing fingers at her.

Ruth felt petrified. She looked across at the other table hoping that Mia would see her plight and come to her rescue, but Mia was so intent on dealing with her own clients that she took no notice at all of what was happening.

The dispute seemed to be growing worse by the minute and as the noise increased she was relieved when Mr Todd himself came in to see what was going on.

The man disputing the number of counters she'd given him strongly defended what he'd said and kept pointing at Ruth and telling Mr Todd other things that she couldn't understand.

'I handed him exactly twenty red counters, which was what he asked for and paid for,' Ruth stated firmly.

'He claims you grabbed hold of his hand and insisted he should open it and that by doubting his word you insulted him when he complained,' Mr Todd interpreted.

'I simply wanted him to open his hand to let me count them,' Ruth said indignantly.

'Aah!' His face clouded. 'To him that was an insult because he thought you were calling him a liar.'

'Of course I wasn't! I wanted to check how I could have made such a mistake, that was all.'

'Then you had better apologise to him . . .'

'Apologise!' Ruth's cheeks flamed. 'No, I will not apologise. He should be the one apologising to me for the way he's behaved,' she declared angrily.

The row looked as though it was going to start up all over again. Men were pointing and waving their arms to emphasise what they were saying and tempers were becoming worse by the minute as they began to take sides.

Ruth had no idea what the outcome would have been had one young man not held up his hand and called out to them to stop and listen. Opening his hand he showed them two red counters and then pointed down to the floor near where they were all milling around and squabbling.

Ruth found herself trembling as, once more, a heated discussion broke out. Then, to her great relief, Mr Todd turned to her with a beaming smile.

'Two counters have been found on the floor,' he explained. 'One of you must have dropped them as you passed them between you. We will say no more about it. I have apologised on your behalf.'

The rest of the evening passed without incident, but from then on Ruth was doubly careful. She stacked the counters on to the table in front of the purchaser each time and insisted that he should check that they were the right number. She watched eagle-eyed as he counted them and then made sure that he picked all of them up.

Mr Todd was waiting for her at the end of the evening when she was about to leave.

'Your wages for your work tonight,' he said as he held out a small brown envelope.

She looked at him apprehensively expecting him to add, 'I won't need your services any more.'

To her surprise he didn't. Instead he asked, 'Can you work three nights a week? Wednesday, Friday, and Saturday? Can you do that?'

She hesitated for a brief second, wondering if first of all she ought to find out how much was in the little brown envelope. Then the thought that whatever it was it would be better than nothing made her smile and nod in agreement.

Once outside she stopped under the nearest lamp-post in Bute Road and opened up the envelope. She drew in her breath with excitement when she found that there were two florins inside. If she could earn that much, three times a week, it would be more than she was earning for a full week's work in his tailoring shop. The difference that was going to make to them was so overwhelming that she felt like crying with relief.

Then she almost jumped out of her skin as someone tapped her on the arm. Quickly she screwed up the envelope, hoping they hadn't seen the money which she tried to hide in the palm of her hand as she swung round to see who it was.

The man who stood there was only of medium height and very thin. Even in the street light it was easy to see that he was Chinese. Her first thought was that he was about to steal her money; he'd probably been in the gaming room that night and knew she'd be paid when she left to go home and had seen Mr Todd hand her the envelope.

As if reading her thoughts he said in a quiet sing-song voice, 'My name is Chan, I saw what happened tonight. I was the one who said he'd found the counters.'

'Oh! Well, thank you, Chan, I'm glad you did; it saved the day for me,' she said nervously.

'I did not find them, though. Those two counters were not on the floor by your table. They were mine; ones I had bought from you earlier in the evening.'

Ruth frowned. 'I'm not sure I understand. Why did you do that when you don't know me?'

'The man who accused you of cheating is known as Ho Sing. He's a very bad man; a rogue and a liar. Ho Sing was out to make trouble for you.'

'Why on earth should he do that? I've never seen him in my life before,' Ruth said, bemused.

'That is what he does. He enjoys mortifying people. It puts them in his power. If the counters had not been found, then he'd still have forgiven you. He would have told Mr Todd that he didn't want to make a fuss and beg him not to sack you.'

Ruth shook her head completely mystified.

'So what power could that possibly have given Ho Sing over me?' she asked. 'I would have been grateful not to lose my job, of course, and I would have thanked him, but surely that would have been the end of the matter?'

'No, not at all. Ho Sing would then have power over you. He would have asked you to do many other things for him, bad things that would get you into trouble with the police.'

Ruth laughed dismissively. 'He'd have been very disappointed, then, because I wouldn't dream of doing anything that I thought might be against the law.'

'Oh, but you would, Ruth', Chan told her sadly. 'That is the way he works.'

'I'd refuse. I've already told you that.'

'If you didn't do as he asked then he'd see you were reported again to Mr Todd and accused of being a thief. He has many devious ways of doing this. Next time Ho Sing would not have been the one who accused you of cheating. He would arrange for one of his gang to do it instead and then he would step forward and remind Mr Todd of the fact that you'd once cheated him.'

'So now, Chan, I am in your power instead of being in his,' Ruth commented.

'No, no, not at all. I like you very much. From this moment on I will try and protect you as much as I can, but you must be on your guard always.'

Before Ruth could think of a suitable answer Chan had gone, melting away into the darkness as if he'd never been there.

Feeling very uneasy and nervous because she was sure that she was being watched, Ruth hurried home. She needed time to think over what had happened before she decided what to do.

She wouldn't say anything tonight, she

resolved, since she didn't have to go back until Friday. If she still felt concerned and undecided about what to do after thinking it over, then she'd talk to her dad about it and see what he advised.

The matter worried Ruth and when she did mention it to her father, Tomas agreed with her that it was a serious matter. He also thought that the opportunity to earn so much extra money made it far too tempting to throw in the job so soon.

'I can understand you feel apprehensive about what might happen in the future, cariad, but at least you've been warned,' he pointed out. 'Mind, though, as this man Chan has told you, it's important that you're on your guard all the time you're there.'

'Do you mean against Chan as well?' Ruth questioned looking worried.

'You should be on your guard against all of the men who frequent the place,' he cautioned. 'Chan might seem helpful and claim to be looking out for you, but then again he might also have an ulterior motive.'

'I'll be careful, Dad.' She laid a hand on his arm. 'I promise, so don't worry about me.'

He covered her hand with his. 'Mind you do, I know how much we need the money but don't stay there if you're frightened or feel you are in any danger.'

Chapter Nineteen

Ruth had been working three nights a week as well as doing her daytime job for almost a month before there was any trouble. It all happened so suddenly that she was taken completely by surprise. One minute she was handing out counters in Mr Todd's gaming room, the next the place was plunged into darkness and she found a hand clamped over her mouth and a voice which she thought she recognised as Chan's hissing, 'Keep still and stay quiet.'

The next thing she knew was that she was being bundled unceremoniously into a cupboard and the door shut. In the room outside she could hear a babble of voices, some were raised in protest, but by far the loudest were the authorative voices, easily recognisable as being police officers, ordering everyone to stay where they were and to put their hands on their heads.

The raid lasted for almost an hour; to Ruth imprisoned in the cupboard, where it was becoming hotter and stuffier by the minute, it seemed to go on for ever. By the time Mr Todd came and opened the door and helped her out she was gasping for breath and felt as if she was going to faint.

'I'm going to let you out into the alley at the back. You must go straight home and tell no one what happened here tonight. Do you understand?'

She nodded, still far too breathless to reply. Her knees felt weak and she knew she was shaking.

'You must go straight home and say nothing to anyone about what has happened here tonight,' he repeated. 'Come to work tomorrow morning as usual. Understand?'

'Yes, yes,' she gasped. 'I'll do whatever you say. Can I go now?' she pleaded.

'You will remember to say nothing,' he repeated yet again as he opened the door into the alleyway, signalling her to wait while he checked that it was all clear. Then, putting a finger to his lips, he gave her a little push to hurry her on her way.

As the door closed behind her Ruth paused for a moment to lean up against the wall to get her breath. She still felt scared. Remembering his warning she scurried down the alleyway, keeping close to the wall so that she was in the shadows until she came out into Bute Road. Then she took to her heels and ran as though the devil himself was after her.

Although she'd been warned to say nothing to anyone about what had happened she was in such a state of shock that Tomas immediately suspected something was wrong.

'Has that fellow Chan being bothering you?' he demanded worriedly as she collapsed into a chair, her shoulders shaking, and buried her head in her hands.

'No, Dad, nothing like that at all,' she gasped.

'What's wrong then, cariad, why are you in such a state? You look as if you've seen a ghost or been held up at knife point.'

'Give me a minute to make myself a cup of tea and get my breath back and I'll explain.'

'You sit down, I'll brew some tea and then I want to know what's happened to make you like this,' he said firmly.

'I've been warned not to say anything, but if I don't tell someone then it will haunt me all night and I won't be able to sleep. I've never been so scared in my life.'

Tomas listened in silence, nodding his head from time to time as, in a shaky voice, she told him the details about the eventful evening she'd experienced.

'I suppose you know why the police raided the place?'

'Because gambling is illegal?'

'Yes, and so are the drugs they hand round there. I'd heard rumours about the place long before we moved here.'

'You never told me! You could have warned me, Dad, and I would never have taken on the evening work. I might have been arrested tonight,' Ruth said indignantly.

'Yes, I should have done so,' he admitted shamefaced. 'I was tempted to do so, my lovely, but the thought of being able to pay our way and wipe out all our debts was too great. I thought if I did tell you about it then you wouldn't want to go and work there.'

'You're certainly right about that! Still, it's no good thinking about what we should or shouldn't have done. Let's hope nothing like that ever happens again. At least we've paid off all our debts and bit by bit we're managing to redeem some of the things we pawned when we moved in here.'

'Yes.' He gave a cynical laugh. 'And let's hope they won't have to go back into pawn again in order for us to make ends meet over the next few weeks.'

Ruth looked puzzled. 'What do you mean?'

'There will be no more evening work for you from now on, cariad. The police will insist on Mr Todd closing his gambling place down.'

Ruth felt very taken aback. 'Are you quite sure about that, Dad, or are you simply guessing?'

'He'll be lucky if he doesn't have to face charges. The police are as hot as mustard on that sort of thing. They're bound to prosecute, and it will not only be him but everyone else they found on the premises. You've had a lucky escape. Whoever pushed you into that cupboard was looking out for you.'

'I'm pretty sure that it was Chan who did that,' Ruth told him thoughtfully.

'Well, he did tell you that he'd look out for you and it seems he has done just that. Let's hope he doesn't get too long a sentence because the police are bound to have found him on the premises.'

Ruth spent a restless night, tossing and turning and thinking about Chan and what it would do to him if he was given a prison sentence. She wondered why he'd taken such a risk.

The next morning she received an even bigger shock. When she turned up for work it was to find the building still surrounded by police and they refused to let her go in.

'You must let me through, I work here,' she told the constable who was barring her way.

He studied her in silence for a moment then took a notebook out of his top pocket. 'Can I have your name, Miss?'

'Ruth Davies. I work in the tailoring shop. I've been here for several months now.'

'So you're a tailor, are you?' He raised his eyebrows quizzically, staring at her as if not believing what she said.

'Well, not really a proper tailor,' she explained, 'I do some of the more menial jobs like taking out the tacking stitches and hand sewing. Then with a smile she confided, 'One of these days I'm hoping to become a machinist.'

'Well, it won't be here, I'm afraid,' he told her bluntly. 'This place is being closed down.'

'Does that mean you'll be putting Mr Todd and all his staff out of work?' she asked heatedly. 'What are we going to live on if you do that?'

'That's not my problem, Miss. You'll have to find a job somewhere else,' he added, snapping shut his notebook and putting it back in his pocket.

Tomas was as upset as Ruth when she returned home and told him what had happened.

'I can't say that I'm surprised, though,' he said morbidly. 'I did tell you that the police were tartars about things like that. It's not the tailoring they're bothered about, it's what goes on behind the scenes. It happens all over Tiger Bay.'

'What do you mean?'

'When people like Mr Todd open up what seems to be a respectable business it is only a front for something else. Up in the attic, or in a poky room at the back of the main premises, they always seem to run some other enterprise.'

'You mean a gambling room?'

'Sometimes it's gambling like Todd was doing. Others have drug dens, or betting organisations and no one knows if their runners are doing messages for the legitimate business or for what's going on behind the scenes.'

'Even so, Dad,' Ruth protested as she poured them both another cup of tea, 'the tailoring business was genuine. He made suits and coats and even uniforms.'

'Of course he did. That's how he managed to get away with the gambling. The police must have suspected he was doing more than that, though, and they must have been keeping an eye on his premises so as to know when to carry out their raid.'

'Perhaps someone informed them,' Ruth said as she stirred her tea thoughtfully.

'That's more than likely. There are always rival gangs ready to do that so that they get the customers. As I said last night, you've been very lucky not to have been arrested.'

'Not so lucky, though, because it means that I've not got a job now and it looks as though we're going to have to pawn all our stuff again,' she said miserably.

'Cheer up, cariad. You'll find some other sort of work in next to no time.'

Tomas was wrong. For two weeks Ruth tried desperately hard to find herself a job, but without any success. Then she had a surprising stroke of luck. She was coming home when she spotted a wallet lying in the gutter and when she picked it up she found that there were four one pound notes inside it.

The temptation to remove the money and then throw the wallet back into the gutter was so strong that she found herself trembling. Instead, she thrust it into her coat pocket and then looked round guiltily, wondering if anyone had seen her doing so.

When she reached home she was in two

minds as to whether or not she should say anything to Tomas. The money would keep them going for a couple of weeks, she reasoned, and by then surely she'd have managed to find some work.

Making sure that he couldn't see what she was doing she took the wallet out of her pocket and looked inside it again. As well as the money there was a card with the name Samoni written on it followed by an address. She studied it for several minutes, knowing that it must be the owner of the wallet. It meant that she'd no excuse whatsoever for not returning both the wallet and the money.

If she did take it back then he might give her a shilling or two as a reward; then again, he might simply say thank you and not give her anything. If she said nothing and kept the wallet, they'd be able to pay the rent and she'd be able to buy food for the three of them and some cough medicine for her dad.

She decided to sleep on it rather than make a hasty decision, but half an hour later it was worrying her so much that she put her hat and coat back on and set off to return it.

The address was a café in St James Street and the smell of cooking as she went in the door made her almost faint she was so hungry. When she asked for Mr Samoni, a greasy-looking, rather portly man wearing a blue-and-white striped apron and a chef's hat came out of the kitchen to see who was asking for him.

Hesitantly, Ruth pulled the wallet out of her pocket and explained about how she'd found it. The look of pure joy on his face made her feel better because she could see it meant a great deal to him. He was so eager to have it back he almost snatched it from her hand.

She expected him to check the money to see that it was all there, but he seemed to be more intent on opening up a flap she hadn't noticed and delving into it with an anxious look on his face, which changed into a beaming smile as he pulled out a tiny sheet of paper with something listed on it which she couldn't read.

Only then did he look at the money. Pulling out one of the notes he handed it to her. 'Thank you, thank you so much. Now, sit down,' he ordered, waving her towards an empty table. 'You must have something special, something that I cook for you myself, so tell me what it is you would like.'

Although she was so hungry that she would have eaten almost anything he cared to put in front of her, Ruth shook her head. 'I must get home, I have to make a meal for my father and sister when she comes home from school,' she explained.

'Then wait one moment while I give you something to take home for them,' he insisted. 'First tell me your name.'

'Ruth Davies.'

'Hurry home, Ruth Davies, it should be eaten while it is still hot,' he told her as he handed her an enormous parcel that smelled so wonderful that it made her mouth water. 'Thank you again for returning my wallet. I hope you enjoy your meal. If there is anything else I can do to reward you, then you have only to say.'

'You've been more than generous,' Ruth told him with a smile. Her eyes filled with tears as she took the package from him. This would be a real treat, better than anything they'd had for ages.

'Good! Now, you still look sad, so are you quite sure there is nothing else I can do for you?' he persisted.

'Not really; not unless you can give me a job,' Ruth told him ruefully.

'A job?' He looked at her in surprise. 'Tell me what sort of job you want.'

'Anything, really.' She smiled wanly. 'Washing up, helping to prepare things in the kitchen . . .'

'You mean working here?' He studied her for a moment. 'Certainly not in the kitchen, but what about as a waitress?'

Ruth's face lit up with enthusiasm. 'I would like to do that even better.'

'Wonderful. I know you to be honest and I feel here' – gravely he thumped his chest – 'that you'll be hard-working,' he told her. 'Can you start tomorrow?'

Half an hour later she was at home and as the three of them tucked into the delicious selection of food that he'd given her, she explained to Tomas and Glynis how she'd found the wallet and what had happened afterwards.

'It just shows you that honesty pays, cariad,' Tomas mumbled, his mouth full. 'This is the best meal we've had in ages,' he added, smacking his lips.

'Do you think you'll be able to bring food like this home every night if you're working there?' Glynis asked as she helped herself to another succulent piece of cooked meat.

'I very much doubt it! This is some of the very best and most expensive food on his menu.'

'There must be leftovers now and again; things that won't keep until next day,' Glynis persisted.

'She's right and he may sell those off to his staff quite cheaply,' Tomas agreed hopefully.

'Does he serve cakes and puddings in his café as well?' Glynis asked eagerly.

'Glynis! Stop getting your hopes up. I've no idea at all. If he does, I'll buy the most sickly one I can find with my first week's wages and bring it home for you,' Ruth laughed indulgently.

Chapter Twenty

Working as a waitress was much more strenuous than Ruth had expected it to be. Her day
at Samoni's café started at eight o'clock in the
morning and she was on her feet until six
o'clock at night except for a short break at
midday.

There seemed to be a constant stream of
customers throughout the day so she never had
a chance to rest her aching legs or hot, tired
feet. The only good thing about being so busy
was that it made the day pass quickly.

She ate her main meal of the day after the
midday rush was over, sitting at the end of the
preparation counter in the back room with all
the cooking going on around her. Very occasionally she found time to grab her hat and coat
and go outside for a walk as far as Clarence
Road Bridge and back in order to have a breath
of fresh air.

One of the assets of the job was that often
when she left for home in the evening, Mr
Samoni would hand her a parcel of food which
he didn't think he'd be able to sell that night
and which wouldn't keep until the next day.

Glynis was always delighted when this

happened and couldn't wait to see what was in the parcel. She was downcast when Ruth returned home empty handed.

'It's all right for you,' she'd say with a sulky expression on her nine-year-old face, 'I bet you had something really lovely to eat at midday and all I had was a jam butty.'

Ruth herself felt quite upset when she'd nothing to bring home to them because she knew her father needed good food. He was in such poor health and what she brought home was always far better than what she could ever afford to buy.

Although she was working full time they still had to watch how they spent their money and try and balance it between food, coal and gas after they'd paid their rent.

As winter progressed, her father's cough became steadily worse. Sleeping on the floor was no longer an option because of all the draughts, so he wrapped himself up in a blanket and his topcoat and curled up in the one and only armchair which he pulled close to the banked-up fire.

Next morning he'd be so stiff that he could hardly move, but he steadfastly refused to let Ruth and Glynis sleep on the floor.

'I can have a nap on the bed any time during the day while Glynis is at school and you're out at work,' he'd protest peevishly whenever Ruth mentioned it.

'Well, you say that, but how often do you

take a nap? You seem so tired and worn out that I don't think you bother,' Ruth scolded.

'Stop nagging me, cariad,' he would tell her irritably. 'I don't need as much sleep as you do because I don't go out to work; in fact, I don't do anything very much to make me tired.'

She knew this worried him because he felt he was a burden and no matter what she told him to try and make him feel differently, it had no effect.

Ruth had been looking forward to Christmas because by then she was confident that they'd be free of debt. By agreeing to work later in the evenings in the run up to Christmas, she also hoped to be able to earn enough extra money to be able to reclaim a few of their possessions from the pawnbroker's.

She was so exhausted when she finished work on Christmas Eve that when she arrived home all she wanted to do was soak her aching feet in a bowl of hot water and then fall into bed and sleep.

Mr Samoni had given her a hamper of left-overs as she'd been leaving so she knew they had enough food to last them over Christmas. She didn't care what she ate – sleep was of far greater importance – but she did make the effort next morning to hand over the presents she'd bought for her father and Glynis.

Glynis was delighted with her grey pleated skirt and thick red wool jumper and immediately put them on. Ruth insisted that Tomas should put on his new dark tweed waistcoat and made him promise that he'd wear the thick grey socks the next day and the grey woollen muffler every time he went out.

Glynis decided to go out as soon as they'd finished their meal, mumbling something about meeting her friends. When Ruth protested that they should all be together for the day, Glynis promised she'd be home again quite soon.

Tomas fell asleep almost immediately and he looked so thin and exhausted that Ruth wondered if keeping an eye on Glynis was perhaps proving too much for him or whether he was still missing her mother, despite the fact that these days he never mentioned her name.

After she'd cleared away the remains of their meal and washed the dishes Ruth decided she might as well take a nap herself.

It was so dark outside when she woke up again that she thought it must be the middle of the night. She was about to snuggle down under the covers again when she realised that Glynis wasn't in bed alongside her and she wondered where on earth she could be.

Still in a daze, she remembered that it was Christmas Day and that she'd only been having an afternoon nap. Pulling herself off the bed she moved across the room to light the gas ring under the kettle so that she could make herself a cup of tea. As she did so, she glanced at the alarm clock on the mantelpiece and was shocked to she that it was almost eight o'clock.

'That can't be the right time!' Ruth exclaimed out loud. 'Have you seen Glynis, Dad? She promised that she wouldn't be out very long.'

Tomas was sitting in the armchair by the side of the fire which was almost out. His chin was resting on his chest, and he didn't even stir when she spoke to him.

'What a way for all of us to spend Christmas Day,' Ruth sighed as she lifted up the half-empty tin kettle, put it on the gas ring, and tried to light the gas. There was a spluttering and hissing, but the flame refused to ignite. She tried once more and then realised that there was probably no gas.

She groped inside the jar they kept on top of the meter for a couple of pennies to feed it, but the jar was empty. Frowning as she realised she'd handed over her last two pennies to the tram conductor the night before, she went over to her father and jogged his arm to waken him to see if he had any coins for the meter.

As she did so he slumped forward in the chair and she quickly put out her hand and grabbed hold of his shoulder to stop him falling any further.

'Dad!' Her voice rose as she realised he wasn't responding. She felt his brow, which was cold and clammy, and picked up one of his hands – it felt lifeless. She placed her hand inside his shirt to see if she could feel his heart beating, but there wasn't even a flutter and his skin was cold to the touch.

'Glynis! Glynis, where are you?' she screamed in frustration, but there was only silence.

She had no idea what to do. She needed a doctor to confirm that there was nothing more that could be done for her father, but she didn't know how to get one. Opening the back door she went out into the yard, hoping that she might find someone out there, but it was completely deserted.

Ruth felt panic stricken; she realised that because it was Christmas Day the pub was shut and all the men who usually frequented it were all at home with their families.

She rushed back in to check on her father again and see if there was any change, but he was still crumpled up in the armchair as lifeless as a rag doll.

Although she knew there was nothing more she could do for him she still didn't like to leave him, and so she sat there holding his lifeless hand, watching the clock as the time slowly crept towards nine, anxiously waiting for Glynis to come home.

It was a quarter past nine before Glynis came in. She had a look of defiance on her face as she burst into the room, obviously expecting a telling off. She stopped, closing the door quite quietly and staring at Ruth as if afraid to ask her what was happening.

'I want you to go and ask someone how we can get hold of a doctor,' Ruth told her.

'Why do you want a doctor? What's the matter? Is there something wrong with Dada?'

'I'm not sure. He . . . he's collapsed. Go on, hurry up and get some help.'

'I don't know where to go for a doctor. Whom should I ask?'

'What about the friends you've been with until now, wouldn't they know?'

'They've all gone home and they don't live near here,' Glynis said evasively.

'Then ask anyone. See if you can find a policeman; he'd be able to tell you.'

'A policeman!' The alarm in Glynis's voice struck an uneasy chord in Ruth's mind, but she felt this wasn't the time to start asking Glynis questions.

'Couldn't I stay here and you go and find someone?' Glynis prevaricated.

Ruth hesitated. Then, afraid that once Glynis realised that Tomas was dead, she might panic, she shook her head.

'I've made him comfortable so I'll come with you,' Ruth told her.

Glynis paused for a moment then nodded. She wrapped her scarf around her neck and linked her arm through Ruth's.

They found a policeman almost immediately. When Ruth told him that her father needed a doctor he shook his head. 'I don't think you're likely to find one who'll come out at this time of night. Perhaps it would be best if you took your father to the infirmary. Can you manage to do that?'

Ruth shook her head as she stared up at the tall, sandy-haired man who looked as if he should be playing rugby, not wearing a policeman's uniform.

'Perhaps I can help you to get him on a tram,' he suggested; 'they're still running.'

'No, I think it's too late to do that.' Her voice dropped to almost a whisper as she looked uneasily in Glynis's direction. 'I'm pretty sure he's dead.'

The policeman's green eyes widened. 'Are you positive? Would you like me to come back with you and make sure?'

'Yes, if you would.'

'Of course. I'm Constable Morgan, by the way,' he told them as they reached their room and he went over to where Tomas was in the chair. Ruth and Glynis watched in silence as he felt for a pulse in his neck and then shook his head sadly. 'I'm afraid you're right, Miss. I'll have to report it, of course.' He pulled out his notebook from his top pocket and began taking down details.

White-faced, Glynis stayed as far away from them as possible in the overcrowded room. When the policeman asked her if she'd been there at the time her father took ill she shook her head and bit down on her lower lip.

'She was out with friends,' Ruth told him. 'She's only just come in and I sent her out again straight away to see if she could find someone to help.'

'I see.' He scrutinised Glynis thoughtfully after he had written down her name in his note-book. 'Glynis Davies? Don't I know you from somewhere?' He frowned.

She didn't answer, but stared back at him boldly, almost as if defying him to say any more.

'How old are you, Glynis?'

'I'm nine, but I'll be ten next September,' she told him sulkily.

'So what do we do now, do we arrange the funeral?' Ruth interrupted quickly, anxious to bring things back to the matter in hand.

'You'll need a doctor's certificate confirming that he's died from natural causes,' the constable told her. 'Leave it with me and I'll see what I can arrange.'

It was a terrible start for 1925. They kept the funeral as simple and as cheap as possible, but even so Ruth found that it meant getting into serious debt.

She was so utterly confused about what to do that she welcomed the advice of Nora Rhys, the landlady who owned the pub above their basement room, and she was grateful when she offered to arrange for her to borrow enough money to cover the funeral expenses.

'I've got this friend, Mylo Norris, who's a

moneylender and he'll let you have it at a special rate as a favour to me,' she promised.

It was only afterwards when she read through the paper she'd signed agreeing to the terms of repayment, that Ruth realised that it was going to take her at least a year to pay it all off. She also discovered that if she defaulted at any time then she'd be penalised and have to pay even more.

For a fleeting moment as she stood at the graveside with Glynis and thought about all the responsibilities she now had to shoulder on her own she wished that it was her, not her father, who was being lowered into the black earth.

In many ways she blamed herself for all the terrible things that had befallen them. If she hadn't been foolish enough to listen to Glyn Jenkins none of this would have happened. She'd been old enough to know right from wrong, but she'd let him sweep her off her feet.

If that hadn't happened and she hadn't become pregnant her mam and dad might still be alive and they'd probably still be living in their lovely little house in Harriett Street. Or she might even be married with a home of her own, she thought wistfully.

The mistake she regretted more than anything was not telling the truth about Glynis. If she'd stood up to her mam and insisted on them telling him, as well as the rest of the world, the truth about the baby, then things might have been so different.

Her dad would probably still have gone to the Front, because that was something over which they'd no control. He might even have suffered shell-shock as a result and been invalided out, but he wouldn't have died believing that Glynis was his child and reproaching himself because he'd thought that having her had been too much of a strain for Caitlin and that was what had caused all her health problems.

Going out to work and living in such squalid conditions was what had been the underlying cause of her mam's ill health. That and the worry of bringing up Glynis even though she'd done all she could to play her part in looking after her when she was a baby.

It was only after Glynis was old enough to start school that the real trouble had begun. She'd not only become cheeky and hard-faced, but at times she was almost impossible to control. That was only to be expected when you remembered that they were living in Tiger Bay and that it was regarded as the roughest and slummiest part of Cardiff, Ruth thought dejectedly.

Now she was going to have to bring Glynis up single-handedly and, without her father in the background to impose some sort of authority, Ruth suspected that Glynis would be running wild in next to no time.

She knew so little about the friends Glynis went out with because she never brought them home. She was so vague about where they lived when Ruth questioned her that there was no way of checking what they were really like.

Now, there'd be no one at all to look after her when she came home from school and she'd be on her own all through the school holidays. This would mean she could get up to all sorts of mischief, Ruth thought worriedly.

She felt a frisson of fear as she remembered the policeman's puzzled look as he'd studied Glynis and his comment, 'Don't I know you from somewhere?'

Glynis had certainly looked scared and even though she'd brazened it out by shaking her head and staring at him defiantly Ruth knew he was not entirely convinced. She'd felt relieved when the incident had passed off without him asking her any further questions.

She wondered if that had been because her father's death was of much greater concern and Constable Morgan had been trying not to distress them more than he had to, but she thought it was probably time she sat Glynis down and had a heart-to-heart chat with her. She really did need to impress on her that from now on they had to stick together and that she was relying on her to behave herself while she was out working.

Chapter Twenty-One

Ruth was at her wit's end trying to cope with Glynis. She was cheeky, insolent, moody, tearful, resentful and down right bad-tempered.

There were complaints from the pub landlady, Norah Rhys, about her rude remarks to the customers when they came down to use the lavatory in the yard outside. Nora also claimed that along with a gang of other little hooligans Glynis shouted out names after the men when they were coming into the pub or leaving it.

Playing out in the street, even swinging from the lamp-posts or kicking a ball up against a wall might be overlooked, but some of the other things they got up to were a source of annoyance, especially to those who were the victims of their mischief.

There were also complaints about the noise Glynis and her friends made when they were playing together in the neighbouring streets after school and the fact that they constantly rang people's doorbells and then ran off.

Ruth frequently reminded her of their chat and cautioned her again that if she didn't stop misbehaving someone was going to report her to the authorities and then there really would be trouble. Whenever she did this, Glynis merely shrugged and looked disinterested. Or else retorted, 'I don't have to do what you say because you're not my mother.'

It was at times like this that Ruth longed to tell her the truth, that in fact she was her mother, but she never did so because she felt she couldn't break the promise she'd made to her own mother when Caitlin had been dying.

No matter how much Ruth tried to please her she invariably failed. If she ignored her then Glynis resorted to tantrums, throwing things around, and banging the door to make her presence known. If she rebuked her, and asked her to behave, then Glynis answered her back as rudely as she possibly could.

If she made a special effort to cook something she knew Glynis loved then it was pushed to one side or picked over and half of it not eaten. It sickened Ruth to have to sit there and watch.

If she suggested taking her out on a Sunday it was never where Glynis wanted to go and she either sulked or behaved atrociously, drawing attention to herself in the worst possible manner, so that Ruth felt uncomfortable or even embarrassed.

Ruth tried to be patient, telling herself that it was the girl's way of dealing with Tomas's death. She was prepared to ignore her rudeness, but one thing she refused to overlook was Glynis's timekeeping.

'You're only nine,' she pointed out. 'You simply must come in earlier at night or we'll be having someone reporting you to—'

'That hulking great copper with the big feet,' Glynis sneered. 'You liked him, didn't you?' she sniggered. 'I bet you'd believed every word he said.'

'Depends what he had to say,' Ruth told her mildly. 'He was certainly very polite and I was grateful for his help. He seemed to recognise you, or at least your name,' she added thoughtfully.

Colour rushed into Glynis's thin cheeks. 'They all say that.' She scowled. 'It's their way of frightening you.'

'They all do?' Ruth looked puzzled. 'How many policemen do you know?'

Glynis gave her a scornful look. 'How many policemen are there in Tiger Bay? Some days you see dozens of them.'

'Only when there's some sort of trouble. That's what they're there for, to keep order and protect us.'

'You talk a load of rubbish.' Glynis yawned. 'I'm going to bed since you keep saying I need more sleep.'

'What about a hot drink and some supper?' Ruth suggested as she moved the kettle into the glowing heart of the fire and took a loaf out of the bread bin. 'I bought some honey today. I know how much you like it.'

'Keep it. I'd sooner have conny-onny. Anyway, I told you, I'm going to bed.'

'You must be hungry, it's almost eight o'clock and you haven't been home since you came out of school,' Ruth pointed out patiently.

'So?' Glynis stared at her belligerently.

'Then you must be hungry. All you took to eat at midday was some jam sandwiches . . .'

'And they were horrible, like everything else you give me. I've had fish and chips, if you must know; a great big paper full with lots of salt and vinegar on them.'

'Fish and chips!' Ruth looked bemused. 'Where on earth did you get the money to buy those?'

'You'd like to know, wouldn't you?' Glynis retorted with a triumphant smile.

'I most certainly would, and I think it would be a good idea if you told me,' Ruth said firmly.

'Well, I'm not going to, and you can't make me,' Glynis declared cheekily.

Ruth sat down in the armchair and patted the arm of it invitingly.

'Come and sit down. There's no need to act like this. I know we're both missing Mam and Dad, but since we've only got each other now we really do have to be friends and pull together. You know I have to go out to work otherwise we'll have no money to pay all the bills, but I must have your help; I need to know that you are safe and sound.'

'You don't need to worry about me; I can look after myself,' Glynis responded.

'No, cariad.' Ruth shook her head. 'I'm afraid

you can't. You're far too young to take decisions or to do just what you like. I don't know what's got into you lately. Nothing I do seems to please you and you look like a ragamuffin most of the time. You don't wash properly, you never even take the trouble to comb your hair unless I'm there to make you, you're certainly not eating properly, and I'm worried about the friends you go around with because I don't know them.'

'What do you want me to do, ask them to come for Sunday tea?' Glynis sniggered.

'If you ask them to come home with you then I'd have a chance to meet them.'

'You wouldn't like them and they wouldn't like you,' Glynis told her. 'You'd start asking them all sorts of daft questions and then I'd never see them again.'

'Have you ever been to any of their homes?'

Glynis looked at her contemptuously. 'We don't like gown-ups. We know what we want to do and how to spend our time and we don't want any mums and dads or anyone else interfering.'

'Then let's hope you don't go playing pranks that might lead you into trouble with the police,' Ruth said quietly.

Glynis didn't answer. She went out of the room muttering to herself and slamming the door noisily behind her.

Although she was extremely worried about it Ruth found that there was another matter which was equally troubling: finding the money to keep up the regular weekly payments demanded by the moneylender.

After some haggling Mylo Norris had agreed she could skip the first week's repayment, but he said he'd have to charge interest and when she discovered how much that was she was determined not to let it happen again. But it had. First, it had been shoes for Glynis because the ones she was wearing were far too small for her and were cramping her toes very badly. She might be able to make do with second-hand clothes, but Ruth refused to even consider buying her someone else's cast-off shoes.

This time she bought sturdy black leather ones, hoping they'd last. She'd even made sure they were on the large size and put a piece of cotton wool in the toes of them. Glynis hated them.

'They're horrible,' she complained. 'They make my feet look twice the size they should be and they're so heavy that they come off when I run.'

'Then you'll have to walk,' Ruth told her sharply. 'What's more I expect you to take care of them. No kicking at tin cans or stones because I don't want to see the toes all scratched.'

Two days later Glynis came home in tears, and without one of her new shoes.

'What do you mean you've lost it?' Ruth asked exasperatedly. 'How can you lose one of your shoes? You don't have to take them off in school, do you?'

'I lost it on the way home, stupid!' Glynis sobbed.

'Here, sit down, blow your nose, wipe away your tears and try and tell me the whole story,' Ruth ordered, handing her a clean handkerchief.

Although she stopped crying Glynis offered no explanation about what had happened.

'Come on, I'm waiting,' Ruth told her.

'I lost it in the canal.'

'In the canal!' Ruth exploded. 'What were you doing down there? You know I've told you never to go near the place. How could you possibly lose it there?'

'I was kicking something into the water and my shoe flew off, that's how I lost it,' Glynis said sulkily. 'I told you they were too big for me,' she added, pouting.

'So what were you kicking into the water?'

There was a long silence, but when she saw that Ruth was still waiting and determined to have the whole story, Glynis rolled up the sopping-wet handkerchief and threw it angrily back at Ruth. 'I was kicking a cat in.'

Ruth felt horrified, but tried to keep her tone reasonable as she asked, 'On your own?'

'No, there was a crowd of us on our way home from school. One of the boys dared me to do it and that's when it happened. The cat and my shoe went into the water together.'

'This poor cat . . . did someone manage to get it out?'

'Of course not, it was dead. It was lying on the towpath; that's why we kicked it in.'

'And no one tried to save your shoe?'

'Save it! You should have been there; it went down like a brick. Splosh, splosh. First the cat and then the shoe.' She grinned as if remembering the event with glee.

'So what are you going to wear to school tomorrow?'

Glynis shrugged. I don't know. I'll have to stay home or else go barefoot, won't I?' She giggled. 'Unless I can wear a pair of yours,' she added as an afterthought.

'I've only got the pair I stand up in,' Ruth said quietly. She looked at the cheap alarm clock on the edge of the mantelpiece. 'I suppose there might be somewhere open at the Hayes, or even in Bute Road.'

'It will soon be summer so can I have sandals this time, ones that fit me?' Glynis pleaded.

'You'll have to take whatever I'm lucky enough to find you,' Ruth told her crossly. 'They'll probably be second-hand ones because I can't afford to buy another pair of new shoes, or sandals; not when you don't take care of them.'

'If you're buying them from a stall up the Hayes then I ought to come with you to make sure they fit because you won't be able to take them back and change them,' Glynis pointed out.

'How do you imagine you can come with me when you've only one shoe? I'll simply have to see if I can find something that I think will fit you and hope for the best.'

'My shoes were too big for me, that's why one of them fell off,' Glynis pointed out sulkily.

'In that case, I'll get lace-up ones and you can make sure they're always done up so tight that they can't fall off. Understand?'

'I could come with you if I wore your slippers,' Glynis said craftily.

'Don't be ridiculous,' Ruth told her exasperatedly, 'they're not suitable for going out in and they'll be miles too big for you.'

'Not if I put on Dad's old socks. They're ever so thick and will make my feet as big as yours.'

'Very well,' Ruth sighed. 'It's a pity you didn't think of that trick with your shoes, then they wouldn't have fallen off when you were kicking dead cats into the canal,' she added caustically.

The second-hand sandals were shabby and therefore quite cheap, but having to buy them so soon after paying out for the new shoes made inroads into the money she'd put aside for the tally man. When Mylo Norris called once again, Ruth found she was only able to make a partial payment.

'I don't think it is fair that you charge me interest on the whole lot that I borrowed because I've paid off quite a bit of it already,' Ruth pointed out. 'Surely I should only have to pay interest on the amount that's still outstanding.'

'No, my lovely, that's not the way I do things, I'm afraid. Every time you don't make a full payment, I charge you interest on the whole debt. I explained all that to you when you took

253

out the loan. Good of me to let you have it in the first place, because I could see you'd no collateral to offer me.'

'Collateral?' Ruth frowned. 'What do you mean?'

'Not much here of any value, that's what I mean,' he said, looking round with a critical eye. 'There's absolutely nothing here worth me taking away to try and sell if you should stop paying me altogether, if you get my drift.'

'There's no question of you taking anything from here, Mr Norris,' Ruth told him hotly.

'I'll be forced to do so if you don't pay me, my lovely. Perhaps you should think about getting some extra work, a part-time job of some sort to bring you in some extra money if you are finding it hard to pay. Have you asked Nora upstairs for work?'

'Mrs Rhys?' Ruth shook her head. 'Why should I do that?'

He smiled ingratiatingly, his narrow weasel-like face beaming. 'You'd be on the spot, see, when they're busy. Nip up there after the little one's in bed and pull a few pints; all nice and handy. Do you want me to have a word with her?'

Ruth shook her head, 'No thank you, it's really of no interest to me because I already have a job.'

'Then perhaps you should find one that pays you better,' he sniffed as he handed her back her payment book.

* * *

Over the next few days Ruth thought about it several times. It was certainly an idea, but she still found that her feet and legs were aching at the end of one of her shifts at the café so she wasn't at all sure that she wanted to do a job in the evening where she'd be on her feet for yet another couple of hours.

There was another drawback; she didn't like the thought of leaving Glynis to her own devices until eleven o'clock at night. She seemed to be getting into even more trouble lately; the incident with the dead cat was not the only misdemeanour and she didn't want someone informing the school that it was because she was never there to look after her.

At the back of her mind was the incident when Constable Morgan had seemed to recognise Glynis. Nothing more had come of that, but Ruth couldn't forget about it, especially when Glynis was late coming home from school and it was impossible to find out where she'd been.

If she only worked in the pub late in the evening, after she knew that Glynis was in bed and asleep, perhaps it would be all right, she told herself. The extra money would certainly be very welcome, so perhaps she ought to ask Nora Rhys if she was interested in part-time bar staff.

Chapter Twenty-Two

For the first couple of weeks Ruth found that, although very tiring, working as a barmaid in the late evening was working out well. She would hurry home from her shift at the café, prepare a meal for herself and Glynis which they could sit down and eat together, and then, as soon as she'd cleared up and made sure that Glynis was either in bed or about to get into bed, she would nip upstairs around half past eight for a two-hour stint behind the bar.

By that time of night it was usually very busy and once again she found herself rushed off her feet, this time serving foaming glasses of beer instead of food. By the time she rolled into bed herself, every bone in her body was aching with tiredness.

Sometimes she felt so worn out that sleep eluded her and she'd lie awake worrying about how long she was going to have to go on doing bar work before the arrears on the loan were paid off.

As the days grew longer, however, Glynis rebelled so much against having to come in so early and not being allowed out again afterwards, that Ruth worried about whether she was doing the right thing by working in the evenings since she seemed to be making Glynis so unhappy. It was as if there was a barrier between them; one which, no matter what she did, she couldn't surmount.

Knowing that things couldn't go on the way they were since she was becoming almost as morose as Glynis, she insisted that they had a long talk and tried to come up with some sort of workable arrangement.

It took a lot of arguing on both sides, but in the end they agreed that if Glynis came home for her evening meal straight from school then as soon as she'd helped to wash up she could go out again to play until eight o'clock.

For a few weeks this new arrangement worked quite well. There were the odd lapses when she wandered off with her friends after school instead of coming straight home, but Ruth tactfully overlooked these and was prepared to be lenient as long as Glynis was trying to cooperate.

The big problem that loomed ahead, however, was the school holidays. Ruth realised that for the whole of August she'd have to leave Glynis on her own all day as well as most of the evening and she was extremely worried about what she might get up to. Glynis might be streetwise and capable, but Ruth knew she wasn't really old enough to look after herself.

She tried to plan ahead, leaving a meal all ready for her to eat and also a list of shopping and other little jobs to keep her occupied some of the time.

If the weather was good then obviously she'd be out playing; it was where she might end up that Ruth was afraid to contemplate. She knew that, despite all her warnings, Glynis still played down by the canal; it seemed to be a popular meeting place for the rowdy bunch she went around with most of the time.

The first week of the school holidays passed without any incident apart from a torn dress, a lost hair ribbon and a grazed knee, which was of no real consequence.

The second week was a different matter altogether. Ruth had only been at the café for an hour when Mr Samoni sent for her to say that he wanted to see her in his office.

Puzzled, she ran her hands over her hair to make sure it was tidy, straightened her apron, and checked that her collar was smooth as she hurried up the back stairs to find out what he wanted her for.

The moment she walked into his office and saw a policeman standing there she had a premonition that it was something to do with Glynis. Her heart thudded uncomfortably as she recognised Constable Morgan and she saw how gravely he was looking at her.

'Has something happened to Glynis?' The words were out before Constable Morgan had a chance to speak.

'She's at the police station; I think perhaps you should come down there.'

'Is she hurt? Has she been in an accident?' Ruth asked worriedly.

'No, it's nothing like that.' His mouth tightened as if he didn't want to say any more. 'Can you spare Miss Davies for about half an hour, Mr Samoni?'

'If it's absolutely necessary, then it looks as though I have no choice.' Her boss frowned.

'I'll be as quick as I possibly can,' Ruth promised.

The moment they were outside the café Ruth wanted to know why he needed her to go to the police station.

'We were called to a shop in Bute Road this morning to apprehend Glynis and a group of other children who were stealing. It's not the first time they've been reported to us.'

'For stealing! Surely not.'

'She and her friends were stealing sweets, chocolate bars and cigarettes.'

'I'm sure there has been some mistake. What would Glynis want with cigarettes? She's not ten years old yet,' Ruth exclaimed, looking up at Constable Morgan defiantly.

'It's not a mistake, Miss Davies. As you know, your sister has been in trouble several times before.'

'Not for stealing,' Ruth stated angrily.

'No, other times it has been for various minor offences and we've let her and the rest of the

259

bunch off with a caution. This time, though, the shopkeeper who reported it said it was not the first time he'd caught them pilfering from his shop. He was fed up with it and wanted some action taken.'

Ruth shook her head. 'I still think there's been some mistake,' she argued. She felt dismayed; Glynis had seemed so compliant lately and they'd been getting on so well that she couldn't believe she'd gone back to her old ways, yet deep down she was afraid that this might be the case.

'There's no mistake.' His voice was so firm and authoritative that Ruth knew it was pointless trying to defend Glynis any more. She blamed herself; Glynis wasn't old enough to be on her own all day with no one supervising what she did. Yet how could she earn enough money to keep a roof over their head and buy food if she didn't go out to work?

'I don't know what to say,' she conceded. 'I still think there's been a misunderstanding of some kind.' She took a deep breath. 'So what will happen now?'

'I very much doubt if she will be let off with a caution. She will probably have to appear before a magistrate and as she's only nine years old . . .' He let his voice fade away without committing himself to any judgement.

'You think she might be sent away to an approved school?' Ruth's voice rose in horror at the very thought of that happening. 'Surely not for a first offence!' she protested.

'It's the first time she's been reported for stealing, but she has been cautioned a great many times over other things – by both me and other officers. The offence which stands out in my mind is the incident over the cat.'

'You mean the one she kicked into the canal?'

'So you know all about it?' he said in surprise.

'She lost one of her shoes, kicking the cat in. I was very cross about it because I'd only bought them for her a few days earlier.'

'Probably not nearly as upset as the person whose cat they'd killed,' he said in a disapproving voice.

'Killed! Glynis said the cat was dead when she kicked it in. It was lying on the towpath and . . .' She paused. 'What do you mean when you say "killed"?' she demanded, her voice laced with dread.

'Your sister and the crowd she runs around with tormented the cat by tying tin cans on it and then they put a piece of cord around its neck and throttled it. After that they set fire to it and then your daughter kicked it into the river in an attempt to hide the evidence. Someone on one of the barges saw what happened and reported it to us.'

'No, I don't believe she'd do such a thing!' Ruth exclaimed in a horrified voice. 'She told me that the cat was dead and lying on the towpath and someone dared her to kick it in.'

'She's only told you her version – only half the story, in fact,' he said grimly. 'This is not the first instance of brutal behaviour; usually it's some poor stray dog that they tie tin cans on to, or else bait it with sticks to make it howl. They're a really vicious little mob, Miss Davies, and I'm surprised you allow your little sister to play with them. She's certainly become a lot more wild and aggressive since your father died,' he added reprovingly.

'Does that mean you've been keeping an eye on her?' Ruth asked indignantly. 'It might have made more sense if you'd warned me about this crowd before she got into so much trouble,' she added sharply before he could answer.

'Well, I would have thought you would know the children she associates with; most parents would have made sure a child of her age had suitable friends.'

'Are you suggesting that I'm not looking after her properly?' Ruth retorted hotly. 'Let me tell you, I have Glynis's welfare at heart, but as I'm her only relative I have to go to work in order to keep a roof over our heads.'

'Surely you could find someone to look after her during the school holidays. Leaving her on her own all day, it stands to reason that she's bound to get into mischief.'

'We're not from around here,' Ruth told him, 'I know very few people and there is no one she can stay with.'

Constable Morgan rubbed a hand over his chin thoughtfully. 'I don't like to see a young girl like that running around with such a wild mob. They're all known to the police and sooner or later most of them will end up in Borstal. Surely you don't want her to be sent away to an approved school?'

'Of course I don't! I've explained the situation, though.' She bit her lip. 'Couldn't you put in a good word for her?' she pleaded. 'If you can get her off this time then I promise I'll keep a closer eye on her and make sure that she's never in trouble again.'

Constable Morgan looked at her speculatively. 'Oh yes, and how will you manage that?'

Ruth shrugged her shoulders uncertainly. 'I'm not sure right now, but, believe me, I'll do all I can; I certainly won't be letting her roam the streets with that crowd again. I knew they were rowdy and I suspected that they got up to all sorts of mischief like swinging from the lamp-posts and that sort of thing, but I certainly didn't imagine anything as serious as this.'

'They're villains in the making and I'm afraid Glynis is often the ring leader. The trouble is that their parents don't even seem to care when they are in trouble; well, most of them don't. That's probably because very often their dad's inside more than he's at home and their mothers can't cope with them.'

'It's not like that in Glynis's case,' Ruth protested.

'You do let her run wild,' he reminded her.

'I certainly won't do so in future,' Ruth told him quickly. 'That's a promise, so will you speak up for her, explain to the magistrate or whoever decides what happens? You have my assurance she won't be in any trouble again.'

Ruth spent an anxious few days waiting to hear what was going to happen to Glynis. The moment she brought her home she sat her down and had a long serious talk.

She not only dealt with the matter of stealing, but also with what had happened to the cat as well, and she explained what the outcome would be if she ever did anything like that again.

Glynis sat in sullen silence, stubbing her toe into the rag rug in front of the grate, avoiding Ruth's eyes and humming to herself in a tuneless monotone all the time Ruth was speaking.

'Are you listening to a single word of what I'm saying?' Ruth asked sharply.

'Yes, of course I am,' Glynis said, pouting.

'Good; then in that case, I hope you understand how serious a matter all this is?'

Glynis didn't answer. Instead, she burst into tears, flinging herself into Ruth's arms and crying hysterically almost as if her heart would break.

'I love you, I love you,' she sobbed. 'I don't want to be sent away. I only did it to make the others notice me because you didn't seem to care any more . . .'

'Hey, stop this, cariad,' Ruth said in alarm. 'Of course I love you, I'll always love you because you're very special to me; the most precious thing in the whole world. I'll always take care of you, no matter what happens,' Ruth told her.

She hugged her close, smoothing her hair, kissing the top of her head, and trying to calm her. She wondered for one wild moment whether or not this was the time to tell Glynis that they weren't merely sisters, but that she was her very own daughter.

Taking a deep breath she hesitated, wondering what would be the best way to explain it to her. Glynis was already very upset and to reveal something so traumatic at this moment might be unwise, she reasoned. It might only disturb her further and make her feel even less secure than she did now.

Instead, she nursed her and comforted her, almost as if she was a toddler, rocking her gently in her arms while she reminded her of all the good times they'd had together.

'Those times are all so long ago,' Glynis snuffled. 'It's not like that now. I've no one to talk to while you're at work; that's why I do so many bad things; it's to make the others listen to what I say and to take more notice of me.'

'You're getting into trouble with the police, though; can't you see that?' Ruth pointed out.

'Only when they catch us,' Glynis told her with a gulping giggle. 'Usually we're too clever for that, or we run faster than them.'

'Not any more,' Ruth sighed. 'Constable

265

Morgan knows you too well now; he knows all about you and he'll be keeping an eye on you. If you ever do anything wrong again he'll have to do his duty and see that you are punished.'

Although Glynis promised that from now on she would behave herself and even stop playing down by the canal and going around with the rough crowd she regarded as her friends, Ruth realised that it wasn't going to be easy for her, not if she was left on her own all day.

'Haven't you any nice friends? Isn't there any little girl who is your special friend at school?' Ruth asked hopefully. 'Someone you could go and play with each day while I'm at the café?'

Glynis shook her head. 'No, not really. Not many of the girls are allowed to come out with me because I play with the boys and all the girls' mums say they're too rough.'

'So tell me, which of the girls do you sit next to in class?' Ruth probed.

'No one in particular,' Glynis told her sulkily. 'None of them like me because they say I smell and that I've got nits, so they don't want to be next to me or play with me.'

'What utter rubbish; we both know that's not true!' Ruth exclaimed heatedly as she smoothed Glynis's hair back from her tear-stained face and kissed her.

'Mind, from the way you look at the moment, I suppose they might think so,' she teased gently. 'I think you'd better go and wash your face and brush all the tangles out of your hair.

While you're doing that I'll cook something really special for our lunch and then this afternoon I'll take you to the park.'

Glynis grinned. 'Do you really mean it? I thought you'd be going to work.'

'Well, I suppose I should; I can't afford to lose my job at the café, but I'll take a chance and stay here with you today and hope Mr Samoni understands.'

'What about the rest of the holidays? I get ever so fed up being on my own. I wish you could be here with me.'

'I know, cariad, but I have to work because we need the money. Tomorrow, I promise I will have to talk to Mr Samoni and see if I can make some sort of arrangement for the rest of the school holidays.'

Chapter Twenty-Three

Mr Samoni wouldn't listen to a word Ruth said when she went in the next morning. Angrily, he pointed to the door. 'You can go; you are unreliable. Yesterday I let you take time off and you didn't return. I was left without help in café. It's not good for my business.'

'Please, let me explain,' Ruth begged.

'No, I don't want to hear. I don't want policemen visiting here. That, too, is very bad for my business,' he insisted.

'It won't happen again,' Ruth promised. 'Everything's been sorted out.'

'It won't happen again because you won't be here,' he told her firmly. 'Now go.'

Realising that it was useless to argue any further, Ruth shrugged her shoulders in despair and walked towards the door. She paused and turned, intending to make one last plea, but Mr Samoni shook his head and pointed unrelentingly at the door.

Glynis was still in bed when Ruth arrived home. 'Come on sleepy-head, you can't spend the rest of your holiday sleeping,' she chided.

'Why not?' Glynis yawned pushing her hair back from her face and rubbing sleep from her eyes. 'There's not much else I can do without getting into some kind of trouble. Anyway, what are you doing back here? I thought you were going to work.'

'So did I,' Ruth sighed. 'Mr Samoni thought differently.'

Glynis shot up in bed. 'You mean he's given you the day off?' she asked jubilantly.

'The day, the week . . .'

Glynis looked dismayed. 'You mean he's sacked you! That's awful!' she exclaimed. 'He can't do that?'

'I'm afraid he can,' Ruth sighed. 'He's the boss and it's his business, so he says who can work for him and who can't.'

'Was it because that policeman came there about me?' Glynis asked looking crestfallen.

'Yes, that did have something to do with it; that and my not going back to work as I'd promised.'

'Then it's my fault.' Glynis's face crumpled and tears trickled down her cheeks.

'Hey, hey, don't worry about it, cariad. I'm glad he doesn't want me to work; it means I can be here with you. Come on, get dressed. It's a lovely summer day, so we'll go out somewhere. I've put the kettle on, so hurry up.'

Glynis rubbed the back of her hand across her eyes, and sprang out of bed. 'You're the best sister in the whole wide world,' she babbled, flinging her arms around Ruth and hugging her.

Her words brought a lump to Ruth's throat and for a moment she was again tempted to tell her the truth about their relationship.

The moment passed; Glynis was already suggesting how they could spend their day and rushing to wash her face and get dressed.

As Ruth poured the boiling water from the kettle into the teapot she was filled with a mixture of relief and guilt. She ought to tell Glynis the truth, but what good would it do? What did it matter what their relationship was as long as she was always there for her? No one, sister or mother, could love Glynis more than she did.

Even as the thought went through her mind doubts flooded in. Was she keeping as careful an eye on her as she should? From what had happened recently it didn't seem like it, she thought despondently. Would Glynis have behaved differently in some way if she knew she was really her mother?

Would it give her more authority? Or would the shock of such a revelation make Glynis lose trust completely and cause her to behave even more badly?

Perhaps she ought to wait until their life was more settled. By then Glynis might have overcome her disruptive tendencies and life for both of them might have become more calm and organised.

For the moment, however, getting through the school holiday without any more incidents involving Glynis and the law and earning enough to meet their overheads were top priority.

The realisation that she'd lost her job at the café and with it her regular wages was a considerable blow. The only money they now had coming in was what she earned in the evenings from working up in the pub bar. That would barely cover their rent, so what was she to use to buy food? And, above all, she needed money to pay off the arrears she owed to Mylo Norris.

Perhaps if she explained the situation to Nora Rhys she'd overlook the rent for a few weeks if she promised to pay her back the moment Glynis returned to school and she was able to look for another full-time job. Nora might even be able to persuade Mylo Norris to do the same since she'd claimed that he was a good friend of hers.

It was almost closing time before Ruth mentioned the matter to Nora. They were waiting for the last few drinkers to finish their beer so that she could wash up their glasses and then tidy around and be finished for the night.

'I don't think that's a very good idea at all.' Nora frowned when Ruth asked if she could delay paying the rent. 'You've got to pay it sometime, so why let it mount up? Anyway, I need it every week. I told you that when you moved in.'

'I know, but I've lost my job at the café and

what you pay me here at nights isn't enough to cover everything.'

'Well, don't blame me,' Nora said huffily. 'You only work a couple of hours each evening; what do you expect me to pay you?'

'I know I'm getting the right amount for the job, but I can't afford to pay you rent and buy food on that much,' Ruth pointed out. 'It's only for the school holidays. Once they're over and Glynis is back in school, I can find a full-time job again.'

'You could put in some more hours working here in the pub. Myra is taking her kids away to stay with her mother for a couple of weeks, so why don't you come in and do her shift in the middle of the day?'

'That would be great.' Ruth smiled. 'When would you like me to start?'

'Tomorrow. Be here at half past ten, and you'll finish at three, so you'll have time for a good break before you come back again in the evening.'

Ruth was relieved by the temporary solution, but Glynis was far from pleased when she told her.

'What about me? That means that I'll be left all on my own again and you promised you'd stay home and that we'd go out every day during the school holidays,' she said, pouting.

'We will go out every day. I'll be finished by three in the afternoon, so we'll have plenty of time together. We'll go out every day; exactly as I promised.'

'I'll be on my own until then, though,' Glynis muttered sulkily.

'You can have a long lie-in every morning and while I'm at work you can do the shopping and heat up some soup or make some sandwiches for us to eat when I come in. Then we can go out and stay out as late as you like.'

'No we can't,' Glynis retorted. 'You have to go back to work again at half past eight in the evening.'

'True, but by that time you'll be tired and ready for bed, so you won't miss me.'

'It's not fair, though.' Glynis scowled. 'I want you to be at home all the time. I hate being on my own.'

'Life isn't fair, I'm afraid,' Ruth told her resignedly. 'By that time I'll be tired as well, remember, and yet I'll have to spend another couple of hours on my feet serving customers who expect a quip and a ready smile from the barmaid.'

Ruth didn't feel any happier about the arrangement than Glynis did. She longed to extract a promise from her that she wouldn't sneak out while she was working and meet up with the gang of children she'd been mixing with before, but she didn't want to let her feel she didn't trust her. All she could hope was that sometime during her shifts she'd be able to sneak a few minutes off to pop down and make sure that Glynis was safe and sound.

By the time her first wages were due, Ruth was reduced to pawning her only decent coat in order to put some food on the table. Her relief at receiving her wages was tempered by the fact that it seemed to be considerably less than she'd anticipated.

'I've deducted your week's rent, so what you've got there in your hand is all yours,' Norah Rhys stated, seeing the look of dismay on Ruth's face.

Ruth blinked back her tears and nodded. She felt too choked to speak.

'Perhaps you should have deducted what she owes me as well,' Mylo Norris commented with a sly grin as he held out his glass and indicated that he wanted it refilled.

Ruth checked the money in her hand before putting it into her pocket. There was barely enough there to keep them in food for the week.

'I'm afraid I won't be able to pay you anything at all this week, Mr Norris,' she said stiffly as she placed his glass under the pump.

He let out a low whistle of concern. 'That's bad, very bad. Things can't go on like this. If you haven't got the ready cash, then we'll have to think of some other way of paying off the debt,' he said thoughtfully as he took his foaming glass of beer from her.

She waited for him to say something else, but from then on he ignored her and she was too busy attending to other customers to even wonder what he'd been on about.

It wasn't until she was about to finish her evening shift that he spoke to her again.

'You haven't paid me anything at all this week,' he said, holding out his hand.

'You heard what I said to Nora about there not being enough left in my wage packet to keep us in food for the week. I thought you understood that I wouldn't be able to pay you anything,' she replied.

He shook his head. 'I thought you were just being melodramatic; or else that it was a way of insinuating to Nora that she wasn't paying you enough.'

'Nora's been very good to me,' she defended, then added pointedly, 'She's been far more understanding than some people.'

'Well, perhaps I should do the same as Nora, then, and offer you some work; something to bring you in more money so that you can pay me what you owe me.'

'What sort of work can you offer me? If you think I am going to go round banging on doors and threatening people with what will happen if they don't pay up—'

'Ssh! You'll ruin my reputation if anyone hears you talking like that,' he admonished. 'No, I have a much better idea of how a pretty young girl like you could earn some money. Far more than you will ever earn as a waitress or a barmaid. What's more it could mean that you could be at home all day to keep an eye on that naughty little sister of yours. I've heard about the sort of trouble she gets into. Next time she's accosted by the law they won't let her off with a mere caution, you know.'

Ruth did know. Constable Morgan had already said much the same thing and she was well aware that it was only because of his intervention that Glynis hadn't ended up before a magistrate or in an approved school as it was.

'So what was it you had in mind?' she asked tentatively.

Mylo took a long time to reply. As he drained his glass and put it down on the counter she began to think he'd only been jesting and felt annoyed that she'd let her hopes rise.

'Don't rush off at the end of your shift; I'll be back and I'll have a word with you then,' he told her as he straightened his tie and moved towards the door.

Puzzled, she finished collecting in the glasses and washing them up ready for next day. As she emptied the ashtrays and spittoons and washed them out, she kept wondering what sort of work he was talking about. She had no training and no qualifications whatsoever; all the dreams she'd once had for the future had died long ago.

There was no sign of Mylo Norris as she placed the neatly folded towels over the pumps, and she could see that Nora was watching her as if wondering why she was dallying. Normally she scuttled off as soon as possible once her shift was finished.

As she went out through the back door into the passageway that led down to the basement, she found Mylo waiting for her.

'Well? Have you given it any thought?'

'Given what any thought? You never said what sort of work you had in mind,' she reminded him.

He grinned slyly. 'I thought you'd guess when I said it was the right sort of work for a pretty girl like you.'

'I've no idea what you're talking about,' Ruth said, frowning.

'Entertaining men, of course. Chatting to them, making them happy. You must know what I mean. If you didn't want to meet them at home, then I know of one or two little clubs where you could work. You'd be well paid, so why not give it a try?'

Ruth put her hands over her ears as she hurried towards the basement.

'Go away, I don't want to talk about such things,' she gasped. 'You've insulted me by even suggesting that I consider doing something like that!'

'Insulted you!' He laughed coarsely. 'Your sister's a thief, you live in a hovel, and you scrape a living as a barmaid, so how can I insult someone like you?'

'By suggesting that I should become a prostitute, that's how,' she flared.

As she reached her door he grabbed hold of her. 'That's about all you're fit for,' he hissed. 'Mind, whether you'd be any good at it is another matter,' he taunted.

'Let go of me or I'll scream,' Ruth threatened, her voice quavering as she tried to push him away.

'If you scream you'll waken that little sister of yours and that wouldn't do, now would it?'

'And it will bring Norah Rhys rushing down here to see what's happening.'

'Don't you worry about Nora. She knows all about it; she was the one who told me to proposition you. She also said it might be a good idea for me to check out the goods first.' He leered, grabbing hold of her again and thrusting his hands under her skirt.

She hadn't meant to scream, but the moment she felt his hand on the bare flesh of her thigh it was an involuntary reaction. Kicking, sobbing and struggling desperately, she did everything in her power to fight him off, but she was no match for his strength or his determination to make her yield.

She felt herself growing weaker and knew that there was absolutely nothing she could do to stop him taking whatever liberties he wanted. She fought against the waves of darkness that seemed to be sweeping over her, petrified that at any minute she was going to faint and then she'd be completely at his mercy.

The sound of another male voice close by

terrified her. She'd thought there was only Mylo to contend with, but now it seemed he had an accomplice.

It was a different sort of voice, though; not oily and smug, but authoritative. The next moment, Mylo had released his grip; there was the sound of blows and an agonised groan from him. Then strong arms were holding her and helping her in through her door and a voice that seemed vaguely familiar was assuring her that there was nothing more to be frightened about.

Chapter Twenty-Four

'What you need is a cup of tea to steady your nerves,' Mervyn Morgan told Ruth as he helped her on to a chair and then picked up the tin kettle to put it on the gas ring.

Ruth was still trembling but she smiled weakly as she nodded in agreement. His voice was so concerned that she felt a sense of relief that someone cared about what had happened.

'I'd love one, Constable Morgan, but there's probably no gas. I hadn't any money for the meter,' she added apologetically.

'That's soon solved.' He delved into his trouser pocket and brought out a handful of small change. 'I'm off duty, by the way, so you can call me Mervyn.' He grinned as he liberally fed some coins into the meter.

Shocked though she was by what had happened, Ruth had noticed that he wasn't in uniform and that without his helmet she could see that his sandy hair was quite wavy and that he wore it brushed back from his forehead. He looked a lot more handsome out of uniform and not nearly as official. He was wearing dark grey flannel trousers, a plain, light grey shirt and a tweed jacket, and she found herself thinking how fortunate she'd been that he'd been on the spot when she so desperately needed help.

Unless, she thought uneasily, he was keeping watch on her because she was on the wrong side of the law, or at least Glynis was, and he was doing his job even though he wasn't on duty.

She waited until he'd poured out their tea before saying anything else. Then as she accepted her cup from him, she murmured rather shyly, 'It's good of you to be so concerned.'

He frowned darkly and concentrated on stirring his tea. For a moment Ruth wondered if she'd overstepped the mark and he was annoyed for some reason.

'I was in much the same situation myself a few years back,' he said ironically.

'Really?' Ruth stared at him wide-eyed. 'I don't understand. In what way?'

There was another silence as Mervyn seemed to contemplate whether or not to tell her the details. Then he gave a deep sigh. 'It would be good to talk about it,' he admitted.

'Go on, then.' Ruth waited expectantly, calmer now her ordeal was over.

'I wasn't born in Cardiff, but about twenty miles away in the Rhondda. A small mining village called Cwmbran.'

'I've heard of it.'

'My father, and his father before him, was a

miner, and so I was expected to follow in his footsteps. He'd started down the old pit when he was twelve, sitting there in the darkness, opening the doors as the loaded trucks came through. Hour after hour he sat there, poor little devil, no one to talk to, alone with his thoughts and fears.

'In time, as he grew up, he graduated to a man's work; became a member of the pit choir, lived and loved. He married a local girl who became my mother. They had two sons. I was the eldest; my brother Ieuan was six years younger than me, though, so he was never a real playmate. I was always made to feel responsible for him, keep an eye on him, and so on.'

He smiled, as though reliving earlier days. 'We were a happy fulfilled family, mind. We all attended chapel on Sundays because Father was a lay preacher. He was also a great organiser. There were chapel outings to the seaside, concerts, celebrations at Easter and Christmas. He was a warm, loving, caring sort of man, who wanted the whole world to be as happy as he was.'

'You're talking as if it was all in the past, don't you still see him?' Ruth frowned.

'Yes, all in the past,' Mervyn sighed. 'There was an explosion; the whole of his shift was trapped down there in the bowels of the earth. My mam waited with me and Ieuan at the pithead for hours and hours. When Dad was finally brought out he was dead.'

'How terrible.' Ruth reached out and touched Mervyn's hand in an expression of sympathy.

'Poor Mam! It was the end of her world. She tried to be brave, but without him there to support her she went to pieces. I tried to do what I could to help her, but I couldn't take his place; no one could. Her heart was broken. Possibly, given time, she'd have pulled through if it hadn't been for my little brother.'

'He missed his dad?'

'Yes.' Mervyn dropped his head into his hands. 'He missed his dad and he went off the rails. Dealing with Glynis has brought it all back. It's like living through it all over again,' he admitted. 'Young Ieuan became involved with a crowd who led him astray. He became their ring leader and got into so much trouble that it broke my mam's heart.'

'She died?' Ruth asked in a whisper.

Mervyn nodded. 'Not because my father had died, or because Ieuan went off the rails, mind. No, she died because of me.'

Ruth looked confused. 'I don't understand. Go on, tell me what happened.'

Mervyn shook his head. 'I've already said more than I intended.' He stood up, fastening the buttons on his tweed jacket as he prepared to leave.

'No, please.' Ruth reached up and laid a hand on his arm. 'Finish what you were telling me, Mervyn . . . you can't leave me not knowing the outcome.'

283

He pulled away. 'Better you don't know. You've enough problems of your own without listening to mine.'

'Sit down and I'll make us another cup of tea,' Ruth told him, ignoring what he'd said. 'You can finish telling me what happened while we're drinking it.'

Ruth listened in silence as Mervyn told her how Ieuan had taken his own life.

'He was only twelve and I'd made him feel that he was a failure. I kept telling him that he was a disappointment to our mam and a disgrace to Dad's memory. I should have hugged him, comforted him or shown brotherly love in some way and helped him to face up to life. But no, I gave the poor young boyo a tongue lashing and he couldn't take it. Instead, he took his own life; hung himself from the banister and it was my mother who found him.'

Ruth felt aghast, but she didn't know what to say. She waited in silence for him to continue.

'Mam had left him in bed while she went out to do the shopping; when she came back his body was swinging from the top banister rail. She collapsed on the hall floor, right underneath his body. A double tragedy, and it was a double funeral, barely a year after my father's death.' He shuddered, almost as if he was living it all over again.

'I couldn't face the pit after that, or the house where I'd been born, or the village where I'd grown up. I came down here to Cardiff and for a while I did any sort of work I could find. Then I decided to join the police force.'

'That's a very sad story, but it wasn't your fault that things ended so tragically,' Ruth assured him gently.

'You're wrong; it was very much my fault. I couldn't see that he was crying out for help, that he wasn't really a rogue. He needed help and guidance, the same sort of law and order that I've found by joining the police.'

Ruth looked at him, frowning. 'Why have you told me all of this?' she questioned. 'Is it because you think I'm not showing Glynis the sort of guidance she needs? Is it because you think that Glynis is not simply going off the rails, but crying out for help?'

Mervyn nodded. 'She's your sister and Ieuan was my brother. You have the chance to help her, while I can never do anything more for him. I left it too late, but you still have the chance to save Glynis from coming to harm or ruining her life.'

As Ruth shook her head, he once again stood up. 'It's none of my business; I shouldn't have said anything.' He ran a hand through his hair in an exasperated way. 'Now you're upset. I shouldn't have said anything. I'm sorry.'

'It's not that. I'm grateful for what you've told me; truly grateful. It must have been a big effort to confide in me like that when I'm more or less a stranger.'

'No.' He took her hand and held it between both his own. 'You're not a stranger, Ruth . . . I'd like us to be friends. Somehow I feel as if I've known you for ever; that's why I want to help you.'

Ruth felt her pulse quicken. He was right, there was an empathy between them; whether it was because they'd shared a similar fate or whether it was something that went deeper that drew them together she wasn't sure, but she felt more at ease with Mervyn Morgan than she had with anyone else in her life. So much so that she wanted to unburden her own conscience like he'd done; she wanted him to know the truth about her own past. It would be such a relief to tell someone.

'Mervyn, there is something I'd like to tell you, something to do with Glynis that no one else knows about.'

'Go on.'

It was Ruth's turn to hesitate.

'You don't have to bare your soul simply because I did,' Mervyn told her gently.

'No, no, I want to. It's just that I don't know how to start.'

'You said it was to do with your sister.'

'She's not really my sister,' Ruth blurted out. 'Glynis is my daughter.'

'Ach y fi!' Mervyn looked at her startled. 'Your daughter? She doesn't call you Mam.'

'That's because she doesn't know that I'm her mother, and she must never know. Please!

You must promise never to breathe a word to her about it.'

'Don't worry I won't, I'll respect your secret. Do you want to tell me more?'

In a flat, unemotional voice, Ruth told him how she'd been seduced as a thirteen-year-old schoolgirl and how, to save their family from disgrace, she and her mother had connived while her father was in the army to let him and everyone else think that Glynis was his.

'And now they've both died without the truth ever being revealed?'

'That's right; my father never knew. There were many times after my mother's death when I wanted to tell him. He was constantly reproaching himself because he thought she'd borne Glynis so late in life that it had proved to be too great a strain on her and that was why she'd died.'

'Yet you never told him?'

Ruth shook her head. 'He died before I had the chance to do so . . . the time never seemed to be right.'

'And Glynis still doesn't know?'

'No, and I'm sure it would unsettle her even more if I told her at the moment.'

'Why should it? You are very close, so surely it would be even more comforting for her to know that in fact you weren't just her sister, but her mother.'

'No,' Ruth said stubbornly. 'She must never know. It would destroy her. She'd never be able to trust me or anyone else ever again if she knew I'd been lying to her all these years.'

Mervyn nodded slowly. 'Yes, I understand your reasoning, but I'm still not sure that you're right,' he said dubiously. He looked at his watch. 'I have to be on duty at six and it's well after midnight, so I must be going. Will you be all right?'

'Yes, of course I will and . . . and thank you for what you did. I'm not sure what would have happened if you hadn't been there.'

'I can imagine, though,' he said grimly. 'Anyway, take care of yourself, cariad, and I'll look in again and make sure everything is all right, if that's all right with you?'

'I'd like that,' she told him quietly.

Ruth thought a great deal about what Mervyn had said long after he'd left, but she was still convinced that she was handling things the right way. When she went to bed, she gazed down at Glynis who was lying there with her thumb in her mouth, deep in sleep and looking as innocent as a baby.

No, Glynis trusts me, and if I tell her the truth she might not, and I might lose all control, lose her, Ruth assured herself as she slipped into bed beside her.

She slept late the next morning, so late that there was no time for her to talk to Glynis before she went up to do her morning stint behind the bar.

When she walked into the bar she found Nora Rhys in a furious mood.

'So you've turned up,' she commented, folding her brawny arms across her ample bosom. 'Well, I must say, I wasn't expecting you to show up today.'

'I'm not late, am I?' Ruth asked.

'Late! It has nothing to do with you being late. I didn't think that you'd have the nerve to show your face up here; not after your night of whoring.'

Her face going scarlet, Ruth swung round as she heard Mylo Norris's voice behind her.

'Yes, Mylo's told me all about you and that fancy man of yours.' Nora looked at her contemptuously. 'Stayed all night, did he? Well, let me tell you this right now, if there's one thing I won't stand for, it's a barmaid with loose morals. Gives the place a bad name, and I stand to lose customers that way. Once the wives get a sniff of what's going on they start to wonder if their old man might be the next one to be propositioned; they have a barney and she stops him from coming here.'

Ruth faced Mylo Norris. 'What have you been saying?' she demanded angrily. 'You told me that it was Nora's idea—'

'I told Nora the truth, that's all,' Mylo interrupted, not giving her a chance to speak. 'I told her that you propositioned me and when I turned you down then you accosted another young chap who happened to be passing by.'

'Happened to be passing by?' Ruth repeated in a withering tone of voice. 'I live in a basement, so how on earth could anyone be passing my door?'

'No, I suppose I got that bit wrong.' He leered. 'Anyway, you were lucky because he seemed to take a shine to you and to be more than willing. Did he stay all night?'

'I'm not interested if it was a quickie, a one-night stand or a regular,' Nora butted in. 'I don't want you working here and I don't want you on the premises,' she ranted. 'You may only live in the basement, but I'm not having that turned into a knocking shop. I want you out.'

Ruth choked back her tears, determined not to let Nora see how upset she was. 'I'll go when I'm ready,' she said defiantly.

'And don't forget that I want every penny of the money you owe me,' Mylo demanded.

'Forget it, let her go,' Nora insisted. 'I'll see you're not out of pocket; you can have the wages I owe her.'

'Will that cover it?' Mylo frowned.

'I don't give a damn whether it does or not, I want her out today,' Nora insisted, 'her and that kid sister of hers. Next thing she'll be on the game as well.'

Chapter Twenty-Five

Ruth felt as if the bottom really had dropped out of her world this time. The trouble and worry over Glynis had been bad enough, but to find herself being accused of being a prostitute by Nora Rhys was a bitter pill to swallow.

She suspected that Mylo Norris was at the bottom of it all because she'd rejected his advances. He'd spun a fabricated story to Nora and had egged her on into thinking the worst and advised Nora to turn her out.

She explained the situation to Glynis as she stowed their clothes and few belongings into a battered old fibre suitcase, and desperately tried to think where they could go because she'd hardly any money. Nora owed her for a few days' work, but after what she had heard her say to Mylo she knew the chances of her handing it over were so remote that she decided it was useless asking her for it.

'Is it because of me?' Glynis snivelled as she folded up her skirt and passed it to Ruth to put in the case.

'Of course not!' Ruth stopped what she was doing to give Glynis a hug. 'Don't worry about it, we'll find somewhere else to live, somewhere far better than this mouldy old place.'

Even as she said it Ruth wondered why she didn't tell Glynis the truth; after all, she was going to know quite soon. Nevertheless, she tried to keep her spirits up, joking with Glynis as they packed the remainder of their stuff into an old canvas shopping bag.

It was now almost mid-afternoon and, after taking one last look around to make sure they hadn't left anything behind, Ruth picked up the suitcase and handed the shopping bag to Glynis to carry as they headed for Bute Road.

'So where are we going? I'm starving,' Glynis stated as Ruth hesitated, not sure whether to head towards the city centre or towards the docks and further into Tiger Bay.

'Right, then shall we find a café and have a hot drink and something to eat while we make our minds up about where we want to go?' Ruth suggested.

'I thought you already had somewhere planned!' Glynis said aghast.

'No, not really,' Ruth admitted. 'Come on, we'll talk about it while we eat.'

Far from being upset by the news Glynis seemed quite excited and even told Ruth not to worry because she could solve their problem easily herself.

'So what have you in mind?' Ruth asked as she watched Glynis hungrily eating her fill of fish and chips and wondering how she was going to be able to feed her and find a cheap room or some sort of lodgings for them on the few shillings in her purse.

'We've no money, have we?' Glynis pronounced. 'So we need to look for somewhere to stay that isn't going to cost us anything.'

'Yes, and the only place I can think of where we can do that is in a shop doorway,' Ruth admitted. 'It's a good job it's summer; at least we won't freeze to death.'

Glynis pulled a face and gave an affected shiver. 'You don't really want to do that, do you?'

'No, of course I don't, but I don't know what else we can do . . .'

'But I do,' Glynis interrupted. 'The gang I've been going around with use this old warehouse near the canal as a meeting place. They'd let us stay there for a couple of nights or perhaps even longer, if they knew we'd nowhere to go.'

'You mean the crowd who got you into so much trouble? The ones that Constable Morgan said I was to make sure you never mixed with ever again?'

'That's right.' Glynis nodded. 'You don't want to listen to him; he's just a bobby doing his job. Anyway, he doesn't know about this place, we made sure of that.'

'I know you're trying to help, but I don't think it would be a very good idea,' Ruth said shaking her head disapprovingly.

'It would be much better than a shop

doorway because if we do that we'll get moved on by the police if they spot us,' Glynis reminded her.

'I'd sooner we found a room somewhere, even if it is only for one night,' Ruth protested.

'The warehouse would be better and it would cost us nothing,' Glynis argued.

'Where did you say it was?' Ruth asked dubiously.

'It's near James Street canal. Why don't you sit here while I go and see if I can find some of my friends and check out if they'd mind us staying there?'

'No, I think I should come with you. If I sit here any longer I'll have to buy another cup of tea,' Ruth told her as she stood and picked up their suitcase, ready to leave.

'Well, only part of the way, then,' Glynis insisted as she grabbed hold of the canvas bag. 'When we get near there, you wait with the case and bag while I make sure if it's going to be all right,' Glynis told her as they headed towards James Street.

Glynis seemed to be gone an awfully long time and Ruth was beginning to get worried as she waited on the almost deserted towpath by the side of the murky canal. The few people who passed by looked at her curiously without speaking, so that when a tall lanky lad in scruffy flannels and a jumper that was full of holes approached her it took her all her courage not to scurry away.

'Your name Ruth?' he called out diffidently when he was a few feet away.

'Yes.' Ruth clutched at her handbag, holding it tight against her chest as if she was afraid he was going to take it from her. Inside it was her purse and the few shillings she still had left, as well as her most treasured possessions: the photos of her mam and dad and of Glynis when she was a tiny tot.

'Come on, then; this way.' He grabbed hold of her battered suitcase and the canvas bag and without waiting to explain or even to see if she was following, he set off with such a long loping stride that she found it difficult to keep up with him.

He led her away from the canal bank and when they were almost at the far end of Margaret Street he suddenly tuned down a dark alleyway. Ruth hesitated, scared to follow in case he attacked her, but she was also afraid to let him out of her sight in case he made off with her belongings. Taking a deep breath to try and control her fear she hurried after him.

At the end of the alleyway, when they came to a stop facing a crumbling old brick wall that had the gaps filled in with sheets of galvanised iron, she found herself trembling.

'Come on. You'll have to squeeze in through this hole,' he told her. 'Mind you don't cut yourself; the edges are rusty. It's there to keep us out,' he added with a mocking laugh.

Putting down the case he held the rusty sheet

steady with one hand as Ruth edged sideways through it into the yard beyond where barrels, crates and all sorts of other containers were piled up. At the far end was a ramshackle wooden shed with a tin roof.

Even though the daylight was now fading it still took Ruth a couple of minutes to adjust to the darkness as he took her inside the shed. When she could see, she found she was being stared at by a couple of dozen pairs of eyes. Most of them were boys, aged between twelve and sixteen. They were all untidy, grubby and their clothes were virtually in rags. There were two or three girls there, and Glynis was sitting with them, chattering volubly as though explaining what was going on.

Glynis jumped up the moment she saw Ruth and came over to her, taking her arm and pulling her towards the group of girls.

'This is my sister, Ruth,' she told them.

They stared at her vacuously; no one spoke.

'Magya, Bronwen, Karyn and Selina,' she announced, pointing out each girl in turn.

'Hello, it's nice to meet you at last,' Ruth murmured.

The girls said nothing but stared at her suspiciously.

Glynis pulled her across to the other side of the room where the boys were watching what was going on in sullen silence.

'This is Owen, who came to fetch you. I won't bother you with all the other names because

you'll never remember them,' Glynis told her.
'If you want to know anything, then ask Owen;
he's in charge here.'

There was an uneasy silence. Ruth wasn't sure
what to say even though Glynis seemed to be
quite at home with the motley gang, but there
were a great many things she wanted to know.
Glynis had said that they'd be able to tell her if
any of their families had a room to rent out, but
most of this crowd looked as though they were
either homeless themselves or else lived in such
dire poverty that there would be little chance
of that.

'Does anyone know where we can get a room
for the night?' she asked, looking questioningly
at Glynis.

'Damnio di, you've got one. Are you saying
this isn't good enough for you?' Owen
demanded.

He looked so annoyed that Ruth felt taken
aback. 'No, of course not; this will do us fine.
I didn't know this was it,' she floundered.

Horrified to think how low she and Glynis
had sunk she tried to conceal her dismay
as she looked around the filthy shed with its
festoons of cobwebs. There were bound to be
rats as well as mice and cockroaches here, she
thought with a shudder. Yet, for all that, it was
better than a shop doorway which appeared to
be the only alternative.

'There's a bucket behind that door over there
if you need it,' Owen told her. 'It used to be

the manager's office,' he sniggered, 'but we've put it to a better use. If you want a wash, then you can use the tap there, which has cold water; or there're some public toilets with a washbasin down by the Pier Head.'

'Time for a brew,' Selina announced. She moved across to a Primus stove at one end of the room and after a short struggle to get it going, placed a battered tin kettle on it.

The assortment of mugs and big cups were all chipped or cracked, but no one else seemed to notice so Ruth accepted the cup of hot, strong, sweet tea gratefully. Some of the boys began smoking, rolling up their own from a pocketful of butts they'd collected earlier and sharing the results between them.

In no time at all the shed was full of acrid smoke and Ruth wondered how on earth she and Glynis were ever going to sleep in such an atmosphere.

It was almost midnight before the last of them left for their homes. The atmosphere was still smoky, but Ruth was so tired that within minutes of settling down on the assortment of old mattresses and covering themselves over with the oddments of blankets that the gang had found for them, she and Glynis were both asleep.

Ruth wakened at first light, disturbed by the sound of a lorry in the yard outside. For a moment she couldn't think where she was or what she and Glynis were doing lying fully dressed on a pile of stinking old mattresses in a filthy shed.

She reached out and clutched at Glynis's arm nervously. 'Are you awake?' she whispered. 'There's someone outside.'

Glynis was alert immediately, holding a finger to her lips. Together they listened to the sound of men's voice, then various clanging noises as if a lorry was being loaded.

Once, when someone started to open the door to come into the shed, they froze in anticipation of what would happen if they were discovered. Then someone outside shouted something and the sound of footsteps receded. A few minutes later an engine started up and they could hear a lorry driving away.

They looked at each other in relief and then both of them started laughing.

'Good job we didn't undress last night,' Glynis giggled, pushing a straggle of curls back from her face.

'We're lucky that whoever it was didn't come in here,' Ruth pointed out. 'It was a near thing.'

'I don't think Owen knows that a lorry comes into the yard or he'd have warned us.'

'Well, we're safe for the moment, but perhaps we should try and find somewhere else before tonight,' Ruth said cautiously. She opened her bag, fished out her purse, and counted out its meagre contents.

'Perhaps we should tidy ourselves up and go out and get something to eat,' she suggested.

'Will we have enough left for a room if we do that?' Glynis asked worriedly.

'I doubt it, cariad,' Ruth sighed. 'I'll have to find work of some sort. Let's go and eat and we might be able to think more clearly then.'

'We'd better hide our stuff away before we go out,' Glynis warned as she lugged the big suitcase over to one corner and slid it behind a pile of old crates. The gang won't touch them, but since it seems other people know about this place, we can't be too careful. We ought to try and find out what they were doing here and what it was they were loading on to their lorry.'

Outside was grey and drizzly and the yard looked more drab and dismal than it had the previous night. As they walked along the towpath towards James Street, Ruth shuddered as she looked down in to the murky dark waters of the canal. There were a couple of barges moored alongside and men were unloading them.

The only cafés open that early were the ones used by workmen. The food was good and cheap, but the surroundings were rough and ready.

Ruth was conscious that there were a good many glances their way as they ordered bacon and eggs and cups of hot tea.

The man who served them, a swarthy dark haired man with blue marks on his face that indicated he was an ex-miner, seemed to be run off his feet and Ruth took her courage in both hands and went up to the counter to ask him if he needed help.

'Why, my lovely, can't you afford to pay for your grub, then?' he replied, grinning.

'Of course I can pay,' Ruth said confidently. 'I do need a job though, quite urgently.'

'Get your coat off, then. There's a stack of dishes out in the kitchen that need washing up. Is she going to help you?' he asked nodding in Glynis's direction.

Ruth was taken aback; then she thought quickly and decided that it would be much better for Glynis to be with her than hanging around outside on her own for the rest of the school holidays. 'Of course she is; we always work as a team,' she affirmed.

'Good!' He held out his hand. 'I'm Dai Pritchard. What're your names, then, girls?'

'I'm Ruth and my sister's name is Glynis,' Ruth told him as she shook hands with him.

'Right ho, I think I can remember that. Go on, then; get cracking, the pair of you.'

The kitchen was a shambles. After washing up the stack of mugs, plates and dishes, Ruth and Glynis spent the rest of the morning doing their best to restore some semblance of order.

'Damnio di, this place looks like a little palace,' Dai remarked when he came through at the end of the morning rush. 'You'd better take a break now, the pair of you, and have something to eat, you must be utterly famished.'

The hot, thick lamb stew was better than anything they'd eaten for weeks and they both enjoyed it.

'It's a pity we can't go on working here for a bit longer,' Glynis sighed as she wiped round the deep plate with the remains of the crusty bread he'd served with the stew.

'I heard that,' Dai told them.

'So what's your answer, then?' Glynis asked, giving him a cheeky grin.

'I don't know, really. I don't stay open all day. I serve breakfasts and hot meals up until four o'clock. No call for hot food later than that, see,' he explained.

'Working here in the mornings would suit us just fine,' Ruth said quickly.

Dai ran his hand through his hair. 'It seems strange that two nice girls like you should want this sort of work,' he said in a puzzled voice. 'You're not from around here, are you?'

'What does that matter?' Glynis asked.

Dai shrugged. 'Stands to sense that if you have to come very far, then you won't be getting here early enough in the morning. I need help from six at the very latest, because a lot of the men working on the docks come in for their breakfast before starting their day shift.'

'We can be here in time,' Ruth assured him.

He shrugged again. 'Then I've nothing to lose, have I? Tell you what, come as a team, seven shillings a morning and all you want to eat. Can't say fairer than that, now can I?'

He waited expectantly as they looked at each other and then grinned when they both nodded in agreement.

Chapter Twenty-Six

Ruth and Glynis settled into a routine that suited them both. Ruth kept the kitchen clean, did most of the washing up, and Glynis dashed to and fro with plates as the orders came thick and fast.

From six in the morning until mid-afternoon they worked non-stop, apart from a few minutes when they managed to either make a bacon butty or pick up a sausage from the pile that were already cooked and ready to go out on the plates.

Dai worked even harder. He'd already been there an hour before they arrived in the morning and in that time he'd cooked a mountain of bacon and sausages, which he kept warm in the ovens, and had heated two great cauldrons of beans which were over a low heat all morning. In addition he had a huge pan of cawl simmering away, with potatoes and either cabbage or carrots boiling in readiness for when someone demanded an alternative hot meal.

Somehow he managed to take orders and serve at the same time. How he'd coped before they'd started to give a hand Ruth couldn't imagine. At the end of the morning, when things slackened off and they were able to stop and have their own meal, the pots, pans and cauldrons were all practically empty.

After they'd cleared up and gone home, Dai went out to shop for fresh supplies and then came back to do some of the preparatory work in readiness for the next day.

'I don't know how he does it,' Ruth exclaimed as they went back to the warehouse and she slipped off her shoes and lay down on the mattresses to rest her aching legs. Even Glynis admitted to feeling tired, but she usually revived well enough to join her friends in the evening to gossip and laugh and joke until they went off to their own homes.

At the end of their first week, Ruth was tempted to move away from the warehouse and find somewhere better to live. After paying out for the necessities they needed to live where they were she had almost thirty shillings in her purse, certainly enough to rent a room, but Glynis was more cautious.

'Perhaps we ought to stay here a bit longer until we're sure that Dai is going to keep you on and I can go back to school,' she said thoughtfully.

'I wanted to find a room and get settled in before you had to back go to school, so that we'd know which one you'd be going to,' Ruth pointed out.

'They're all the same.' Glynis shrugged. 'It won't worry me which one it is.'

Ruth agreed to think about it and also to let Dai know that she'd be working there on her own in future.

Dai was far from pleased when she told him. 'You said you worked as a team.' He scowled. 'How are we going to manage without young Glynis?'

'You managed well enough before,' Ruth pointed out. 'Don't worry, I'll work doubly fast,' she said, smiling confidently.

He still wasn't appeased. 'Young Glynis moved like greased lightning,' he muttered. 'You realise that if she isn't here, your money drops to three shillings.'

'Three shillings!' Ruth looked at him indignantly. 'You can't expect me to work from six in the morning until mid-afternoon for a measly three shillings. You've been paying us seven shillings a day.'

'That was when there were the two of you working together as a team.'

'If I'm prepared to do the work Glynis was doing, as well as my own, so I should still be getting seven shillings,' Ruth argued.

Dai shook his head. 'Oh no!'

They argued heatedly, but Dai refused to give in. Eventually, they compromised, agreeing that he would pay her four shillings a day and she could take home any left-over food for Glynis.

Although she capitulated Ruth felt devastated. It was only a few pennies over half what they had been earning, and it made moving into a room of their own precarious. When she told Glynis she immediately wanted to stay away from school and to return to work, but they both knew that was risky. If the school authorities got wind of it and the school board man came nosing round, then there'd be real trouble, especially when he found out where they were living.

'Let's give it a try,' Ruth suggested. 'If it doesn't work out we'll have to make new plans. When I finish at Dai's around mid-afternoon I'll spend an hour or so looking for something else.'

'Don't talk daft. After doing my job as well as your own you'll be far too tired to do that,' Glynis pointed out.

'Rubbish! Without you to worry about, cariad, I'll be as fresh as a daisy,' Ruth laughed. 'Don't forget,' she added brightly, 'I'll be bringing food home for you each day as well; that will be an added bonus so we'll be able to save every penny I earn towards moving.'

Two nights later as Ruth and Glynis and a group of others, who'd heard about the nightly 'feasts' and come to take part, were enjoying a pot of cawl that Ruth had brought home with her, there was a hammering on the rickety door. It burst open before anyone could reach it and two police constables and a sergeant strode in.

'Stay where you are,' the sergeant boomed. 'Which one of you is going to tell me what's going on?'

'We're eating our supper, mun,' Owen said, pushing back his chair and turning to face the police.

'You're trespassing.'

'Not doing any harm, though, are we?' Owen muttered. 'Not making a noise or anything,' he added lamely.

'That's not the point. All of you are guilty of breaking and entering these premises.'

'Hold on, mun! There's no question of that. The door was open so we came in here for shelter, that's all. What harm is there in that?'

'As I said before, you're trespassing.' He nodded towards the two constables who stayed on either side of the door to make sure that no one tried to escape then, slowly, but thoroughly, he walked round the shed, poking his baton into the pile of mattresses and every cranny he could find.

'You're wasting your time; you won't find anything here that shouldn't be here,' Owen told him.

'I'll be the judge of that. You speak when you're spoken to,' the sergeant told him. 'There've been quite a few robberies round here lately and you lot fit the descriptions we've been given.'

'Hey, mister, stop poking around our things and tossing them on to the floor,' Glynis protested as he opened the battered fibre suit-case and hooked out the contents with his baton.

'Shush!' Ruth shook her head and gave Glynis a warning look, but it was too late.

'Ah, so they're your things, are they? So what are your clothes doing in a place like this, and what are all these mattresses for?' He looked round suspiciously. 'Some disgraceful carryings on here, I can see, and I take it you're the one in charge,' he snapped, glaring at Ruth.

'Will you let me explain?' Ruth said quietly. In a low, modulated voice, although inwardly she was seething with a mixture of fear and anxiety, she tried to explain to him that they were using the shed as temporary accommodation until they could find a room to rent.

'A good story,' he said dismissively, 'but it won't do. You needn't worry about accommodation; we'll find some of that for you tonight and probably for a good many nights to come,' he added grimly as he looked across at the constables and signalled them to come forward.

'We'll be taking these two into custody,' he stated, indicating Ruth and Glynis, 'so take them over by the door out of the way while Constable Rogers helps me to deal with the rest of this mob.'

While he was doing this, Owen had given a nod to the rest of them and the moment the two constables moved away from the door they scarpered quickly and without a sound.

'Well, go after them!' the sergeant bellowed.

Before the two constables were out into Margaret Street everyone had vanished. They raced to the towpath but there was no sign of them. They could only assume they had made off down one of the many alleys or back streets, and decided that giving further chase was a waste of time.

'Not a sign of them,' one of the constables reported slightly shamefaced. 'Still, we've got these two so that's something,' he added hopefully.

'Over here, you two.' The sergeant scowled and moved to a far corner of the room so that Ruth had some difficulty in hearing what was being said.

'It's a waste of time taking these two in. You heard what they said; they're sleeping rough while they look for a room. Leave them here and keep watch on the place in case any of the others come back. Understand?'

Returning to where Ruth and Glynis were waiting to see what he was going to do, he told them harshly, 'I'm letting you off this time, but I want you out of here. You've got two days and then we'll be back and if you haven't moved on you'll be arrested.'

Ruth nodded, but said nothing and as Glynis was about to speak she squeezed her arm and shook her head.

She gave a long gasp of relief when all three policemen left. 'That was a narrow escape,' she breathed. 'Now we really must do something about finding somewhere else to live.'

One by one the gang came back, sneaking in

so quietly that they were all back in the shed before either Ruth or Glynis were aware of what was happening.

By this time the cawl was stone cold so Ruth made mugs of cocoa for them all and told them what the police had said.

'Two days,' Owen said thoughtfully. 'They'll be watching the place and since they're intending to use you as a bait to try and catch us we'd better stay clear from now on.'

Most of them agreed and accepted his reasoning, but Cefn Lewis, a hulking great fourteen-year-old with a scar down one side of his face, was not so easily persuaded.

'It's your fault,' he stormed, rounding on Glynis. 'We should never have let you and your sister stay here. I've seen you being friendly with the cops; they're using you as a decoy.'

'There's rubbish you talk,' Glynis flared back at him. 'I have no more to do with cops than you do. I run a mile when one comes in sight.'

'Oh yes.' He leered, his face contorting with anger. 'And what about Constable Morgan, then? I saw you toadying up to him.'

'You're so daft, Cefn Lewis, that you talk like an idiot,' Glynis told him. 'Constable Morgan caught us pinching, didn't he? You lot scarpered and left me to face the music. Course I talk nicely to him. He let me off, didn't he, and that means the rest of you got let off as well.'

'She's talking sense,' Owen agreed. 'Even so,' he added, 'they're watching us, and like I've said, and I think that agreeing to let you stay on here was because they hoped the rest of us would think it was safe enough to come back and join you. They thought that if we did that then they'd be able to get the whole lot of us at once. The best thing we can do is break up for a while and lie low.'

Half an hour later they'd all vanished again as silently as before. As soon as she was sure that they were on their own Ruth suggested it was time for bed.

'I still have to be at the café by six,' she reminded Glynis.

'And I'm coming with you.'

'You'd better not. If you stay away from school there'll be trouble,' Ruth warned.

'One or two days won't matter, and I'll be scared to go there on my own. Dai will be glad of the help especially when we tell him it isn't going to cost him anything,' Glynis giggled.

Ruth lay awake for a long time. She kept wondering if there was any way she could get in touch with Mervyn Morgan; but even if she could, would he be able to tell her what to do?

Even as the thought went through her mind she wasn't at all sure whether it was a good idea or not. She had neither seen him nor heard from him since she'd confided in him that Glynis was her daughter, not her sister as everyone believed. There was even a niggling doubt at the back of her mind as to whether he'd been rather shocked to learn that she was an unmarried mother. Also, he'd probably heard about the raid on the warehouse by his colleagues, so perhaps he was deliberately avoiding her.

Dai had already heard about the police visit and he wasn't pleased. He demanded to know the reason and the moment he heard they'd been sleeping in an old warehouse he decided he didn't want either of them working in his café.

'I'll give you the money that's due to you and then I want you off the premises,' he told Ruth.

'It's the middle of the morning, you'll be rushed off your feet in half an hour so, now we're here, wouldn't you like us to stay just for the morning?' Glynis asked hopefully.

He shook his head. 'I can't take that risk,' he muttered as he handed Ruth the few shillings he owed her. 'Here, kid.' He thrust a bacon butty and a couple of over-cooked sausages towards Glynis. 'Now get out, the pair of you, and don't come back again.'

They went back to the warehouse and packed up their belongings and spent the rest of the day trailing round Tiger Bay searching for somewhere to stay. Always they met with blank refusal when they were unable to provide two weeks' rent in advance.

'I've enough for a week,' Ruth kept assuring them, 'and I'll be working before the next lot is due.'

'You're strangers, we don't know if we can trust you,' was the standard response as, time after time, they were turned away.

As evening approached and they'd still not found anywhere to stay Ruth began to panic. Where could they go, what were they to do? she kept asking herself. It would soon be dark, there was a nip in the air, and a fine drizzle was soaking them to the skin.

Glynis had shared her sausages with her, but they were now both cold and hungry and Glynis was not only flagging but yawning with tiredness.

'Come on,' Ruth said decisively. 'There's only one place I can think of where we can get shelter and that's in one of the shopping arcades in the centre of the city.'

'I can't walk that far, not with all the stuff I have to carry,' Glynis whinged.

'Then we'll get a tram.'

'That's a waste of money,' Glynis argued.

'In that case, we'd better start walking.'

As they trudged over Clarence Road Bridge, along Corporation Road and then turned down Aber Street on to the Taff Embankment, they both admitted they wished they'd taken a tram.

'Perhaps we could sneak into the railway station and spend the night in the waiting room,' Glynis suggested.

'No,' Ruth shook her head, 'we'd probably be found by one of the porters and turned out.'

'We could always say we'd missed the last

313

train and were waiting for the first one next morning.'

'They'd want to see our ticket,' Ruth pointed out.

'So where are we going, then?' Glynis asked sullenly. 'My feet are hurting and my legs are aching and I'm hungry.'

'I thought we agreed it would be one of the arcades where we'll be out of the wind and rain. We'll find a shop doorway somewhere about the middle and settle down there until morning.'

The David Morgan Arcade was closed for the night and protected by iron gates. Queen Street Arcade and St Mary's Street Arcade were still busy because some of the shops in them were still open.

'So what do we do now?' Ruth asked in dismay. 'It wasn't such a good idea after all, I'm afraid, cariad.'

'We could go round the back of Howell's and see if we can find somewhere there. Now that the shop itself is closed the lorries won't be delivering or taking things out until early in the morning.'

'We won't find much shelter there, though, will we?' Ruth said worriedly. 'If it rains we'll get soaked through.' She frowned. 'What's more, it's probably the sort of place the police will patrol just to make sure there's no one trying to break in. Perhaps we'd be better off going back down Bute Street.'

'What about behind the big buildings in Mount Stuart Square?' Glynis suggested. 'The big coal office are there and the doorway to that is huge. We could find a spot behind one of the pillars and no one would see us.'

'How do you know that? We've never been to Mount Stuart Square,' Ruth said in surprise. 'I don't even know where it is.'

'I can show you. I know where it is, I've been there a couple of times,' Glynis told her.

Ruth wanted to know more, but she thought it best to say nothing for the moment. Not for the first time she realised that there'd been quite a lot going on in Glynis's life that she knew nothing about.

Chapter Twenty-Seven

The polished slate floor was rock hard and icy cold. Although they'd managed to find a hideaway behind one of the stone pillars where it seemed impossible that anyone would spot them, Ruth still couldn't settle to sleep. Glynis, tired out by all that had happened, slept soundly, snuggled up against Ruth for warmth.

Somewhere towards dawn Ruth dozed off only to be wakened by a heavy hand on her shoulder and a man's voice demanding. 'What's going on here?'

Startled awake Ruth groaned inwardly as she recognised the blue uniform. Once again the police had found them. As she struggled to her feet her movement disturbed Glynis who was immediately wide awake and alert.

The moment she heard the policeman state that they were vagrants, and that he was taking them in, Glynis took fright. She'd already heard the other police threaten what would happen to her if they were taken into custody and the thought of being sent to an approved school was more than she could face. She'd heard too many tales from the mob she'd been mixing with about their experiences when that had happened to them and she had no intention of ever being sent to one of those places.

As the policeman pulled out his notebook and began asking Ruth for their names and Glynis's age, Glynis began edging away around the pillar looking for a way to escape. 'Keep him talking,' she whispered to Ruth, 'I'm off. I'll be all right, don't worry about me.'

Ruth tried to restrain her, but it was too late and she was torn between running after her to try and stop her in case she ended up in worse trouble, and keeping the policeman talking in the hope that he wouldn't realise she'd gone.

When he noticed that Ruth was standing there on her own he was furious. 'You must have seen her go,' he accused. 'You do realise it's only making things worse for the pair of you?'

When Ruth said nothing his eyes narrowed. 'Come on,' he ordered sharply as he put his notebook away, 'pick up your belongings, I'm taking you in.'

At the police station she was made to wait and then she was interrogated all over again until her head was swimming and she wasn't even sure what she was saying.

'Don't start thinking that's the end of the matter,' he told her when Ruth breathed a deep sigh of relief because it was over. 'I didn't say that I was going to let you get away with it. I want your sister brought back here. Off you go, then.' He looked at his watch. 'Make sure you're back before two o'clock, because that's when my shift ends.'

As Ruth bent to pick up her suitcase, his hand shot out and stopped her. 'Oh no, missy, I'm not that twp. Your case, and the rest of your baggage, stays right here.'

'You mean you don't trust me to return?' Ruth exclaimed indignantly.

'I'm doing you a favour by looking after it all for you instead of making you take it with you,' he told her smugly. 'Now stop wasting time and get along and find that young sister of yours before I change my mind and put you in a cell.'

Ruth decided not to argue. She had no idea where to start looking, however. She was quite sure that Glynis wouldn't go anywhere near the pub in Bute Road, or the café where they'd worked but, apart from that, she could be anywhere, she reflected.

She felt that the best place to start looking was probably in the James Street area from Clarence Road Bridge along the towpath by the side of the canal. It was just possible that Glynis had gone back to the warehouse in the hope of finding some of her friends.

Her search proved futile. There was no sign of Glynis and the few familiar faces she met hadn't seen her either. She'd no idea where to look next, so she continued up Corporation Road, along the Taff Embankment as far as the Hayes. There was still no sign of Glynis there or in any of the arcades, and there was no one she recognised to ask if they'd seen her at all that day.

The morning went so quickly and she felt so footsore and weary that Ruth was at her wit's end wondering what to do for the best. If she didn't return to the station by two o'clock then the constable would assume she wasn't coming back and would alert someone to the fact that both she and Glynis were missing.

What would happen then, she wondered? Would all the police on duty in Cardiff be alerted and told to watch out for them? And what about her suitcase with all her possessions in it, which was still at the station? Without that she only had what she stood up in.

Why, oh why, had it been a strange policeman who'd found them and not Mervyn Morgan? He'd have listened to her explanation that they'd nowhere to stay and that it was only for one night they were taking refuge in the doorway.

Thinking about him only made her more depressed. She hadn't seen him since the night she'd told him that Glynis was her daughter. She bitterly regretted telling him, but she'd really thought that as he was so warm and friendly and a man of the world, with such a wide experience as a policeman, he'd understand.

She kept wondering if he'd gone back to the

pub, found she'd gone, heard that she was living in a disused warehouse, and decided he didn't want anything more to do with her.

Going back to the police station was pointless, she told herself when her search continued to be fruitless. It would mean that she'd probably be taken into custody and poor little Glynis would still be roaming around on her own. The best thing she could do, Ruth decided, was to forget about her suitcase and continue looking for Glynis.

She felt so tired and hungry that she bought a sandwich and a mug of hot tea from a stall in the Market hoping that it would revive her. As she ate the sandwich she tried to reason out where Glynis could be. She even found herself wondering if she had gone to school, hoping that if she resorted to her normal routine everything would work out right for her.

Fired up by the idea, she finished her mug of tea and set off towards the school in Bute Road. If she hurried she'd be there just as they were coming out. It was a long shot, but somehow she felt sure that was what had happened.

Her hunch was right; as the children came out of school she spotted Glynis tagging along in the rear. She looked so woebegone and miserable that it made Ruth's heart ache. As she called out to her, holding out her arms, Glynis ran over to her, hugging her with relief.

There were tears on both their faces as they drew apart.

'I've been worried sick about you, cariad,' Ruth said in a reproving voice.

'I thought I'd go to school because it was probably the last place the police would think of looking for me,' Glynis told her with a weak laugh.

'It was certainly the last place I thought of,' Ruth agreed. 'I've scoured the whole of Tiger Bay looking for you and half the city as well. I've been up and down all the arcades and the Hayes and everywhere I thought you might be. I even went back to check you weren't at that old warehouse in Margaret Street.'

'There's twp of you! You should have known that I wouldn't be silly enough to go back there; it was probably one of the first places the police went looking for me.'

'No, they haven't been looking for you at all, cariad. They sent me to find you.'

'So does that mean they've let us off?' Glynis asked cautiously.

'No.' Ruth shook her head. 'I was supposed to get you back to the station by two o'clock, before that constable went off duty. I couldn't find you, though, so I don't know what's happened. I imagine he's reported both of us as missing.'

'So what are we going to do now, then?'

'Go back to the police station and explain that I've only just found you, I suppose,' Ruth said worriedly.

'If we do that then they'll put us in prison for being vagrants,' Glynis muttered, her face white with fear.

'What else can we do? All our things are there; he kept our suitcase and the canvas bag to make sure I did go back.'

'Haven't you got any money at all?'

'Only a few shillings.'

'Have you enough to buy something to eat?' Glynis asked hopefully. 'I'm starving,' she added, rubbing her stomach to emphasise just how hungry she was.

'Let's get right away from here and then I'll count it out and see how much I have left,' Ruth said, looking over her shoulder anxiously almost as if expecting a heavy hand to come down on it at any minute.

'Where are we going, then?' Glynis asked, kicking a can into the gutter.

'Stop doing that,' Ruth told her irritably. 'We don't want to draw attention to ourselves. Come along; let's get away from here in case someone who knows us spots us. Let's head for the city centre. There're so many people about there that it'll be easy to get lost in the crowds. If we see any policemen then we can always turn down one of the arcades and come out in another street.'

It was a long walk and they were both tired, but Ruth was so concerned that they might be seen by a policeman that she insisted they went as far as Queen Street, just to be on the safe side.

As they came out of the arcade, the bright September sunshine had already turned to a cold drizzle that made both of them shiver. Ruth stared around, anxiously wondering which way would be safest, but Glynis's attention was already drawn towards huge placards outside the Queen's Cinema.

'Look!' she squealed. 'Charlie Chaplin's on in *The Gold Rush*. Oh, do let's go and see it, Ruth.'

'Don't be twp, Glynis. We can't waste money on something like that when we're both hungry and haven't even got enough to pay for a room,' Ruth protested.

'It will be warm and dry inside and if we go in now we can sit there through all the performances; we could have a sleep, even.'

'I thought you were starving hungry,' Ruth reminded her. 'If we go to the pictures then we most certainly won't have enough money to buy us a decent meal.'

'I'd sooner watch Charlie Chaplin and have a laugh,' Glynis assured her. 'Come on, let's go and see how much the cheapest tickets are and if we've enough money. Please, Ruth; we both need a laugh to cheer ourselves up.'

As she looked at Glynis's eager face Ruth's resolution to be strong and sensible faded. Glynis was right. There'd been nothing but hardship and misery in their lives for such a long time that a good laugh would be like a tonic. The chances of finding a room that night were remote and, sooner or later, she and Glynis would have to report back to the police station, so what did it matter?

'Come on, then, but don't blame me if you're too hungry to enjoy the film,' Ruth told her after she'd paid the cashier for one and a half tickets in the cheapest seats.

Although it was not yet five o'clock there were a good many people inside when they went in. The lights were still up and the organ playing as they took their seats.

Glynis insisted they sat near an aisle. 'We'll move as soon as the lights go down,' she whispered.

'Move?' Ruth frowned, not understanding what she was planning to do.

'Move to the back, to the better seats. There're some doubles right at the back. If we can get one of those, we can cuddle up together and you can have a sleep if you get fed up with watching the screen.'

'Don't be twp,' Ruth scolded. 'Those seats are three times the price of these.'

'I know! That's why we've got to wait and why I wanted to sit near the aisle. When the usher sits down to rest her feet for a couple of minutes, we can sneak back there.'

The front seats were practically full almost before the lights dimmed and the trailers started. As Glynis had said, once everyone was settled the usher moved to her own special seat to have a short rest before there were any new arrivals.

'Come on.' Glynis nudged Ruth in the ribs. 'This way.'

Ruth hesitated, but as Glynis started to move towards the back of the cinema she felt forced to accompany her. The last thing she wanted was to lose sight of her again, but it worried her that Glynis could be so devious.

The double seat was much more comfortable than the one they'd been in at the very front of the cinema, but Ruth was on edge in case the usherette realised they'd moved and asked to see their tickets.

We'll deal with that if it happens, she told herself as she settled down beside Glynis and let herself become absorbed by what was happening on the big screen. She had only seen Charlie Chaplin once before and in next to no time she found herself laughing at his silly capers and escapades and momentarily forgetting her troubles.

Towards the end of the main picture other people started to arrive and a smartly dressed young couple pushed past them to get to the next seat. As they did so the girl dropped the box of chocolates she was carrying, and because it was already partly opened some of the contents fell out and dropped by their feet.

Glynis swiftly leaned down and began to pick up the sweets. She unwrapped a couple of them and stuffed them into her into her mouth before straightening up. Then, very politely, she hand the rest to the girl who was now settled into her seat.

'You dropped your chocolates,' she whispered. 'I managed to find some of them, but there may still be some of them on the floor.'

'Well, I certainly don't want them if they've been on the floor,' the girl told her haughtily, pushing Glynis's hand away and turning her back towards her.

'I don't think they're dirty,' Glynis assured her.

'I still don't want them. Stick them in the ashtray or put the box under the seat,' the girl insisted.

'I'll eat them if you're sure you don't want them,' Glynis muttered as she settled back into her own seat. 'Here,' she whispered as she slipped Ruth a couple of chocolates wrapped in silver paper from the handful she was still holding. 'They're lovely.'

The chocolates were very rich and creamy and they had a delicious fruity centre. Ruth ate the two she'd been given and saw that Glynis was steadily munching away with obvious enjoyment. She felt worried, wondering just how many of them she was eating and hoping that they wouldn't have any ill effect on her, seeing that she had eaten nothing else all day.

When she tried to warn her that they might upset her, Glynis only laughed and said that they were all gone now, so it was too late to try and stop her eating them.

Ruth said no more, pleased to see that Glynis was enjoying herself so much. This is how it should be all the time, she thought. She was far too young to be feeling unhappy because she didn't live in a nice home and enjoy good food.

Glynis was so thin and, in her raggedy second-hand clothes, she looked unkempt. No wonder the girl who'd been sitting next to them in the cinema hadn't wanted her sweets back when Glynis had picked them up for her. Sadly, she suspected it was not so much because they'd been on the floor, because after all each of them had been individually wrapped, but because Glynis had handled them.

Chapter Twenty-Eight

Although they'd arrived at the Queen's cinema well before five o'clock they stayed until about ten minutes before the end. They'd seen the big picture through twice as well as most of the supporting programmes. As Glynis had said, it was warm and comfortable there so neither of them had suggested moving.

With the few pennies she had left Ruth had intended getting them some fish and chips so that they wouldn't feel hungry during the night since, once again, they were going to have to spend it in a shop doorway. Now she wondered whether the greasy fried food, coupled with the rich chocolate, might be too much for both of them.

When they did come back out into the street it was to clear skies, a bright moon and a keen early autumn breeze.

'It's a pity we couldn't have stayed in the cinema for the rest of the night because I'm feeling cold already,' Glynis sighed as she tucked her arm through Ruth's and snuggled up close to her.

'That's probably because you're hungry and, of course, you've no coat,' Ruth sighed. 'Never mind,' she went on cheerfully, 'we'll find a fish-and-chip shop. I've enough money to buy one portion so we can share it between us.'

At the mention of the words 'fish and chips' Glynis gave a gasp and a noisy heaving sound and was suddenly violently sick.

'Oh heavens! That's all those chocolates you've been eating,' Ruth sympathised.

Before Glynis could answer she was sick again and Ruth did her best to keep her calm, clean her up and ignore all the people who stood and stared at them, or went out of their way to avoid the mess that Glynis had made.

'Now, then, what's going on here?'

At the sound of a familiar voice Ruth's heart pounded wildly. It was a voice she'd given up hope of ever hearing again. Her face was scarlet with embarrassment as she looked up unable to believe that it was Mervyn Morgan.

Her pulse raced as their eyes met; he was looking so stern and official in his policeman's dark blue uniform, his sandy hair hidden under his imposing helmet, that she found it hard to believe he'd once been so warm and friendly towards her.

'I'm so sorry about the mess,' she said rather lamely, putting a protective arm around Glynis's shoulder.

'That's not important,' he said dismissively. 'Is Glynis feeling all right now?'

His voice was so concerned that Ruth felt her senses spin and soar. He didn't sound the slightest bit unfriendly or disparaging.

'Does she need to go to hospital?'

'Heaven's no! It's nothing serious. We've been to the cinema and I'm afraid Glynis ate too many chocolates while we were in there,' she explained.

'I see! Then the best thing you can do is get her home,' he suggested. He turned away, telling the curious onlookers to move on. When they'd done so he turned back to Ruth and Glynis. 'Come along, I'll walk with you. Where are you living now?'

When she hesitated, Mervyn went on, 'I know you've moved out of that basement room in Bute Road because I've been looking for you so that I could explain why I haven't been around for a while. I was sent to help out some-where else; it was all such a rush that I didn't get a chance to let you know that I was going to be away.'

'Oh!' Ruth felt nonplussed and speechless. She was dismayed by all her bad thoughts about Mervyn Morgan. He hadn't been censorious about what she'd told him about Glynis after all. She'd completely misjudged him.

'So where are you living now?' he asked again.

'We're not living anywhere,' Glynis blurted out. 'We were picked up by the police last night and accused of being vagrants because we were sleeping on the steps of the coal offices. I expect the same thing will happen again tonight because Ruth says it will have to be a shop doorway or some old shed down by the canal.'

'Duw anwyl! This is terrible,' Mervyn exclaimed. 'Where are all your belongings?'

'At the police station,' Ruth told him. 'We were more or less arrested earlier on, but Glynis ran away and the constable who'd detained us said I was to go and find her and bring her back before his shift ended at two o'clock this afternoon. He kept our suitcase and the rest of our stuff. It was his way of making sure that I went back there, I suppose,' she added dolefully.

'You haven't been back?'

'Well, no. I didn't find Glynis in time so there didn't seem to be much point.'

'That's because I went to school,' Glynis tittered. 'I thought that would be the very last place the police would come looking for me.'

'I had a hunch she might do that so I went and met her from school and—'

'We went to the cinema to see Charlie Chaplin because we knew it would be warm in there.'

'And you bought chocolates instead of a meal.' He frowned. 'That wasn't very sensible.'

'We didn't buy them!' Glynis babbled. 'Some woman sitting next to us dropped them on the floor and when I picked them up for her she said she didn't want them.'

He nodded gravely. 'And so you ate them so that they wouldn't be wasted.'

'No, I ate them because I'd had nothing to eat all day and I was hungry,' Glynis told him with a cheeky grin.

Mervyn looked rather taken aback and looked at Ruth as if for confirmation. When she gave an almost imperceptible nod his mouth tightened into a grim line.

'I think we'd better start by trying to find you somewhere to stay tonight.' He raised his hand to silence Ruth as she started to explain that they didn't have enough money to do that. 'Leave everything to me,' he told her brusquely. 'There's a café not far from here where you can get a meal even at this time of night. I'll take you there and while you're getting some proper food inside you I'll see what I can do to get you fixed up with somewhere to stay.'

An hour later he was back to collect them and to escort them to Christina Street off Loudon Square. There he introduced them to Mrs Price, a small buxom woman in her late forties who had coal-black eyes and plump shiny cheeks.

'This is Mrs Price,' he told them, 'and she's letting you have a room and the use of her kitchen.'

'We can't possibly afford to stay here, not even for one night,' Ruth protested in a whisper to Mervyn as they were taken up to a fairly large room that held a double bed at one end and a table and two chairs at the other. There was also a large built-in cupboard, a chest of drawers and a washstand with a jug and bowl on it.

'Of course you can. It's all fixed,' Mervyn told her.

Glynis was already exploring the room and uttering little sounds of delight. 'Do we have to come back to the police station tomorrow?' she asked, pulling a face.

'I'm afraid so, if you want all your belongings back,' Mervyn Morgan told her. 'I'm pretty sure the charges will be withdrawn, however, once they know you have a respectable address.

'We really can't afford to stay here, you know,' Ruth repeated worriedly as she accompanied him to the door. 'I haven't a job, so there is no way I can pay the rent.'

'We'll sort all that out in the morning,' he told her, patting her arm reassuringly. 'Now both of you get some rest. After your escapade last night you must be very tired.'

Since they'd none of their own things they had to sleep in their underwear, but Ruth made sure that their outer clothes were hung up so that they wouldn't looked too creased the next morning when they went to the police station.

Glynis couldn't get into bed quickly enough she was so tired. The supper they'd eaten had taken away her feeling of nausea and all she wanted to do was sleep.

Much to her surprise Ruth also fell asleep almost as soon as her head touched the pillow; long before she'd had a chance to try and work out what she was going to do from now on and where they were going to live. She slept so soundly that she was barely awake before there was a knock on their door and she found Mrs

Price, the landlady, standing there carrying two covered plates.

'I was told to bring you up a cooked breakfast at about eight o'clock. Hope you're ready for it.

'Usually I expect you'd prefer to get your own, but for this morning, everything being strange and that, Constable Morgan suggested I should do it for you.' She smiled as she put the plates down on the table together with knives and forks.

'Now you get started; I'll nip back down and bring you up a pot of tea; it's all ready.'

The appetising smell of fried bacon, egg, sausage and bread roused Glynis and within minutes the two of them were tucking in with gusto.

'Take your time and eat it more slowly,' Ruth warned. 'I don't want you to be sick again.'

'Don't worry, I'm not going to waste a meal like this,' Glynis promised, her eyes shining with pleasure.

'We still have to report to the police station, remember,' Ruth warned as they sat back replete.

'I could face anything after that,' Glynis said grinning. 'Anyway, it seems we'll probably get let off, so there's nothing to worry about,' she added confidently.

'Or else we might get an even longer sentence for indulging in a cooked breakfast and spending the night in a comfortable room when we can't afford to pay,' Ruth pointed out primly. 'Come on, we'd better get ourselves washed and smartened up because we have to be there for ten o'clock.'

They were both feeling very nervous when they arrived at the police station, but to Ruth's great relief Mervyn Morgan was waiting outside on the corner near the police station when they arrived.

'Sleep well?' he asked

'Wonderful; the most comfortable bed I've slept in for a long time,' Ruth assured him.

'And we had a lovely cooked breakfast,' Glynis piped up.

'Good, and now you're all ready to face the music, are you?' he asked.

Ruth shuddered. 'Are they going to be very harsh on us?' she asked fearfully.

'Not if you do as I tell you,' he told her quietly. 'When they ask where you live, then give the address in Christina Street where you stayed last night.'

'Surely they'll check up and find out we were only there for one night,' she said worriedly.

'No, they'll find out that you've already paid two weeks' rent in advance,' he told her.

She looked at him in dismay. 'You mean that's what you've done?' she said in a disbelieving voice.

He nodded.

'That's very kind of you, but I can't possibly afford it. I haven't got a job and that room—'

335

'Ssh!' He shook his head to silence her. 'You'll have a job,' he told her confidently. 'You've an interview at two o'clock and by tomorrow you'll be working as an usherette at the Central Cinema. You do know where that is?'

For a moment Ruth looked bemused.

'I do. The Central Cinema is that one at the Hayes, isn't it?' Glynis said excitedly.

'That's right. You'll be working there from ten in the morning until six at night. What's more, I've arranged that when Glynis comes out of school each afternoon she'll come there and stay in the staff room until your shift is finished.'

Ruth stared at him in disbelief. 'I don't understand how you've managed to arrange all this so speedily.'

'I'll explain everything later,' he promised. 'I don't think it's a good idea to be seen talking to you at the moment, but I felt it was important that you get your story right and convince them that Glynis is being properly looked after,' Mervyn pointed out. 'If they think that she's running wild when she comes out of school, they may insist on taking some sort of action. Remember, she's been in trouble twice quite recently, so this is very important.'

'None of the things you've told me to tell them is true, though,' Ruth gasped. 'They're bound to find out when they check up on what I've told them.'

'It's all true because I've made sure it is,' he

told her firmly. 'Now, you go along inside and report to the sergeant on the desk before they send someone out looking for you. Keep your wits about you and tell them what I've told you.

'Remember, you've got to convince them that you only intended sleeping rough for one night and that the reason was because you couldn't move into the room you've rented in Christina Street that night as you'd expected to do.'

As Ruth and Glynis started to walk towards the police station he called after them to wait a moment.

'If you see me when you're inside the station, don't speak to me or appear to recognise me,' he warned. 'Do you understand what I'm saying?'

Ruth assured him they did.

'I'll call round this evening and you can tell me how you got on,' he told Ruth before he walked briskly away leaving them to report as they'd been told to do.

Chapter Twenty-Nine

Ruth found their interview with the station inspector, a craggy-looking man in his late fifties, both embarrassing and irritating. He stared at them critically with hard grey eyes when they were shown into his office and he indicated curtly that she was to sit in the straight-backed chair facing his desk and Glynis in a chair against the wall.

Even though she followed Mervyn's advice and explained that it had been an emergency because they'd not been able to move into their newly rented room right away, he still didn't seem very convinced.

'So this new address will be a permanent one?' He frowned, studying her speculatively.

Ruth nodded, not daring to speak in case he could detect the uncertainty in her voice. She certainly hoped that it would be permanent, but so much depended on whether she really did have the job at the cinema Mervyn had told her about.

The inspector consulted the notes in front of him yet again. 'Your sister, Glynis Davies, has been in trouble on numerous occasions,' he reminded her. 'We have several reports concerning her bad behaviour.' He studied the papers on his desk more closely. 'I see that on numerous occasions she's been responsible not only for terrorising people and damaging property, but has also been the culprit of various other misdemeanours. We can also link her name to that of a gang of unruly children who've caused mayhem throughout Tiger Bay in recent months. She's been associating with them for some considerable time and, according to my information, she's the ring-leader. How do you explain all this?'

'That's all in the past,' Ruth defended. 'It was because she was constantly getting into trouble with those children that we've moved away from the pub in Bute Road, where we were renting a room in the basement, to somewhere where she's less likely to mix with the wrong sort of children.'

He still didn't look very convinced, so she plucked up the courage to risk telling him about the interview she had for a new job at the Central Cinema at the Hayes.

His frowned deepened. 'So your sister will be left to her own devices every afternoon after she comes out of school.'

'No! Glynis will be coming to the cinema straight from school each afternoon and staying there until I finish work and then we'll be going home together.'

The inspector listened in silence, making notes from time to time and frowning heavily as he did so. He then asked her a great many more questions concerning Glynis and several times Ruth felt that he was trying to catch her out and make her contradict herself.

When he'd finally finished, he kept her waiting on the edge of her chair while he read through all his jottings once again. This took him so long that she was beginning to think that the whole idea of ever starting afresh was hopeless.

Ruth's feeling of despondency increased when he finally looked up and then delivered a solemn lecture on her responsibilities as Glynis's guardian. When he'd finished he said he wanted to talk to Glynis on her own and asked Ruth to wait outside.

Out in the passageway Ruth stood as near to the door as possible, trying to hear what the inspector was saying. She was silently praying that Glynis wouldn't answer him back in a cheeky fashion, or say anything that could incriminate them any deeper, or mention Mervyn Morgan by name or say that he was a friend.

The deep rumble of the inspector's voice made it difficult to hear his exact words, but he seemed to be reprimanding Glynis for her past behaviour and delivering warnings and covert threats about what would happen to her in the future if she offended again. She also heard him tell her that the crowd she'd been associating with in the last few months would only get her into trouble and that she was to have nothing more to do with them.

Ruth felt on tenterhooks the entire time this was going on. When he finally called her back into his office, she saw that Glynis was looking subdued and sulky as they sat through another long sermon about her behaviour and its possible consequences.

It was almost midday by the time he'd finished with them both and then they had to wait another half an hour before their suitcase and canvas bag were returned to them.

'I have to get to the Hayes by two o'clock,' Ruth said worriedly as they headed back to Christina Street. 'Whatever happens, I don't want to be late for my interview.'

'Why don't you catch a tram and go straight there and I'll take these things home,' Glynis suggested.

Ruth shook her head. 'You'd never manage them both on your own. Come on, we'll make it. What are you going to do, though?' she asked worriedly. 'I can hardly take you with me, so perhaps you'd better go to school.'

'I'll be all right. I can stay up in our room until you get back,' Glynis told her.

'On your own?'

'Well, that's better than being out roaming the streets, isn't it?' Glynis said sulkily. 'I'll be good and keep out of trouble from now on, I promise,' she added contritely.

As they reached Christina Street and let

themselves in Mrs Price came out of her kitchen before they could go up the stairs. Her round face was beaming as she greeted them. 'Mervyn Morgan called round this morning,' she told them.

'Really?' Ruth looked perplexed. 'I wonder why? He knew I wouldn't be here.'

'He said you might be in a bit of a rush when you got back and asked me to have something ready for you to eat as you had to go out again. It's all ready, so as soon as you've taken that case up to your room, come and get it.'

Before Ruth could protest or indeed say anything more, Mrs Price had gone back into her kitchen. Ruth and Glynis looked at each other, bewildered.

'Come on, let's do as she says,' Glynis urged, 'I'm starving, so I hope it's something good.'

The hot savoury homemade cawl served with rounds of crusty fresh bread was very welcoming and both of them tucked in.

The minute Ruth had finished her stew Mrs Price put a cup of freshly poured tea in front of her. 'Drink that up, cariad, and then get on your way,' she bustled. 'Now don't you worry about young Glynis,' she assured her, 'because she can stay here with me for as long as she likes. When she's fed up with my company, then she can go on upstairs to your room if she wants to.'

'That's very kind of you, but—'

'Off with you now, cariad! That Mervyn will scold me if he hears you were late for your appointment. He said I was to make sure you left here in plenty of time for it. I've got some books here that will keep young Glynis occupied. I take it you like reading?' She smiled, looking in Glynis's direction.

'As long as they're not anything to do with school work.' Glynis grinned.

'No, cariad, nothing at all like that, Story books that my own children enjoyed reading when they were about your age.'

'Great! I'll love them,' Glynis enthused.

'I still have a read of them myself sometimes; they remind me of the old days before they left home,' she sighed.

'Well, if you're quite sure it isn't too much trouble, then thank you for your help,' Ruth said gratefully as she pushed back her chair and stood up.

She felt very nervous about what lay ahead and it was a great relief to know that she needn't worry about Glynis. She'd taken to Mrs Price in a big way and the jocund, motherly woman seemed to already have a soft spot in her heart for Glynis.

Or was it Mervyn that Mrs Price was so eager to please? Ruth wondered as she took out a clean blouse and skirt from her suitcase and changed into them. He certainly seemed to have an awful lot of influence with her to be able to persuade her not only to rent them the room, but also to put herself out so much for them, she thought wryly.

It took her only a few minutes to get ready, though she wished she had something smart to wear instead of her shabby navy skirt and white blouse that was fraying at the collar.

All she could hope, she thought, as she called out a quick goodbye to Mrs Price and Glynis before she left the house, was that the coming interview would go as smoothly as everything else in her life seemed to be doing at the moment.

From deep despair she was now on cloud nine and all because of the help she'd had from Mervyn Morgan, Ruth mused, as she boarded a tram. The icing on the cake would be if the promise of a job at the Central Cinema really did come true. If it didn't, then she'd no idea how she was ever going to pay back the money he'd paid out, or what she and Glynis would do when the two weeks were up and they had to move on.

As she went over all the events of the past week or two she realised that she'd let herself get downhearted for nothing. It had all been in her mind when she'd believed that Mervyn had walked away from her because she was an unmarried mother. He'd done nothing of the sort; she should have been more trusting.

Once again she wondered if perhaps it would be better to tell Glynis the truth. Since she was making a fresh start, then perhaps this was the right time to be honest with her.

Her interview was a mere formality and her

introduction to the new job was not nearly as arduous as she'd feared it might be. The woman in charge of the usherettes, Olwyn Vaughan, was neatly dressed in a black dress with a cream lace collar, and her pepper-and-salt hair was short with a Marcel wave. She was calm, kind and reassuring; so much so that Ruth found her nervous tension was dispelled within the first few minutes of meeting her.

She hadn't been at all sure what the job would entail, but after asking her a few simple questions to find out if she'd had any previous experience Olwyn Vaughan made it all sound so easy that Ruth found she was actually looking forward to starting work.

'Our girls are all expected to wear white blouses and black skirts. We supply the apron that goes over them and the fancy hat, but the rest of it is up to you. I said black, but that dark navy skirt and the blouse you have on at the moment will pass for the present, so don't worry if you haven't got a black skirt.'

'What about shoes?' Ruth asked anxiously. She looked down at her sturdy black shoes with their button bar over the instep and hoped they would be suitable.

'You need to wear comfortable ones, because you'll be on your feet a lot. And remember, in the dark, people often stand on your toes, so make sure they're sensible ones; perhaps something like you're wearing at the moment,' Mrs Vaughn advised. 'Now if you'll come with me,' she said standing up, 'I'll take you into the auditorium and we can see how well you adjust to the conditions and the darkness and I'll introduce you to the girls you'll be working with.'

Ruth wanted to ask if that meant she had the job, but she was afraid to do so in case the answer was 'We'll let you know', or she appeared so eager that Mrs Vaughan had doubts about her suitability.

'As well as showing people to their seats using this,' Mrs Vaughan told her as she handed her a powerful torch, 'you'll be expected to help with the refreshments in the interval. You won't find that very difficult as all the lights are on then so you can find your way around without any trouble.'

They walked into the darkened cinema and Ruth felt very nervous. As she stumbled a couple of times, and bumped into the edge of one of the seats, Mrs Vaughan whispered, 'Use your torch until your eyes become adjusted. Remember to keep the beam down on the floor when you switch it on, though, because you don't want to accidentally shine it into someone's eyes and dazzle them.'

When they stopped for a cup of tea half an hour later, it seemed from what Mrs Vaughan told her that, like Mrs Price, she had a warm affection for Mervyn Morgan. She not only knew him, but also seemed delighted to be able to help him by finding work for a friend of his.

Even so, Ruth felt it was necessary to enquire

if it really was all right for Glynis to come there straight from school each afternoon as Mervyn had told her it would be.

'Indeed it is. I agree with what Mervyn said; it's not sensible that a girl of her age should be left to her own devices, especially with the darker nights. And on Saturdays, she can sit in the cinema and watch the screen while you're working, so that will help to pass the time for her,' she added kindly.

Ruth felt in a dream as she walked home. How could one man organise so much in such a short space of time? she asked herself over and over again. He really was enabling her to make a fresh start as she longed to do and now it was up to her to put the past behind her and make a new life for herself and Glynis.

She couldn't have done any of it without Mervyn's help and she couldn't wait to thank him; she'd be indebted to him for the rest of her life.

Glynis seemed to be able to tell from the moment she stepped over the doorstep that things had gone well. She flung herself into Ruth's arms and hugged her tightly.

'You've got the job, you've got the job,' she carolled happily. 'Now we can stay here for ever.'

Ruth returned her hugs and nodded at Mrs Price from over the top of Glynis's head.

'Well, that's all settled then.' Mrs Price smiled. 'Mervyn will be pleased. Pity he wasn't still here to be the first to hear it.'

'He's been here again?'

'Yes, he was waiting to find out how you'd got on, but he had to go back to the station. He said he'd see you later,' Glynis told her excitedly. 'When do you start work?'

'Let's sit down and have a cup of tea and then Ruth can tell us all about it,' Mrs Price suggested. 'The kettle's boiling.' She stopped abruptly and looked questioningly at Ruth. 'That's only if you want to, of course. Me and my big mouth! You mightn't want to talk to a complete stranger about such matters.'

'Stranger?' Ruth looked around the room, her eyes twinkling. 'I can't see any stranger here.' She held out a hand towards Mrs Price. 'I think of you as a friend, a very kind one, and I always shall.'

Chapter Thirty

As Christmas 1925 approached, Ruth thought that life couldn't get much better and that she'd never felt so happy. She smiled to herself every time Mervyn dropped by as she recalled her mother's gloomy prediction that no man in his right mind would give her a second glance if he knew the truth about Glynis. Yet Mervyn not only knew the truth about Glynis but he also liked her and insisted they took her with them when they went out.

She still had to watch her spending but with careful budgeting she was able to buy a lot more things than she'd ever done in the past. Glynis was a reformed character and hadn't been in trouble once since they'd moved to Christina Street. She'd changed in every possible way. She no longer looked like a little ragamuffin, but took a great interest in how she was dressed.

Now that she had a regular wage packet Ruth looked for bargains on the second-hand rails for both herself and Glynis as she walked through the Hayes each day. She enjoyed being able to buy the occasional skirt, jumper or dress for Glynis. She became so friendly with the stall holders that often they kept something aside for her to see before they put it out on the rail.

She was enjoying her job as an usherette. The other girls were all friendly and Mrs Vaughan was always ready with helpful advice if she had a problem.

Glynis seemed settled at school and eagerly looked forward to spending her Saturday at the cinema. She no longer came there each afternoon when she left school, however, but went straight back to Christina Street where she stayed with Mrs Price until Ruth came home from work.

It was a pattern that had evolved gradually and without any coercion on either side. Glynis had become very fond of Mrs Price and liked being spoilt with little treats of cake or biscuits and lemonade when she arrived home from school. Mrs Price seemed to enjoy her company and her chatter and hearing all about what had gone on at school that day.

Within a very short time Glynis had learned all about Mrs Price's family and had even discovered why Mrs Price was so fond of Mervyn Morgan.

'She told me that her son Lloyd got into trouble while he was at school, but that thanks to Mervyn Morgan he wasn't sent to a reform school; instead, Mervyn made sure he behaved himself and now Lloyd is in Australia,' Glynis reported.

The story brought a smile to Ruth's face because it also answered the question she'd been constantly asking herself, which was why Mrs Price was always so anxious to please him.

Mervyn had become equally prominent in her own life, Ruth thought with amusement. He was such a stalwart friend and asked for nothing in return. Sometimes she longed for him to be more than a good friend. There were occasions when she dreamed of what it would be like to be kissed by him or even to be held in his arms.

Whenever this happened she scolded herself for her foolishness and reminded herself that it was only because he was a copper that he was so concerned, and that he was only doing what his job demanded.

Yet, at other times, she really did feel that their friendship was rather more special than that. It certainly was to her and when Mrs Price commented that she seemed to be seeing a lot more of him these days than in the past, it invariably brought a lift to her spirits.

Christmas was only a few weeks away and she wondered if perhaps Mrs Price would be interested in inviting him to call in on Christmas Day, perhaps even have a meal with them.

This year it was on a Friday so, since the cinema would also be closed on Saturday, it meant she was going to have a really nice break which would be lovely.

She toyed with the idea for days, wondering if she dare mention it to Mrs Price. In the end there was no need. One afternoon, she called in after work to let Mrs Price know she was home and that it was time for Glynis to come upstairs.

'Mrs Price says that I can stay down here with her all day when we break up from school at Christmas,' Glynis announced, her face wreathed in smiles.

'Are you sure she won't be in your way?' Ruth asked looking enquiringly at Mrs Price.

'No, I won't be,' Glynis assured her. 'We're going shopping together and we're going to have our Christmas dinner down here with her,' she added excitedly.

'Hold on, Glynis, hold on,' Mrs Price protested. 'Give me a chance to talk to Ruth; she may not want to come; she may have made other arrangements.'

'I can't think of anything that would be nicer.' Ruth smiled. 'Are you sure you really want to do that? It's not a case of being talked into it by Glynis, I hope?'

'No, it was my idea, cariad,' Mrs Price admitted, 'but I intended to be a bit more tactful when it came to asking you. I didn't want you to feel that you had to accept.'

'I think it's a lovely idea,' Ruth told her gratefully. 'As long as you let us share what we have with you. I shall look forward to the three of us sitting down together.'

'Well, hold on a minute; it won't be only just the three of us here at Christmas,' Mrs Price told her quickly. 'I've invited Mervyn to join us when he comes off duty. He'll be on his own otherwise, see. You don't mind too much, do you?' she asked anxiously.

'I don't mind at all,' Ruth told her. 'It will be very nice to have him here.'

'We'll be like a real family,' Glynis chipped in. 'Can we have presents and everything?'

'Wait and see.' Mrs Price smiled. 'If you're very good and help me with the shopping and all the extra work, then we'll make it the best Christmas ever,' she promised.

It would be the best Christmas ever if all they did was sit down to bread and cheese as long Mervyn was there with them, Ruth thought happily.

It would also mean that she would look forward to 1926 with even greater enthusiasm. If it was anything like the past couple of months then it would be confirmation that at long last they were over all their troubles and the future really was going to bring them the happiness and security she longed for.

For now, she intended to focus on Christmas. Even though Mrs Price would be taking care of all the cooking there'd be plenty of other things she could do to help. She also wanted to make it special in other ways. This would be the first time since she could remember that she'd be able to afford to buy presents. Not only for Glynis, but also for Mrs Price, to thank her for all she'd done for them. She also wondered about buying a present for Mervyn; nothing too ostentatious, because she didn't want to embarrass him, but she'd like to give him a memento of some kind from her and Glynis as an expression of their gratitude.

From now on, she resolved, she'd save something each week out of her wages and she'd also keep her eyes open for any suitable gifts when she was walking through the Hayes. Many of the stallholders there had already started displaying their Christmas wares. She could, of course, wait until the very last minute to buy things in the hope that by then they'd have reduced their prices, but if she did that, although she might pick up a bargain, she might also miss something that was suitable.

It was a dilemma she quite enjoyed. Contemplating which was a suitable present was half the fun; that and smuggling it home afterwards and hiding it away so that neither Glynis nor Mrs Price was aware of what she'd bought.

They seemed to have plenty of secrets of their own. The two of them were often whispering together, or Glynis was giggling about something. Ruth pretended not to notice, realising that it was all part of the excitement for Glynis.

The two of them were also full of plans about what they were going to cook for their special meal on Christmas Day. Mrs Price said that if Glynis was going to help her that meant that Ruth would have to entertain Mervyn.

Ruth rather thought that she was getting the better part of the deal although she never mentioned a word of this to either of them. It did make the forthcoming festivities all the more exciting for her, though.

Christmas Day turned out to be everything Ruth could possibly dream about. Mervyn was with them for Christmas dinner and it was a momentous occasion; one that Ruth knew would live in her memory for ever.

It had started almost before she was awake that morning. After Glynis had finally gone to bed on Christmas Eve Mrs Price had helped her to fill one of Glynis's socks to go on the end of the bed ready for when she woke next morning.

Ruth had bought her a comic, a new hairbrush, some hair ribbons and slides, a little box of sweets and two shiny new pennies to go into the toe of it. Mrs Price insisted on adding a few walnuts, a tangerine and a shiny red apple.

When Mervyn arrived he praised the colourful paper chains that festooned the room, which Mrs Price and Glynis had made out of strips of coloured paper. There was also the special garland that Mrs Price had used every year since her own children were small and which opened up like a concertina into a rainbow of brilliant colours and stretched all the way across the top of the fireplace.

She'd also bought a small fir tree which stood in a bucket by the window. They'd covered the bucket in bright red crêpe paper and hung all sorts of baubles and silver stars that Glynis had made at school on to the tree. At the very top was a celluloid doll in a stiff white dress, carrying a shiny silver wand.

Glynis had helped dress the tree and she thought it was the most beautiful thing she'd ever seen. All morning she kept rearranging the tiny balls of cotton wool and silver paper that they'd tied on to it so that it would look perfect for when Mervyn arrived.

The presents they had for each other were all wrapped in brightly coloured paper and had been placed underneath the tree. Every so often Glynis would surreptitiously squeeze the ones with her name on them and try and guess what might be in them.

Mrs Price spent the morning bustling around, laying the table and spasmodically attending to things in the kitchen. She refused to let Ruth do anything.

'Your job is to entertain Mervyn when he gets here; leave all the cooking to me and all the arranging to Glynis, now that's an order,' she told Ruth when she offered to help. 'I can't be doing with people under my feet when I'm trying to get a meal ready; I only lose my rag or forget what I'm supposed to be doing.'

'Well, shall I make up the fire so that we have a good blaze going when he arrives?' Ruth suggested.

'Certainly not! That's my job. We can't have you getting any dirt on that pretty new red dress you're wearing. It looks lovely on you, by the way. The colour suits you. You should never wear black or pale colours; that red brings the colour to your cheeks.'

'What about my new jumper and skirt, don't you think that they're pretty?' Glynis asked as she did a twirl, making her short pleated skirt swing out.

'Yes, they are and you look lovely in them, but mind you don't spill anything on them. You'd better put a pinny on before you come out into the kitchen to help me bring things in for the table so that you don't get them splashed or marked.'

'When are we going to see your new dress?' Ruth teased. 'I know you've got it on, but you're wearing the biggest overall I've ever seen so it's impossible to tell what you have on underneath it.'

'And that's the way it's going to stay, cariad. I'm not taking this overall off until I have dished up the meal and I'm ready to sit down at the table with you all. I'm not taking any chances. One splash of grease and it would be ruined.'

By the time Mervyn arrived everything was in place and looked very festive. The candles were alight, the table was laid, and there was a colourful cracker beside each plate.

Mervyn had brought presents for them all and these were added to the pile already under the tree. Glynis was so excited that she could hardly sit still. She wanted to open them before they had their dinner, but Mrs Price told her very firmly that unless she ate everything on her plate she wouldn't be opening any of them at all.

Christmas Dinner itself was such a splendid occasion that, momentarily, Glynis forgot all about the presents. Mervyn carved the plump chicken which was cooked to perfection, as were the roast potatoes and parsnips and the others vegetables that Mrs Price served.

They pulled their crackers and Mrs Price put a hand to her chest when each one of them gave a loud bang, declaring that it was enough to give her a heart attack. Nevertheless, she was smiling happily and put on the coloured crêpe hat that was inside hers.

Afterwards there was Christmas pudding which Mrs Price had made over a month earlier.

'I helped to make this,' Glynis told them excitedly. 'I stirred it and I made a wish.'

'Shush!' Mrs Price held a finger to her lips. 'If you tell us what you wished, then your wish won't come true.'

'I can tell you, though, because it has already come true,' Glynis told them blithely. 'I wished that Mervyn would be here on Christmas day because I knew it would make Ruth happy and he is here.'

Ruth felt her cheeks burning as she looked across at Mervyn on the other side of the table, wondering what he must be thinking, but his face and voice were both very serious as he said, 'Thank you for doing that, Glynis. It's exactly what I would have wished myself if I'd had a chance to stir the pudding.'

Once the remains of the meal were cleared

away they made themselves comfortable and declared they were so full they couldn't eat another thing.

'You'll have to do so later on because there're mince pies that Glynis helped to make and a Christmas cake that she helped me to ice,' Mrs Price told them.

'Can we open our presents now?' Glynis whispered to Ruth who looked questioningly at Mrs Price before answering.

The next hour was a medley of rustling as the colour wrapping paper was taken off, followed by exclamations of delight or surprise, or both, as the present inside was revealed. The pile around Glynis was by far the largest and she sat entranced by all the wonderful things she'd been given, her eyes shining with delight.

'Come on,' Mervyn said, smiling, 'tell us all what you've got there, then.'

'There are so many things I don't think I can,' Glynis sighed.

'Shall I help you?' he suggested.

'I'll pass them over to you one at a time and tell everyone what they are as I do it,' she said, beaming.

'A jigsaw, a book, a doll, some other puzzles, some games, a scrap book, another new jumper, a scarf and some woollen gloves,' she announced.

'What a wonderful pile of presents,' Mervyn enthused. 'Shall we play one of the games?'

Glynis frowned and nodded at the same time.

'Right, so which one is it to be? Which one of them is your favourite game?'

Glynis bit her lip and looked doubtful. 'I don't really know because I've never had any games like this before. I don't know how to play any of them.'

'That's soon solved,' Mervyn told her cheerfully. 'I know how to play them, so I can show you. Shall we start off with Snakes and Ladders? That only needs two players.'

'Can't we try one that we can all join in together?'

'When you've learned that one then we'll try one of the others,' he promised.

'That sounds like a good idea,' Mrs Price agreed. 'I'll go and wash up the dishes.'

'I'll come and help you,' Ruth said quickly, getting to her feet and heading for the kitchen.

'You'll have to wrap yourself up in one of my big overalls, then,' Mrs Price told her. 'When we've finished I'll make us all a nice cup of tea and then we'll all join in a game with you, Glynis,' she promised.

The evening ended fairly early because Mervyn was due on duty but it was fun and laughter right up to the moment he left because when he said goodbye he insisted on kissing all three of them under the mistletoe.

'The kiss you gave Ruth was twice as long as the one you gave me,' Glynis teased him as he finally took his leave.

Chapter Thirty-One

Christmas had been such a memorable occasion that even though they saw nothing at all of Mervyn for the next few days because he was on duty the memory of the lovely time that they'd all had together was something Mrs Price, Ruth and Glynis talked about constantly.

Glynis loved all her games and was always begging Mrs Price and Ruth to play with her; it soon became their favourite way of spending their evenings.

Ruth was aware that apart from sleeping in their own room she and Glynis spent very little time up there and it began to worry her that they were impinging on Mrs Price's good nature and privacy.

When she mentioned the matter, however, Mrs Price shook her head and assured her that she thoroughly enjoyed their company and wouldn't have it any other way.

'I've been on my own far too much over the past few years and I've become very lonely and depressed. I thought there'd never be a family around me ever again,' she confessed. 'Having you two here, and the visits from Mervyn Morgan, has brought a real joy into my life. I've a lot to thank Mervyn for,' she added with a deep sigh.

Ruth tactfully remained silent, waiting for Mrs Price to explain, only if she wanted to do so. She'd already told Glynis about Mervyn helping her son, but Ruth didn't want Mrs Price to think they'd talked about her behind her back.

There was a long silence and Ruth was about to go up to her room when Mrs Price said, 'Have you time for a cuppa and a chat?

'Of course I have, but only tell me if you want to do so,' Ruth told her.

'It would do me good to talk about it,' Mrs Price said quietly as she bustled around setting out cups and saucers for them both.

'It all happened about five years ago. My two boys were still living at home with me. The eldest, Twm, who'd just turned twenty at the time, was on the point of getting married and the younger one, Lloyd, was restless and, I think, a bit jealous of all the fuss that was going on over the forthcoming wedding.

'I was scrimping and saving and doing my utmost to help Twm get set up in his new home. Only two rooms, mind you, but to him and his bride it was going to be their first home and, naturally, there were a lot of things needed to make it comfortable. In the midst of all this, Lloyd, who was apprenticed as a plumber, lost his job. It seems he'd been stroppy over something, answered the boss back, and that was that; immediate dismissal.'

Mrs Price paused and dabbed at her eyes. Ruth stretched out a hand and patted her hand. 'Don't say any more . . .'

'No, I want to. It'll get it off my chest, cariad. Been bottled up for too long. It's not the sort of thing you want to stand on a street corner talking about, now is it?'

'Take your time, then.' Ruth smiled, sipping her tea.

'I should have paid more attention to Lloyd,' Mrs Price sighed, 'but I was caught up in all the wedding plans and simply told him that the best thing he could do was go back and apologise and ask them to take him back. He only had another six months or so to go before he'd get a certificate to say that he was fully qualified.

'Saying that to Lloyd was like a red rag to a bull, I can tell you! I thought no more about it. He went out and came home each day at his usual time; he handed over his money at the end of the week and I thought everything was fine. The only thing that did bother me was that he was out every night of the week and I had no idea where he was going. Well,' she sighed deeply, 'I didn't at the time, and when I did find out it was too late.'

Ruth put her cup back on to the saucer and frowned. 'What do you mean?'

'Mervyn brought him home about one o'clock in the morning. He'd caught him breaking and entering a shop in the centre of Cardiff.'

'He was stealing!'

'He was about to, but Mervyn caught him before he had a chance to take anything.'

'He didn't arrest him?'

Mrs Price paused and bit down on her lower lip. 'What I'm going to tell you now is in the strictest confidence. If it got out it might mean trouble for Mervyn, but since you're such a good friend of his I know you won't let that happen.'

'Go on. Whatever you tell me will be between the two of us,' Ruth assured her.

'Mervyn gave him a good telling off, but he didn't report him. He said he was in with a bad lot and the best thing he could do was stop going round with them.'

'Did Lloyd agree with this?'

Mrs Price shook her head as she reached out for Ruth's cup to refill it.

'When Lloyd said he was afraid to break away from them because of what they might do to him, Mervyn suggested that perhaps he should clear off to Australia or Canada and start afresh before he ended up with a jail sentence.'

'What happened?'

'We sat there for hours talking it over. I didn't want him to go, of course. With Twm moving out it was like losing both my boys at one go. Terrible!'

'He did go, though?'

'Eventually. There was further trouble. The gang suspected what had happened and tried to bully him into carrying out another robbery. They kept telling him that Mervyn was a softie and wouldn't arrest him, and that if they found out when Mervyn was supposed to be patrolling and picked a shop there, Lloyd would be safe enough. They kidded him up no end and he fell for it.'

'Did he get caught?'

'Mervyn caught his accomplices, but Lloyd managed to get away, whether by good luck or not I'll never know. Mervyn came round a few days later and advised Lloyd to take his advice and leave for Australia as quickly as he could, before the case came to Court, because he was pretty sure that the other boys were going to squeal and say he'd been with them.'

'This all happened before the wedding?'

Mrs Price shook her head. 'There was no wedding. The bride-to-be's family got wind of it and made their daughter call the whole thing off; they told Twm they didn't want jail birds in the family.'

Ruth looked shocked. 'Lloyd wasn't a jail bird, though, he hadn't been arrested.'

'No, that's true enough, but they were very moral, God-fearing people, and they decided that there was bad blood in our family.'

'Surely the girl could have stood up to them if she really loved Twm.'

'That's exactly what I thought,' Mrs Price declared triumphantly, 'but Twm wouldn't see it like that. He knew how domineering her father could be so he accepted their decision. He was heartbroken, mind you; so much so that he decided to go to Australia with his brother. The pair of them went and from their letters I think they're settled and doing all right. It was such a wrench, losing both of them like that.'

'There must be times, though, when you resent Mervyn's interference. If he hadn't suggested Lloyd going to Australia then they'd still be here with you.'

'That's true, but it was better than my Lloyd ending up inside. It gave both of them a fresh start and I've got Mervyn to thank for that, bless him.'

'Quite a bold decision for him to make, though, wasn't it?'

'Indeed it was. He'd not long started out as a policeman and if he had turned Lloyd in as a suspect then it would have earned him considerable praise.'

'Showing so much consideration, however, earns him even more praise in my estimation,' Ruth told her.

'And in mine!' Mrs Price added fervently. 'I'd do anything to help that young man and I think there are a good many other people who feel the same.'

Although Ruth said nothing to Mrs Price it made her wonder if he had done some similar sort of service for Mrs Vaughan, which was why she'd been prepared to give her a job even though she hadn't the right sort of experience or a reference of any kind.

It made her own friendship with Mervyn even more special and as she remembered the brief but enchanting moment when he'd kissed her under the mistletoe at Christmas she harboured the hope that he had feelings for her, just as she had for him.

New Year's Eve should provide the answer, she told herself. He was off duty and had asked her to go to a dance with him at the City Hall. She had never been there before and was worried about what she was going to wear since she'd nothing suitable for the occasion.

On the spur of the moment she confided in Mrs Price and was amazed at the delight on the older woman's face.

'That's wonderful,' she enthused, hugging Ruth excitedly. 'I know you like him and from the way he looks at you I know he has feelings for you!'

'He probably feels sorry for me,' Ruth said, blushing. 'It's the sort of good turn he would do, isn't it?'

'Sorry for you, cariad! What utter nonsense. He wouldn't ask you to something as grand as that unless he'd a very good reason. I'm as pleased as if it was me going.' She smiled. 'Now don't go worrying about Glynis; I'll keep her entertained and see she gets off to bed once we've seen the new year in. We'll do it properly, with a lump of coal and so on, so don't you worry about her; she'll enjoy herself. A lot of the neighbours will be popping in to wish me a Happy New Year; she'll love all the comings and goings.'

'Heavens! I hadn't given a thought to Glynis,' Ruth exclaimed in dismay. 'Are you sure you won't mind her being with you?'

'Of course I won't, I've just told you so. Now, what are you going to wear?'

Ruth's face fell. 'I don't know, it's a bit of a problem. I haven't got a proper evening dress or a dance frock. I've never needed them before,' she added with a deprecating little laugh.

'Don't worry about it, cariad. I've got just the thing. You're not a lot taller than me so it should fit you a treat.' She held up a hand as Ruth was about to speak. 'Don't worry, cariad, I wasn't always as plump as this. Let myself go since the boys have gone. I sit and eat things I shouldn't and it shows.' She smiled, patting her ample stomach. 'Now wait here a minute while I go and fetch it. If you don't like the colour or the style then say so. It's just an idea.'

Ruth waited apprehensively. The last thing she wanted to do was offend Mrs Price in any way, but she really couldn't see herself wearing one of her dresses.

Mrs Price returned a few minutes later carrying the dress over her arm. It was wrapped in a sheet and Ruth couldn't see it properly, or even what colour it was.

Almost reverently Mrs Price unwound the sheet to reveal its contents and Ruth gasped in amazement. The dress was in a shimmering oyster colour and the material was so delicate and smooth that it was the loveliest thing Ruth had ever seen.

'It was meant for the wedding, though I'd probably never have got round to wearing it because it would have outshone the bride's dress, but when I saw it I fell in love with it.'

'It really is beautiful,' Ruth admitted, 'but I couldn't possibly wear it. I'd be scared of spilling something or catching my heel in it.'

'Nonsense! At least see if it fits you. Come on, try it on. Slip your blouse and skirt off and pop it on.'

As Ruth slid the delicate material over her head and then smoothed the fitted bodice and the folds of the long skirt into place, she sensed that it fitted her like a dream. On her, it was only ankle length, but it still looked perfect. On Mrs Price it would have been sweeping the ground.

'Fits you as if it was made for you,' Mrs Price told her. 'You look absolutely lovely. Nip upstairs into my bedroom; there's a big mirror in there and you can see yourself full length. Here' – she held out Ruth's blouse and skirt – 'you'd better take these and change into them if you want to keep the dress a secret until the night of the dance.'

Upstairs Ruth pirouetted in front of Mrs

Price's cheval mirror admiring both the dress and how she looked in it. Would Mervyn like it or would he think she was overdressed?

It was a special New Year's Eve dance, some people would call it a ball, so how could she be overdressed, she told herself. She'd never worn anything quite so exquisite in her life and even if the whole evening was a flop, simply wearing such a wonderful dress would be a tremendous boost to the start of 1926.

For the rest of the week she schemed, planned and daydreamed about what she'd wear with it, how she'd do her hair, and all the other things that would contribute to it being the most wonderful occasion of her life.

When she explained to Glynis that because she was going to a dance with Mervyn, Mrs Price had said she could spend the evening with her, Glynis was ecstatic.

'Will you ask her if I can stay up later than usual because I want to see the New Year in,' Glynis pleaded. 'I've never done it before, and I really want to.'

'She already knows that and she's planned all sorts of things to welcome in 1926, so you needn't worry,' Ruth assured her. 'She's looking forward to it as much as you are.'

'Will we still be up when you get home?'

'I'm not sure about that because I don't know what time the dance ends. It certainly won't end until after midnight and then we might have difficulty getting home. We may even have to walk. If Mrs Price says you are to go to bed, then you must go; no arguments, mind.'

Mervyn had said he'd come and pick her up at eight o'clock, so at seven she left Glynis with Mrs Price and went upstairs to get changed. She wanted to be on her own and even though everything was ready she wanted to give herself plenty of time.

'Call me if you need any help,' Mrs Price whispered. 'I'll make sure Glynis is busy with something down here so that she doesn't see you until you're ready. I can't wait to see her face,' she chuckled.

Ruth spent a long time putting on her make-up and doing her hair before she finally slipped into the dress. Her first impression still held; it looked beautiful on her and transformed her from an ordinary working girl into someone special.

Mrs Price had given her a pair of silk stockings and she'd managed to find a pair of cream satin court shoes on one of the second-hand stalls in the Hayes that fitted her perfectly.

Mrs Price came out into the hallway as she came down the stairs and her gasp brought Glynis running to see what was going on. They both stood staring wide-eyed at Ruth as if unable to find the right words to express what they were feeling. She could tell from the look in their eyes, though, that they approved.

'There's posh you look,' Mrs Price breathed.

'You're ever so much prettier in that dress, it's lovely,' Glynis said in awe.

The reaction from both Glynis and Mrs Price was important, but the final test, the one that really mattered to her above all others, was Mervyn's reaction when he came to collect her.

The stunned look of admiration on his face told her all she needed to know. With the utmost care he took her in his arms, pressing his lips gently to her brow in a tender kiss. `You look absolutely radiant, cariad,' he breathed.

Chapter Thirty-Two

There was already a huge crowd at the City Hall when they arrived. So many people, and all of them so beautifully dressed, that Ruth felt very shy. Nervously she made her way to the ladies' powder room to change from her walking shoes into the elegant satin court shoes she'd bought specially to compliment her dress.

Mrs Price had loaned her a pretty little cream moiré evening bag but she was so on edge, and her fingers felt so clumsy, that when she opened it she almost spilled the lace-edged handkerchief and the other few items that were inside it.

Only once she was on the dance floor, in Mervyn's arms as they circled to the strains of a waltz and he whispered how lovely she looked and how proud he was to be her escort, did she finally manage to relax.

When they paused for refreshments, she didn't really need the glass of wine he brought over to the little table for her; she was already euphoric. As she sipped it she felt as if she was in a dream, which she never wanted to end. It was the most momentous occasion in her life and she was so bursting with happiness that she was almost in tears.

The rest of the evening passed in a haze of happiness and was over far too soon. When the chimes to mark midnight sounded and Mervyn took her in his arms, kissed her and wished her happiness for the coming year, she returned his kiss with fervour.

'I think it might be a very special year for us, don't you?' he murmured softly, a twinkle in his eye.

She didn't know quite what to say; she wasn't sure how serious he was, so she smiled and nodded and whispered, 'I hope so.'

They returned home arm in arm. Mrs Price had allowed Glynis to stay up so that she, too, could wish them both a Happy New Year. As they all hugged and kissed, Ruth felt a lump in her throat. It was such a special moment that she longed to tell Glynis the truth; tell her that she was not really her sister but her mother.

She wasn't sure why she held back, but a few minutes later she was glad that she'd done so since it might have burst the wonderful bubble of happiness that encased them all. It would not only have been a startling revelation, but a tremendous shock to both Glynis and Mrs Price.

Glynis was quick to notice that when Mervyn finally left he not only kissed Ruth goodnight, but also held her in his arms for quite a long time.

'I'm not sure when I'll see you next because I haven't seen the duty roster for next week,' he told her, 'but I'll be round.'

The look in his eyes told her more than mere words; promises for the future – their future.

Long after she was in bed, and Glynis was sleeping soundly beside her, Ruth was still reliving the excitement of the evening, recalling the glittering lights, the gorgeous frocks, and, above all, the sheer joy of being held in Mervyn's arms.

Remembering the more tender moments between them brought tears to her eyes, but they were tears of happiness. Her last thought as she drifted off to sleep was that, as Mervyn had said, it was going to be a momentous year for them both.

The New Year started off well; Mervyn was a regular visitor to Christina Street and he and Ruth also went out on their own once or twice a week. So much depended on what shift he was working and whether or not he was free at the same time as she was.

Occasionally on a Sunday they'd take Glynis out to Roath Park, and they'd promised to take her to Barry Island as soon as the weather was warmer.

'We must wait until it's warm enough to be able to sit on the beach,' Ruth pointed out.

Glynis was hoping that it might be possible to do so at Easter.

'I'm not promising you, mind,' Ruth warned her. 'Good Friday is on the second of April, and it may still be far too cold then to go anywhere like that.'

'What about on Easter Monday, then?' Glynis begged.

'Wait and see what the weather is like and, of course, it will depend on whether Mervyn is on duty or not.'

'We could go without him; we could take Mrs Price instead.'

'We could, but she sees so much of you that perhaps she'd prefer to have a whole day to herself,' Ruth said, smiling.

Shortly after Christmas, when the weather had become damp and very cold, Mrs Price had suggested that it might be better for Glynis to continue to come straight home from school and have a hot drink in front of the fire and stay with her.

'It would be much better for her than having to trail all the way up to the Hayes and then wait in the staff room at the cinema for you to finish work,' she told Ruth.

Ruth had looked doubtful, aware that it would mean that Mrs Price would be tied to a routine that she might later regret. When Glynis heard the idea she was so eager, however, that, finally, Ruth was talked into agreeing to the arrangement.

'It really does make good sense,' Mrs Price told her. 'I'm here on my own, so why not let her come and keep me company? Don't you worry about her, I'll find plenty to keep her occupied. She can help me get an evening meal ready for all of us.'

Before Ruth could protest she went on quickly, 'That also makes good sense. No point in me cooking for myself; half the time I don't bother, but if I have to prepare a meal for the three of us, then it makes it worth doing.'

'You already get our breakfast before we go out in the morning,' Ruth reminded her.

'Well, it's quicker and easier than you trying to do it and getting yourselves ready at the same time. It makes a nice start for the day if the three of us can sit down together, and I enjoy doing it.'

After a great deal of discussion and argument, Mrs Price finally agreed to letting Ruth pay her to provide breakfast and an evening meal for them as well as herself.

At first Ruth felt a little guilty about letting her do all the work, but she soon realised what a boon it was to know that when she came home there would be a hot meal on the table within a few minutes and that she didn't have to shop or cook to make it all possible.

Very often there was the added pleasure of Mervyn's company as well, and while she and Mrs Price did the washing up, he'd entertain Glynis, playing board games with her until it was time for her to go up to bed.

At this point Mrs Price would decide she wanted an early night too, and after they'd all had a cup of cocoa, she would leave them together, sitting in front of the glowing fire.

During the next hour, as she sat cradled in Mervyn's arms, listening to his plans for their future together as they watched the dancing firelight, Ruth would feel so safe and content that it was magical. All her past traumas would fade into oblivion as they shared precious moments of sheer happiness.

When she told him how much Glynis wanted to go to Barry Island at Easter he agreed with her that they ought to invite Mrs Price to accompany them.

'She's the nearest we both have to family,' he said with a smile, 'and I'm sure that in her eyes we are her family.'

'She does more for us than most mothers would,' Ruth agreed. 'I'll tell her and Glynis tomorrow. They'll get as much enjoyment out of talking about it as going there. Glynis has never been to the seaside. I'd been several times by the time I was her age. We used to be taken there on a Chapel outing and as a school trip each year. Mind you' – she pretended to shiver – 'we had more sense than to go at Easter. We preferred it to be a hot day in July or August.'

'It will have to be on the Monday,' Mervyn warned her, 'and, if it's a nice day, it's going to be pretty crowded no matter what sort of weather we have.'

'That's all part of the fun, isn't it?' Ruth smiled.

Glynis was delighted when they told her and so was Mrs Price. The two of them began planning what sort of food they'd have to bake and what sort of sandwiches to make for their picnic.

'You won't have room for any ice cream or sticks of rock when we're there,' Ruth teased.

'We'll make room for an ice cream cornet,' Glynis assured her, 'and we'll bring back a stick of rock to remind us of our day out.'

As it happened, Easter Monday dawned bright and sunny, but there was still a sharpness in the air which made Ruth insist that they must all wrap up warm.

'You can always take it off if you're too hot, but if you haven't got a scarf, you'll be shivering and complaining that you're half frozen and that will spoil the day for all of us.'

Mrs Price provided a large wicker basket to put all the food in and Ruth was glad that Mervyn was there to carry it because it weighed so much. As soon as they arrived at Barry Island he found a sheltered spot near some rocks and left Ruth and Mrs Price there while he and Glynis went to find some deck chairs.

Glynis didn't give them time to get settled. The tide was going out and she was eager to start walking over the dappled sand and explore the beach.

'I'll go with her while you sort out what we're going to eat. Once we've lightened the load then we can all go for a walk if you want to do so,' Mervyn suggested.

The air was bracing and both Ruth and Mrs Price were glad they'd dressed warmly. As far as they were concerned it was much too cold to be tempted to paddle although a great many people were doing so. Children had taken off their socks and shoes and loved it, but most of the adults were content to walk along the water's edge merely keeping a watchful eye on the children to make sure they didn't venture too far into the sea and end up in trouble.

Many families grouped nearby were using the rocks as shelter by forming their chairs into a circle as a barricade against the buffeting wind so that the smaller children could build sand-castles or simply dig in the sand.

Later, after they'd eaten, they walked along the beach and Glynis insisted on taking off her shoes and socks and paddling, jumping back in alarm every time an incoming wave caught her legs.

By mid-afternoon, even Glynis was begin-ning to feel the cold and was happy to go along with Mervyn's suggestion that they should find a café where they could all have a hot drink.

Knowing how much Glynis was looking forward to an ice cream, Ruth agreed that she could have one to eat as they walked along, provided she also had a hot drink later on.

There was a sigh of relief from Mrs Price when they found a café not too far from the beach and she was able to get out of the cold. They were lucky enough to find a window seat and Mervyn insisted they had hot buttered toast as well as either hot tea or cocoa.

Warm once more, they explored some of the many shops and stalls piled high with buckets and spades, seaside mementoes, sweets and magazines. Glynis bought her stick of rock and Mervyn bought a huge bag of humbugs for them all to enjoy on the train on their way back to Cardiff.

Despite the sharp wind they all agreed that it had been a lovely day out.

'Can we do it again at Whitsun?' Glynis asked. 'The weather will be warmer then and we can all go in paddling. Mervyn says he'll teach me to swim next time we come here.'

'We'll see. It's a long way off, so we don't have to make up our minds at this moment.'

'Why can't we? It will be something to look forward to,' Glynis argued.

'Well, we don't know what shift Mervyn will be on for one thing,' Ruth pointed out.

'We don't have to decide on the actual day,' Glynis told her. 'I get a whole week off school at Whitsun so it can be any day of the week.'

'Then we'll say yes, we'll try and come, though we're not sure which day. Will that do?' Ruth said firmly.

'I suppose it'll have to.' Glynis grinned cheekily, looking happy now that she had a definite answer. 'How long is it until Whitsun? Is it six weeks?'

'Something like that,' Mervyn agreed. 'I'll

book it into my diary,' he told her seriously, 'and as soon as I know which days I'll be having, we'll set a firm date.'

Although this kept Glynis happy, all three of them knew that there was always the chance that, even though he was due to be off duty, some crisis might arise and all their plans would be changed.

'You do understand that it's something I have no control over? It's one of the drawbacks of the job, I'm afraid, but you could always go on your own, of course,' Mervyn said to Ruth.

He repeated all this later that night, after both Mrs Price and Glynis had gone to bed and they were sitting on their own. 'The uncertainty of when I might have to be on duty unexpectedly is the one drawback that makes me hesitant about asking you to be my wife,' he told her softly.

She looked at him startled. It was the words she'd dreamed of hearing him say, but the sombreness of his voice disturbed her. 'What do you mean?'

'Would you be able to cope with never knowing if I was coming home on time or not, or if I was suddenly sent away for several days at a moment's notice because there was trouble somewhere?'

'As long as I knew you were coming back to me, then of course I could,' she whispered.

'Does that mean you'll marry me?' he asked awkwardly.

'Are you asking me?'

He pulled back and ran his hands through his hair. 'You must know I want to marry you, but I've never done this sort of thing before and I don't really know the right words or how to go about asking.'

She looked at him in amusement. 'Keep on trying,' she whispered. 'The answer will be "yes", no matter how you put the question.'

It was his turn to look startled. 'You mean it, don't you?' he laughed.

The next moment he was holding her close, kissing her passionately and whispering that she'd made him the happiest man alive.

'There's just one thing,' she told him, leaning away from him so that she could look at his face as she asked. 'Glynis will live with us until she's old enough to support herself.'

'I'd taken that for granted,' he assured her. 'She's your daughter and I shall think of her as mine, and I'm pretty sure she'll accept me as her dad . . .'

'Hush!' Ruth placed her finger on his lips. 'You're forgetting that she still thinks of me as her big sister. I still haven't found the right moment to tell her that I'm her mother, but I will, I promise; when the time is right,' Ruth told him quietly.

'When are you going to tell her about us and that we're going to be married?'

'Soon! Once I've got used to the idea,' she answered softly.

'It might be a good opportunity to tell her that you are really her mother,' he suggested.

Ruth looked startled. 'Perhaps,' she said. 'I'll have to think about it.'

Mervyn pulled her back into his arms, stroking her hair. 'And when are you going to set the date for our wedding,' he whispered, his voice warm with pleasurable anticipation.

Ruth frowned. 'We ought to tell Glynis and Mrs Price first, don't you think?'

'Yes, as long as it doesn't take you as long to do that as it has to tell Glynis that you're her mother,' he teased.

'So when would you like us to be married?' she parried, overwhelmed by the suddenness of it all as she looked at him with raised eyebrows.

She loved Mervyn so much that the thought of being his wife had such a reassuring feel about it that it filled her with excitement and longing.

'Tomorrow? A week's time? I don't mind as long as it is very soon.' He grinned impatiently.

'Be reasonable!' she laughed. 'There are all sorts of arrangements to be made. We'll have to find somewhere to live, for one thing; somewhere with two bedrooms because Glynis will be coming with us, remember.'

That problem was easily solved. As soon as they told Mrs Price that they were planning to get married she immediately suggested that they moved in with her.

'It will be so much better for Glynis if you do that, she insisted. 'If you move into a strange house, she'll feel lonely and you two will resent having her underfoot all the time. Move in here and things can go on much the same as they do now. She can spend all the time she wants in with me. There's a small bedroom she can have all to herself so she'll be over the moon about that and I'll really feel that I've got a family around me again.'

Chapter Thirty-Three

They decided on a fairly quiet wedding. Ruth's boss, Mrs Vaughan, and Mrs Price were to be the witnesses and Glynis was Ruth's attendant.

'I wanted to be a bridesmaid really,' she protested. 'I wanted to wear a pretty frock and to carry flowers.'

'You still can,' Ruth assured her. 'Next to the bride you'll be the most important person there.'

'And will you be wearing a long white dress and a veil?'

'No, I'll be wearing the lovely dress that Mrs Price lent me to go to the New Year's Eve ball in,' Ruth told her. 'She's said I can keep it and it will always bring me good luck, so I think that's the right thing for me to wear on my wedding day, don't you?'

'Will Mervyn be living here with us all the time afterwards?' Glynis pondered.

'Yes, he will. The only difference will be that my name will be Mrs Morgan.'

'So really nothing will change,' Glynis said with a sigh of relief.

'Well, you'll be getting a new bedroom all to yourself. You can decorate it exactly the way you want to and we'll make sure it's all done and ready before the wedding.'

Although Glynis was excited about this she confided in Mrs Price that she was also a little bit worried that Ruth wouldn't perhaps love her quite as much as she did now.

'There's a load of old nonsense you're talking, cariad,' Mrs Price reproved her. 'Of course Ruth will love you just as much. She always will. She's your sister; she's loved you all your life. The only difference is that you'll have Mervyn there to love you and care for you as well.'

The wedding was fixed for 1 May, which was the first Saturday in May. It was happening so soon that they were all a little stressed out with all the things that had to be done before then.

Mervyn also had other worries. There was unrest amongst the miners and there was talk that a strike was imminent.

'If that happens then I'll be expected to do extra duties and I may be called in at any time,' he warned. 'It's Whitsun only three weeks later and I was hoping we could keep our promise to Glynis and take her to Barry Island again, but I'm not at all sure if I'm going to be able to or not.'

'Perhaps it would be better if we don't mention it to her, then?' Ruth frowned.

'I'm not too sure. She was really keen to go there again. It would be something for her to look forward to, and make up to her for the fact that the two of us will be going away for a week on our own immediately after our wedding.'

'Then why not tell her about Barry Island and about the strike as well and she will understand that it can't be an absolute certainty,' Ruth suggested.

When Mervyn mentioned another trip to Barry Island it did bring a spark of interest into Glynis's eyes, but her face fell and she shrugged her shoulders trying to hide her disappointment when he warned her that a strike was imminent and that if it took place he might have to do extra duties.

Later in the day, when Ruth and Mrs Price talked about the proposed trip, Glynis ignored what they were saying. When Ruth spoke to her directly she took no notice and Mrs Price gave Ruth a little warning shake of her head.

Later, when they were on their own and Mrs Price explained that she thought it was best to leave Glynis to work things out for herself, Ruth agreed with her.

'She's feeling a bit jealous at the moment, poor little dab,' Mrs Price said consolingly. 'It's only natural when she's been used to having you all to herself all her life.'

'I suppose you're right,' Ruth agreed. 'Nevertheless, I do find it worrying to see her so upset. Let's hope that all the excitement over our actual wedding will cheer her up.'

'Oh it will, don't you worry about that,' Mrs Price assured her confidently.

The wedding certainly did cheer them all up. Everything went like clockwork and both Ruth and Mrs Price made sure that Glynis received plenty of attention so that she wouldn't feel out of things.

The week away at a hotel in Penarth which Ruth and Mervyn had planned as their honeymoon had to be cut back to a long weekend but it was still memorable.

Their first night together was something Ruth knew she'd never forget. Mervyn's tender lovemaking stirred her deeply. It was a thrilling revelation of what love could be like and the answer to all her hopes and longings. It made her realise that what she'd experienced before with Glyn Jenkins had been mere infatuation.

The luxury setting, the panoramic view from their bedroom window and the sheer joy of being together in each other's arms, made her wish they could have stayed there for ever.

The threat of a miner's strike had become reality and as the repercussions began to spread throughout the country she had to resign herself to seeing very little of him.

Within days volunteers were manning the trams and buses because the drivers and conductors were out on strike. Soldiers were on duty at the ports to help unload ships and keep the food supplies moving. Not only Cardiff, but also the whole country, seemed to be in a state of upheaval.

As she worked, Ruth watched the Pathe News showing the disruption that was taking place everywhere and she listened to the announcements with increasing dread as there was more and more friction between those on strike and those in authority.

Newspaper headlines screamed of the disruptions that were taking place. Miners from the Valleys made their way down to Cardiff and all traffic was halted as they marched four- and five-deep down St Mary's Street.

Later there was violence when fights and general scuffles broke out along the route and trams and other vehicles were overturned. The police struggled to restore order.

Ruth was frightened to walk home when her shift ended and she was truly thankful that Glynis still went straight back to Christina Street when she finished school and didn't come up to the Hayes to meet her.

Even so, she was unprepared for the news when she reached home that Mervyn had been hurt in one of the frays and that he was in the Cardiff Infirmary.

'They say that his leg is broken and at least one of his ribs, poor dab,' Mrs Price sympathised.

'How can you possibly know?' Ruth asked in bewilderment.

'It's all in the *South Wales Echo*, cariad,' Mrs Price told her, holding up the evening newspaper so that she could read the banner headline.

'And they actually mention him by name?' Ruth exclaimed in amazement.

'No, no, of course not, but from the descrip- tion it can't be anyone else. Here' – she handed the paper to Ruth – 'read it for yourself; it's him, all right, isn't it?'

It wasn't so much the report but the picture of what had taken place that sent Ruth's heart racing. Unless Mervyn had a double, the policeman trapped under the back of an over-turned vehicle was Mervyn, there was no doubt at all about it.

She tried to keep her voice calm as she looked up and her eyes met those of Mrs Price. 'Well, it does look like him,' she agreed. 'You say he's been taken to the infirmary; I'd better go and find out how he is. Are you coming with me, Glynis?'

For a moment she thought that Glynis either hadn't heard her or was refusing to answer.

'Come on, Glynis, go with Ruth, there's a good girl. She needs someone to be with her in case it is Mervyn. I want to stay here in case he manages to send someone round with a message.'

There was utter chaos at the hospital. So many people had been injured, some more serious than others. When they asked for Mervyn Morgan at the main reception they were brushed aside and told to wait. Finally, when Ruth pointed out that he was one of the policemen who'd been brought in and that she was his wife, it brought some attention from the overworked clerk on the reception desk.

Even so it was almost two hours before they

were allowed to see Mervyn. He'd already had an operation and had barely recovered from the anaesthetic, but there was a look of relief on his face when they were admitted to his bedside and told they could spend ten minutes with him.

'Are you going to get better?' Glynis asked bluntly.

'Of course I am, but it will take time,' he told her in a groggy voice. 'I'm counting on you to look after Ruth for me until I am well enough to come home and when I do come out, the three of us will go to Barry Island for the day,' he added as he struggled to focus on her.

'When you said you mightn't be able to come there with us at Whitsun because you might be on duty, did you think you might get hurt?'

'No, but then I didn't know for sure that there was going to be a strike, did I? It's just that being a policeman means you have to be on duty whenever they ask you to be,' he told her weakly.

Before Glynis could say any more the nurse was back to check on his pulse and temperature. 'Mr Morgan is still very ill so I think you should leave now before you tire him any more,' she told them firmly.

'Mrs Price made me promise to remind you that as soon as you are well enough to come back to Christina Street we'll both help Ruth to look after you until you're better,' Glynis told him as she said goodbye.

He smiled, but his eyelids were already

drooping and as she paused in the doorway to look back at him Ruth could see that he was already asleep again.

Mrs Price was both relieved that he was going to be all right and upset that he had to stay in hospital.

Ruth visited him every day after she'd finished work at the cinema. His leg was causing him no trouble, but he'd received internal problems from being crushed which caused grave anxiety.

There were nights when she couldn't sleep for thinking about him, reliving their past happiness and silently praying that he'd pull through and have no lasting ill effects. When she visited him he always seemed to look so pale, his face so etched with pain, that her heart ached for him.

After making the one visit Glynis refused to go to see Mervyn again, either with her or Mrs Price.

'I don't like hospitals,' she told them both.

'None of us do and I'm quite sure that Mervyn doesn't like being in there; that's why we have a duty to go and see him and try and cheer him up,' Mrs Price told her.

'I'll draw him some pictures and I'll write notes to him, but I'm not going in there again,' Glynis told them stubbornly. 'I have nightmares afterwards because I'm afraid Mervyn is going to die.'

By the time the strike was over and all the

workers, with the exception of the Welsh miners, had returned to their jobs, Mervyn was making good progress. The country was still trying to recover from the financial turbulence the strike had caused and there were shortages and gloomy faces everywhere.

Although Ruth never bought a newspaper she was always well aware of what was happening from the Pathe newsreels at the cinema. She reported the facts daily to Mervyn because he was now well enough to take a keen interest in what was going on in the outside world.

When he was discharged he was still very weak; he had to walk with crutches and his body was heavily bandaged.

'I have to go back twice a week to have my dressings changed, but they said as long as I had someone looking after me then I could leave,' he told them.

'You've got someone looking after you, no worries there, boyo,' Mrs Price told him happily. 'We'll wait on you hand and foot, all three of us; you won't want for a thing.'

She was as good as her word. She wouldn't let him lift a finger. Ruth was equally attentive and when she wasn't working spent every minute of her time with him.

The only one who didn't do very much for him was Glynis. He tried to coax her to play board games with him, but she merely shook her head and walked out of the room.

At the weekends when she wanted to go out

394

and Ruth said they ought to stay and keep Mervyn company, she sulked.

'Leave her, just ignore it,' Mrs Price advised. 'I think she's jealous of all the attention we're giving Mervyn. I suppose we haven't been taking much notice of her since Mervyn came home from hospital.'

As Mervyn grew strong enough to go out for a short while, and even walk as far as the park in Loudon Square and sit under one of the trees, Ruth was dismayed to find that Glynis didn't want to go with them.

'I don't want to sit there and watch you two holding hands and listen to you fussing over him. I'd sooner go for a walk on my own,' she stated.

Ruth found this rather hard to believe, even though, reluctantly, she accepted it.

It was August before Mervyn was able to discard his crutches and manage with a walking stick. His internal injuries were now better and he was putting back the weight he'd lost and beginning to look quite well again.

'We'd better have that day out at Barry Island,' he suggested one Sunday dinner time. 'What about next week?'

'A great idea as long as it's not raining,' Ruth agreed. 'We'd like that, wouldn't we, Glynis?'

Glynis smiled and nodded but showed no real enthusiasm. Ruth put it down to the fact that she'd said 'as long as it's not raining', and Mervyn attributed her indifference to the fact that he'd let her down by not being able to take her at Whitsun as he'd promised.

Although there were several wet, cloudy days, at the beginning of the following week by Thursday the skies were clear once again and it was very hot and sunny.

'It will be lovely on the beach if it stays like this,' Mervyn enthused. 'You ladies had better make sure you get some sun hats. Are you going to try swimming in the sea this time, Glynis?'

She shook her head. 'No. I haven't got a swimming costume.'

'Then you'd better hurry up and buy one,' he told her. 'Why don't you walk up to the Hayes with Ruth on her way to work tomorrow and see if there is anything there that you like?'

'If you don't find anything then I'll look for one with you when I go out shopping,' Mrs Price offered.

The next morning, however, Glynis had already gone off on her own by the time Ruth was ready to leave for work.

'She really shouldn't disappear like this without telling us where she's going,' Ruth grumbled.

'Well, it is the school holidays and she's almost eleven, so I suppose she thinks she's grown-up enough now not to be treated like a baby,' Mrs Price commented.

Ruth was already late leaving so she said nothing, but it irritated her that Glynis could be so thoughtless and she worried, remembering all the trouble she'd been in before. She resolved to have a word with her when she got home.

So many other things happened during the course of the day that it had gone out of her mind by the time she finished work. When she arrived home Mrs Price was already organising what they'd need to take on their trip the next day so she took it for granted that Glynis was looking forward to their day out.

They were all up early on Bank Holiday Monday; the morning had all the promise of a glorious day to come. As soon as they'd finished breakfast, Mrs Price began making the sandwiches and packing the luncheon basket.

'Don't make it too heavy now, I'm not as strong as I was last time,' Mervyn joked. 'You'll have to take turns and help me to carry it.'

By nine o'clock they were ready to leave; all of them except Glynis.

'She must still be up in her bedroom titivating herself up,' Mrs Price commented.

Ruth shouted up the stairs for her to hurry up and come down.

When Glynis still didn't put in an appearance Ruth dashed up to see what was keeping her. The bedroom was empty.

Puzzled, she came back downstairs wondering if she'd slipped out to buy a comic to read on the train, even though she thought that was highly unlikely.

'Neither of you sent her on a message, did you?' she asked Mervyn and Mrs Price.

'Of course not, why on earth would we do that?' Mrs Price said sharply. 'Isn't she in her bedroom, then?'

Ruth shook her head. 'No, and I can't for the life of me think where she can be.'

They all looked puzzled, but before they could work out where Glynis might be she walked in through the front door.

'We've been looking everywhere for you,' Ruth scolded. 'Where have you been?'

'Outside in the lavvy,' Glynis told them with a wide-eyed innocent look.

'But the back door is locked!' Mrs Price exclaimed.

'I know! It wasn't when I went out there, but when I tried to come back in it was. I hammered on the back door but you took no notice so I had to walk all the way round to the front door.'

'Well, you're here now and that's all that matters so shall we get started or it'll be time to come home before we get there,' Ruth interposed as she picked up the picnic basket and headed for the door.

She was pretty sure that there was more to it than what Glynis had said and she could see that the others didn't believe the story either. It seemed a pity to spoil the day when they'd all been looking forward to it so much, but she'd certainly want an explanation from her later.

Chapter Thirty-Four

There was something about Glynis's story that worried Ruth because she didn't feel it rang true. It buzzed around in her mind like a trapped bluebottle and she couldn't get rid of it.

Each time she looked across at her as they sat on opposite sides of the carriage on the train to Barry Island, she was aware of how smug Glynis looked. It was as if she was hugging some special secret and although she ignored them all she seemed to be in a happier mood altogether. The tiny frown between her eyes that had been so prevalent for weeks now seemed to have vanished.

As no one else seemed to notice any change in Glynis, Ruth tried to tell herself she was imagining things.

Because it was such a lovely day, warm and sunny, the beach was already crowded when they arrived. The spot by the rocks that they'd picked for themselves when they came at Easter was already taken so it took them some considerable time to find somewhere to set up their deck chairs.

Once that was done Ruth offered to go

paddling with Glynis while Mervyn and Mrs Price relaxed and took care of all their belongings.

As they approached the water Ruth reached out and took hold of Glynis's hand. 'We'd better hang on to each other in case we slip or something,' she explained when Glynis made to withdraw.

The water was cold but refreshing and as they listened to the laughter and chatter going on all around them Ruth relaxed and told herself to stop worrying. Glynis was not only growing up fast but she was advanced for her age; it was only natural that she had moods.

To see her now, her frock tucked up into her knickers, splashing in the shallow water, giving little screams when a larger than usual wave hit them, she looked carefree enough, Ruth thought happily.

The rest of the day went so well that after they'd enjoyed their picnic lunch and Glynis said she wanted to go and explore on her own, Ruth made no protest. Her only caution was that she didn't stay away too long and that she made a note of exactly where they were sitting so that she wouldn't get lost.

An hour later, when she hadn't returned, she began to feel anxious and wondered if she should go and look for her. Mervyn and Mrs Price were both dozing, so she felt she shouldn't do so without telling them. She didn't want to waken them so she tried to remain calm as she sat scanning the beach looking first one way and then the other in the hope of seeing Glynis in her bright red summer dress.

It was an hour later before Glynis returned. She looked so happy that Ruth didn't have the heart to tell her off. When she asked casually if she'd had a good walk, Glynis smiled and nodded, but didn't say where she'd been or what she'd seen.

The rest of their day passed without incident. They left for home earlier than most of the other people because Mervyn looked tired although he refused to admit it.

On the train Mervyn slept for most of the journey back to Cardiff and as soon as they arrived home he went straight to bed. Ruth took him up a hot drink, but he was already asleep. She thought his face looked flushed but she decided that it was probably the effects of being out in the sun all day so didn't attach too much importance to it.

The next day he was running such a high temperature and his breathing was so harsh that on her way to work Ruth went to the surgery and left a message for the doctor to call in.

By the time she returned home in the early evening Mervyn was delirious and the medicine the doctor had prescribed seemed to be doing no good at all. Mrs Price was beside herself with worry and she and Ruth took it in turns to sit up with him all night so that someone would be on hand all the time to bathe his fevered brow and give him sips of cool boiled water.

By morning the fever had begun to dissipate, but he was still too weak and ill to even sit up in bed unaided. Ruth was tempted to stay home from work, but Mrs Price insisted that since Glynis was on holiday from school they could manage.

It was several weeks before Mervyn was up and about again. By then Glynis was back at school and things were more or less back to normal; except where Glynis was concerned.

She'd changed so much that half the time Ruth simply couldn't work out what was the best way to deal with her. There were times when she was dreamy, times when she was grumpy, but always it was as if she was holding back in some way; as if she had some deep secret or grudge. Ruth traced it back to the night when she'd walked in on her and Mervyn as they were discussing getting married and put it down to the deep unease and jealousy this had caused Glynis.

Even so, she reasoned, that was quite a long time ago and she should have adjusted to the fact by now. In any case, it had made no difference whatsoever to the way Ruth treated her or behaved towards her.

Since her eleventh birthday was only a few days away she asked Mrs Price if she would mind if Glynis invited two or three of her school friends to tea as a special treat.

'That sounds a fine idea to me,' Mrs Price enthused. 'She hasn't been looking too happy lately. I think her nose has been put out of joint by all the attention we've been giving Mervyn; it's almost as if we've been ignoring her. Perhaps a little tea-party will put us all back in her good books.'

Glynis certainly did brighten up when the idea was put to her. Then she frowned and asked: 'Does it have to be school friends?'

'Well, no, but I didn't think you knew anyone else well enough too want to invite them.'

'Well I do,' Glynis said, scowling.

'You've never mentioned them,' Ruth told her mildly, 'but I don't see why you can't invite whoever you want to.'

'I will, then,' Glynis told her and the scowl had gone and she looked almost pleased.

'The seventeenth is on a Friday so her little party will have to be in the evening or else you'll miss it,' Mrs Price said. 'Unless we leave it until the following Sunday.'

'Sunday might be best,' Ruth confirmed.

'Shall we tell her or ask her?' Ruth asked smiling.

'Leave it me, I'll talk to her about it when she comes in from school tomorrow and get it settled then. I'll tell her that if it's on the Sunday we'll have more time to bake some cakes together. She used to love helping me in the kitchen, but she hasn't done so lately.'

'Oh?' Ruth looked puzzled. 'Why's that?'

'Well, she's never here. She pops in from school and then she's off out again with her friends.'

'You never mentioned that before.'

'No, but then there's been so much else on my mind with Mervyn being so ill and needing so much attention. Anyway, I thought you probably knew.'

'No, I thought she was coming straight home from school as we agreed,' Ruth said, struggling to control her anxiety. 'I wonder where she's been going?'

'Out with her friends, like I said.' Mrs Price stopped speaking and a look of dismay crept into her face as her hand went up to her mouth. 'Oh, my dear, because of the trouble she used to be in both you and Mervyn wanted me to keep a close eye on her. Oh dear, oh dear, I've let you both down.'

'Nonsense, you've done nothing of the sort.' Ruth's anger faded as she saw how distressed Mrs Price was. 'She's probably made a whole heap of new friends; I'm sure she'd never mix with that old crowd again, so don't worry about it. Anyway,' she added brightly, 'we'll be meeting some of her friends on Sunday and then can see for ourselves that everything is all right.'

'I do hope so,' Mrs Price said fervently. 'Perhaps we shouldn't let Mervyn know what's been happening. Apart from the fact that he'd be very cross with me it might worry him in case she is mixing with the wrong sort again.'

'Agreed. Not a word,' Ruth promised. 'I'll look forward to meeting her friends and I'm perfectly sure they'll all be very nice children.'

Although on the surface it seemed that they were both quite happy about the situation Ruth suspected that in actual fact Mrs Price was as anxious as she was and would be glad when it was all over.

Glynis eventually told them that she'd decided to ask two girls and three boys.

'Boys?' Mrs Price raised her eyebrows. 'You'll only be eleven, Glynis, aren't you too young to have boys as friends?'

'There are boys as well as girls in my class,' Glynis told her, going red in the face and looking uncomfortable.

'I know that, but you don't sit together and you have to use separate playgrounds and different entrances when you go in and out of school.'

Glynis looked rather taken aback. 'How do you know that?' She frowned.

'I had boys of my own, that's how I know, and I also remember that they never bothered to be friends with any of the girls while they were at school,' Mrs Price told her primly.

'Are you saying you don't want me to invite boys to come here to tea?' Glynis asked sulkily.

'No, no, of course not,' Ruth intervened quickly, giving a warning glance towards Mrs Price. 'Of course we want you to invite them. You'd better tell us all their names though.

Are they the same age as you, or are they younger or older?'

'If they're in her class then they'll be the same age, surely,' Mrs Price commented.

'One of the boys isn't, he's a bit older,' Glynis admitted.

After that she didn't seem to want to talk about the party and turned to Mervyn who'd been sitting quietly in the background, listening but saying nothing.

'Would you like play a game of Ludo?'

'Good heavens!' He looked surprised. 'You haven't wanted to play board games with me for ages, what's made you suddenly change your mind?'

'Don't play if you don't want to,' Glynis told him huffily. 'I thought you might like to, but if you don't then I'm going out.'

Before Mervyn or any of them could answer she'd banged out of the front door and they could hear her feet pounding on the pavement as she ran down the street.

'She's never invited anyone to tea before so I expect she's feeling nervous about it all,' Ruth said lamely. Inwardly she was more than a little concerned by Glynis's strange behaviour and wondered whether the birthday party was a good idea or not. It was too late now to call it off and if she did, it would probably only create even more tension. Remembering what had happened to her when she was only thirteen, she couldn't help wishing that

Glynis hadn't started showing an interest in boys.

Glynis spent a long time upstairs getting ready for her party, putting on the new dress Ruth had bought her for the occasion. The blue-and-white spotted bodice had puffed sleeves and the plain blue skirt skimmed her knees. The colour suited her and the style certainly made her look more grown up.

Mrs Price had bought her some lisle stockings, the first she'd owned, and when she put them on she walked with tremendous care because she was nervous in case she laddered them.

Mervyn had bought her a pretty silver bracelet and a tiny silver star on a matching chain. As he fastened it on for her Glynis's eyes shone with unconcealed delight.

When her girlfriends, Mina and Petra, arrived at four o'clock she was as excited as any young girl could be as they admired her dress and jewellery and gave her their presents. Mina had brought her a dainty lace-edged handkerchief and Petra gave her a pretty little bottle of scent which she opened right away so that they could all have a dab of it.

The three of them chattered and giggled as they speculated on whether the boys would come or not.

They did come. Brennan and Garfield arrived together, both of them looking rather sheepish in their best clothes. When the third boy,

Dafydd, arrived ten minutes later Ruth thought he looked older than the other two, but decided that perhaps it was because he was taller and was wearing long trousers.

It was apparent right from the start that Dafydd was Glynis's special friend. From the moment he came into the house she seemed to ignore everyone else and spend all her time either looking at him or trying to say or do something to attract his attention.

He was a very good-looking boy, with very thick straight black hair, deep-set dark eyes and a forceful jaw line, but there was something about him that disturbed Ruth.

The more she looked at him the more positive she was that she'd seen him somewhere before. It troubled her so much that she was determined that as soon as she was able to have a quiet word with Mervyn she'd ask him if he felt the same way. She was worried in case he'd been one of the boys in the gang Glynis had been mixed up with when she'd got into so much trouble.

The food went down well. The boys especially appreciated Mrs Price's ham sandwiches and all the home-made cakes. Glynis had shaken her head when they'd suggested the jelly and blancmange that was customary at children's parties so Mrs Price had made a huge trifle instead.

'It's the same ingredients, jelly and custard, except that there's cake in it as well,' she told

Ruth with a smile. 'Looks more grown-up like that, I suppose, and it's just as easy to make.'

It was also equally popular, especially with the boys. All three of them accepted second helpings which brought a smile of satisfaction of Mrs Price's face because she always liked to see her efforts being appreciated.

The games planned by Mervyn to keep them entertained after their meal were not so popular. He'd thought pinning on the donkey's tail while blindfolded, pass the parcel and musical chairs would be great fun, but as soon as he saw them he realised that the games were far too childish, especially for the boys.

For half an hour they simply sat around talking. Ruth could see they were getting fed up and, from the mutterings she overheard, she suspected they were on the point of leaving. Knowing how miserable this would make Glynis she racked her brains as she and Mrs Price cleared away the debris of their meal to think of some way of keeping them all entertained.

'Would anyone like to play a game of snap?' she suggested, placing a pack of cards on the table. 'Mervyn's in charge,' she added, giving him a wink.

Half an hour later and they'd progressed from Snap to Rummy, and from then onwards no one seemed to want to leave. At about nine o'clock, Mrs Price brought in mugs of cocoa and a plate of biscuits and asked if they would mind packing up their game so that she could use the table.

When they finally agreed that it was time they all went home Glynis accompanied them to the door to see them off. She was gone such a long time that Ruth was on the point of going to see where she was but Mervyn stopped her.

'Give her a few minutes, cariad,' he said softly. 'She's saying goodnight to that nice boy she invited.'

'You mean Dafydd!'

'Of course. Couldn't you see how much she liked him?'

'Yes, I could, and I wanted to ask you about him. His face seemed familiar, I'm sure I've seen him before somewhere and I wondered if he was one of the boys in that gang that caused so much trouble.'

Chapter Thirty-Five

From the moment she met Dafydd and realised that he wasn't a boy from school but that he was already working, Ruth felt worried, remembering her own youthful experience, and she tried to persuade Glynis to stop seeing him.

'He's far too old for you, cariad,' she said firmly, 'I think it would be best if you didn't have anything more to do with him.'

Ruth wasn't sure if it was his name, although Jenkins was a pretty common one, or whether it was his appearance – the black wavy hair and dark eyes – but there was something about him that struck a chord and made her uneasy.

She pondered on it for weeks, trying first of all to talk to Glynis to see if she knew anything about his background that might bear out what she was thinking, but Glynis was suspicious of her interest and seemed to be careful about how she answered.

Ruth felt certain that Glynis was still meeting him and simply couldn't leave the subject alone. She was constantly trying to work out how she could persuade Glynis to talk about him without divulging why she was so interested.

Every time she drew a blank she became

more and more worried. Finally she asked Mervyn if he could find out more about Dafydd just in case Glynis was still seeing him.

'Of course I'll check through our files at the station, but I've already told you that I didn't recognise him. As I said before, he seems far too respectable a sort of boyo to have been involved with any of the tearaways I've been involved with. Mind you, boys do change as they grow up so he might be a completely reformed character and that's why I can't place him. What did you say his surname was?'

'Jenkins. I don't think that is much of a clue, though, because there are countless people called Jenkins in and around Cardiff.'

'And in the whole of Wales, if it comes to that,' Mervyn agreed with a laugh.

Mervyn could turn up nothing detrimental at all about Dafydd Jenkins but the matter still troubled Ruth although she now kept her worry to herself.

It was several months later when Mervyn brought the matter up again.

'You remember that young boyo that Glynis invited to her birthday tea last year? Well, I heard today that he comes from Cathays where you once lived. There's a coincidence now. I wonder if that's why you thought you recognised him. Mind you, he'd only have been a tiny tot when you lived in Harriet Road.'

Ruth stopped what she was doing and the colour drained from her face. 'Can you find out if his father was ever a school caretaker?' she asked in a strained voice.

'Of course I can, my lovely. Remind me when I go on duty tomorrow and I'll check it out and have the answer when I come home at the end of my shift.'

Ruth was in torment all day. The more she thought about it and remembered what Dafydd had looked like, the more certain she was that his father would be a school caretaker and that his name would be Glyn Jenkins.

'He's not a school caretaker these days,' Mervyn reported, 'but his name is Glyn Jenkins and he used to be one. Do you know him, then?'

Ruth couldn't speak and she clutched at the back of the nearest chair for support.

'Come on, cariad, what's the matter? I would never have told you if I'd known that it was going to have this effect,' Mervyn said worriedly. 'Oh, Duw anwyl!' He also looked stunned as the truth dawned on him. 'Glyn . . . Glynis . . . that's it, isn't it? That's what's upsetting you; it's what made you believe you'd met Dafydd before. Damnio di. He's . . . he's . . .' He shook his head in disbelief as he stared at Ruth.

'Yes,' her voice was barely a whisper. 'You're right, Mervyn. His dad is also Glynis's dad. That's why Dafydd seemed so familiar. He looks very like his dad, although, of course, Glyn was a fair bit older than Dafydd when I knew him, but the resemblance is very strong both in his colouring and in that determined jaw-line.'

Mervyn ran his hands through his hair in a gesture of despair. 'So what do we do now? Do you really think she's still seeing him?'

'I'm sure she is.'

'Then we'll have to tell her; tell her the whole truth, in fact.'

Ruth nodded distractedly. 'I know, I should have listened to you and told her years ago that I was her mother and not let her go on thinking of me as her sister.'

'Let's be practical about it. You did what you thought was best at the time. You had no idea that a situation like this would ever arise, but now it's time to put matters right and tell her not only that but about who her real father was as well.'

Finding out whether Glynis was still meeting Dafydd wasn't easy. At first Glynis did everything possible not to tell them and then, when she eventually did, she tearfully accused them of trying to stop her seeing him.

'So it means you're still meeting him even though we asked you not to do so?' Ruth said unhappily.

Glynis avoided their eyes.

'We asked you before not to do so, now we must insist that you stop seeing him,' Mervyn told her gravely.

'Why? You're jealous. You don't want me to be happy. You took Ruth away from me and now you're trying to stop me seeing my boyfriend. I hate you; I hate both of you,' she stormed.

'Glynis, listen to me.' Ruth put her arms round the girl's shoulders and gently stroked her hair. 'There's a very good reason why you can't go on seeing Dafydd. It's something I should have told you about a long time ago.'

Glynis looked puzzled. 'I don't know what you are on about.'

'I hope you will understand after I tell you the whole story.'

'Go on then!' Glynis pulled away impatiently. 'I'm listening, and it had better be good if you think it's going to stop me seeing Dafydd.' She scowled at Ruth ominously.

Glynis looked shocked and upset by the time Ruth finished telling her how she'd been seduced by Glyn Jenkins when she was only a schoolgirl and how, to save her family from disgrace, she and her mother had covered things up by saying that the baby was Ruth's sister.

'You've been lying to me all these years,' Glynis exclaimed in an anguished voice. 'I don't believe it; I don't want to believe it. You just want to get rid of me so that you can be with him!' she sobbed pointing an accusing finger at Mervyn.

As she dashed out of the room and they heard her running up the stairs Ruth made to go after her, but Mervyn held her back. 'Leave her, cariad,' he begged, 'she probably needs to be on her own to think all this through. It's an awful lot to take in all at once.'

As she sat sipping the cup of tea that Mervyn made for her Ruth felt full of guilt. 'If only I'd told her earlier on,' she mused, 'this situation could have been avoided.'

In the days that followed Ruth lost count of the number of times she wished she'd told Glynis the truth years ago because even after Glynis had recovered from the shock she was still very bemused.

'So Dada wasn't really my proper dad?' she persisted time and again in a puzzled voice.

'No, he was your grandfather and Mam was your grandmother,' Ruth explained.

'Why did he let me call him Dad, then?'

'Well, he didn't know; he thought he was your dad.'

'You knew, so why didn't you tell him? Why didn't you tell all of us?' she said angrily. 'Now I don't know who I am. I always liked being your sister, but I don't think I want you for a mam.'

Those words above all others cut Ruth to the quick. She'd done everything in her power to be a mother to Glynis, even putting her own happiness on hold. She wouldn't even have accepted Mervyn's proposal unless he'd agreed that Glynis stayed with them and Glynis had seemed to like him so much. Now she was jealous and confused and it was all her fault.

Mrs Price also seemed quite taken aback by the news although she was far more sanguine about it. She thought it had been wrong to let

Tomas believe he was Glynis's father especially when he felt so guilty about his wife dying and blamed himself.

'Mam knew the truth,' Ruth pointed out, 'and she made me promise never to tell. I wanted to tell him and there were several times when I almost did; in fact, I intended to a few days before he died, but then I was too afraid that it might upset him so I said nothing.'

'Well, it's certainly upset young Glynis,' Mrs Price told her sharply. 'Poor little thing, she doesn't know who she is these days.'

'I know, and, believe me, I'd do anything to help her to understand,' Ruth agreed. 'She looks so woebegone that it breaks my heart to look at her.'

'Yes, I agree with you about that, so can I give you a piece of advice?' Mrs Price asked cautiously.

'Of course you can!'

'Well, it's only my opinion, of course, but I think the last thing you should do is make Glynis call you Mam. She's called you Ruth all her life, remember.'

Ruth looked startled, and then nodded her head in agreement. 'I think you're right. I'll probably only ever be Ruth to her,' she added a little sadly.

Although she hoped that once Glynis was over the initial shock things would return to normal, Ruth was dismayed to find that it was not the case.

Glynis seemed to be in a daze, as if she wasn't sure of anything any more. The once bright, buoyant girl was now withdrawn. Nothing seemed to interest her; she had no appetite and even when Mrs Price cooked special meals for her she only picked at them.

As well as telling Mrs Price, Ruth had also gone along to the school to explain matters to Glynis's teacher and to account for why there might be a change in her attitude for a short while.

'I could see that there was something wrong,' Miss Hodges commented. 'When I asked her if she wasn't feeling well she shook her head and wouldn't answer so I thought that perhaps someone in the family had died. I can understand now why she is so upset and withdrawn. It must have been a very great shock for her.'

'She hasn't taken the news too well,' Ruth agreed. 'I'm sure she'll be back to normal in a few weeks, though.'

Ruth's optimism wasn't fulfilled. Glynis remained withdrawn, secretive and suspicious of everyone and Ruth blamed herself even when Mervyn pointed out that having met Dafydd she was bound to feel drawn towards him.

'After all, they are related, they're half-brother and half-sister, in fact, and so very close in age that it stands to reason that they're going to be attracted to one another.'

'I wonder how he's going to react when he

finds out the truth? That's if she's still seeing him, and I'm pretty sure she is.'

'It probably depends on who tells him. We can hardly expect Glynis to be the one to do that.'

'Heavens no!' Ruth exclaimed. 'I wouldn't expect her to have to do that. He has to be told, though.'

'Let's leave matters as they are for the moment,' Mervyn advised. 'Let's deal with Glynis first. She's so upset that she might decide she never wants to see him again and there'll be no need for us to take the matter any further.'

On that point Mervyn was very wrong. A couple of weeks later when Glynis didn't put in an appearance at breakfast time, Ruth went up to her bedroom to see if she had overslept. She found the room empty. When she saw the note lying on her bed she guessed what it would say even before she opened it.

As she'd anticipated, it told them that Glynis was running away and that they shouldn't come looking for her.

'I'm sure she's run away to be with Dafydd,' Ruth said worriedly.

'You're probably right but we simply can't let them be together,' Mervyn agreed. 'Have you any idea where they might have gone?'

'No idea at all. We don't even know where Dafydd lives because you said he no longer lived at home.'

'That's true; it must be in this area for them

to have met in the first place. We could try by asking those two girls who came to her birthday party. Surely they'd know; girls confide in each other about those sorts of things.'

Ruth went round to see Mina and Petra, but neither of the girls had any idea where Dafydd lived.

'He doesn't come to school, see,' Petra told her. 'Anyway, why don't you ask Glynis, or won't she tell you?'

When she explained that Glynis had run away to be with Dafydd both girls looked stunned.

'I know she liked him a lot and still does, but she's younger than me and my mam would half kill me if I did a thing like that.'

'Do you think that the two boys you brought to the party would know where Dafydd lives or where he works?'

Neither of the girls thought so but they agreed to go and ask them to come and let Ruth know if they found out anything at all.

'Let it drop,' Mrs Price admonished reproachfully. 'You've got a right bee in your bonnet about this young boyo and no mistake, but she'll be back given time.'

'I know that, but surely you must see the implications. He's Glynis's half-brother and I'm sure the longer we let them be with each other the greater the heartbreak there's going to be in the end.'

'You've told her that he's her brother and I'm

pretty sure that she's told him all about that by now. Give them time to come to terms with it all and, since he's older than her, he'll persuade her to come back home. Everything will turn out all right, you'll see,' Mrs Price said confidently.

It was a sleepless night for all of them. Mervyn was due on early shift so after she'd seen him off to work Ruth went up to Glynis's bedroom to have another search to see if she could find anything that might give her a clue as to where she might have gone. There was absolutely nothing. No address, no note of any kind from Dafydd, but it was apparent that Glynis had taken all her most treasured possessions with her, as if she never intended coming back again.

This fact above all others reduced Ruth to tears and as she confided in Mrs Price later in the morning it really looked as though history was going to repeat itself.

'I was not much older than she is when I fell for Glyn Jenkins,' she confessed. 'A silly schoolgirl with a crush on an older man. She could so easily end up as an unmarried mother like me.'

'You're talking nonsense, cariad,' Mrs Price told her sharply. 'For one thing, that Glyn Jenkins was a lot older than Dafydd; he was old enough to know better. Anyway, it's an entirely different set of circumstances. As I said before, she's bound to have told him by now that she's his half-sister, so she'll not come to any harm, not with a respectable boyo like he appeared to be. She'll be back home again in a couple of days looking sheepish and hoping you aren't going to scold her too much,' she forecast.

On that point Mrs Price was only partly right. Glynis did return of her own accord, but she was far from sheepish; she was very angry and bitter.

'We went to Dafydd's home because we hadn't enough money to pay for a room anywhere, but when he told his dad about who I was, and that I was his half-sister, he refused to let us stay there.'

'Well, I can understand that,' Ruth sighed.

'He asked me a whole lot of questions and then seemed to take a dislike to me. I think it was because I told him that if we couldn't stay there then we'd sleep rough. I told him it wasn't too bad and that we'd had to sleep in doorways and in an old warehouse when I was only a little kid because you'd no money.'

'Oh, Glynis!' Ruth pulled her into her arms and hugged her.

'I don't know what his dad said to him after that,' Glynis went on, struggling away from Ruth, 'because they went into another room and Dafydd wouldn't tell me, but I know it was something bad about you, Ruth. If you'd told me the truth years ago, none of this would have happened,' she said looking at Ruth accusingly.

'It still may have done,' Ruth defended. 'You

could still have met Dafydd along with other friends and have felt there was a special charisma between you and chosen him as your boyfriend,' she pointed out.

'I still like him a whole lot, better than any of the other boys that I know,' Glynis sighed. 'Do I have to stop seeing him? Couldn't we still be friends?'

'You don't have to stop seeing him, but I think it would probably be better if you did, now that you know the truth,' Ruth said quietly. 'His dad doesn't want you to have anything more to do with each other, does he?'

'No,' Glynis pouted, 'but perhaps if you went to see him and talked things over, he wouldn't mind about Dafydd and me being friends . . . after all, we are brother and sister.'

'No.' Ruth shook her head emphatically. 'That's not a good idea.'

'Please,' Glynis wheedled, looking at her with tear-filled eyes.

'No.' Ruth shook her head firmly. 'That part of my life is over. I've made a new life now. I'm happy and I hope that now you know the truth you'll be able to put all this behind you and make a new life for yourself just as I've done. If Dafydd wants to visit us occasionally I'll try and accept it,' she conceded.

Glynis tossed her head defiantly. 'I'll never forget Dafydd and I'm never going to call you Mam, so don't think that I am,' she said stubbornly but with less force behind her words.

'I don't expect you to, but I do hope that, deep in your heart, you will always remember that I'm your mother, and that no one can ever love you more than I do.'

She held her arms wide and after a moment's hesitation Glynis responded and was hugging her. 'You may be my mum, but I'll always think of you as the best sister ever,' she murmured tearfully as Ruth held her tightly.